What critics are saying about

SUPERNATURE

"The plot sucks you in and doesn't let go . . . if you enjoy a suspenseful sci-fi thriller, then Supernature is an excellent choice."
~Roger Wilson
Author of 'Phantom Four: Children of the Grave'

"The story goes full speed ahead . . . I stayed up way too late one night finishing a chapter!"
~Ami Blackwelder
Hot Gossip Hot Reviews & Author of 'The Hunted of 2060'

"This is a great science fiction read!"
~ Barbara Hightower
The World of Book Reviews

"This book gave me the creeps, but held my interest."
~ Brenda M. Lisbon
The RAWSISTAZ™ Reviewers

"Supernature, is a jam-packed roller coaster ride of fun for lovers of science fiction."
~ M. Champagne
Author of Bittersuite: Songs of Experience

SUPERNATURE

**Science opened up the door.
Now nature has a plan to control the ways of man**

H.V. LYONS

LYONS & GRANT
MULTIMEDIA LLC
NEW YORK

First edition, July 2010
First Trade edition, October 2011

Edited by Roslyn Dames & Cameron Cook

Cover design by DivineTree Publications
www.divinetree.com

"SUPERNATURE" the song composed by M. Cerrone © 1977

Published by Lyons & Grant Multimedia LLC, New York
visit our website at www.LGMmedia.net

Printed in the United States of America

Library of Congress Control Number: 2011909894

Paperback edition:
ISBN-13: 978-0-9837172-0-1
ISBN-10: 0-9837172-0-6

ePub edition:
ISBN-13: 978-0-9837172-2-5

To my little Angel
Alexandra Elizabeth Lyons
May you rest in peace by the lord's side
Love you always, through the tears
Your Dad –

To my father:
You have always been my hero and without your guidance, love
and dedication to family I could not have become the man that I
am today. It's because of you that my mind and imagination
have been open enough to be able to write a story such as this.
For that invaluable gift I thank you.
Your Son –

Acknowledgments

Alvin Grant
Shanell Lyons
Michael and Sasha Flash
Chauncie Brooks
Nazario Gonzalez

Table of Contents

Blessed are the meek:
For they shall inherit the Earth.

Matthew 5:5

Prologue

"Don't go too far," Jose yells to the two children.

"Okay Papi," says 7-year-old Diana as she and her little brother run off with the dog, "We're just going over there to play with Pepe."

"Stay where we can see you," says Maria Hernandez with a concerned voice as her children play on the outskirts of the forest in the Arizona Desert.

"Yes Mami."

The two children and the dog run off to play among the brush, excited about their afternoon arrival at the camping grounds.

The 3-year-old retriever, Pepe, is also excited about the prospect of playing fetch with the children. The dog's tail wags with great enthusiasm as he waits for Daniel to throw the ball. Daniel rears back and tosses the soft rubber ball over a large bush. The instant the ball leaves the 5-year-old's hand Pepe darts off into the bush after it.

"Pepe, get the ball boy! Go ahead--get the ball," yells Diana at the top of her lungs as the dog takes off in the direction of the reddish-brown boulders and dense, high stretches of brush.

A well-trained dog, Pepe dashes off into the woods and disappears but instead of immediately returning with the ball as is his habit, Pepe began barking wildly from within the forest.

"What is it boy?" Diana yells, craning her neck to catch even a glimpse of the beloved pet. This is very unlike Pepe, and Diana is beginning to get a little scared. In a tone as firm as her fear allows she cries, "Come here Pepe! Come here!"

But the typically obedient dog doesn't return, only continues to bark from somewhere deep within the undergrowth and towering clusters of maple trees.

"Pepe?" says Daniel. He looks up at his sister with a puzzled expression, dark brown eyes narrowed with concern. "Why won't he come out?"

"I don't know," Diana murmurs. She glances over at her dad, who is transferring a few of his deliciously seasoned hamburger patties from the cooler to the grill. Their mom has just finished setting up the folding table and chairs for lunch and has disappeared inside the camper. They only have a few minutes of last-minute fun before they'll be made to sit down and eat. She turns to Daniel and says excitedly, "Let's go get him!"

"Okay!"

She takes her little brother's hand and walks into the woods following the sound of the barking dog. As they walk deeper and deeper into the woods calling Pepe's name the distant sound of the dog barking grows steadily nearer.

"Pepe! Pepe! Come here, boy!"

Woof! Woof! Woof!

The two children exchange glances, Daniel looking downright worried. Rarely have they heard Pepe bark in that manner. The friendly dog only barked like that when there was some kind of threat, or he was feeling protective. The sound made the two pick up speed.

"Over there. I heard him over there," yells Daniel as he breaks away from his sister and darts even deeper into the woods.

A flash of white Converse sneakers and Daniel disappears into the forest—Diana loses sight of her little brother.

"Daniel, No! Come back," cries Diana as she races after him.

But Daniel ignores her, in hot pursuit of his dog. "Pepe! Pepe! Where are you?" cries Daniel.

He runs through the forest until he comes to a small clearing near a tall maple tree. Adjacent to the tree is a large mound of earth with a large hole on the top, tapering almost like a rounded pyramid about two feet high and partially covered with vegetation. Daniel walks up to the mound slowly, looking up at it as his sister runs up to stand beside him, panting heavily with her hands on her hips.

"Daniel we have to get back. Mami and Papi are going to be mad," she sternly tells him.

"Wait, I hear Pepe! Listen." Daniel cocks his head to the side and listens attentively. The little boy gets to one knee, and draws closer to the mound in order to listen.

Diana follows suit, listening carefully. She finally hears a faint barking which seems to be coming from underground. She gasps, looking at Daniel in horror. The little boy looks up at her, solemn and sad. The two children slowly move closer to the mound of earth and it becomes clear through the scattered soil and break in vegetation that their dog apparently fell down the opening atop the great swell of earth.

"We should go back and get Papi. He could get him out!" Diana says with more confidence than she felt in her heart.

Daniel, still ignoring his sister, gets to his feet and looks about the clearing until he finds a long dead branch at the base of the maple tree. Daniel returns to the mound and pokes the stick down into the hole, turning it this way and that. Suddenly, the children hear their dog bark fiercely, as if under some kind of attack, followed by a great yelp of pain, then complete and ominous silence.

"Pepe! Pepe!" Daniel leans forward and shouts down the hole. The boy lies on his stomach, crawls toward the top of the mound and thrusts his hand in.

Daniel, No!" hollers Diana, reaching out her hand in protest. But it is too late. Something grabs Daniel's hand and pulls him into the hole so quickly the boy hasn't a chance to scream. Diana screams in pure terror as Daniel is dragged away into the darkness that claimed Pepe.

Jumping into action, she manages to rush to the hole just as her little brother's white Converses are dragged up the mound, leaving tracks in its rich soil.   Before his body disappears completely beneath the ground, Diana dives toward the opening and just manages to grab his jean clad legs, pulling with all of her might.

"Papi! Papi! Help me please," she screams at the top of her lungs, hoping that somehow her father can hear her back at the campgrounds. Too far away for her parents to hear her cries her pleas are lost among the maple trees as she hangs on to Daniel's trembling body. She screams until she grows hoarse, until she realizes that no one can hear her, and no one is coming. "Papi! Please," she pleads softly as she begins to sob. Within minutes, whatever thing got Pepe has dragged Daniel's now limp body down into the dark depths and Diana's arms are now deep inside the hole, still clinging to little Daniel's legs. She feels herself losing the battle with whatever has a hold of her brother. But Diana refuses to let go of Daniel.   Steady streams of hot tears have etched pale streaks in her dust and grit covered face.

Still holding on to her brother's legs, Diana suddenly feels something crawling up her back. Unable to see what it is, she feels a sensation akin to pinpricks, traveling steadily up her spine. Reflexively, she attempts to swat the object from her back with one hand, letting go of one of Daniel's legs in order to do so. Immediately, a searing pain shoots through her small body, with a throbbing so intense it paralyzes her, leaving her unable to move or even scream. As Diana's muscles tense from some powerful and alien substance, her breathing grows more erratic. An odd sensation overtakes her limbs and she can do nothing as she feels Daniel slip, little by little, then completely from her grip. Blood trickles from her nose and eyes as the girl coughs up large clots of blood. Conscious yet unable to react, Diana merely remains silent as her vision reddens with blood.

Suddenly, something sharp grabs and pierces the flesh of her arm which is now limp inside the hole. It jerks her hard, pulling her deep inside the belly of the mound of earth.

At the campground Jose Hernandez has just finished grilling some hot dogs and hamburgers. The aromatic scent of charcoal mingled with meat fills the air. His wife is napping in the camper and he calls to her, "Maria, get the kids--the food's ready!"

Maria groans, stretches, and swings her feet from their propped position on the narrow camper sofa, before emerging, barefoot, to stand in the doorway of the vehicle. Stretching once more, Maria steps down from the camper and looks off in the direction of the forest just a few yards away.

"Diana! Daniel! Time to come in! Diana! Daniel!"

Maria sighs and calls the children again, in a sterner tone this time. Failing to get a response, Maria walks over to the edge of the forest where she last saw the children playing. With one hand on her slender hip, Maria says sharply, "Diana! Daniel! Time to come in!" She waits a few more minutes then says, "Pepe! Pepe! Here, boy!"

Upon hearing his wife's repeated calls, Jose looks up from the grill and notices that there has been no response from his kids. Growing slightly irritated, he quickly wipes his hands on his apron and takes great strides to join an increasingly worried Maria. Jose walks over to the edge of the forest where Maria is standing and shouts, "Diana, Daniel vienen aquí ahora!"

After a moment or two, the two parents stop yelling and listen attentively. There is no sign of Pepe's boisterous bark, or the delighted sounds of the children exploring the forest. All the two can hear is the sound of the wind brushing through the woods.

They stand frozen in the campgrounds listening, hoping to hear their children's voices, but the only sound they hear is silence.

"Diana…Daniel! Diana, Daniel, where are you?"

Mystery in the Desert

It's 9:00 am on the Fourth of July weekend and the temperature is already in the upper nineties.

Highway Patrol Officers Cliff Johnson and Brad Williams are on patrol down Route 377, also known as Dry Lake Road.

In the Apache-Sitgreaves National Forest of Arizona the sky is clear and blue but the air is still. There are only faint sounds of life: a few birds, a few bugs, but mostly stillness.

"Quiet," Officer Williams comments, as he drives the vehicle. Equally unusual is the fact that he already has to crank up the AC.

Officer Johnson doesn't reply beyond a grunt of agreement, looking out onto the monotonous stretch of desert-like land that they have been assigned to patrol ever since the two Hernandez kids went missing.

Normally during this time of year this area is teaming with life. The forest is home to over 400 species of wild life and it spans over two million acres of untainted wilderness with more than thirty lakes and reservoirs and more than 680 miles of rivers and streams.

Once two separate forests, Apache-Sitgreaves is now managed as one. It runs along the Mogollon Rim, which defines the southwestern edge of the Colorado Plateau, the White Mountains in east-central Arizona and extends partially into New Mexico.

A favorite forest for tourists, hikers and nature lovers, the Apache-Sitgreaves terrain ranges from a desert-like environment on the outer perimeter to an interior of thick rich vegetation. The heart of the forest is lined with aspen, maple, and pine trees and is populated by deer, wild turkeys, elk, eagles and osprey. Among the smaller animals found in the area are rattlesnakes, squirrels, roof rats and black widow spiders. During the summer months the sounds of the forest usually play like a living orchestra. Birds sing, crickets chirp, frogs croak all playing their part of a natural ensemble. All this while hawks slowly circle over head and rabbits quickly scurry through the bush. But today the music is silent, the sounds are few and the feeling in the air has an eerie stillness to it and the two patrol officers can't help but feel uneasy in what has been their normal route for about four years now.

This long deserted highway that is now under Officer Williams' and Johnson's jurisdiction stretches through the Sitgreaves portion of the forest from the small frontier town of Holbrook all the way to the mountain community of Heber-Overgaard.

Patrolling Route 377 may be part of their daily routine now but it wasn't always. Originally, their job was to assist vacationers who were lost or had car trouble along the thirty-three miles of road. But over the past two years things have changed because of the unusual high number of missing persons being reported in and around the area. In addition, many ranchers along the outskirts of the forest as well as the neighboring Native American communities have complained about missing cattle, unexplained horse and livestock mutilations, and other strange occurrences. Last year's incident with the Hernandez kids put everyone on alert. A five-year-old little boy and his seven-year-old sister disappearing without a trace and two hysterical parents was more than enough for people to decide that this area needed to be watched closely. And with no bodies or evidence of foul play ever recovered, it only served to keep every one more on edge. So Officers Johnson and Williams set out early each morning, driving their white and blue

Crown Victoria police interceptor up and down Route 377 and keeping their eyes peeled for anything out of the norm.

Today it's early on a holiday weekend and nothing seems particularly noteworthy except for the heat and the unusual stillness in the air. They're traveling south down Dry Lake Road towards its intersection with Route 277, with Brad driving and Cliff riding shotgun. It's a dry stretch of road lined with small shrubs, cactus and rocky sand. There is no real tree line in this part of the forest which is more desert-like than anything. The largest shrubs found in the area only grow to about five feet.

Cliff, a few years younger than Brad at age 32, reaches for the patrol car's radio as his partner, muscle-bound and athletic, drives. He takes a sip of coffee in his right hand then clicks on the mic in his left saying, "Dispatch this is forty-nine."

"Go ahead, forty-nine," replies the voice over the radio.

"Heading south on Route 377. All's quiet, nothing to report."

"Ten-four, forty-nine."

Cliff runs a hand through his close-cropped blond hair, still staring out of the window as he takes another sip of coffee, "Sand, nothing but sand as far as the eye can see. Damn, I'm getting tired of this," he mumbles in between sips of coffee and adjusting his six foot muscular frame in his seat. Yet all of his cop's intuition tells him that something isn't quite right out here, and he keeps his eyes fixed on the passing outskirts of that forest that had swallowed those kids. Cliff didn't have children, but having helped raise his younger siblings had fostered a protective side to him that made him want to get his hands on--

"What's the matter with you?" asks his partner, a friendly African-American with ten years on the force. Officer Williams could sense that something was wrong.

"Nothing," Cliff answers, eyes still fixed on that eerily still forest.

"Nothing? You barely said a word all morning. What's eating you?"

"Nothing," repeats Cliff, still staring out of the passenger side window.

"Come on, how long have we known each other, five, six years? You don't think I don't know when something's bothering you?"

Cliff takes another sip of coffee and mutters, "It's nothing--I'm alright."

In an attempt to lighten things a bit Brad comments, "You know they say when you're having problems it's always good to talk to an elder," Cliff turns and frowns at Brad, "and since I'm the oldest you should feel comfortable confiding in me," he glances over at Cliff and flashes a wide grin.

"You gotta be kidding--you're only six years older than me Bradley," says Cliff as he turns back to the window.

Brad's brow furrows with frustration as he lifts his blue baseball style cap and scratches the barely-there, closely cropped wool on his head. He replaces the cap and mutters, "Just trying to help," before focusing back on the road ahead and drives on.

Officer Williams is trying not to take things personally, knowing this dry stretch of desert road, bleak forest and now a brooding partner could easily get you down if you let it. They've been driving in silence for twenty minutes and have just passed a sign which reads, 'DESPAIN RANCH ROAD NEXT RIGHT.'

Brad glances over at his partner and observes Cliff still staring out of the passenger's side window at the bushes whizzing by along the plain two lane stretch of road.

Brad decides to give it another go and launch full-steam ahead into a conversation.

"You know you and Doris really should have come by the barbecue last night, we had a ball. Pat kept asking, 'where's Cliff and Doris? Where's Cliff and Doris?'" Cliff says nothing but continues to sip his coffee, "we didn't shut the grill down till 12:30," he again glances over at his partner waiting for a response, but nothing.

Undeterred Brad continues, "Woodberry came, Hernandez was there, Singletary came over, Brown and his wife showed up. Simmons came with another new girlfriend, I think that's the third one this month, and even the Sarge came through for a while. Oh and you're not going to believe this but Pepper showed up. You know that muscular dyke from the SWAT unit? And she brought her girlfriend with her, a drop dead gorgeous blonde with big tits. I had to stay at the grill so Pat wouldn't catch me staring at her. But no Cliff and no Doris."

After another slow sip Cliff mutters, "Doris and me had a fight."

Progress!

With a slight grin Brad replies, "What! Again? What is it with you guys anyway? And I bet it was over something stupid, wasn't it?"

"Yeah, you're right it was."

"All right what was it this time?"

Cliff looks over at Brad's grinning, mahogany-brown profile then takes another sip before explaining, "It's like this. We were going to come to your party. I was already dressed and watching the end of the heavyweight ultimate fighter match. She's in the bedroom taking forever to get ready. Then she comes out, stands in front of the TV and asks me if her new dress makes her look fat."

Brad winces and interjects, "Wait a minute let me guess, you said, YES."

Cliff shrugs his shoulders and looks at Brad like a little puppy that soiled the carpet and replies, "Well, yeah!" Brad bursts into laughter as Cliff tries to explain, "Well it did make her look fat. What was I going to do lie?"

"Then what happened?"

"She threw a beer can at me. Hit me right in the back of the head. That shit still hurts," says Cliff as he reaches under his cap and rubs a spot on the back of his head.

Brad laughs even more, "And I bet the two of you spent the rest of the night making up, right?"

A long devilish grin forms across Cliff's face, "Man it was great!"

"You know it never fails with you guys. I think you both are crazy. I think you guys just start fights just so you can have make-up sex."

"Come on man you have to admit, make-up sex is great!"

"Yeah I'll admit that but me and Pat never fight as much as you guys. You guys are crazy."

"Come on man we're not that bad."

"Are you kidding me? What about last year's Christmas Party?"

"Okay, we were both a little drunk."

"Halloween?"

Cliff gives a devilish smile and says, "We made up after that."

"And Cancun?"

"Come on now you can't talk. What about that time we caught you and Pat at Sunset beach?"

"What?" Brad's dark-brown eyes widen in mock innocence.

"Last year in Jamaica? You remember now?"

"Oh boy, here we go again. If I told you once I've told you a thousand times we weren't doing anything. We were just holding each other."

"In the nude?"

"It was a clothing optional beach!"

"Okay, and?"

"Nothing, we were just enjoying each other's company," says Brad in a sheepish tone of voice.

"I'll say you were enjoying a whole lot more from where I was standing."

"Oh shut up. It's bad enough you saw my wife naked."

"And that's not all we saw. Doris couldn't stop laughing," replies Cliff as he begins to laugh out loud.

"Alright, alright, that's enough," says Brad in a serious tone.

"What's the matter is somebody getting sensitive?"

"Well how would you like it if someone caught you and your wife--?"

Brad trails off, glancing out of the driver's side window for a moment, before putting his eyes back on the road.

"You and your wife doing what?" interrupts Cliff.

"Nothing."

"Ah hah, I got you! Come on, admit it already! The two of you were doing it on the beach weren't you?"

"Oh grow up. Hey, what about the time you tried your uncle Bill's Viagra and had a five-hour erection? Now that was funny," Brad begins to laugh uncontrollably, "I'll never forget the phone call: 'Hello, Brad? It's getting bigger! It hurts and it won't go down'," Brad laughs so hard he has to wipe tears from his eyes.

All mirth dissolves from Cliff's face.

"Hey, that wasn't funny. That really hurt."

Brad chuckles, "I bet it did. I don't know why you took that stuff in the first place. And how did they make that thing go down anyway?"

"I had to go to the hospital man; you know how embarrassing that was?"

"I can imagine."

"Yeah after the doctors stopped laughing they pulled out this super long needle and stuck me."

"Stuck you? Where at?"

"In my dick! Can you believe that! In my dick! It hurt like hell!"

"What? They stuck it in your dick?"

"Yeah, they said they had to drain out all the blood." Brad begins to laugh even louder while slapping the steering wheel with his hands.

As Brad shakes his head, laughing heartily, something catches Cliff's eye through the passenger side of the patrol car. At first he thought it might be some rags strewn by the side of the road but as the vehicle approached, he knew it had to be a body. A small body. Could it be a child? Another kid?

He reaches over and nudges Brad's muscular forearm, pointing. "Hey, hey, hold on a sec. Slow down partner." The urgency in his voice causes Brad to sober up immediately.

Brad slows the vehicle and now they could both see a small framed figure lying on the ground about 200 yards off the side of the road partially obscured by some shrubs.

After slowing down the vehicle Brad leans over his partner to get a closer look while pulling the car off of the road.

"What is that? Is it a body?" asks Brad.

Cliff still squinting replies, "Jesus I think it is," he swings open the door just as the car comes to a stop and jogs off toward the figure on the ground. Brad jumps out and follows. As the two men approach the figure they notice a bare-footed young woman in her early thirties lying on her stomach. She's very pale with short dark hair, wearing a pair of badly torn jeans and a ripped tee shirt, both lightly splattered in blood. Her eyes are closed and the left side of her face is in the dirt. Parts of the woman's face and arms are dark red, dry and clearly sun burnt. She is also covered in dozens of small cuts and scratches. As the two officers examine her they also notice that her feet are dirty, bleeding and blistered. On her right cheek and on her right forearm there are what appear to be large reddish swollen abscesses both about the size of golf balls. The abscesses are dry, peeling and slowly leaking a yellowish puss. Cliff looks down at the woman and softly calls out to her. "Miss, can you hear me? Miss?" There's no response. The woman just lies there very still and breathing slowly, showing little sign of life. Cliff kneels down and checks her neck for a pulse with two expert fingers, "She's alive! But just barely, better call it in."

Brad unhooks his portable radio from his belt and calls the dispatcher as he briskly walks around the area looking through the bush, "Dispatch, this is car forty-nine, over."

"Go ahead forty-nine," the radio crackles back.

"Ah, we have an eleven forty-seven on route 377 about one mile south of Despain Ranch Road, requesting Medevac ASAP, over."

"Ten-four forty-nine, requesting Medevac for eleven forty-seven, route 377, one mile south of Despain Ranch Road, there's already a chopper in the area, ETA about twenty minutes, do you copy?"

"Ten-four Dispatch, twenty minutes."

Brad walks back over to Cliff and the woman and hunkers down next to them, "Chopper will be here in twenty. What do you think happened to her?"

"I don't know. Her breathing is very slow and she's covered in all these cuts almost like she's been in a fight with a cat."

"Damn, she does look real tore up," adds Brad.

Cliff looks at the wounds and twists his face, "Have you noticed that odor?"

"Yeah, smells like she was sprayed with vinegar," Brad slowly scans the area around the woman, "strange, this is real strange. You hear me partner?"

Cliff looks up at him slowly, "I know what you mean."

For fifteen minutes the two officers sit with the female while they wait for the medical helicopter to arrive. They check her back pockets for any signs of identification and repeatedly check her pulse and breathing. As Cliff kneels by the girl's side Brad searches the surrounding area for any clues as to what might have happened. He follows some partial tracks from the woman leading south but only manages to find blood spattered foot prints in the sand. While kneeling down to study one print he stops and looks around slowly. The silence they noticed earlier seems especially oppressive now. *What could have happen out here?*" He thinks to himself.

He begins to scan the area more intently. There's nothing around, normally in this part of the forest there are birds over head, flies buzzing around, even the occasional scorpion scurrying by. But today there's nothing but silence. The stillness unnerves Brad and he stands up and begins to make his way back towards Cliff and the woman. Just then Brad's radio crackles to life, "Car forty-nine, Car forty-nine this is Medevac two, do you read?"

"Go ahead Medevac two this is forty-nine, what's your ETA?"

"We are five minutes out forty-nine, Just thought you should know we just flew over a camper off the side of the road about two miles south of your position. Appears to be abandoned, could belong to your Vic."

"Ten-four Medevac two, we'll check it out as soon as you clear station."

"Ten-four forty-nine."

Brad approaches Cliff and kneels beside him, "Chopper will be here in five."

"Great."

"The chopper spotted a camper down the road. Could be where she's from. We should check it out when we're done."

"Right!"

"How is she?"

"Still no response, no movement, nothing, and her breathing is getting even slower. You find anything?"

"Naw, no clues, but…I don't know, it seems a little weird but remember I mentioned how quiet it is out here? Something's not right."

Cliff slowly looks around and scans the area then turns back to Brad, nodding, "Yeah it's pretty quiet today isn't it?"

"Yeah, a little too quiet if you ask me. It's giving me the creeps."

"I know exactly what you mean. Like, it's kind of--"

"--Dead," his partner finished.

In the background the low rumbling sound of the four bladed Bell 407 helicopter can be heard approaching. The sound steadily grows louder as the red and white chopper slowly appears overhead. The pilot hovers for a minute while he looks for a clearing to land. Brad covers his eyes and Cliff angles his broad, muscular frame in an effort to shield the young woman as the machine kicks up a cloud of dust. The skilled pilot softly lands the helicopter just in front of the officer's patrol car on the side of the road. As the engine slows to an idle, two paramedics dressed in bright orange jump suits jump out, one carrying a medical kit and the other a portable gurney. Both wear pilot helmets and multi-pocketed vests loaded with bandages and other small medical tools. They run over to the two officers and their victim.

Dave, a short stocky seven-year veteran of the Medevac service, crouches beside the young woman on the ground. His partner Nancy, a thin light skinned young woman with freckles, quickly runs to the other side and applies the inflatable bag of a portable blood pressure machine onto the woman's left arm.

Dave examines her body, being careful not to move her too much as the extent of her injuries are as yet unclear. While wearing protective gloves he examines the abscesses on her face and arm.

"Damn! I've never seen anything like this before. How long has she been like this?"

Scratching his head Brad responds, "Don't know, we've been here for about twenty minutes. Don't know how long she's been lying here before that."

While closely examining her burnt skin Dave then says, "Must have been at least an hour by the look of these sunburns."

Cliff then jumps in, "Have you noticed the odor? Kind of like vinegar."

Dave leans closer to the woman and sniffs, "Seems to be coming from these big sores."

Suddenly a steady beeping emits from the blood pressure machine. Nancy checks the LED display and calls out its readings.

"Blood pressure's 55 over 40!"

Dave looks up, "Not good, not good at all"

"Is that very bad?" asks Cliff with a look of concern.

"Yes it is, very low, probably due to dehydration. She could slip into a coma if we don't get her some fluids and to a hospital ASAP!"

Nancy pulls an IV bag of clear fluid out of her medical kit and attaches it to the woman's arm.

Dave pulls out a small light from his vest and shines it into the woman's eyes as he pulls them open with his other hand, "Her eyes are dilated and her breathing is erratic and with the low blood pressure she's in real bad shape. We have to get her out of here now. Come on, give us a hand."

"Where're you going to take her?" asks Brad.

"The trauma center at Lincoln Hospital in downtown Phoenix. We can be there in about thirty-five minutes."

Dave gently lifts the woman over to one side as his partner Nancy slides the portable gurney under her back. The two officers assist the paramedics in lifting the woman up and carrying her to the waiting helicopter. After securing her inside of the copter the two officers back away and watch as it slowly rises into the air and speeds off.

Brad turns to Cliff and says," I don't know what's going on but we need to check out that camper."

"You're right, let's get a move on it. Someone has to know what happened to her."

The two officers enter their patrol car and speed south down Route 377 with lights flashing and sirens blaring. About two miles down the road they come upon a thirty foot motor home parked about 200 yards off the side of the road among some light brush. Brad spots the camper's tracks and follows them up to the rear of the vehicle. He cuts the engine and kills the lights as the two men cautiously step out of the patrol car.

With their hands on their weapons they slowly approach the right side of the motor home. The camper, a Bigfoot 3000 series Class C motor home built around a Ford E-450 chassis, is white with brown stripes and has the side door wide open, broken and hanging off the bottom hinge. The windows along the side of the motor home are also broken. Brad and Cliff exchange knowing glances, silently encouraging one another to proceed with caution. As the officers approach the camper they notice debris scattered around the campground: torn clothes, broken furniture, and trash.

Cliff moves alongside the camper and presses his back against the wall of the motor home on the left side of the open door, Brad approaches from the right. Both men draw their weapons as Brad yells out toward the opening, "This is the police, is there anyone in there?" After a pause he continues, "Is there anyone in there?" after no reply he motions to Cliff as he aims his gun toward the dark interior. Cliff, with both hands on his weapon quickly swings into the motor home as Brad follows.

Inside, to the right there's a small dinette and the cab of the vehicle with a small bunk bed on top. Dishes and papers cover the floor. Bloodstains are splattered all over dishes and up the walls in no particular order; some stains are even on the ceiling. To the left there's a small bathroom, with a missing door, and a narrow hallway leading to the back bedroom, also splattered with dried blood. Cliff looks at Brad grimly and mutters through clenched teeth, "Jesus, what the hell happened in here?"

"Looks like one hell of a fight," Brad replies, his voice barely above a whisper.

The two men slowly and carefully walk around the ransacked area, shuffling through broken dishes and torn papers. After finding nothing more than broken furniture and splattered blood on the walls, Cliff, with his gun held up and pointed, cautiously moves toward the rear of the camper. He moves down the narrow hall with Brad following close behind. They cautiously push the bedroom door open and gasp at the horror within. Lying on a blood-soaked bed are the remains of a white male in his early thirties. The thick stench of blood and death hang heavily in the hot Arizona air. There are no legs, just a right arm, a head, and most of a badly mangled torso torn from the rib cage down with the spine still intact. The head is disfigured and covered with gashes and scrapes similar to the ones the young woman had. The man's face is cut up and the left eye is hanging out of its socket by a few veins. The left arm is missing and appears to have been ripped out at the shoulder. In the right hand is a Glock-19 9mm semi-automatic handgun and on the bloodied bed are about fifteen 9mm shells. The room is in a shambles and bullet holes pepper the walls. Flies swarm the inside of the room and crawl all over the body. Brad and Cliff struggle for breath at the horrific sight. In their line of work both men have seen death but nothing as grisly as this. This body was ripped apart!

Brad's eyes widen and his mouth drops open in shock, before he quickly whips out a handkerchief and covers his mouth and nose. Cliff steps back from the bed with the back of his hand over his mouth, trying to control a gag reflex. He re-holsters his gun and unclips his radio. "Dispatch, this is car forty-nine, over." There's a moment of no reply so he tries again. "Dispatch, this is car forty-nine, over."

"Go ahead forty-nine," the voice on the other end answers back.

"Dispatch we have a one eighty-seven on Route 377 about four miles north of Route 277"

"Ten-four forty-nine, one eighty-seven on Route 377"

"Requesting CSI, possible connection with earlier eleven forty-seven."

"Ten-four forty-nine, notifying CSI, please stand by."

As Cliff holds the radio Brad re-holsters his gun and moves around the bed, being careful not to disturb anything. On the left nightstand at the head of the bed he finds a photograph and calls his partner over to look at it.

"Looks like this is our Vic's place alright."

Cliff looks down at the picture. It's a photo of a couple in their early thirties sitting under a tree with a little boy. The woman is the same one they found up the road. She has an air of quiet confidence about her, with excellent posture and an aura of strength. The man by her side is clearly the same one as the one on the bed—at least, what is left of him.

"And we have another problem on our hands," comments Cliff.

"What's that," says Brad as he examines the photo closer.

"What's wrong with that picture, Brad?"

"Ah, shit! Where's the kid?"

"Right, hopefully he got away like his mother."

"Cliff, remember what shape she was in?"

"I know. How old do you think he is?"

"Looks about eight or nine."

Cliff's jaw tightens and he shakes his head.

"Jesus, Doris has a niece that old. You remember Tammy?" He shakes his head again and looks away. As he does so he happens to glance at the floor by the night stand and notices a black rectangular object.

"What's this?" After pulling on rubber gloves Cliff picks up a battered and bloodstained black wallet and looks inside. "Damn!"

"What you got there, partner?"

"Looks like our Vic here is an FBI agent."

"You're kidding!"

"Naw, Agent Allen Henderson, look for yourself," he holds the open wallet for Brad to see.

There was a photo of a nondescript man in glasses and a white collared shirt. It appeared to be the same man in the photograph on the nightstand and in the messy pool of blood, bone and the remnants of organs on the bed.

"Man, this case keeps getting weirder and weirder. And did you notice the odor in here?"

Cliff nods his head, "Sure did, vinegar."

"Just like the woman."

Cliff's radio squawks to life, "Car forty-nine, Come in forty-nine."

"This is forty-nine go ahead," Cliff answers.

"CSI in route to your location. ETA thirty minutes. Command advises to secure the area."

"Uh, ten-four dispatch. Please advise command that victim is FBI and we may also have a missing child."

"Ten-four, forty-nine, will advise."

"Well looks like we're stuck here for awhile. Better make the most of it."

"So much for a quiet holiday."

Both officers leave the motor home and walk quickly to their patrol car. Cliff snatches several rolls of caution tape out of the car and hands a few to Brad. The two hurriedly rope off the area around the camper attaching the tape to the trees and brush around the camper. They work quietly while wondering to themselves what could do such mangling damage to the man inside.

Cliff keeps thinking about the little boy somewhere out there, with a dad who clearly died fighting and a mom who seemed about to lose the fight for her life.

After they finish they return to their vehicle, lock the doors, and wait without another word for the Crime Scene Investigators to arrive.

After about ten minutes another patrol car pulls up behind theirs. Driving it is Officer O'Brien, a young two-year rookie and in the passenger seat is Watch Commander Lieutenant Maddox. The gray haired Maddox is a twenty-year veteran who was part of the investigation of the disappearance of the two missing Hernandez kids that Brad and Cliff worked on. He's a pot bellied stone-faced bull of a man with a head of white hair who's known for being tough on the officers under his command but for some reason he seems to have a soft spot for both Brad and Cliff.

After seeing the newcomers exit their vehicle Brad and Cliff exit their own.

"Lieutenant," says Cliff as he nods to the approaching Maddox.

"Johnson, Williams," Maddox nods back, "so what do we have?"

Brad and Cliff slowly glance at each other for a moment.

"Well? What is it?" Maddox asks impatiently.

Cliff steps forward, "Lieutenant, we have a real mess in there," he says as he points toward the camper, "first we found this unconscious woman up the road and then we traced her back here and find a bloody massacre. We also think there might be a missing little boy! This is the craziest thing we've even seen!"

"Alright, alright calm down," Maddox turns to O'Brien, "Let's check it out to see just how bad it really is."

Cliff glances over at Brad.

"You want to know how bad it is. Lieutenant it looks like someone put that guy through a wood chipper!" shouts Brad, "I mean he's missing his whole body from the waist down!"

Maddox and O'Brien give each other a glance of disbelief.

O'Brian looks at Brad and comments, "Come on guys."

Cliff and Brad just stare at him in stoic silence.

Seemingly unconvinced about the level of savagery reported, Maddox and O'Brien move to enter the motor home to examine the scene for their selves. After barely five minutes the two men hurry out of the camper with a look of repulsion on their faces. O'Brien vomits beside the camper, and then gasps, "Who or what could have done that?"

Maddox, mopping the sweat from his forehead, nose and upper lip looks at Brad and asks, "No other clues? No sign of what happened to the boy?"

The heat was starting to weigh down on them. The heat and the silence. Brad removes his blue baseball cap to wipe perspiration from his brow before pulling the hat low over his brown eyes. "No, nothing," he replies.

"You know the feds are going to be all over this one. They don't like it when something happens to one of their own."

"You think it could be some kind of terrorist attack?" asks Cliff.

Maddox looks at Cliff and says, "Don't know. These days anything's possible. Remember when those terrorists cut that guy's head off on the news? You never can tell these days. But what I do know is that we're going to need more help out here."

Maddox glances over at Cliff and says, "Johnson, Get on the horn and call Air Search and Rescue we need some eyes in the sky if we're going to have any chance at finding that kid."

Just then in the distance a faint siren could be heard growing steadily louder. Maddox stares south down Route 377, "Sounds like the cavalry's finally here."

O'Brien, Brad and Cliff turn and look toward the sound. Off in the distance they can see the oncoming procession of law enforcement vehicles. Rolling up to the site are five patrol cars, two vans from the K-9 unit, a coroner's wagon and a large black truck, which is the mobile lab of the Crime Scene Investigation Unit. Brad and Cliff quickly assist the arriving officers in setting up a command post near the crime scene. Over the next two hours the area becomes alive with even more personnel and vehicles as they gather around the abandoned motor home. Police helicopters buzz overhead as they crisscross the forest area searching for the missing young child. K-9 teams plow through the bush with great, muscular dogs. An Amber Alert is broadcasted to help find the little boy.

Later in the day, Maddox is discussing a game plan with Cliff and Brad as they pore over a map of the area when a black Ford Expedition pulls up to the command post with dark tinted windows. The passenger side door opens, and a burly man with wide-set brown eyes, short dark-brown hair and a neatly trimmed moustache emerges from the front passenger seat, astute eyes quickly surveying the area and personnel with an air of authority. He's wearing a dark-brown suit and tie with a stark white shirt. From the driver's seat comes a tall, striking woman with fine, shoulder-length auburn hair who appears all-business and no-nonsense. She is wearing a black business suit with a white open-collar blouse and dark sunglasses. With a long, gazelle-like stride, she comes around the front of the vehicle, checking out the command post and the bustling activity of the technicians and officers. When she removes her glasses, Cliff notices her piercing hazel eyes.

Maddox stops and looks up, recognizing them at once.

The highly esteemed Special FBI Agents Debra Hill and Clarence Daily stride forward and greet Maddox with hearty handshakes. Maddox introduces Cliff and Brad then escorts them over to the mobile lab so that they can take a look at the police and lab reports that have been generated so far. Special agents Debra Hill and Clarence Daily expertly examine all of the evidence found and are so in sync that they finish one another's sentences as they draw conclusions.

These are two of the best special agents in the Phoenix field office. They have worked together for over ten years and during that time have accumulated an impressive investigative record. As a team they have solved some of the toughest cases to date. Hill 42, daughter of an ex FBI Agent with a master's degree in criminal psychology usually serves as an FBI Profiler or lead investigator. She's direct and tough as nails, standing 5 feet 6 inches, slightly shorter than Daily. Her partner, Daily, age 40, has a master's in Criminal Justice. He can be just as intense as Hill but has a much lighter demeanor.

After Daily and Hill have had an opportunity to review the evidence and touch base with the technicians working in the mobile lab, they meet outside of the camper with Brad and Cliff.

"So you two are the ones who found Agent Henderson and his wife?" asks Hill.

"Yes ma'am," replies Cliff partially distracted by forensic technicians buzzing around them taking photographs of the camper and surrounding area.

"We've read your report," comments Hill as she takes some notes on a small notepad, "very thorough. Good work gentlemen."

"Thanks," responds Cliff.

Hill then says to Cliff, "I know you wrote everything in your report but can you tell me in your own words what led you to discover the body?"

Daily's brown eyes narrow as he sizes up Cliff and Brad. Brad stiffens and draws himself up to his full height.

"Well we—Brad and I-- were on our regular patrol down Route 377 when I saw something about 200 yards in the bush. So me and my partner ran over to investigate and that's when we found the woman."

Hill pauses from taking notes, glances up at Cliff and squints her eyes.

Cliff noticing her look stutters, "Uh, I mean, Mrs. Henderson."

Daily and Hill briefly exchange glances before Hill looks back down at her notepad and continues writing. Then in a serious and direct tone she asks, "What time was this?"

"Around 9:20."

"What was her condition when you arrived?"

"She was unresponsive and breathing sporadically."

"She smelled like vinegar and was covered in cuts and bruises," added Brad.

Cliff then continues, "We called for EMS and had her air lifted to the Lincoln Trauma Center."

In the same serious tone Daily asks," Did she ever regain consciousness?"

"No Sir," reports Cliff, "not while she was with us."

Hill continues, "Has anyone had a chance to follow up on her condition?"

Brad and Cliff look at each other then Brad responds, "No I don't think so."

Hill makes a note of that then responds, "No problem, we'll check her out. Lincoln Hospital is right down the road from our Phoenix Field Office. Is there anything else you can tell us about this case?"

Brad nods his head no as does Cliff.

"No not really. I think we told you everything," says Cliff, "and from what we've heard very little of what the CSI team has found can explain what happened in the camper or what happened to the little boy."

Hill closes her notepad and puts it in her pocket; "Well I guess that's it then. We'll take over from here," she extends her hand to thank the officers, "thanks for your help."

"Wait a minute!" exclaims Brad as Hill shakes Cliff's hand, "Listen we know this is your case but we'd like to know what the hells going on here. I mean do you think this could have been something related to a case he was working on, was it the mob, or terrorist? Come on you could tell us something."

"My partner's right," adds Cliff, "There's been a lot of strange things going on in these parts for a while now and for once we'd like to get some answers."

"A lot of strange things?" Daily interjects.

Cliff goes on to share the unexplained events that have taken place in the area like the mutilation of livestock and horses, missing cattle and persons, and of course, the two Hernandez children who had disappeared. Daily nods, listening intently and mentally recording the information while Hill jots down some notes.

Hill sighs, raising an eyebrow as she glances over at Daily, who gives her a quick nod.

"Okay fair enough," she says, "I'll tell you all we know, which really isn't much," Hill reaches back into her pocket and takes out her notepad. She flips through a few pages then stops and reads, "The dead agent's name is Allen Henderson. He was thirty-three years old and has been an agent for the past eight years. He was currently assigned to the downtown Phoenix field office and was on vacation with his wife Laura age thirty and their ten year old son Billy," Hill flips through a few more pages, "we checked his case load and interviewed his partner and found nothing that suggests this incident could have been connected to anything he's been working on," she closes the notepad and sighs, "so you see we know about as much as you do which amounts to nothing."

Just then O'Brien, who was with a group of officers across the road opposite the camper, runs over and interrupts, "Johnson, Williams, A chopper just spotted something about twelve miles south west of here. Looks like the boy! Maddox is getting ready to leave! He thought you might want to know."

"Thanks," exclaims Brad as the two officers race off behind O'Brien towards a waiting white and blue police helicopter.

As they approach they see the Lieutenant Maddox stepping into the craft.

Brad yells out over the deafening noise of the helicopter, "Lieutenant! Mind if we come along?"

Maddox turns around and stares at the two men for a moment.

Brad pleads, "Come on Lieutenant, give us a break."

Maddox grins then waves the officers in.

"Have room for us too?" shouts Agent Daily as he scrambles up behind the officers.

Maddox nods his head sarcastically and yells, "Alright, alright come on."

Once secured in the chopper Cliff turns to Maddox as they lift off, "How in the world did the kid get twelve miles out?"

"Hell if I know. We figured he'd been missing for over six hours so I guess it's possible to get that far."

Brad looks at Cliff and says, "Shit if I was that kid and saw what happened back at that camper I'd be in Los Angeles by now."

"I'd be right behind you partner."

After the group is secured in the chopper it lifts off and speeds towards its destination. As the helicopter flies over the forest Cliff stares out of the window observing the rough terrain below. He wonders to himself what could have happened here. What could have frightened this child enough to run blindly through a darkened forest? What could have injured his mother and brutally mutilated his father? What or who could have done this?

As the helicopter touches down all of the law enforcement officers jump out and converge at the edge of the forest. Cliff looks up and notices that a little distance away another chopper is hovering over a densely wooded section of the forest. Finally a third helicopter with medical personnel arrives and lands a few yards behind theirs.

"That's where he is," Maddox shouts trying to be heard over the deafening sound of the three helicopters in the area. He's pointing in the direction of the chopper hovering over the woods about 300 yards away.

Once the medical personnel join the team Maddox takes the lead, "We'll have to cut through here," he says as he enters the dark woods. The other members of the group follow him, struggling to make their way through the thick bush and undergrowth. They continue on till they are almost under the hovering helicopter.

"There he is!" shouts Brad while pointing towards a large maple tree. Under the tree is a small boy with long dirty brown hair, curled up in the fetal position clutching a red and blue Spiderman backpack. He's wearing a blue hooded sweater, blue pajama pant with white trim and unlaced sneakers without socks. He's just lying there with his eyes closed. As the group slowly approaches three paramedics from the second chopper push pass them and run over to the boy to begin checking his vitals. Brad, Cliff, Maddox and the two agents follow forming a semi circle around the boy. With the search and rescue helicopter still hovering overhead, one of the paramedics' turns to Maddox and shouts, "He's alive!" A collective sigh of relief is felt throughout the group.

Maddox unclips his radio, "Dispatch, this is Search Team Alpha."

"Go ahead Alpha."

"Alert command, the boy has been found. Repeat, the boy has been found."

"Good news Alpha."

"We're airlifting him to Lincoln Trauma ASAP."

"Ten-four Alpha, will advise."

He then looks down at the paramedics as they begin strapping the young child to a stretcher.

"Is he going to make it?" he shouts over the noise of the hovering helicopter.

One of the paramedics shouts back, "Looks like he's suffering from dehydration and shock. Doesn't look like anything's broken, his blood pressure looks good but we'll know more when we get him to the hospital."

While the medical team continues to secure the child to the stretcher Brad picks up the backpack that had fallen from the boy's grasp. He unzips the bag and pulls out a large clear plastic box, the type fisherman use as bait and tackle box. The rectangular box is about one foot long, six inches high and just as thick. Inside he can see what appears to be a very large insect. While standing next to the tree he holds it up to the sun to get a better look, "Wow, look at this."

Cliff comes over for a closer look, "Is it dead?"

Brad shakes the box and the insect's body rattles about, "Yeah, but what is it?"

"Don't know never seen anything that big before, must be about ten inches long."

"When I was a boy I used to do the same thing. My mother used to have a fit for bringing bugs into the house," adds Brad.

"Looks like we got ourselves a junior bug collector," says Cliff as he flashes a brief smile.

Brad smiles and shoves the box back into the backpack while they carry the boy back to the waiting helicopters.

Once they have the child secured on the Medevac copter Cliff approaches Maddox while he stands in the doorway of the helicopter, "Lieutenant, we'd like to follow this one through."

"Listen you guys…" he pauses in mid-sentence as he notices the look of determination on their faces.

Then Brad interrupts, "Lieutenant, remember the missing Hernandez kids?"

Maddox shakes his head yes.

"That really kicked our asses. It's still an open case. We'd like the chance to at least close this one."

Maddox gives them both a look that says he understands. Finally he says, "Go ahead fly back with the boy. I'll send someone to pick you up later."

The two men smile as they enter the chopper, getting pats on their backs from Maddox as they pass him.

As the chopper's engine revs up Maddox yells, "While you're there you might as well check up on the condition of the mother."

Brad and Cliff both give him thumbs up.

Agent Daily, standing behind Maddox shouts, "We'll meet up with you guys at the hospital. The FBI's chopper is on its way to pick us up."

The two men nod their heads and close the door to the helicopter and strap themselves in. The Red and white vehicle lifts off, spins around 90 degrees, lowers its nose and speeds off over the forest towards Phoenix.

The flight to the hospital is uneventful and quick. After about twenty minutes they are approaching the landing pad on the rooftop of Lincoln Hospital in downtown Phoenix. As the helicopter touches down one of the paramedics swings the door open and is greeted by the hospital's medical staff, a team of two doctors, three orderlies and a nurse. Together they transfer the boy to a hospital gurney and quickly wheel him towards the trauma unit with Brad and Cliff in close pursuit. They cart the young child down a long hall and through a pair of large swinging doors, which serve as the entrance to the trauma ward. Just as Cliff is about to enter the ward a grey-haired man in his mid-sixties wearing a white doctor's jacket and a stethoscope around his neck runs up from behind him and grabs his arm, "Excuse me, but are you the officers who found the woman on the road this morning?"

Cliff shakes his head, "That's us. We just found the woman's son they just took him in there."

"Well I'm Dr. Taylor and I thought you should know that she woke up a few minutes ago and she's asking for her child. I didn't know what to tell her and I was told that you may want to question her first."

"Thanks, where is she?"

"Just one flight down in recovery, I'll take you there."

Brad turns to Cliff and says, "Listen you go ahead I'll stay with the boy just in case he wakes up too."

"Alright then see you in a few," Cliff turns and follows the doctor as Brad pushes open the swinging doors to the trauma ward and enters with the boy's backpack slung over his right shoulder.

Cliff follows the doctor down the stairs and onto the next floor. From there they travel through a maze of corridors that finally lead into the recovery ward. The ward consists of a nurse's station followed by a hall lined with ten private rooms. As they walk down the hall Cliff can hear all manner of monitoring equipment beeping and buzzing from one room to another. Finally they reach the last room at the end of the hall and slowly open the door. Lying on the bed is Laura Henderson. Two IV bags are attached to her left arm. Wires from an EKG machine snake all over her body and the steady beep of her heart monitor dominates the atmosphere in the room. Cliff almost doesn't recognize her; her face looks much fuller than it did when he found her on the road. It is still red from the sunburn but he can tell that some type of ointment had been applied. Bandages now cover the abscess' on her face and arm, the smaller cuts and scrapes of her face and body have also been cleaned and now don't look as bad as they did earlier. Her breathing is stronger and she appears to be sleeping.

Dr. Taylor turns to Cliff and says softly, "Good thing you found her when you did she was severely dehydrated but the weirdest thing was that she had a large amount of formic acid in her system. We had to work quickly before her body's systems started shutting down."

"Formic acid?"

"Yes formic acid. It was mainly concentrated around those large wounds she has on her face and arm."

"How does somebody get formic acid in their body? I never even heard of that kind of acid. Can you buy it? I mean what is it used for?"

"Well commercially it's used as a preservative or an antibacterial agent in livestock feed but in nature it's found in some insect stings."

"Insect stings? You mean she could've been stung by some kind of bug?"

"That's right. I looked it up and I found that it's found primarily in ants."

"You mean to tell me ants did this to her?"

Dr. Taylor chuckles, "No, no, it would take tens of thousands of ants to give her the amount of formic acid we found in her system. No, I'm afraid ants couldn't have done this. I'm sure there's an logical explanation to what happened to her," he walks over to the side of Laura's bed and leans over her, not noticing that Cliff was still frozen at the door. Dr. Taylor speaks to Laura in a calm voice, "Mrs. Henderson? Mrs. Henderson? There's someone here to speak to you."

She slowly begins to stir as Dr. Taylor turns toward Cliff, "We had to sedate her. When she woke up she started screaming and shouting nonsense."

Cliff slowly approaches the bed, "What kind of nonsense?"

"She was screaming about bugs. She said bugs were everywhere. We thought at first she was on some type of drug, like Angel Dust or something."

Cliff ignores the doctor's comments and says, "What kind of bugs Doc? Could she have meant ants?"

Dr. Taylor pauses for a moment and slowly turns back towards Cliff with a curious look as if the question caught him off guard. He then turns back to Laura and says slowly in an unsure manner, "I don't know…um, maybe." He pauses again before curtly saying, "I know what you're thinking and as I told you before ants couldn't have done this type of damage," he turns back to Laura and gently places a hand upon her shoulder. "Mrs. Henderson can you hear me?"

Laura slowly opens her eyes and looks up at the doctor, "Doctor did you find him? Where's my baby? Where's Billy?" she asks in a tremulous voice.

"Billy's fine now. We're taking care of him upstairs," comforts the doctor.

"I want to see my boy. I want to see Billy. I want to see him! Is he alright? Did he get away? They didn't get him did they?" tears begin to roll down her face, "Where's Allen?"

She looks around the room as though searching for her husband.

"Allen? Allen? Oh Allen! Nooooo! Nooooo!"

She turns her head into the pillow and sobs bitterly.

Cliff slowly comes closer and leans over the bed, "Mrs. Henderson? Mrs. Henderson my name is Officer Johnson my partner and I found you on Route 377 this morning. Can you tell us what happened to you, ma'am?"

Laura turns toward Cliff slowly and wipes her eyes then reaches up to squeeze his hand.

"Thank you. Thank you so much. I want to see my baby! Where's Billy?"

"He's just fine ma'am. He's alright, their taking real good care of him. You can see him soon."

"Thank God. Oh thank God!"

"Can you tell us anything Mrs. Henderson? Anything at all that can help us?" Cliff presses.

Mrs. Henderson visibly struggles to calm down, gradually becoming quiet and taking deep breaths. As she collects herself, she hugs herself tightly, looking away from Dr. Taylor and Cliff as she wrestles with her thoughts. With a far-off look in her eyes she whispers, "Bugs…"

Dr. Taylor isn't sure he has heard correctly. "Excuse me?"

Mrs. Henderson shakes her head, running a hand through her short, dark hair before saying more emphatically. "Bugs." She looks up at Dr. Taylor, eyes rather unfocused. "Bugs!"

"What do you mean, bugs?"

Laura looks down at her hands, now trembling in her lap, turning them this way and that as though she didn't recognize them. Cliff observes that this was not some drug-induced hysteria--something had frightened this woman so badly, she was a far cry from the serene, composed woman he glimpsed in that nightstand photograph.

She takes a deep breath and turns to Cliff with a wildly frightened look in her eyes, "There were these big bugs, okay? They were everywhere, biting and--and stinging us." Mrs. Henderson pauses, putting a hand to her forehead as though she can't quite believe the words she herself is uttering. After another deep breath she continues, "My husband and Billy found a dead one the day before and put it in a box," she attempts a wry smile but her lips only tremble as though she is about to burst into tears again. Dr. Taylor puts a hand on her shoulder to comfort and encourage her, with a slight nod. She looks up at him then back to Cliff, continuing, "Billy said he wanted to show his friends when he got back. He's in the cub scouts and they like stuff like that. Everything was alright till this morning. Billy was sleeping in the bunk over the cab and me and Allen were in the back room."

Laura's face grows grim again. "Then early in the morning we hear Billy screaming at the top of his lungs. So we –my husband and I-- run into the kitchen and they were everywhere. They were all over Billy, the walls, the ceiling everywhere. Everywhere!" Laura bursts into tears again, covering her face with her hands.

Sobbing hysterically she continues, "They just started jumping on us and, and, and biting us. They were all over, everywhere! Everywhere…" Laura collapses into sobs, falling back upon the pillows with her hands over her face.

The heart monitor machine attached to Laura which has been steadily increasing begins beeping faster. Dr. Taylor moves to her side and sits on the bed next to her. He gently touches her shoulder in an attempt to comfort her, "It's okay Mrs. Henderson, everything's going to be alright. Just try and relax."

"You're doing great, Mrs. Henderson," adds Cliff.

After a few minutes the beeping begins to return to its normal rhythm. As she slowly regains her composure the doctor and Cliff exchange glances of disbelief and shake their heads.

After a few more moments Laura continues in a weary voice, slowly wiping her eyes, "Allen started screaming for us to get out! He was covered with the things. He just kept screaming GET OUT, GET OUT. I just grabbed Billy and ran out of the camper. They were still all over us…it was horrible. We just ran and ran and ran. We were fighting off the bugs and calling for Allen. Next thing I know there's screaming and gunshots coming from the camper. I kept calling for Allen but…he never came." She puts her hands over her face again and sobs.

"Allen, my God Allen." She lowers her hands and looks up at Dr. Taylor. "What happened to Allen? Is he ok?"

Doctor Taylor and Cliff glance at each other again, neither man wanting to be the one to tell her the grisly details of her husband's death.

Cliff tries to change the subject, "Mrs. Henderson do you have any idea what kind of bugs these were?"

Nodding her head she says, "I don't know. They looked like ants. Like big giant ants."

Cliff takes her hand in his and says, "Thank you so much Mrs. Henderson. You've been a tremendous help. Get some rest now, OK?"

Mrs. Henderson nods, exhausted, and lays back on the pillows, closing her eyes. "Find Allen…" Her voice trails off sadly.

"Mrs. Henderson, we're doing everything we can to…help your family. I'll be back a little later—I'm going upstairs to check on your son." Dr. Taylor smiles warmly.

Mrs. Henderson looks up at him with a look of hope in her eyes. "Thank you! Oh, thank you doctor."

Dr. Taylor pulls the hospital curtains around Laura's bed and they exit the room. Once outside, Cliff turns to Dr. Taylor and says, "Doc, I need to talk to my partner right away! Can you direct me back upstairs?"

Dr. Taylor looks at him askance but recovers quickly. "Sure follow me."

The two men hurry upstairs to look for Brad. On the way the doctor asks Cliff, "What do you think of her story?"

"I don't know, but we did find a big dead ant like bug in her kid's backpack."

Dr. Taylor stops briefly, looking at Cliff. "You're kidding!"

"I wish I were. My partner has the backpack now. Didn't you say that formic acid comes from ants?"

"Sure, but giant ants … that can kill people? That's incredible."

After Cliff pushes open the door to the trauma ward he spots Brad across the room talking to another doctor. Brad looks up and notices Cliff and Dr. Taylor at the entrance and motions for them to come over.

As they approach Brad points to the doctor at his side, "This is Dr. Green he just completed the autopsy on Allen Henderson. Doctor this is my partner."

The two men shake hands, "You two know each other?" asks Cliff while pointing to the two doctors. Dr. Taylor reaches out his hand to Dr. Green. "No I'm afraid not. How'd you do? I'm Dr. Taylor I've been helping Mrs. Henderson through her recovery."

Brad continues, "Dr. Green was just filling me in on what he found during the autopsy. Cliff you're not going to believe this.

"Oh really, wait till you hear what I found out!" exclaims Cliff.

A look of surprise and wonder sweeps across Brad's face then Dr. Green begins, "Well as I was telling your partner Mr. Henderson could have died any number of ways. First and of course the most obvious was the fact that he was missing his lower extremities. Most of his major internal organs are missing including intestines, liver, and kidneys, all gone. His lungs were punctured and here is the real mystery. Are you ready for this? He was filled with enough formic acid to kill ten men."

"Formic acid? Like the kind found in ants?" says Cliff in a matter-of-fact kind of way.

Dr. Green pauses with a puzzled look on his face, "Ants? Well yes ants I believe ants do sting with formic acid but not in this quantity."

"What are you getting at partner?" asks Brad.

"Doc and I just came from interviewing Mrs. Henderson and she claims to have been attacked by a swarm of giant ants."

Brad looks down at the side of the boy's bed where he had placed the backpack and slowly picks it up. Then quietly says, "Like the one in here?"

All four men bend closer to get a better look as Brad slowly pulls the plastic box out of the bag.

"Incredible!" exclaims Dr. Green.

"We thought it was some harmless exotic bug the boy found," explains Brad.

Then from behind them a female voice yells out, "What'cha got there, boys?"

The men snap their heads around. Coming through the swinging doors of the trauma ward walking briskly towards them are FBI Agents Hill and Daily.

"I think we just got a lead in the case," explains Brad.

"Really?"

"But, you're not going to believe it." adds Cliff nodding his head.

"Try me."

She walks up and shakes the hands of the two doctors.

"Hello, I'm Special Agent Hill of the FBI and this is Special Agent Daily. So, what have you found?"

Looks like you got yourselves one weird case here," Dr. Taylor notes.

"Really?" replies Agent Hill.

"Straight out of the X-Files," comments Brad.

Dr. Green looks around the trauma unit; there are doctors, nurses and orderlies scurrying about tending to various patients. He then realizes that opening the box here and examining its contents may not be a good idea.

"Why don't we go down to my lab to discuss this and examine the evidence?" interrupts Dr. Green.

"Good idea, Doc," adds Cliff.

"Come on follow me."

The team follows Dr. Green out of the trauma unit and down a lengthy hallway. Along the way Agent Daily turns to Brad and says, "So what's so special about this evidence you've found?"

"Trust me you won't believe it even when you see it."

Hill frowns and Daily shakes his head with a little half-smile on his face as though the patrol officers were starting to wear on both of them.

The group stops in front of a bank of elevators and Dr. Green presses the down button. "My lab's down on sub-level two."

Not one who likes to be kept waiting, Agent Hill says, "Okay, enough beating around the bush. What exactly have you have found?" Those piercing hazel eyes demanding answers.

Brad glances at Cliff as the elevator bell rings and the doors open. As they all step in Brad says to Agent Hill, "It was ants."

Agent Hill's eyes narrow, while Agent Daily's half-smile widens into a fully condescending sneer. "What did you say?" Hill demanded.

"Ants, it was ants," repeats Brad, hearing for himself how crazy it sounded.

"You're kidding?" replies Hill as her pretty face contorted in disbelief mingled with impatience.

"Yeah ants--big ones."

The doors to the elevator close as Hill stares at Brad with a puzzled look. Brad opens the backpack and slowly pulls the box halfway out of the bag. Hill looks down at the box and the highly disciplined and self-controlled agent can't help but gasp. "Look at the size of that thing!"

Daily walks over and takes a look, "Holy shit!"

"You mean to tell me this killed Henderson?" says Hill.

"According to Mrs. Henderson, there were hundreds of them," adds Dr. Taylor.

Brad pushes the box back into the bag.

"And based on the amount of formic acid found in his remains it would take that many ants of that size," continues Dr. Green.

As the elevator bell rings the doors open on the third floor and a few people step into the elevator. The door closes as Hill steps back against the rear wall of the elevator. She exhales, "Wow, this is crazy."

Everyone remains silent as the elevator arrives at the second sub-level. They follow Dr. Green around a few corners and enter his lab, a small room with a two-tiered shelf filled with beakers, test tubes, jars of chemicals and testing equipment around the back three walls and file cabinets with a desk in the front. In the middle of the room is a large metal examination table. The group surrounds the table as Brad opens the backpack and removes the plastic box. He gently places it on the table. Dr. Green puts on some rubber gloves then steps forward and opens the box. Using a pair of tongs he gently removes the dead insect and places it on the table beside the box. The ant is brownish-black in color, has six long legs and two thin transparent wings attached to its mid section. On its head there are two large black tear-shaped eyes along with two long antennas curled around like the horns of a mountain goat. Its legs are curled underneath the body the way insect's legs curl up when they die.

"Are ants supposed to have wings?" asks Cliff.

"Only the new queens and males do. The queens lose them after they mate," explains Daily.

Everyone looks at him as if surprised by his knowledge of the creature. He looks at the group and shrugs his shoulders then says, "What? I saw it on the Discovery Channel."

Dr. Green turns his attention back to the ant on the table. He gets a ruler from one of the shelves and begins to measure the carcass. "Hmm. Eleven and a half inches. Anybody know how big these things normally get?" He looks around the group for a response. The group then turns and looks at Agent Daily.

"Hey I don't know! I just saw that one show and all of those ants were barely an inch long."

"I think we can all agree that an eleven-inch ant isn't normal," says Dr. Taylor.

"But how come we haven't seen them until now?" asks Brad.

"You know, I'm beginning to wonder if these things were responsible for the disappearance of the Hernandez kids last year," Cliff says to Brad.

Dr. Taylor looked at him quizzically while Hill and Daily knowingly recalled the information they shared with them at the camper. Cliff proceeds to fill the physician in: "It was a case we worked on last year. Two kids disappeared without a trace about five miles from where the Henderson's parked. We never got any leads on the case. It was terrible, a five-year-old kid and his sister, just a couple of years older than him just vanished into thin air."

"Pet dog, too," Brad added.

Everyone looks at him and he adds, "Not to mention about a dozen or so other cases of missing people going back the last five years. Who knows how long these things have been around?"

Just then Agent Hill makes a suggestion, "You know we're not going to get any answers here. None of us are experts in this area. Why don't I send this specimen to our Washington forensics lab maybe they can tell us something?"

"That's a good idea, but in the meantime we need to warn the public if there's a nest of these things on the loose," states Dr. Taylor.

"You may be right, Dr. Taylor, but we don't want to panic people," Hill replied.

"Screw that--these things are killing people!" exclaims Brad.

"I know, Officer Williams," Agent Hill begins, "But can you imagine the widespread hysteria this would cause. We have to do this responsibly. I think the first thing is for you to get in touch with your superiors. Explain to them what we've found and have them quietly begin setting up a quarantine zone around that trailer. I'll advise the FBI and the EPA about the situation and find out from them what course of action to take."

Brad nods his head in agreement and says, "Alright! Sounds like a plan." He motions to Cliff to follow him out of the lab. As the two officers leave the lab, Brad unclips his radio and begins calling Lieutenant Maddox.

Dr. Green returns the dead insect to the plastic box and hands it to Agent Hill who places it back into the backpack, "I hope you know what you're doing," he says.

"I hope so too," she responds as she takes the backpack.

As the two agents leave the hospital they notice a black Crown Victoria parked out on front. Sitting on the hood of the car reading a newspaper is a tall well-dressed balding man. It's their Supervising Agent Mark Spinner. Standing next to him is Special Agent Barry Griffin. Griffin sees them approaching the car and nudges Spinner's arm with an elbow, "Here they come."

Spinner quickly looks up and folds the paper, sticking it under his arm. "Find out anything?"

"We need to hurry sir. We definitely have a situation here," she opens the rear door of the car and quickly gets in as Daily follows. Spinner, sensing the urgency of the matter jumps in on the passenger side as Griffin runs around to the driver's side with keys in hand.

"What's going on?" says Spinner as he buckles his seat belt.

Hill reaches over the back of the seat and hands him the backpack. "What's this?" he slowly begins open it and pulls out the plastic box as Griffin drives out of the parking lot.

"We believe that a nest of these things killed Agent Henderson and possibly several others in the area," reports Hill.

Spinner peers through the box, "Jesus!"

Griffin glances over while driving and blurts out, "What the hell it that?"

He swerves the car but quickly regains control. Griffin glances at Spinner who gives him a stern look. Griffin snaps his head around and continues to drive.

"We think it's some kind of mutated ant, sir," continues Hill, "There could possibly be a whole colony of these things in the forest. I'd like to get this one over to our lab in D.C."

"Good call, Debra. When we get back to the office I'll call the local law enforcement and coordinate closing down that section of the forest."

"That's already begun. The two officers that were with us are informing their people as we speak."

"Good. Then get a call out to the EPA and you may even want to inform the CDC."

"Yes, sir!"

He slides the box back into the backpack, "Step on it, Griffin!"

"Yes, sir!"

Griffin turns on the siren as they speed down Indianola Ave. towards the Phoenix Field Office of the FBI. When they arrive Daily prepares the ant specimen for shipping to Washington D.C. as Hill puts in a call to the EPA and the CDC.

The next morning Agent Hill is in her office preparing to meet with the other law enforcement personnel out at the Henderson's camper, which has become a mobilization point and base of operations for the multi agency task force that is forming to hunt down and destroy the nest of killer ants.

Hill's office is a veritable hive of activity. Subordinates come in and out with new data reports and processed lab results. The walls are plastered with local and regional maps highlighted with key areas pertinent to past and recent events in the forest in an effort to discern some kind of patterns. Hill's desk is piled high with photos and folders, and the pile seems to just be getting bigger. The phone seems to ring steadily but she has a couple of people on hand to assist with the calls and continue processing data received via computer and satellite observations of the area.

To keep the public out of the area officials from Hill's FBI office decided to release a fake story about a tanker filled with toxic waste that has overturned on Route 377. The report is released to the media who is told that it may take several days to clean up the spill. An onsite team has proceeded to cordon off a ten-mile ring around the Henderson's camper and is in direct contact with Hill's team at the office in order to keep feeding consistent information to the media.

Having delegated instructions to her team via its coordinator, Agent Hill prepares to head down to the site, putting on her dark blue field jacket with big white FBI letters printed on the back. She then picks up her government issued Glock 9mm hand gun and slaps in a full clip just as Agent Daily walks in carrying a small brown bag, nearly running into a senior staff member who is on his way out.

"We got some visitors here from the Environmental Protection Agency," Daily announces.

"Already? Wow that was fast. What's in the bag?"

"How long have you been up?"

"I don't know eight or nine hours maybe."

"And when was the last time you had something to eat?"

"Clarence I don't know. You know how it is when I get into a case."

"Yeah I do," he hands her the paper bag, "tuna salad, extra mayo, lettuce and tomatoes on rye just the way you like it."

Hill smiles and takes the bag from him. "What would I do without you? I promise I'll eat it as soon as we finish with these guys."

Daily gives her a look of disbelief. Hill looks at him and responds, "I promise I'll eat. Ok?"

"Okay, but I'm watching you."

Hill smiles and says, "Come on let's see what these guys want."

She puts the bag on her desk, holsters her gun and follows Daily out into the waiting area. There she's greeted by two men and a woman all of whom appear to be in their forties and wearing jeans and denim jackets, one of the men smiles at Hill and approaches with his hand extended. He's a Caucasian man with a shiny bald head, wide smile and no facial hair. While shaking her hand he says, "Hi, you must be Agent Hill. I'm Dr. Bloomberg, this is Mr. Cooper," pointing to the man standing next to him sporting long blond hair tied in a ponytail falling down the center of his back, "and this is Dr. Hinds," he points to the only woman in their group, a tall slender woman with short dark hair who is wearing sunglasses.

"How do you do?" replies Dr. Hinds as she moves forward to shake Hill's hand.

"Nice to meet you. I'm surprised that you arrived so quickly. We could use all the help we can get. We were just on our way out to the site to supervise locating and exterminating the nest. How much have you been filled in about the incident?"

The three look at each other slowly and then back at Hill. Dr. Bloomberg steps forward and says in a very diplomatic way, "Agent Hill, with all due respect and discretion, we are not really here to assist you. We are actually here to inform you that this operation is now under the jurisdiction of the EPA and you and your partner have been temporarily reassigned to work with us in a matter of national security. All the paperwork has already been cleared through your supervisor Spinner. You're welcomed to look it over if you'd like."

Both Hill and Daily look at each other with the look of surprise in their eyes. Daily steps forward and says, "Who's us?"

"We're part of a team called the Invasion Task Force," Dr. Bloomberg continues.

"Never heard of it."

"And you never will," adds Dr. Hinds with a smirk.

"Since when did the EPA start developing covert ops?" asks Hill.

Bloomberg cuts in, "Listen I know you probably have a million questions. All of them will be answered I assure you. We have our bird waiting on the pad to fly us out to the site. Our mobile lab is already there and setup. We'll fill you in when we get there along with the other members of the team."

"Give us a sec," says Hill as she and Daily walk back into Hill's office.

"Debra, what the hell's going on?" asks Daily with a worried look on his face.

"I don't know but I'm going to find out," she picks up the phone on her desk and pushes a button. "Hello Spinner this is Hill. I have some people here from the EPA and they're saying.............Yes Sir..........I know Sir but...........Yes Sir..........Yes Sir." She hangs up the phone and looks at Daily.

"What did he say?"

"He says we're to cooperate with them and it's out of his hands. He said the orders come from high up."

"What the fuck is going on?"

"I guess the only way to know is to go along with them."

The two agents reenter the waiting room and head to the heliport with the EPA officials. When they arrive at the pad the two agents stop in their tracks at the sight of the vehicle that's waiting for them, they discover a V-22 Osprey tilt rotor aircraft like the type the U.S. Marines fly. The Osprey is a twenty first century hybrid aircraft. The Jet-black vehicle with a large EPA insignia on its side is about 60 feet long and has a wingspan of around 45 feet. At the end of each wingtip is mounted a three-bladed turboprop engine attached to a transmission nacelle capable of rotating a full 90 degrees. The tilt rotor aircraft can take off like a helicopter when the nacelles are pointed 90 degrees up. Once airborne its nacelles can be rotated forward to convert it to airplane mode, which allows it to be capable of high-speed high altitude flight.

The EPA vehicle looks sleek and impressive sitting on the helipad with its rear-landing ramp down; its props are pointed straight up and are idling with a loud groan. Daily scratches his head and looks at Hill. "You ever rode in one of these before?"

"You kidding? I've never even been this close to one."

As they follow the other team members up the ramp and onto the craft Daily says, "They must have some budget. I hear these things cost about fifty million each."

Then Cooper responds as he steps into the aircraft, "More like seventy million and we have four."

As they sit down and buckle in, Daily and Hill exchange amused glances. Once they are secured in their seats and checked by a crewmember the rear ramp is raised and the engines begin to roar. They feel the vibration of the fuselage as the aircraft begins to lift off. As the Osprey turns east the team can hear the whine of the nacelles rotating forward as the aircraft begins to pick up speed.

After a brief flight the Osprey gently sets down across from the Henderson's camper. The area is alive with personal and vehicles of all type. Members of the military are on post all around the area. There are no signs of the state police or other local law enforcement personal. The entire area has become an armed camp! As the Osprey's engines wind down the rear ramp lowers and the three EPA members walk down along with the two FBI agents. Hill and Daily pause at the bottom of the ramp for a moment and look around in awe of how quickly the large well-equipped camp has been put together.

They are then lead towards a large black fifty-foot mobile command center parked next to the landing area. The command center is attached to a huge black Kenworth tractor. On the top of the command center is an array of satellite dishes and communications antenna. In the middle of the command is a small set of steps leading to a door. Daily and Hill follow the team up the stairs and into the command center. Once inside they find themselves in a hi-tech monitoring room with screens and computers covering both walls. To the left are four people sitting at the monitors and appear not to notice the team walk in. To the right a thick glass wall with a door leading to a small conference room complete with a table surrounded by ten chairs. Hanging from the far end behind the table is a large flat screen monitor and on the opposite wall are several maps. Above the large monitor is the word INVASION painted in large white letters.

As they near the door to the conference room Daily notices that patrol officers Cliff and Brad are seated at the table. They're talking to a man seated across from them. He is an older black man possibly in his early sixties sporting a salt and pepper beard who is well-dressed with long slightly gray dread locks falling to just about the middle of his back and wearing a pair of horn rimmed glasses. On the table in front of the man is a stack of thick file folders.

As Bloomberg opens the thick glass door he motions for them to take a seat.

Hill looks down at Brad and Cliff sitting at the table, "Officer Johnson, Officer Williams, what are you boys doing here?"

"Looks like we've been recruited," replies Cliff, "and you?"

"Same here," says Hill as she takes a seat next to Cliff.

As the rest of the team begins to find seats the well-dressed black man stands up and in a deep commanding baritone voice says, "Hello lady's and gentlemen, I know you have a lot of questions and I hope I'm able to answer them all. But first allow me to introduce myself and my team. My name is Professor Richard Hamilton and I'm head of a top secret team from the Environmental Protection Agency known as the INVASION Task Force."

"Invasion?" Daily exclaims.

"Yes. Actually it's an acronym which stands for Invasive Noxious & Violent Alternative Species Investigation Operative Network."

"Invasive?" asks Hill.

"Noxious?" Daily murmurs.

"You mean like the ants?" adds Brad.

Just then a pleasant-looking young black man dressed in jeans and a short-sleeved yellow designer shirt with the collar turned up walks in carrying a laptop and some papers in his hands, "Sorry I'm late," he says in a slightly nervous tone. He pulls up a chair and sits down quickly, avoiding eye contact with Professor Hamilton while he opens up his laptop.

Hamilton pauses for a moment staring sternly at the young man, "Nice of you to make it Troy," he says in an irritated tone. Hamilton then turns his attention back to the members at the table.

"Let me first introduce the members of the task force and explain our mission. Maybe then things will become clearer."

He begins his introductions by pointing at Dr. Bloomberg, "I believe most of you have already met our Ecologist Dr. Bloomberg." Bloomberg smiles and waves his hand, "This is our Environmental Engineer Simon Cooper," Professor Hamilton says while pointing at Cooper, Cooper nods his head, "Next is our Biologist Dr. Karen Hinds and Toxicologist Jacob Forrester," he presents them with an open palm and the both of them give a brief wave, "and the tardy youngster over here is Troy Phillip, our resident Technology Specialist," Troy gives a comical salute before seeming to immediately regret the gesture before the serious group. He looks down sheepishly.

"What's your background?" Hill asks Professor Hamilton.

"Well I'm an entomologist."

"A what?" asks Cliff.

"An entomologist, I study insects."

"Well, that's exactly what we need but damn! What's up with all the hi-tech gear?" asks Brad.

"And since when does the EPA recruit FBI and police officers?" adds Hill.

Prof. Hamilton slowly removes his glasses, folds them and places them on the table, "Before I begin let me tell you that everything I'm about to say to you is considered top secret by order of the President himself," Brad and Cliff take a quick glance at each other as does Hill and Daily, "How many of you have heard of a company named Gen X Technologies, Inc.?"

Everyone nods their heads to acknowledge that they have heard of the company but Brad raises his hand and says, "Aren't they the one's that had that big explosion at one of their plants in South America some years back?"

Hamilton continues, "One and the same. Actually it was about ten years ago in Ponta do Seixas, Brazil. Now let me tell you a little story about Gen X Tech. As you may or may not know they are the largest and most successful Biotechnology Company on the planet. They employ over 100,000 people worldwide. They're the ones that developed the world's first truly synthetic blood and synthetic skin for burn patients. And as you might have heard in the news they recently developed a technique to clone and grow human body parts from stem cells at an accelerated rate for people awaiting organ transplants. Well ten years ago they had a facility in Brazil where they were working on a growth acceleration compound called SF-20. When mixed with food the compound was supposed to accelerate the growth hormones found in most complex organisms."

"Did it work?" asks Daily.

Professor Hamilton chuckles wryly. "Oh, it worked alright. Perhaps a little too well."

"What do you mean?" says Hill with a puzzled look.

"Let's just say it had some unexpected…side effects," Hamilton turns to Troy, "You can turn it on now."

Troy presses a few buttons on his laptop computer and the lights in the conference room dim as the flat screen monitor on the far wall comes to life.

"This is some footage we obtained from Gen X Tech's Brazilian research facility before the accident. This chicken is subject Alpha 25."

A video image of a chicken appears on the monitor. The animal looks normal and is seen feeding in a small enclosure. There is a large red tag on one of the chicken's legs. The tag reads A-25. Hamilton motions to Troy. He hits a key on the computer and the video changes.

"This is subject Alpha 25 only two months after being fed SF-20."

The two officers as well as Hill and Daily sit up in their seats to get a better look at the image being shown them. Their mouths drop open as they stare at the screen. On the monitor is a something that looks like a normal chicken. But its proportions are enormous. The animal is walking around the same enclosure as before while a worker is pouring some food into a feeding tray. The animal stands almost as tall as the man!

"Impossible!" shouts Daily.

"How big is that thing?" asks Cliff.

"Over four and a half feet tall," Hamilton says in a calm voice.

"Why would they want to make a giant chicken?" asks Cliff.

"To help cure world hunger. How many people do you think a bird this size could feed?" continues Hamilton.

"Food of the Gods," utters Brad under his breath.

"Excuse me?" replies Hamilton.

"Food of the Gods. It was a book I read in high school. I think it was by H.G. Wells. It's about these scientists that develop this food that makes things grow into giants. It was one of my favorite books as a kid."

"Ahh, yes--I've heard of the story. Yes I guess you're right Officer Williams this was like the potion in the book Food of the Gods," he says as he chuckles with a grin.

Just then Hill interjects, "So this was the unexpected side effect?"

"No, no Agent Hill this was what it was supposed to do," Hamilton looks at Troy and says, "Play the next one."

Troy taps some keys and the video changes again.

"This is Alpha 25 one month later."

The image shows the chicken in the same enclosure but this time it's over ten feet tall. The team watches in amazement for a while as the giant chicken walks around bobbing its head up and down pecking at the floor. After about a minute two technicians walk into the room with a barrel of food, as though part of a routine feeding. Initially the bird pays them little attention as it uses its great beak to groom itself. Suddenly however, the monstrous chicken squawks, red maw opened wide and, with a flourish of great feathers turns and swoops down on both men. The poor men were simply not prepared for the sudden attack and fall over one another in an effort to reach the door. The great chicken slashes mercilessly at the helpless men, its claws ripping into their midsection and tearing them almost in half. They watch in silent horror as the video shows the monster bird proceeding to peck, alternately and with lightning-fast speed at each of the convulsing bodies of the workers, ultimately ripping long, glistening ropes of intestines from their innards as easily as pulling worms from the earth. Other horror-struck technicians attempt to enter the room to try and retrieve the bodies, now bloodied, shredded and still as the towering chicken busily devours long strands of skin and organs. After a few moments the video pauses.

Hill, her already porcelain features even paler now, is the first to respond, with a calm that belies her disgust. "What the hell just happened? It killed those men."

"Yes, as you can see one of the side effects of SF-20 is that it causes the organism to become overly aggressive. But there were other undesirable effects. For instance it doesn't affect all organisms the same way. It is most affective on invertebrates. They also found that the offspring of the animals that were fed SF-20 mutated into uncontrollable organisms. It appears that SF-20 had become a super gene re-sequencer."

"A what?" asks Cliff.

"It has the ability to rearrange an organism's DNA, something that usually takes millions of years in nature. With SF-20 the organism goes through an evolutionary stage in just one or two generations. The project was deemed too risky to continue and was scheduled for termination. But that's when the real problem began. According to Gen X Tech a rival company found out about SF-20 and in an attempt to steal the formula accidently released a cloud of the stuff into the atmosphere. Fortunately SF-20, for some reason that we can't yet explain, has no effect on humans. A few months later we received the first reports of giant fire ants not far from the lab. By the time our government got involved the city of Arara in Ponta do Seixas was over run by the things. After consulting with the Brazilian government a very difficult decision was made to eliminate the threat completely."

"What do you mean completely?" Hill asks in a somber voice.

"The city had to be destroyed. Of course the official story was that there was a terrible explosion at the Gen X Tech facility.

"You mean--? Oh my God...all those people. You killed them?"

"Actually the ants had already killed most of the population."

"How many people lived there?" presses Hill.

"About 12,000 people," answers Hamilton.

"And you had them killed?"

Hamilton stares at Hill with a look of agitation and says curtly, "And just what would have been your solution, Agent Hill? The infestation had grown out of control and the decision was made at the highest level to halt its spread."

"There's something else you don't understand, Agent Hill," Dr. Hinds interjects, "SF-20 just didn't make these ants grow in size. Like Professor Hamilton has told you they've taken an evolutionary jump. They have increased intelligence; they breed faster, live longer. These things are extremely dangerous. If left unchecked they can easily replace us as the dominant species on this planet."

Then Cliff interrupts, "So what's going to happen here? Are we going to just nuke the whole area?"

"No! Oh God, no. Our job here is to find the colony and destroy it. It's as simple as that."

Brad raises his hand, "Professor Hamilton I have a question."

"Yes?"

"All this information is good and all. But what do you need us for? Why were we recruited? I get the feeling that there is more to this story than what you just told us."

Cooper glances at Hamilton and asks, "Professor...if I may?"

"Please by all means," replies Hamilton as he gestures in Brad's direction.

Cooper turns to Brad, "Officer Williams, to be honest...you and your partner know too much."

At that moment Cliff and Brad give each other a worried look.

Forrester then jumps in, "Listen, we can't risk causing a public panic if it got out what was going on."

"Normally we'd take you out and shoot you," says Troy.

"What?" exclaims Cliff.

Hamilton glares at Troy, who cringes and squeezes out a small grin, "Just kidding."

Cooper continues, "You've been assigned to us until we've gotten this situation under control."

"What about our Watch Commander? He knows what is going on?" reports Cliff.

Hamilton clears his throat and says, "Oh, you mean Lieutenant Maddox? He's also been reassigned."

"Besides we could use the extra man power," adds Forrester.

"To do what?" exclaims Daily, "We're investigators, not exterminators!"

Brad chuckles then says, "How much help do you need to squash some ants?"

Hamilton gives him a serious look, "This problem is much more serious than you think. After the incident in Brazil we started to get reports of strange unexplained events occurring all over the world."

"What type of events?" asks Brad.

"Although it has had the greatest effect on insects we have found evidence that suggests SF-20 has affected other organisms as well," adds Cooper.

Dr. Bloomberg stands up holding a thick folder, "You see this? These are the type of things we've been documenting over the past few years," he opens the folder and flips through the papers and stops at one section "You remember a few years ago when the price of wheat products went sky high?"

"Yeah some virus killed most of the wheat crops," answers Brad.

"That was the official story." Professor Hamilton grins wryly.

"In actuality," Dr. Bloomberg continues, "Giant locusts ravaged crops across the mid western United States. They destroyed millions of acres of land before we got them under control."

As they reflect on the enormity of all of this, Dr. Bloomberg thumbs through some more papers and begins again, "Did you hear about the case of five people in New York contracting a rare non contagious form of the Ebola virus?"

As most nod at the recollection Professor Hamilton volunteers, "They were actually attacked in their sleep and eaten alive by mutated roaches."

Daily and Hill exchange horrified glances.

Bloomberg continues, "And recently in Florida a family was attacked by a flock of seagulls. Their injuries were so severe they had to be hospitalized," he throws the folder on the table and sits down.

Hamilton adds, "We've had unexplained disappearances like the Hernandez case you two worked on and a rise in killer bee attacks. This is not an isolated incident, people. That's why we formed the INVASION task force. Our main mission is to investigate any incident that may be related to SF-20 and eradicate it."

Hamilton then turns to Cliff and Brad, "Now because of the sensitive nature of our operations and National Security you have been assigned to our team."

"What about us?" asks Daily.

"We've been following your cases. You and Agent Hill are considered two of the best investigators in your field office. We need you on this task force because over the past four years there has been a spike in SF-20 incidents and they have begun to spread worldwide. There have also been some questions about the operating practices of Gen X Tech. They are a very secretive company and once we get a reign on these biological problems we're going to need your skills when we investigate them."

At that point, Cliff decides to jump in. "I mean, I appreciate that you like our investigative skills but how does that help you find a pack of giant ants? I mean we don't know anything about ants? We're not scientists!"

Hamilton looks at him with a reassuring grin, "We felt it was important that you see what we are dealing with first hand. It may help in your investigation later. Who knows, after a short time with us you may become an expert. Nevertheless I have some information that can help."

Hamilton looks at Troy and nods his head. Troy presses a few buttons on his computer and the room's lights dim and the monitor turns on once again. On the screen is an image of two ants side by side. A small one on the left and on the right one that is more than three times larger.

"First of all, the fire ant is not an indigenous species to North America so it has no natural predators here. On the left is a normal fire ant measuring about one third of an inch and on the right is one of our giants. This one measured a little over four inches long. One queen runs each colony. Normally queens can live up to seven years but we have no way of knowing how long these giants live. We do know from other colonies that we've found that queens can grow to about fifteen to twenty inches in length."

"The one we found was almost a foot long," exclaims Cliff.

"Yes I read the report. We determined that the one you found was a new queen. She still had her wings so that tells us that she hadn't mated yet. You see when a batch of queens are born they leave the nest with the new born males who also have wings."

Troy changes the images on the monitor to display a video of winged queens and males emerging from a nest and flying away.

Hamilton continues, "During the mating flight the strongest male will catch the queen and mate with her. He deposits enough sperm in her to last her for her entire lifetime."

Hill's face twists in disgust, "You mean she's pregnant for life?"

"Yes I'm afraid so. After mating, the male dies and she begins building her nest."

"He dies after one night? Must have been one helluva honeymoon," jokes Cliff.

Everyone chuckles.

"Yeah she must have really put it on him," adds Daily.

"Men," Hill snorts sarcastically. She rolls her eyes as Dr. Hinds smiles.

Hamilton continues on with his lesson, "In a colony, all of the ants are infertile females except of course for the males --or drones as they're sometimes called-- which are only born around the same time as the new queens. There are different classes of ants within a colony. First there are the workers. They are the smallest and do most of the work like building and repairing the nest and caring for the young. The workers of these mutants have measured around four inches long. Next are the soldiers these are the ones that are responsible for the death of Mr. Henderson. They measure around eight to ten inches in length and have large massive mandibles capable of cutting through flesh and bone."

The images on the monitor change again to show soldier ants fighting one another.

"These ants are unrelenting and vicious in their attacks."

"Excuse me Professor but what are mandibles?" asks Hill.

"Jaws, Agent Hill it's their Jaws. They're sharp and serrated," he looks around the room at the entire group, "an ant is a powerful animal people. Don't under estimate them because of their size. These insects have been known to be able to carry objects that weigh over twenty-five times their own body mass. The soldiers also have another weapon. They can inflict a lethal dose of formic acid into their victims. That was the vinegar-like smell you noticed at the scene."

Brad and Cliff look at each other and nod.

Just then a buzzer sounds from an intercom on the desk. Hamilton moves forward and holds down a button on the device.

"Yes, what is it?"

"I think we've found the nest, sir, about fifteen miles out. We have a Humvee waiting for you out front," the voice on the other end crackles back.

"We'll be right out," he takes his hand off of the button and looks at the team.

"Well it looks like Ant Biology 101 is going to have to wait. Let's pack up."

Everyone gets up and leaves the conference room. The two police officers and the two FBI agents leave the trailer as the INVASION team members grab bags and equipment. Outside of the trailer are three Humvees. The front one is already loaded with soldiers, the team including Professor Hamilton pile into the remaining vehicles. As soon as everyone is secured the caravan of Humvees speed off.

They drive through some rough terrain and down small dirt roads and into a wooded area of the forest.   This area encompasses the part of the forest where the desert ends and the vegetation begins. Once the vehicles stop and the team members emerge they find themselves along edge of some densely packed Maple trees. A soldier motions for them to follow and they proceed through the woods. After about ten minutes they come to a grassy clearing with a mound of dirt in the middle. The mound stands about three feet high and has a diameter of about thirty feet. There's a noticeable hole in the middle of the mound. The clearing which measures about a hundred yards in diameter is ringed by about fifty armed soldiers some holding flamethrowers.

"So now what do we do?" asks Cliff.

Hamilton looks over at one of the soldiers. He's an older soldier, well-built, about in his fifties with stripes on his shoulders, "Sergeant!"

The soldier quickly runs over, "Yes sir!"

"Have you found any auxiliary exits?"

"Yes sir, there are two to the east about fifty yards out and another north of here about seventy-five yards. We have them all covered."

"Thank you. Give me a minute before you begin," he then turns back to Cliff, "this is the biggest colony we've found to date, four holes and about two hundred yards in diameter. Which means that it could easily be a hundred yards or more deep."

"How do we fight them?" presses Cliff.

Hamilton just looks away and motions to the sergeant. The solder picks up his radio and is heard saying, "Okay, send them in."

A few minutes later from behind them six men dressed in hooded white chemical hazard suits appear. They are completely covered and have large metal containers on their backs that are connected to a hose and nozzle. They surround the mound and begin spraying a liquid all over the area.

"What is that stuff?" asks Brad.

"It's Deltamethrin. We've used it before and found it's very effective at killing them. It seeps into the soil and attacks their nervous system. It takes a while because the ground has to be thoroughly soaked but we have teams at all of the holes doing the same thing. This time of day it's pretty hot so most of the ants will be in the nest. The flame throwers can take care of any stragglers."

After a spraying of about twenty minutes, Daily feels the ground begin to shake under his feet, "Did you feel that?" he asks Hill.

She looks down and notices that the ground is vibrating, "What's going on?"

Brad glances down then jumps back, "What the fuck? They're coming out of the ground!"

He and Cliff draw their guns as does Hill. The three of them are looking at the ground. Two solders armed with flamethrowers run over and aim their weapons at the ground near Hill. The Sergeant grabs Prof. Hamilton by the arm and pulls him back away from the vibration. But the tremor spreads. It now seems to be under all of their feet. Then suddenly as if triggered by some silent signal, long curled antennae begin to wiggle up through the ground around the perimeter of the clearing looking like thousands of little worms. Ants begin pouring out of the ground from everywhere all at once; around the perimeter of the mound dozens of soldiers are seen stomping, shooting and burning the insects as they appear. The grassy clearing becomes a living swelling mass of brown angry ants. The men with the poison turn their spray on the emerging ants, as do the men with flamethrowers. The ants begin to die but not fast enough. They are coming up faster than the soldiers can kill them. Then unexpectedly four large soldier ants leap onto the back of one of the soldiers with a flamethrower, stinging and biting him on his face and back. He spins around in screaming pain with his finger still on the trigger. A long orange tongue of fire plumes outward, hitting three other men and setting them on fire. More ants jump on their victims as panic begins to spread through the ranks. A signal is given for the team to fall back to the Humvees.

"Sir we need to move. NOW!" shouts the sergeant at Hamilton as he drags the professor by the arm, "Everybody! Head back to the Humvees. MOVE IT!"

Brad and Daily are running along side the professor and the sergeant when up ahead Daily notices something, "Look on the ground over there," in front of them another mass of ants begin to emerge from the ground, "They're trying to cut us off!"

Brad yells, "This way! Follow me," he finds a clear path to the left and waves for everyone to follow him.

"Go! Go! Go!" yells the sergeant as he pushes Hamilton in Brad's direction.

"Ahh!" Brad screams as he falls to the ground with an ant gripping the back of his leg and biting down hard. He grabs the insect and throws it into the woods.

Daily reaches down and helps up Brad just as he notices Hill running towards him, "Debra! Get down NOW!"

Without hesitation she dives to the ground. Daily instantly aims his gun.

BAM! BAM! BAM!

He hits a solider ant just as it leaps into the air towards Hill. She looks back at the dead ant then jumps up and joins the group as they continue to run towards the Humvees. When they reach the vehicles Hamilton, Brad, Daily and Cliff jump in the first one. Hill, Cooper, Bloomberg and the sergeant jump in the second. Hinds, Forrester and Troy are in the third. They all speed off together down the dirt road.

"What just happened back there?" screams Brad, "I thought we had everything under control?"

Hamilton visibly shaken looks at him, "They were ready for us. They organized an effective counter attack," he leans forward to talk to the soldier driving, "Call in the strike!"

"Yes, sir!" the soldier picks up his radio, "This is Baker Charlie Victor the code is Red. I repeat the code is Red."

"What's a code red?" asks Daily.

"An fuel-air bomb, it was on stand-by as a fail safe. It's the largest non-nuclear incendiary bomb we have. It should wipe out the entire colony."

"What about those soldiers still on the ground back there?" says Cliff.

"They're evacuating as we speak. Anyone left behind may become collateral damage I'm afraid," he says softly while looking down at the floor.

They all look at him in disbelief.

"Those men have families, you bastard!" shouts Brad as he grabs Hamilton by the collar.

"Hey, come on, Brad, come on!" Cliff grabs his partner's arm but Brad maintains his grip.

"They've got families!"

"Don't you think I know that!" Professor Hamilton shouts, succeeding in pushing Brad back.

Brad glares at him, fuming.

"You saw what happened back there. They're getting smarter. What do you think will happen if a few queens start a nest in New York or Los Angeles? Huh? What do think will happen then?" Professor Hamilton looks around at them all, grim resolve etched in his face. "We're working against the clock here, gentlemen. And time's running out."

The soldier driving and talking on the radio calls to Hamilton, "Excuse me sir. Command reports five minutes to blast. All personnel are in the clear."

"Thank you, soldier," says Hamilton with a sign of relief.

They pull up to an abandoned picnic area as other vehicles begin to join them. Everyone exits their Humvees and look over the trees in the direction of the nest. The low-pitched sound of a large plane fills the air as a low flying C-130 cargo plane zooms overhead towards its target. After a brief moment of silence a huge fireball mushrooms over the forest followed soon after by a thundering roar.

They clap their hands over their ears and grimace as the earth trembles beneath them. When the ringing in their ears subside, Professor Hamilton looks out over the great, roiling balls of orange-black fire eating its way through blackened matchsticks and scorched earth.

"In a half hour we'll go in and Inspect the area," says Hamilton. The others just stare in the direction of the blast, all of them wondering the same thing: the INVASION task force might have won this battle. *But what about the next one?*

Imperial Beach

Twenty-two-year old Johnny Sanders paces back and forth across the parking lot repeatedly then checks his watch for perhaps the fourth time.

"It's 8:30! Where the hell are they?"

"Come on baby calm down. They'll be here," pleads Christina, a tall and voluptuous 20-year-old brown gazelle with slanted brown eyes and flawless dark-brown skin. Her almondine eyes pleading with athletic Johnny, who just can't seem to stop pacing.

She glances over nervously at their friends, Scott and his girlfriend Judy, both of whom turned 21 this past spring. They don't seem to mind Johnny's little outburst, but Christina Edwards is sometimes mortified by Johnny's lack of self-control, especially around a couple as cool and laidback as Judy and Scott. She at times even envies them. They are so in sync with one another, such perfect complements of one another. Scott is a short, buff, biracial blend of Caucasian and Asian: Chinese with reddish-brown hair. Pretty Chinese Judy, with her sparkling dark eyes, Coke-bottle figure and fairy-thin wisp of a smile, often seems kind of vacant, as though very little is going on under that chestnut brown bod. But she and Scott really seem to be the perfect couple and sometimes Christina wondered about her relationship with Johnny. He was sweet, but he could be a bit of a hothead at times.   On the other hand Scott, sporting a comic-book hero jaw line and the abs to go with it, never loses his cool.

The temperature is a comfortable eighty-five degrees at the beginning of August on San Diego's Imperial Beach. It's the start of the city's annual U.S. Open Sandcastle Competition and at 8:30 the beachfront is already crowded with a large part of the 300,000 people expected to attend. Every year at this time this southern Californian community opens its doors to this unique championship. Professional sand carvers from across the country come here to compete in building elaborate sandcastles for the title of Master Champion Sandcastle Builder as well as cash prizes totaling over $20,000.

About twenty-one miles north of Imperial Beach, Johnny, Christina, Scott and Judy are waiting for their friends Catherine and Andrew in the parking lot just outside of San Diego Mesa College's soccer field. Scott and Judy are both computer science majors, while Johnny Sanders and Christian Edwards are biotechnology and animal health technology students, respectively. They're waiting for a ride from Andrew to head down to Imperial Beach to hang out, get a little sun and catch a few waves. Their brilliantly-colored surfboards litter the parking lot as Johnny continues to pace and curse. He was hoping they would beat the Sandcastle crowd.

"I knew I should've got my brother's truck," Scott murmurs as he updates his FaceBook page with his iPhone. He sighs and looks up at Johnny, who he has known since the seventh grade. "We could've been there already."

Judy takes the phone out of his hand to read what he has written and giggles shrilly. "Scott!" He looks at her impishly and they grin over some private joke.

Scott continues, "Andy's always late. They're probably screwing in the back of the van again." He and Judy try to get comfortable, leaning against the bumper and hood of a Honda Accord, Scott still scrolling through his FaceBook page while Judy appears to be sending messages over her Blackberry.

"We should've been down at IB over an hour ago," complains Johnny, flailing his arms and splaying his hands as if appealing to reason. "And they're having that freaking competition today. It's going to be a madhouse down there."

Johnny, who towers over the rest at six foot four, begins pacing back and forth again, his mid length dreadlocks hanging wildly across his face. Christina is trying to figure out how to get him to just chill. But who could blame him? The beach was going to be packed—Imperial Beach is extremely popular, especially at this time of year.

Although best known for having the best beach sand in the country, Imperial Beach is normally just a busy little beach city of 30,000 residents.

IB, as it is affectionately known as by residents, is mainly a hippy community with palm lined streets, bungalows, villas and over ten miles of beach. It is part of California's San Diego County, and has a long and rich surfing history. Flanked by the Pacific Ocean on one side and the South San Diego bay on the other, this is the most southern city on the west coast and is located about fourteen miles south of downtown San Diego and only three miles northwest of the Mexican border. Just south of Imperial Beach is the Tijuana River National Estuarine Research Reserve which is home to many endangered birds and wildlife. Below this is the Border Field State Park which is a beach so far south that beachgoers in the United States can actually talk to beachgoers in Mexico right across the border.

Christina decides to talk to Johnny again, sauntering up to him with soothing tones. "Come here, baby. Let me help you relax," says Christina as she slowly walks up to Johnny and seductively wraps her arms around his neck. Even though she is rather tall, she still has to stands on tiptoes in order to softly plant a kiss on his full lips. She feels his tension subside as he yields to her feminine fortitude, letting his hands travel up her curves to gently hold her waist.

As Johnny kisses her he mumbles, "Baby, you're just what I needed."

She smiles as the two continue to kiss sweetly.

"Wait a minute," yells Scott's girlfriend Judy, who jumps off of the Honda's hood where she has been perched. She squints in the sunlight, one slender pale hand shading her eyes as she points out a fast approaching blue Ford Windstar mini van with the other.

The vehicle, practically on two wheels, pulls up alongside the four friends with breakneck speed, tires screeching and brakes squealing. Romantic mood dispelled, Johnny's muscular biceps bulge as he folds his arms in disapproval. The driver's side window rolls down and an unshaven young man with long sandy blonde hair sticks his head out and waves while a pretty blonde with big blue eyes sucking on a lollipop leans over and smiles from the passenger seat.

"Hey dudes! Sorry, but we got a little hung up." Andrew says as his girlfriend Catherine giggles.

"Yeah I bet you were hung up all right!" snaps Johnny.

Andrew retorts, "Dude, relax! We're here now, right? Come on, throw your boards and stuff in and let's go."

Scott and Johnny pick up their and the girls' surfboards from the parking lot ground and prop them against the van. As Scott slides open the side door he pauses and grimaces at Andrew. "You know what time it is?"

Andrew just looks over at him and grins in an infuriating manner. Catherine –also known as Cat—seems to be in her own world and is idly twirling the lollipop in her fingers, cheeks hollowed as she absently tongues the candy.

Judy and Christina gingerly step into the filthy vehicle while Scott and Johnny start loading everyone's boards into the van. The floor of the van is littered with gum and candy wrappers, flyers rescued from the windshield of the car, empty Doritos and potato chip bags, soda cans with straws still jutting from them, and even a random sock. The two girls take seats behind Andrew and Catherine. Christina gets settled behind Andrew but as Judy begins to sit, she lets out a shrill yelp, having noticed something on the seat. Her lovely Asian features contort in disgust and she turns toward Christina with a look of pure revulsion, waving her hands frantically as though trying to erase the memory of what she has just seen.

"Eewww! Christina, please tell me that's not what I think it is?" She points to a used condom clinging to the seat. Shocked speechless, Christina looks down at the prophylactic then up at Catherine, who is sitting in the passenger seat as contentedly as the cat having eaten the proverbial canary. She tosses a backward glance over her shoulder, smiles down at the offending object then merely shrugs, continuing to suck on her lollipop.

"You have to be kidding! That is so disgusting," Christina snarls, thoroughly offended.

Andrew turns around and takes a look at the seat.

"So that's where it went," he laughs. Judy is outside of the vehicle again, arms folded with an expression on her face that makes it clear she's not getting in until this is taken care of. Christina and Scott are fed up, but Johnny is cracking his knuckles and looking off into the distance—an indication that he's more than a little shut down and has had just about as much as he can take. His relationship with Andrew has always been a little tenuous, particularly since the "dude" is more Scott's friend than his and he always seems to show up with his empty-headed girlfriend. All Johnny really wants is to chill with Christina, Judy and his boy Scotty.

Seeing that he's the only one who finds any of this remotely funny, Andrew smirks a bit sheepishly and reaches back, picking up the condom and throwing it out of the window to land in the soccer field parking lot.

"You're such a pig!" Christina declares wearily, rolling her eyes. She starts in on Catherine: "And Cat you should be ashamed of yourself!" Catherine just shrugs again. Christina throws up her hands and stares out the side window, not unlike Johnny. She is starting to feel like maybe this is a bad idea. Maybe they should go home. The beach and water was going to be full of kids and tourists anyway.

Still outside of the van, Judy throws her hands up and exclaims, "Well, hello! I need something to wipe off this seat. I'm not sitting in there with all your stuff dripping everywhere. Eewww!"

"Alright! Alright! Here, how's this," says Andrew as he turns around and reaches back to wipe the seat down with a cloth. Judy relents and gets back in the vehicle, sitting as far away from the offending area as possible. She looks back at Scott who gives her a reassuring glance and pokes her shoulder teasingly. She smiles and seems to feel more at ease.

As Scott and Johnny continue to figure out how best to arrange the boards in the back, Christina continues to badger Catherine. "No wonder you guys were late. You mean to tell me you couldn't wait till later? And in a dirty van of all places."

Andrew laughs, "Hey dude, I gotta take care of my baby. You know how it is," he leans over and begins deeply kissing Catherine, "You didn't mind, right baby?" he whispers as Johnny and Scott finally enter the van, backpacks and boards now in place.

Scott looks at the two, shakes his head then glances at Johnny, "Can you believe these two?" He looks back at Andrew, "Hey guys can we get a move on?"

"Alright! Alright! Chill, we're going," says Andrew.

Johnny reaches out and slides the side door closed and the vehicle lurches forward, careening out of the parking lot with a screech before heading south down Interstate 5 towards Imperial Beach.

Scott leans forward from the back seat, "Step on it, man-- we already wasted enough time."

"Chill, dude!" says Andrew. "We'll have plenty of time. Don't worry about it."

"You know how crowded it's going to be today? They're having that sand castle tournament," adds Christina.

"Alright! Alright! I'll hurry, I'll hurry," replies Andrew.

During the drive Judy retrieves a bag of Oreo cookies from her backpack and begins to eat them. How she can have any kind of appetite is beyond Christina. "Anybody want some cookies?" Judy asks sweetly. She has an endearing innocence about her. She leans forward to hand the bag to Catherine, but the busty blond just waves them off.

Christina nudges Judy and says under her breath, "Don't mind her. She's already had her cookies. That's why they were late."

The two girls giggle as Catherine tosses an evil look back at Christina before rolling her eyes and turning back around.

Andrew looks into the rearview mirror and says, "Ah, come on Chris. Ease up a bit. Nobody said anything when you and Johnny got caught naked in the locker room!"

Judy puts her hand over her mouth, "Oooh!"

A scowl quickly forms on Christina's face, "We weren't naked!" she shouts.

Andrew laughs, "I have the pictures!" He glances over at Catherine and now they share a conspiratorial giggle.

"Yeah, yeah," Johnny growls, "Let's just get to the beach, okay?" He reaches out and briefly massages Christina's shoulders. She arches her neck and murmurs her gratitude.

"Yeah, I thought so!" says Andrew as he turns on the radio full blast. The group speeds down to the beach to the sounds of Lady Gaga, Beyoncé and Nicki Minaj. The music puts everybody in a better mood and even Johnny comes out of his funk a bit.

After about a half-hour drive they pull up to an area known as Pier Plaza, an outdoor museum which showcases multi-colored surfboard benches that are adorned with plaques depicting how big waves on the beach impacted surfing in the area from 1937 through the 1950's.

As Andrew pulls into the parking area he stops at the entrance and looks around at the seemingly endless rows of parked cars. "Wow," he murmurs, "There's a lot of people here today."

Johnny just sucks his teeth, shakes his head and resumes sulking.

Scott, staring out of the window at the tourists and their families milling about says, "Well, let's not just sit here. Drive around--we should be able to find parking somewhere."

They drive around the lot slowly with everyone looking for an open parking spot. Finally Judy shouts, "Andy there's a spot right over there--look.

Andrew stops the van and looks in the direction Judy is pointing to then wildly swerves the vehicle around to position it for parking.

Johnny, still upset, comments acidly, "It's about time. It only took us forty-five minutes to find parking. Look, it's almost 10:00! You know how crowded it's going to be out there?"

Andrew doesn't reply, he just backs the van in between two cars in the back of the lot. In the rear of the van Johnny and Scott manage to put on their wetsuits while Andrew pulls his on outside alongside the van.

"Can you help me with the cooler, Judy?" asks Christina as she pulls the large container from the back of the van.

"Sure, no problem," responds Judy as reaches to grab the opposite handle. She looks back at Catherine, "Cathy, you think you can manage the grill?"

Catherine pulls the lollipop out of her mouth just long enough to answer, "Yeah, I got it," then sticks the pop back into her mouth as she moves aside backpacks in the back of the van in order to locate the grill.

When the group arrives at the beach they stop at the entrance. In front of them is a massive sea of humanity. People of all types run back and forth. They throw Frisbees, play volleyball and gather around the sandcastle structures.

Christina, shielding her eyes from the sun says, "Let's set up near the Pier."

"Good idea," says Scott. "That's pretty close to the surfer's section."

The group walks past the historical Imperial Beach Pier. This wooden-planked pier stretches about 2000 feet into the ocean and is very popular among tourists for evening strolls, jogging, pier-fishing or just watching the sunset. At the end of the pier where it forms a unique arrow shape is the Tin Fish, one of the best seafood restaurants in the San Diego area. The group arrives at a point on the beach that divides the surfing section from the swimming section. They stake out their claim in the sand and begin to stretch out their blankets. Scott sets up the small hibachi grill while Andrew opens up the cooler and grabs a zip locked roast beef sandwich from a bed of ice. Christina and Judy sit under the sun in their thong bikinis and begin smearing sunscreen lotion all over their bodies.

Johnny slowly crawls on all fours like a cat towards Christina, "Don't put too much of that stuff on. I don't want you slipping away when I grab you." He crawls up to her and softly kisses her on her remarkably soft lips.

"You don't have to worry about that, baby," she says as she playfully grabs his dreadlocks, pulls him close and kisses him back.

Andrew, finishing a soda he just pulled out of the cooler, looks around the beach, "Hey dudes I'm sorry, you were right--it really is crowded out here."

Johnny inwardly marvels; it's the closest the lanky blond surfer has come to an apology since he met him through Scott a year or so ago. Johnny plants one last kiss on Christina's lips then stands up beside Andrew shrugging in a no-hard-feelings kind of way. "Don't sweat it, we're here--that's what matters. We better get in the water before it gets too late. Come on!" He grabs his board and heads into the surf. Andrew picks up his and follows. Just then Catherine runs up behind him with her board, "Hold up! You weren't going in without me, were you?"

He turns around and kisses her, "Of course not, baby."

Johnny, Catherine and Andrew jog into the water with their surfboards under their arms. Judy, Scott and Christina watch the young, tan and attractive trio from the shore as they run over to the surfing section and hit the water with their boards in front of them, paddling out to sea.

It's a little after ten in the morning and the beach crowds have swelled to over 100,000 people, young and old. Overlooking their safety is a team of forty highly-trained lifeguards perched high on their seven-foot towers. The chief lifeguard on the beach is David Tokushima who has been a lifeguard at Imperial Beach for over eight years and has saved close to a hundred lives. During these special events he is especially vigilant. With so many vacationers and visitors on the beach there is an increased risk of a mishap in or around the waterfront. He keeps a really close look out for teenagers and young drunk college students who have a tendency to do something stupid and dangerous. He tries to stay as focused as possible but there are times when it's hard not to sneak a peek at the young girls running around wearing the skimpiest of bathing suits.

At this point in the day he notices the small cluster of surfers, Johnny and his friends, paddling out further than most people on the beach. This catches his attention as this could be a possible dangerous situation. David puts his set of binoculars to his eyes to assess the situation. They seemed like expert swimmers and he was trying to make a judgment call. All of a sudden while he is focused on the three in the water, his concentration is interrupted by a high-pitched voice from below.

"Hi, Mister Lifeguard!" yells a big-breasted young blonde wearing a thong and a revealing halter-top. She's standing beside his lifeguard tower with a shapely brunette holding a camera. Both of them appear to have been drinking a bit too much.

"Sorry miss, I can't talk to you now," responds David, with a quick glance at the attractive duo.

"Come on; let me get a picture with you! You're a cutie."

"Thank you. But sorry miss, not now."

"Aw, come on. It'll only take a minute," giggles the blonde.

"I hope it takes longer than a minute," jokes the brunette as the two women put their hands over their mouths and giggle.

David looks down at the two smiling women for a moment then back up at the three surfers. Johnny, Catherine and Andrew are swimming deftly now, surfboards under each and he can discern how athletic they were—these weren't amateurs in the least. He convinces himself that the surfers are alright and it can't hurt to take a few pictures. After all there are other lifeguards on duty and a little public relations do make the city look good. He climbs down from the tower and smiles at the two women.

"So, how are you two doing today?" he asks as he places his arm around the blonde.

"I'm just fine now," she responds with a giggle, "Sandy, come on take a couple of us together," as she hugs him back, burrowing her face into his nude pec with mock bashfulness.

The brunette aims the camera and begins to click.

Meanwhile, out at sea Johnny, Andrew and Catherine have arrived at a point somewhere near the middle of the pier. They're sitting up on their surfboards waiting for a good wave to come in.

Catherine looks at Andrew and asks, "Are you sure we're out far enough?"

"Sure, we lucked out. Not too many people surfing today," he looks over to Johnny, "See? We did alright, buddy."

Johnny grins and responds, "Alright, Andy, we'll let you slide this time."

Just then the group spots a distant wave, noticeably larger than the normal set waves. Sensing the coming big wave the three position themselves side by side and wait for the incoming swell. As the large mound of water moves closer the wave bulges up to an impressive size. Without arguing whose wave it is, all three paddle simultaneously once the moment is right and within seconds the three are standing up swishing down its face. Andrew rides the wave high up towards the top of the barrel while the other two speed along ahead of him near its bottom. He spreads out his arms in an attempt to keep his balance, sensing he's not in the right place and is losing speed quickly. The barrel rapidly overtakes Andrew, crashing over his head as Catherine and Johnny watch from further down towards the bottom. For a moment Andrew disappears under the water but soon pops up in the whitewash behind the wave like a blond cork, the wet hair plastered to his head. He looks around bewildered and notices Johnny and Catherine paddling back towards him.

"You okay?" shouts Catherine over the roar of the water.

"Dude, did you see the size of that wave? That was awesome!" Andrew gives her his trademark grin.

"Let's head back out and catch another one," adds Johnny.

The three begin paddling back out to sea.

Back on the beach David is finding it hard to get rid of his new friends.

"You're cute. Do you have a girlfriend?" asks the blonde as she wraps both arms around his neck, preventing him from climbing back up the lifeguard tower.

"No, I don't," he says a little wearily. "But I really need to get back to work."

The blonde takes a plaintive, sing-song tone. "Don't you want to go for a swim with us?"

"I think you girls have had a little too much to drink," David says, slowly pulling her arms off of his neck, "maybe the two of you should stay out of the water for a while."

The brunette runs over and grabs his arm and kisses him on the cheek, "Awww, how sweet he cares about us."

"Alright, ladies that's enough," David says in as firm a tone as he can muster although each woman, undeterred, now grabs him by an arm.

The brunette rubs her hands across his chest, cooing, "You're so big and strong. We should take you home with us!" The two begin giggling as David just stands there, blushing. In a last effort of resolve, he finally pulls away from the girls. They immediately begin mewling their displeasure as David backs away from them, climbing up the ladder of the lifeguard tower. "Alright, how about this? After the festival is over, let's say around six, you meet me at the lifeguard station at the end of the beach and we'll see what happens then?"

The two women look at each other and smile then the blonde says, "All right, we'll be there. Don't be late," the two walk off laughing and giggling, with a couple of backward glances. David turns his attention back to the three surfers out by the pier. He has lost track of where they are so he scans the area until he spots them again.

Back out on the sea, Catherine, Johnny and Andrew are awaiting another wave. They are sitting upright on their surfboards waiting for the set. Andrew is all worked up from the last wave, adrenaline flowing as he gushes a mile a minute. "Did you see the size of that wave? Shit, that was a big one. The next one is mine!"

"Andy, just be careful," says Catherine with a hint of concern.

"You know how I do, baby," he reaches over and gives Johnny a high five. Suddenly there is a great splash and Andrew's arms fly up over his head as he appears to be sucked down under the water. The empty surfboard floats on the surface, but Andrew is gone.

Catherine looks down at his surfboard then around the water nearby, "Andy? Andy? Come on, stop playing around. You know I hate when you do shit like that. Come on, stop it!"

Johnny soon joins in, "Andy? Andy? Andy! Oh shit, where is he?" He dives off of his surfboard and into the water. Johnny takes a deep breath then dives under then after a few seconds' pops up again, "Andy? Andy?" He screams before diving back under the water to look for his friend.

Back at the lifeguard tower David stands up, he can't believe his eyes. One moment there's three surfers in the water and the next there's only two. He reaches under his seat and grabs a 40-inch long foam rubber buoy known as a Peterson Tube. It has a strap attached to it that is used to wrap around victims and pull them to safety. David jumps down from his perch and runs at top speed towards the ocean.

"Oh my God! Oh my God! Where is he?" screams Catherine as she sits on her board. The young woman begins sobbing hysterically. Johnny is still diving underwater looking for Andrew. He stops for a moment to catch his breath while treading water and sputters, "I don't know where he could be!" He wipes a wet hand over his wet face. "This is crazy. He's just gone."

David is now in the water swimming at full tilt towards Johnny and Catherine.

Johnny swims over to Catherine and holds her forearm, giving it an emphatic little shake and looking into her eyes, "I can't find him. He-He's gone." Catherine leans over on her board and buries her face in his neck as the two of them begin to cry, holding one another.

David swims up to them, almost out of breath and gasps, "What happened? Where's your friend?"

Johnny lets go of the still sobbing Catherine and turns toward the lifeguard, arms steadily stroking the water, "I don't know. One minute he was here. Next thing I know, there was a big splash and then he was gone."

David takes a deep breath and dives below the surface. The ocean water is very clear this time of year but he sees nothing. He comes to the surface, takes another breath and tries again. This time he notices something. Something he didn't notice before. There are no fish and the bottom of the ocean seems like a dark fleshy cloud at first glance. But as David realizes exactly what he is looking at, an engulfing wave of horror comes over him. He almost gulps in seawater at the shock of what he has seen.

David surfaces quickly and the look of fear is evident on his pale face. The sight of the frightened lifeguard jolts Catherine out of her grief for a moment and she cries, "What is it? What did you find? What happened to Andy?"

David can barely catch his breath, "Get..get..get out," he says while coughing up water.

"What?" replies Catherine in a puzzled voice, growing increasingly alarmed.

David still coughing up water yells at her, "Get out! Get out of the water. Get out now! Move it! Go!" he points to the beach.

Johnny and Catherine continue to stare at him with a look of bewilderment then at one another.

With a sense of frustration David finally screams, "I said move it!" Suddenly his entire body is quickly pulled under the ocean. Johnny and Catherine scream as they begin paddling back to shore on the ends of their surfboards. David surfaces again flailing his arms about, screaming at the top of his lungs, "Everyone out of the water! Everyone out!" People swimming and surfing nearby turn to look, alerted by the lifeguard's blood curdling cries. "Everyone out of the—" David's words are swallowed up again as he is yanked violently under the water in mid sentence.

An overweight woman in a red bathing suit sporting goggles and polka-dot bathing cap yells in a great, booming voice, "Shark! Shark!" The beach instantly erupts into complete pandemonium.

People begin screaming on the beach and in the water as everyone starts rushing towards the sandy shore. Children are snatched from the water by concerned parents and piggy-back with more expert swimmers. Many people cry out to their friends and family from the beach to hurry up. People in the water cry out in fear, their playful time in the water instantly turned deadly.

As people start frantically swimming towards the beach, individuals begin disappearing from the crowd, plucked under the waves by some unseen force. An elderly Hispanic man and his wife are swimming side by side when suddenly the wife vanishes. A woman floating in an inner tube is pulled right through its middle. A man swimming towards the shore is about to stand up and walk onto the beach when he is violently pulled backwards back out to sea and then under the waves. During the commotion Christina, Scott and Judy run to the edge of the water looking for their friends. Christina cupping her hands around her mouth yells out into the terrified crowd emerging from the ocean.

"Johnny! Johnny! Johnny! Oh my God, Johnny!"

Judy, hands shielding her eyes from the sun, shouts, "Cathy! Johnny! Andrew! Johnny! ... Wait!" she pauses for a second as she spots a familiar image emerging through the mayhem, "Wait! Look over there! Look, there's Cathy."

The three run into the water pushing past the screaming mass of frightened people. Catherine, spotting her friends, drags herself drunkenly out of the water, her eyes red from tears and salt water. Just before she reaches them she collapses but is caught by Johnny who suddenly appears from behind her. He's limping but manages to pick her up and carry her. When their friends reach them Scott takes Catherine from Johnny and carries her rest of the way as Christina smothers Johnny in kisses and hugs. When they reach their blankets, Scott lays Catherine down and sits beside her. Judy sits on her other side. Johnny and Christina sit down near her feet. Christina looks at Johnny with a look of relief in her eyes and softly rubs the side of his face, "I thought I was going to be a widow before being a wife. I was so scared, baby."

He takes her hand from his face and kisses it tenderly, "I know baby. I know."

Christina looks down at Johnny's left leg, "What happened to your leg?" Around his left calf is a series of large round gashes each about two inches wide. The flesh in the middle of the gashes is torn and bleeding.

"I don't know! Something grabbed me out there. It was grabbing everybody. I was lucky to get away," he explains.

Judy stares at Johnny's leg with a look of shock and disgust then suddenly says, "Wait! Where's Andy? Shit, we gotta go back-- we forgot about Andy!"

Johnny slowly turns to her shaking his head from side to side before saying softly, "Andy's gone."

"What do mean?"

"He's gone, Judy, just gone. Something out there pulled him under."

She puts her hand over her mouth as the realization of what he is trying to say sinks in. "Oh my God. No! Oh my God," she whispers as tears begin to fill her eyes. Scott moves to her side and wraps his arm around her. Just then Catherine starts to come out of her daze. She slowly sits up and gazes into the water. All around them are people pushing, screaming and running to get out of the water. But in her mind she doesn't hear a thing. Her mind is blank. All she can think of is to save her Andrew. He must be out there. If only she can find him. She mutters in a low voice, "Andy, I got to get Andy."

Judy hugs her and kisses her on the cheek, "Sweetie, the lifeguards will find him, okay?" She glances over at Johnny for reassurance but he only nods his head slowly signaling that finding their friend is hopeless. Judy sadly looks back at Catherine and hugs her tighter.

"I got to get Andy," Catherine repeats.

"I think she's in shock. We should get her to the hospital," says Scott.

Catherine slowly stands up, "Andy's still out there. I have to get him!"

"No, Cathy. You need to come with us," Judy says as she gently grabs her arm. Then without warning Catherine rips away from her and bolts toward the water knocking into people who are running in the opposite direction. The three take off after her.

When she reaches the water she dives in and begins swimming out to sea. The group wades in up to their waists all while yelling to her to come back.

Finally she stops and turns toward them, "I know he's alive. I know he is!" she shouts back at them, "I can feel it. I know he's--" her sentence is cut off as her body is violently sucked beneath the waves. The group jumps back in shock clinging reflexively to one another. After a few seconds Catherine resurfaces, flailing her arms around and gasping for air, "Help! Help me!" Scott dives in and swims toward her.

Judy yells to him, "Scott! No!" Just then Catherine's body jerks backward as if pulled by a speed boat. Scott immediately stops swimming and treads water, backing up in horror. Her body is ripped through the water like a rag doll. She's dragged for about 100 yards by some unseen force before changing direction and dragged back to where she began. Catherine finally stops a few feet from Scott and stares at him with a dazed look, "Help...," she whimpers just before her body is violently torn beneath the sea for the final time.

Scott begins frantically swimming back to the beach and scrambles out of the water to join his friends. For a moment he is bent doubled over, panting from the exertion of literally swimming for his life. When he has regained his bearings, they all just stand there quietly staring out to sea. Around them are others who have witnessed what had happened to Catherine. Judy sniffles, and then begins weeping quietly, her body shaking uncontrollably. Scott puts an arm around Judy's waist and she throws her arms about his neck, hugging him tightly. And now it is Johnny's turn to hold Christina and calm her down as he holds her close and rubs her shoulder. She sobs into the crook of his neck, completely traumatized. Other stunned and weeping beachgoers begin to gather around on the beach, dazed, shocked, and trying to make sense of what just took place.

Calamari

  In a secluded section of the Davis Monthan Air Force Base in Tucson, Arizona there are two secure hangars set aside for the INVASION Team. Parked out on the tarmac in front of the hangars is a brand-new dark-green custom-built Boeing 747-8, complete with the EPA logo on its tail. This new version of the famous 747 commercial aircraft is longer than the original and is outfitted with the latest in hi-tech monitoring equipment, a mini-laboratory and sleeping compartments for the entire team. It can be refueled in the air and has new high performance engines enabling it to travel quickly to anywhere on the globe. Behind the 747-8 is a Lockheed C-5 Galaxy military transport plane. This is one of the largest planes in the United States Air Force inventory. It's a massive aircraft with a wingspan of two hundred and twenty-two feet and a length from nose to tail of two hundred and forty-seven feet. The C-5 Galaxy has the ability to take off and land in relatively short distances and also utilizes sophisticated communication and navigation equipment that allow it to operate without the use of ground-based navigational aides. This military plane is quite impressive, with a payload capacity of over 200,000 pounds.

  Inside one of the hangars, named EPA One, is the INVASION Task Force, meeting in a conference room at the rear of the building. They have just returned from Chicago's Lincoln Park where they battled an infestation of mutant rats. Thousands of the animals had invaded the area and several people were killed in their homes by the rodents as they slept. By the time the nest was found in an abandoned warehouse, the rats had spread throughout most of the city. Not only had they become extremely aggressive, but conventional poisons no longer had any effect on them. The INVASION task force began utilizing a controversial and experimental type of neurotoxin that managed to quell the tide of mutant rats, immediately reducing their population. Just as it was beginning to make a dent in the problem, the team was called back to the base. The city's officials picked up where the INVASION task force left off; forming a plan that would effectively spread the new biochemical weapon throughout the other districts.

With various mutant species surfacing, it also has become harder to keep the growing incidents hidden from the public. The media was now asking questions, and lots of them. News reports were coming in from all around the country.

In Florida, a man was admitted to the hospital with twelve large painful bumps on the back of his head. When the doctors examined him they were astonished to find he had large insect larvae gnawing into his skull. Further examination revealed that the larvae belonged to mutant Botflies, a fly normally found in the Caribbean, known for laying the eggs of their parasitic larvae on warm bodied animals including humans. The normal Botfly measures about three quarters of an inch but these mutants are over an inch and a half long and their larvae can borrow through bone as well as flesh. The man died during the operation to remove the parasites just as four similar cases emerged in both Florida and Alabama.

On New York's Coney Island beach hundreds of uncharacteristically aggressive seagulls dove onto sun worshipers. Thirty people had to be hospitalized after the attack. Then, in Dallas, a football field size swarm of mutated Africanized killer bees formed a cloud over Randall Park near the Woodrow Wilson High school. They attacked and stung hundreds of people, killing twenty before moving off. The attacks were so vicious that autopsies revealed several of the victims' stomachs filled with dead bees.

The nation's reporters were searching for a pattern in the attacks and the public was starting to show signs of alarm.

Sitting around a large oval table in the conference room is Troy, Dr. Bloomberg, Cooper, Forrester, Dr. Hinds, Cliff and Brad, as well as Daily and Hill. Professor Hamilton stands at one end of the table in front of a large video monitor and a large wall-mounted map of the United States covered with colored pins representing SF-20 incidents around the nation.

"The situation is getting tense. After Lincoln Park we've had incidents in Texas, New York and now, Imperial Beach California. The President is naturally getting pressure from all across the country so now he's putting the squeeze on us to show some results." Professor Hamilton pauses, looking around at the solemn group. "So let's get started. Our first priority is the incident in California." He turns to Dr. Hinds, "Karen, what do we know so far?"

Hinds picks up a folder from in front of her and opens it, "Based on the evidence I doubt very much that this was the work of sharks."

"What evidence?" asks Brad, reclining in his seat.

Hinds looks across the table at Brad and explains, "Well for one thing there weren't any body parts left at the scene." She pauses, looks around at the other members then continues, "When sharks attack people, they usually tear off limbs or chunks of flesh. No body parts have washed up on the beach so far and none of the injuries reported from the survivors have been consistent with shark attacks. Also there were over twenty-five people attacked at the same time along the beach. Sharks don't usually hunt in packs especially that close to the shore."

Brad, now intrigued, leans forward, "So what do you think it could be?" he continues.

"Don't know until we get out there," responds Hinds, enjoying Brad's attention.

Cliff, sitting next to Brad, sighs and says, "So I guess this means we're going to Cali?"

Hamilton steps closer to the table, "Yes. And I need all of you to leave immediately. That's just how serious this situation is."

Brad sits up in his seat, "Immediately? Now wait a minute! We just got back! I need to talk to my wife. She's been sick for the last couple of weeks and is staying with her mother. I was hoping to be able to go home soon. What am I going to tell her?"

Looking at Brad Cliff interjects, "Your wife? What about mine? What am I supposed to tell my wife?" He then turns to Hamilton, and takes a deep breath in an effort to get himself under control. "She was upset when I told her I'd be away working in this outfit from the beginning. She's only been cool about it because I told her that one, I had no choice, and two, Brad was here with me. But she's still worried, Professor Hamilton."

The appeals from the patrol officers appear to have no effect on their leader. "Just tell her exactly what you have been telling her, Officer Johnson: nothing," Hamilton says coldly as he walks around the table. He comes to a stop behind Brad and Cliff, "I don't have to remind you two that this is a matter of national security and that no one outside of this room and the president himself is to have any knowledge of what is happening!" he leans over Cliff's chair between the pair and says quietly but sharply, "Not even your wives. Is that clear?"

Brad and Cliff both glance up at the Professor then at each other and nod their resignation.

Hamilton pauses then stands up straight, "You want to know why we're keeping this so secret? It's because if these incidences get any worse, there'll be chaos in the streets. This nation is in danger of being overrun by mutants and we aren't any closer to solving the problem and if the public knew that, all hell would break loose!" He walks back to the front of the table near the large map, "A little inconvenience is not going to kill your wife, Officer Johnson--not when three hundred million lives are at stake."

Cliff just shakes his head as he leans back in his chair and sighs.

Hamilton goes on, "Okay. As I said I'm going to need the whole team on this one. Kevin will be in charge during the mission. The planes are already waiting out front. You leave in three hours, so pack your gear. You'll be briefed during the flight."

"Aren't you coming along?" asks Hill standing up.

"Unfortunately no. It seems I've been called to New York to meet with some of my international counterparts," says Hamilton, picking up a leather briefcase from alongside the table into which he starts transferring various folders from the table's surface.

"Apparently SF-20 incidents have spread throughout Europe, Asia and Africa. I'm also meeting with some Gen X Tech officials to get information they may have that can help us come up with a global solution. Up until now, they have been slow to cooperate with us. I hope to change their attitude."

"Wow, I had no idea it's gotten that bad," replies Hill as she heads for the large door at the end of the hangar.

Hamilton continues, "That's another reason why it's important to get more data. It can help get us some answers so we can finally put a stop to this thing. I know it's difficult. Believe me, I know," he pauses for a moment as if he is lost in thought then closes his eyes tightly, bends over slightly and holds his chest.

Troy stands up immediately and rushes to his side. Cliff and Brad stand up quickly, both with a look of concern on their faces. Hill stops and turns toward Hamilton, "You okay, Professor?"

Troy pulls one of the chairs closer to Hamilton and helps him sit down. Hamilton sits then takes a deep breath, "I'm alright. Just a little tired," Troy takes the briefcase from him and places it back on the floor as Hamilton looks up at Hill and the others, "Alright, people that's enough. I'm alright. Stop fussing over me. We have a job to do! Let's get a move on!" the rest of the group stands up slowly with their eyes glued on Hamilton. He notices their hesitation and shouts, "Go on. I'm just tired. We don't have any time to waste. Get going--the planes are waiting! I'll contact you when you land. Now move it!" They all turn and quickly follow Hill to the exit leaving only Troy by the professor's side.

Cliff and Brad leave the hangar and head over to a small building next door where they have living quarters. As they cross the tarmac Cliff says to his partner, "I have a bad feeling about this buddy."

Brad giving him a perplexed look answers, "What do you mean?"

"I don't know. I just don't feel right about any of this. This is some real crazy shit we've gotten ourselves into and...I just have a bad feeling that's all."

Brad smiles and throws an arm around Cliff's shoulder, "Don't worry, bro. I know how you're still afraid of the dark so I won't let any mutant monsters get you," he chuckles.

Cliff pushes him off playfully, "Get off me, you nut. You're going to protect me? Who was the one running like a little girl from those mice up in Chicago?"

Brad now with a serious expression of his face exclaims, "Mice? Those were rats, big mutant rats!"

Cliff waves his hands up in the air and begins to run comically on his toes, "Help they're after me! Help!" he shrieks with a high pitched voice.

"I didn't sound like that!" says Brad now embarrassed by Cliff's play-acting.

"Help me! The little mice are going to get me! Help!" Cliff continues.

"That's not funny! Those things could've eaten me alive and you know I'm allergic."

Cliff stops clowning around and looks Brad in the eyes, "Allergic to what?" he says sarcastically.

"Animal fur!"

"Get the hell outta here!" he says as he waves his hands, "As many times as you've been around my dogs, now you're allergic. You're full of shit. You were scared--just admit it," he turns nodding his head and laughing then heads toward the living quarters.

Brad starts after him, "What a minute, I am. I'm allergic to rat fur. It makes me itch," he says as he crosses his arms and scratches his sides.

Cliff smirks, "You were itching all right--itching like a little girl."

"No, I'm serious. I wasn't scared. I wasn't!"

Cliff still laughing pulls open the door to the living quarters and pushes Brad inside, "Come on, scaredy-cat."

Meanwhile, Bloomberg and Hinds are stowing their backpacks in the belly of the 747. Bloomberg secures one of the packs against the wall of the cargo hold as Hinds stands behind him and comments, "I'm worried about Richard."

Bloomberg without turning around replies, "He's just overworked. Hell, we all are."

"It's not just his health I'm worried about, Kevin." She looks at Bloomberg with a look of concern and her hands on her hips, "Don't you think he came down on the cops a little hard?"

Bloomberg, kneeling and with his back still towards Hinds, continues to tighten the straps around the packs but manages to mumble, "What?"

"Brad and Cliff. Don't you think Richard came down hard on them? I mean they shouldn't even be here."

As he finally finishes tightening the packs he stands up, turns to Hinds and takes a deep breath, "Karen, we've been over this before. Richard knows what he's doing."

"Does he, Kevin?" Hinds scolds, "For that matter do any of us really know what we're doing?"

Bloomberg wipes some sweat off of his bald head, "What do you want me to do, Karen? We've had some successes but this whole situation is new territory for everyone involved, even you."

"I know, I know it is," she nods, "but for every success we've had we end up facing two setbacks. We can't go on like this and it's taking a toll on all of us. Look at what's happening to Richard. He's not a young man. This is too much for him," she pauses for a moment and paces around the cargo hold, "I'm just saying that it looks as though this is beginning to wear him down. He's our friend, Kevin, but he's not the man we used to know. He's changed. He's more irritable, more restless and I'm worried about him."

Bloomberg with his arms crossed looks at Hinds and says calmly, "I know what you mean. I'm worried too. But I think it's wearing us all down. What I'm really afraid of Karen is what might happen if we don't slow this thing down and I think Richard has those same fears," he pulls her close to him and hugs her, "We just have to trust in one another and I promise I'll keep an eye on him."

Hinds looks up into his eyes and says softly, "Thank you. I guess you're right. I'm just scared."

"We all are," he responds.

She buries her head into his chest as the two continue to hold each other.

On the main deck of the 747 Cooper and Forrester are assisting Troy in setting up his computer and monitoring equipment.

The two men hold an instrument panel against a console in the lab located just under the cockpit. Troy lies on his back under the console tightening up its connections.

Forrester holding one side of the panel with shaky hands says, "I can't believe it. I've wanted to get to the beach all year and now I get to go and it's infested with man-eating creatures. Just great!"

Cooper looks over at him and smirks, "I know what you mean."

"Do you guys mind holding that steady?" yells Troy from under the console.

"Sorry, Troy," apologizes Forrester as he and Cooper attempt to steady the panel.

"So what do you think it is?" Forrester asks Cooper.

"I don't know. I still think it could be some mutated shark but Karen thinks it's something else," he readjusts the heavy panel in his hands then looks down at where Troy is lying, "what do you think, Troy?"

Troy slides out from under the console with a screwdriver in his hand, "You could let it go now," he says as he stands up and places the screwdriver on the console.

Cooper and Forrester let go of the panel then Cooper turns to Troy and asks him again, "So what do you think? What do you think is in the water out there?"

Troy without looking up begins flipping switches and turning on some of the computers in the lab as he speaks, "It could be anything from jellyfish to giant eels. At this stage nothing would surprise me."

"Giant jellyfish? Damn, that's creepy!" states Forrester.

Troy stops and glances at him for a second, "Whatever it is, a lot of people lost their lives because of it," he walks up to the two men, "we're going to have to be very, very careful with this one," he says it a solemn tone, "You understand me? We're going to be out in the ocean, which adds a whole new dimension to this mission. Things can get out of hand in the blink of an eye."

Cooper and Forrester stand there staring at him both with a look of worry. Troy, noticing their uneasiness, says, "If everything works the way it should, we should be safe but we can't take any chances out there." He turns and goes back to turning on his equipment. Cooper and Forrester glance at each other then quietly leave Troy to finish his work.

The plane takes off on time and heads east toward California to unravel the Imperial Beach Mystery. This 747-8 is a fully equipped flying command center. The upper deck has a small conference room as well as a hi-tech communications center located just outside of the cockpit. The middle of the plane has a fully stocked galley and dining area and the rear has sleeping compartments for the entire team.

During the flight as Hill sits at one of the conference room windows watching the clouds fly by, she wonders what type of terror they'll encounter in California. After a short time she becomes restless and decides to join Daily in the galley. Hill slowly strolls down the spiral staircase from the conference room. She stops at the bottom for a moment and slowly looks around as if to gather her thoughts. She's standing in a small lounge area that lies between the galley and dining section to the rear of the plane and the lab in the front lined with four seats and windows on either side of the staircase. She begins to head for the door to the galley when an electronic sound catches her attention. It's a soft beeping sound coming from behind her. She turns and realizes that the sound is coming from the open sliding door that leads to the lab. Intrigued, she walks over to the lab and looks through the doorway. She scans the room and notices that it takes up quite a lot of space. It seems to extend the entire length of the conference and communications rooms above and possibly even the cockpit. There are no windows and along both sides are computers and monitoring equipment. In the middle is a large desk loaded with all sorts of electronic equipment and parts. At the far end of the lab, which is the nose of the plane, there are several boxes stacked almost to the ceiling.

Hill slowly steps into the room and sees Troy busy at work in front of one of the computers. He doesn't even notice that she has come in. She quietly walks up behind Troy and stares at the young man for a while. Since they first met Hill has admired the youngster's intelligence and charm. She scans his body and notices what a handsome young man he is. She notices the small gold earring in his left ear complimenting his short neatly-groomed afro and the slender build of his six-foot frame, which is always decked out in brand-named designer clothes. A smile grows across her face as she observes how focused and intently he's working, totally unaware of her presence.

"What'cha up to Troy?" She says, softly startling Troy for an instant. He spins around and looks at Hill with his eyes widened like a deer in headlights.

"Sorry, I didn't mean to startle you," Hill says apologetically as she approaches slowly.

"Oh, it's okay," responds Troy as he slowly turns back around and continues his work.

Hill walks over to get a closer look at what he's doing, "So what are you up to?"

"Just calibrating the Nautilus II sensor array software," he replies without even looking up.

"The Nautilus II?"

"Yes, it's our own submersible. It's stored in the cargo bay of the C-5 that's following us. Dr. Hinds is going to use it when we get to California."

"Really? Must be pretty advanced."

"Well, it's based on the famous French Nautile. That's the mini-sub used to examine the wreck of the Titanic. But our design has some beefed-up technology."

Hill smiles and takes a seat next to Troy, "Okay, you've got my attention. Tell me more."

Troy smiles back and hits a few keys on his computer. Suddenly the screen flashes and displays a full diagram of a mini submarine.

"Okay. Allow me to introduce you to the EPA's brand new Nautilus II mini sub. It's forty feet long and holds a crew of four. There's four color CCD underwater cameras, four digital still cameras, both thermal and sonar recognition systems and it has a maximum diving depth of 7,000 meters and a top speed of fifteen knots. Along with the Nautilus we also have Mark-six re-breathers for each of the crew members."

"Re-breathers?"

"Yes, Instead of using regular scuba equipment we're using advanced re-breathers," Troy punches a key on the computer and an image appears displaying the new diving equipment, "This type of system is smaller and lighter. But best of all, it allows divers to go deeper, stay down longer and spend less time decompressing by cleaning and reusing some of the air they breathe out."

Hill leans in toward the computer screen for a closer look, "You're kidding?"

"Nope."

"This is really impressive, how much does all this stuff cost?"

Troy gives her a devilish grin, "Sorry, that's classified."

She gives him a funny look and the two of them share a hardy laugh. He goes on for the next few minutes explaining some of the functions and features of the Nautilus II submersible.

Hill is truly impressed with both the quality and the quantity of knowledge the young man possesses.

"Tell me something Troy, just how old are you?" she asks.

"Twenty-five."

A look of disbelief spreads across her face, "Twenty-five? How in the world did you get mixed up in this mess? You should be out chasing girls and going to parties."

"First of all, I don't need to chase girls," Troy says in a sarcastic tone.

"Really? And why is that?" Hill responds playfully.

Troy leans back and points to his cheek, "Come on have you seen this face?" he turns his head from one side then to the other to show Hill his profile, "The girls are the ones that chase me. You should see my Facebook page. I have to beat them off with a stick."

Hill smiles and laughs, "Well excuse me, Casanova," she laughs again as she leans back with her hands up as if he's too hot to touch. Troy looks at her and blushes. Finally Hill stops laughing and leans into Troy and asks, "No, really, I want to know. How did you end up here?"

Troy smiles, "Well, let's see. I finished high school at sixteen, graduated summa cum laude from MIT at twenty and got my graduate degree at twenty-three and after leaving school I was recruited by my grandfather."

"Your grandfather?"

"Yeah, you know him as Professor Hamilton, I just call him Pop."

"You're kidding! I had no idea," responds Hill in a startled tone.

"Well we don't make a big deal about it and he sure doesn't treat me any different than the other members. I mean, he is very overprotective," Troy smiles as he speaks, "I remember for about a year some organization harassed me to join their group. I think they called themselves the…" he looks up and puts his hand on his chin while trying to remember the facts, "what was the name? Oh yeah, The Academy of New Minds or something like that. It sounded like a cult. Well, Pop went bananas when I told him about them. I don't know what he did but he got them to stop calling."

Hill giggles, "Wow, he really is protective."

"Yeah he is."

"Still it must be a strain on him knowing that you could get hurt working with this team."

"To tell you the truth, I think I worry about him more than he worries about me."

"How's that?"

"Haven't you noticed? His health isn't the greatest. He has a bad heart, he's sixty years old and this operation has been putting a lot of strain on him. But the flip side is that he loves what he does so much that I'm afraid if he stopped he'd die from boredom."

"He's a real workaholic, isn't he?" Hill says understandingly.

"You got that right. Part of why I'm here is to keep an eye on him. He's been more of a father than a grandfather to me especially after my parents died. I don't know what I would do without him," he pauses and gives Hill a serious look, "You know what I mean?"

"Yes I do, more than you know. I felt like that about my father," says Hill in a saddened tone, "I lost him some years ago."

"Sounds like you really miss him," says Troy with a softened voice.

"Yes, he meant everything to me," she then pauses as if to reflect on a thought.

The two exchange glances of understanding and share a moment of silence. Hill then gets up, walks behind Troy and gently rubs his back, "Your grandfather must be very proud of you. I know if you were my grandson I would be," Troy turns around and smiles at Hill. She smiles back then gently kisses him on the forehead, "Keep up the good work. But I think I've taken up enough of your time. I'm going to let you finish what you were doing," she starts toward the door to the galley, "It's been nice talking with you."

Troy gives her a little wave and responds, "Same here."

Hill stops at the entrance and looks back, "Listen I'm headed to the galley to grab a bite. Can I get you anything?"

"No I'm good. But thanks anyway," replies Troy as he turns back to the computer equipment and begins working again.

Hill flashes a grin then turns and heads through the door toward the plane's galley. She steps into the large brightly lit kitchen area where she finds Dr. Hinds and Daily. There are several cabinets lining both sides of the galley. On one side are three large microwave ovens, two coffeemakers, an ice machine, small sink and an elevator that leads to the cargo hold. In the middle of the room is a medium size dining room table surrounded by eight chairs, two of which are occupied by Hinds and Daily.

As Daily, sipping a cup of coffee, notices Hill enter the galley he puts his cup down and motions for her to come over, "Hey Debra, come and join us."

Hill smiles and causally walks over then takes a seat next to Daily who is sitting across from Hinds drinking a cup of coffee.

Hinds takes a sip from her cup then looks across at Hill, "So how's it going, Agent Hill?"

"As well as can be expected, Doctor," Hill responds with a sigh. She then leans across the table toward Hinds, "Can I ask you something, Dr. Hinds?"

Hinds smiles then says causally, "Sure, what's up?"

"Do you really think we have a chance in Hell of slowing these mutations down?" Hill asks.

With a twinkle in her eye, Hinds leans back in her chair and grins at Hill, "First of all, enough with the 'doctor' already--it's Karen," she says, flashing a warm and friendly smile.

Hill smiles back, "Okay Karen, what do you think are our chances?"

Hinds takes a deep breath and replies, "To be honest, Agent Hill--"

"Debra," interrupts Hill with a smile.

"Okay Debra," smiles Hinds as she continues, "I don't really know and I'm scared as hell. I don't know if you've noticed, but the incidents are getting worse and growing in frequency."

"So what can we do?" exclaims Hill while waving her hands in frustration.

"Pray. That's all I can say for now. Pray. But I'm telling you it doesn't look good," states Hinds shaking her head dejectedly as she takes another sip of coffee.

Daily gets up and heads toward the coffee machine, "Well, there's no way I'm letting a bunch of rats and bugs take over the world," he stops in front of the coffee machines and reaches for one of a pair of full pots, "at least not until I've had another cup of coffee," He turns, arching his eyebrows, "you want a cup Deb?"

"Sure, why not," replies Hill. "Anything to eat around here?"

"You bet. We're fully stocked and I know just what you need. How about my famous tuna salad on rye, extra mayo, lettuce and tomatoes?"

Hill smiles as she crosses her hands over her heart. "Oh, you know the way to a woman's heart."

Hinds looks at the two of them and grins.

"One coffee and tuna sandwich coming up! Doctor how about you?" says Daily playfully.

Hinds smiles and says, "No, don't trouble yourself--I'm fine."

Daily pulling down a loaf of bread from one of the cabinets says, "Come on Doc. I promise you I make the best tuna salad you've ever tasted."

Hill reaches over, touches her hand and whispers, "Go ahead. You might as well; he'll bug you until you say yes. That's how he got me the first time," Hill gives her a little wink with her left eye.

"Oh alright, sure. Make me one too," smiles Hinds.

Daily heads to the refrigerator and begins preparing their meal.

"He's a great guy," remarks Hinds to Hill.

"Yeah, that's my partner. I call him my big bear. He's someone I can always count on."

"I've noticed you two seem pretty fond of one another."

"Well, we are. I mean neither of us has much family. We both love our work. We spend a lot time together and have a lot in common."

She looks over at Daily and smiles as she watches him mix the ingredients at the counter. Hill turns back to Hinds, "I guess when you've worked together for as long as we have you're bound to get close."

Daily calls out from the counter at the rear of the galley, "All done, ladies." He opens up one of the cabinets and pulls out a tray.

"Here's my world-famous Daily Tuna Special," he boasts as he carries over the tray with a mug of coffee and two sandwiches. Daily hands Hill her sandwich and mug, "Here you go--just the way you like it with just enough cream and a little sugar," he hands Hinds a sandwich, "and here you are Doc."

"Thank you Agent Daily," she says as she picks up the sandwich.

"No problem, Doc."

Hill smiles and says, "Thanks a lot, Clarence. What would I do without you?"

"You know I always got your back Deb," he pats her on the shoulder and gives her a wink. "And now I'll leave you ladies alone to savor your delicious meal prepared by the master chef."

He bows and leaves the room with his coffee as the two women clap their hands and laugh.

Hinds looks across the table at Hill. "The two of you make a great couple you know."

"What? Clarence? We're just partners, nothing more," Hill smiles as she sips her coffee.

"I know love when I see it honey, and that man has the hots for you! I've been watching the two of you together and it shows."

"Like I said, we're close. Hell, we've worked together for over ten years."

"And how do you feel about him?" asks Hinds.

"I guess I have some feelings for him," says Hill sheepishly as she sips her coffee.

"Some feelings?" presses Hinds.

"Well you know how it is, we work together," explains Hill.

Hinds looks at Hill with a grin as she takes a bite out of her sandwich.

Hill continues, "I don't know. I guess I never really thought about it."

Hinds leans forward, "Listen to me. In case you haven't noticed this world of ours is going to shit and none of us knows how this is going to end, but I can tell you this--it's not going to end well. You got yourself a good man there. Hold on to him. Let him know how you feel. In the end we all are going to need someone by our side. Believe me."

"What do you mean, in the end?" says Hill with a sense of concern.

"Just hear me out. Things are bound to get worse before they get better. Let him know how you feel before it's too late," she takes another bite of her sandwich, gets up from the table and smiles down at Hill, "and he makes one hell of a tuna sandwich!" she says with her mouth full of food. The two women share a chuckle as Hinds stands up and heads to the entrance to the rear of the plane where the cabins are located. She stops at the doorway and looks back at Hill with the sandwich still in her hand, "Remember what I said Debra. I have a good feeling about the two of you."

Hill smiles back as she chews her food, "I won't Karen. I promise."

Hinds nods, then turns and leaves the room.

On the upper deck located just above the lab is the conference room. It's a small space lined with windows on both sides and an oval table in the middle surrounded by chairs. At one end is the cockpit and communications area, which is separated from the conference room by a clear Plexiglas wall, and at the other end is a spiral stairwell to the lower deck.

Sitting in the conference room around the table are Dr. Bloomberg, Cooper, Cliff and Brad going over some of the information gathered about the Imperial Beach incident.

While Cooper is reading some information in a folder he says, "Thousands of people on the beach, twenty five people disappear and not one person saw what did it. Amazing!"

"I know what you mean," Cliff adds as he thumbs through a folder of his own, "this is crazy. I don't know where to begin."

"Hold on. This may be something," exclaims Brad as he sits up with an open folder in his hands, "this kid was admitted into the hospital after the attack with some unexplained wounds on his leg."

"That's as good a place as any to begin," says Bloomberg, "Any name?"

"Yeah, Johnny Sanders and we have his address. I guess Cliff and I will talk to him and see what information we can get."

"Good start," says Bloomberg.

Just then a tall thin young man with blonde hair exits the communications area, enters the conference room and approaches Brad, "Excuse me, Officer Williams?"

"Yes?" answers Brad as he pops up his head and looks at the crew cut youngster dressed in military fatigues.

"You have a call sir. It's from EPA One. They have a communiqué from your wife. You can take it in here," he says as he points to the communications area.

Cliff and Brad exchange a puzzled look at one another. Brad stands up and follows the officer into the communications room.

Cliff returns to looking through the folders nodding his head. He mutters to himself, "Miles away up in an airplane, on a secret mission for the government and she still finds a way to track him down. And I thought my wife was bad."

Forrester from across the table chuckles quietly as he scans through the files in front of him.

Back downstairs Daily is resting in his sleeping compartment, a small room with a twin bed along one wall and a chair, a small desk that folds down from the wall and a laptop computer along the other. Suddenly there's a knock at the door.

"Come in."

The door opens and in walks Hill. She sits down at the foot of the bed as a smile fills Daily's face.

"What's up, partner?" he asks as he lies in the bed with his hands behind his head.

"Not much. Just thought you could use some company."

"Sure can, kick your shoes off and take the load off," he says jokingly.

Hill leans back against the wall near Daily's feet.

Daily senses that she has something on her mind and asks, "So, how do you feel about all of this craziness they've got us into?"

"Clarence, this whole situation scares the shit out of me. None of it makes any sense. I'm an FBI agent not some high-paid bug exterminator. What are we doing here?"

"Helping to protect the public the best way that we can. Listen, I'm just as confused as you are Deb. Ever since we've joined this unit I've seen the weirdest shit I've ever seen in my life and it scares the crap out of me too. But I also know that if this continues to spread a lot more lives will be lost. If I could do anything to prevent that from happening then my work is done."

Hill just stares at Daily and smiles for a short moment then asks, "Clarence, can I ask you something personal?"

"Sure. What's up?"

"Why haven't you ever settled down? I mean for as long as we've known each other I can barely remember you dating anyone seriously."

Daily sits up in the bed and faces Hill who is now nervously looking into her lap. He reaches over and gently takes her hand. As Hill slowly looks up at him he says, "I guess I could legitimately ask you the same thing", Hill looks at him and smiles as he continues, "To be honest I've never really found Mrs. Right."

"You mean you've never had any special person come into your life? Someone you'd like to spend your life with?"

"Well, I can't say I never have."

"Oh really? Who?"

"Hey, what's with all the questions anyway?"

"Come on, just answer me. Who was this special lady?"

Daily turns and sits on the edge of the bed with his head in his hands and his elbows resting on his knees. Then he says softly, "Debra, come on."

"No I want to know," she persists as she moves to his side and puts her arm around him.

Daily looks up from his hands and slowly turns to her. He gives her an innocent look with teary eyes and says softly, "Deb, stop. Don't you know?"

Hill puts her hand over her mouth and softly whispers, "Oh my God, then it's true," she pauses for a moment with her hand still over her mouth, "how long?"

"A long time now."

"Why didn't you say anything?"

"What? Are you kidding? You know what would happen if the bureau found out. You know what their policy is on agents dating each other. I'd be sent to Alaska carving ice cubes and you would probably end up in Maine investigating stolen lobster tails. Besides I was never sure if you felt the same way."

"I guess I always felt something but made excuses to cover my real feelings. I mean, after losing my dad I convinced myself that I didn't need anyone. But I always seemed to want you around and close."

Daily moves closer to Hill, "You mean?"

"Yeah, I guess I've loved you for a long time too," tears begin to roll down her cheeks as the two of them embrace each other. "This is crazy. Hell yeah, I love you, you big bear. I've always loved you, Clarence!"

He squeezes her tightly as they kiss each other passionately. With her arms still wrapped around Daily. Hill looks up at him smiling, "I can't believe we're doing this. This is crazy."

He looks down at her, "You want to stop?"

"No!" giggles Hill as she kisses him again, "what are we going to do?"

Daily still holding Hill, "Let's just take one day at a time."

Hill rests her head on Daily's chest, her arms still around his waist, "I'm just glad we're together," she sighs then holds him tighter, "I'm just glad that I have you."

Back upstairs, Brad has just returned from the communications room. Cliff is still looking over the files when Brad sits beside him.

Cliff looks up, "So what's up, partner?"

"Remember I told you Pat's been under the weather?"

"Yeah. Is she alright?"

"You're not going to believe this man, but…you're going to be a godfather."

"What? You mean Pat's pregnant?"

"Yeah. Finally after trying for so long. You remember how long we've been trying?"

"Holy Shit!" shouts Cliff. He then looks across the table at Cooper and Bloomberg who have just looked up, startled by his outburst, "His wife is pregnant! You hear that! My buddy's having a baby!" he pats Brad hard on his back, grabs him by both shoulders and shakes him as his partner blushes. "This is great, man!"

"Congratulations," says Bloomberg with a big smile as he reaches across the table and shakes Brad's hand.

"Congrats," adds Cooper as he shakes his hand also.

Suddenly Cliff stops and looks at Brad, "Wait a minute, you need to get home. You need to be with Pat right now, not flying around the country fighting monsters. I could take care of this."

"It's alright, buddy I plan to see this through. Besides, she's safe over at her mother's and the base promised me that they'll keep me posted if there are any problems."

"Just the same, I should get in touch with Doris and have her go over there and give them a hand."

"Oh, that's the other thing. I was supposed to tell you that Doris is already over there. Apparently your wife, my wife and my mother in-law are having a good old time while we're away."

"What, are they having a slumber party?" jokes Cliff.

The two of them laugh briefly before Bloomberg interrupts, "I think work can wait for a while," he throws his folder down on the table and stands up. "This calls for a celebration and I hear that the plane's galley has all kinds of goodies. I say we have ourselves a little party. Heck, we could all use a break."

Cooper replies, "You don't have to tell me twice."

The men get up and head down to the plane's galley and begin their celebration. The remaining members of the team soon join them. The news of Brad's forthcoming child helps lighten the mood among the team members. It also helps bring them closer together. For the remainder of the flight they all seem to have a more optimistic outlook on the future.

After an hour and a half in the air a screech comes over the plane's intercom system. "This is the captain speaking. We have arrived at Naval Air Station North Island. We'll be on final approach shortly. All passengers please report to the conference room and secure for landing."

As they take their seats Dr. Hinds looks over at Hill and the two women exchange smiles as they buckle in. Daily glances over at Troy and asks, "What's this Naval Air Station North Island?"

Troy answers, "It's a large naval base on an island off the coast of California about three miles west of San Diego International. It's the best place for us to land and deploy the Nautilus without attracting too much attention. Also it's only a few miles from Imperial Beach."

"Sounds great," replies Daily.

Suddenly the plane vibrates as its engines give off a high-pitched whine during the landing sequence. As the plane's vibrations grow in intensity a nervous look appears across Forrester's face. He grips the armrests of his chair tightly and grits his teeth. Brad looks across at him and gives him a reassuring wink but Forrester's nervousness continues to grow. After a few minutes, the vibrations begin to subside just as the passengers hear the heavy metallic sound of the landing gear lock into place.

There's a slight bump as the plane touches down causing Forrester to let out a small sigh of relief. He nervously looks up to find Brad nodding his head and laughing quietly.

Hinds looks out of the window and watches the buildings of the airfield pass by as the plane taxies toward a secure hangar near the southern end of the base.

A screech comes across the intercom, "This is the captain. Sorry for the rough ride. We ran into a little crosswind coming into the base. You are now free to move about. We'll be disembarking in about two minutes."

When the plane comes to a stop outside of one of the hangars the members begin to head down the stairs onto the tarmac. As they head toward their designated hangar, Cliff turns around to see crews unloading the Nautilus II from the C-5 Galaxy parked next to the 747.

Inside the hangar is a small meeting room in the back complete with a large table, chairs and large maps of the California coast hanging from the walls. Between two of the maps is a large video monitor. The team gathers in the room to outline their plans.

Dr. Bloomberg is standing in front of the seated team members, "Well, we want to cover as much ground as possible in the shortest amount of time. But before we launch the submersible we need to question some of the civilians from Imperial Beach. I need Officers Johnson and Williams as well as Agents Hill and Daily to help out in that department."

Hill takes a quick look at Daily then turns back to Bloomberg and says, "No problem."

Bloomberg continues, "Right, then. Karen you and Troy get the Nautilus ready while the rest of us continue to go over the data we've collected so far. Let's get a move on. There are drivers waiting for you out front."

The team members move with a sense of urgency, each person hurrying to their respective areas. Cliff and Brad get into a waiting black Lincoln Town Car as does Hill and Daily. In Brad and Cliff's car are two waiting Marines. When they get in the Marine driving turns around and asks, "Where would you like to go, Sir?" Brad opens up the folder he is carrying and replies, "32 Towser Street in Serra Mesa. You know where that is?"

"Yes sir, I do." replies the Marine.

"How far is it?" asks Williams.

"Not far at all, sir. Maybe about a half hour ride."

"Alright then, let's step on it," says Brad.

"Yes, sir!"

The car speeds off as does the one carrying the two FBI agents.

About twenty-five minutes later the vehicle arrives at the home of Johnny Sanders. It's a small ranch-style home painted white with an attached single car garage. There's a red Dodge Charger in the driveway.

The two Marines get out as do Cliff and Brad.

"You guys wait here," Brad directs the soldiers.

"Yes, sir," one of the Marines replies as the two continue to stand at attention near the car.

The two police officers, dressed in causal black suits and ties, approach the front door and ring the bell. After a short time Johnny opens the door, "Yes can I help you?"

"Mr. Sanders? Mr. John Sanders?" asks Brad.

"Yes."

The two officers reach in their jackets and show him their EPA ID's.

"The Environmental Protection Agency?" replies Johnny as he reads their identification. He then looks past the officers and notices the black car parked out front and the two Marines, "What's this all about?"

"Mr. Sanders we would like to question you about the events at Imperial Beach," says Cliff.

"I was already questioned by the police at the hospital."

"We know, sir. We just need a little more of your time," explains Cliff.

Johnny hesitates for a moment then looks over at the marines again, "Okay, come on in," the Officers enter Johnny's home as he opens the door wider. He motions for them to take a seat in his living room then closes the door and limps over and sits in a lounge chair facing them.

Cliff begins the questioning, "We understand you were injured during the attack."

"Yeah, on my leg. It wasn't that bad, really. They looked at it at the hospital and just cleaned it up and sent me home."

"May we see?"

"Sure," he pulls up his left pants leg. Cliff and Brad lean forward and take a look at his wounds. Around his left leg are two large bandages one from the knee to the calf and the other from the top of his calf to his ankle. Johnny carefully pulls back both of the bandages and reveals eight large circular scars. Each of the scars is about two inches in diameter. The skin appears chewed and jagged around the outer edge of each scar. The flesh in the middle of each the scars look red and raw and there are signs that scabs are beginning to form.

Brad pulls a digital camera from his pocket and asks, "You mind if we take a few pictures?"

"No, go ahead," says Johnny as he points down to his leg.

Brad gets up and begins snapping photos as Cliff continues to ask questions.

"So how did you get these marks?"

"I was out surfing when my friend was attacked by something under the water. Then one of the lifeguards gets sucked under and all hell breaks loose. I barely made it back to shore myself. Something grabbed my leg while I was swimming. I just kicked and kicked and until I made it safely back to the beach."

"Did you get a look at it?"

"Not a good look," he pauses for a moment as if trying to remember, "you know when my leg was caught I could have swore I saw lights flashing under the water," he pulls his pants leg down as Brad puts his camera away.

"Flashing lights?" queries Cliff.

Johnny continues, "I know it sounds weird but yeah, there were red and white flashing lights. But I couldn't make out what it was."

"Did you hear or smell anything unusual?" asks Brad.

"No not that I remember," he says as Cliff writes his notes on a small pad. Johnny with a frustrated look on his face then says, "Listen, I have a question? What the hell's going on here? Why is the EPA involved in this? What happened to my friends and all those people out there?"

"We're just trying to get answers like everyone else, Sir," replies Cliff.

"Bullshit!" shouts Johnny, "I know a snow job when I see it. That's not good enough. The police don't know anything, you don't know anything! I want some answers. I lost two of my best friends out there and no one knows anything. And now the EPA shows up at my door with the military! Something stinks!"

Brad holds his hands up in an attempt to calm the young man, "Sir, we understand your frustration. Believe me we do. But you must understand that before we can do anything we have to first find out what we are dealing with."

"We're just asking that you give us a chance to get those answers you want. We're going to find out what happened but we just need some time," cuts in Cliff.

"When we find out more information we'll pass it on to you. You have my word," says Brad as he hands Johnny a business card, "If you remember anything you think could help please feel free to call us at that number," Johnny takes the card looks at it briefly then sticks it into his pocket as Brad continues, "and I'd like to say that we're very sorry for your loss, but right now we know about as much as you do."

Johnny just sits there, shaking his head slowly from side to side and mumbles, "This is some shit."

The two officers stand up and prepare to leave. Cliff shakes Johnny's hand, "Thank you again for your assistance."

"Yeah, sure why not?" replies Johnny sarcastically as he gets up and hobbles toward the door.

Meanwhile on the other side of town Hill and Daily are also questioning a witness from the beach. They're sitting at the dining room table of sixty-six year old Jose Ramos. He is a short stout man with thinning gray hair and a potbelly. Standing behind him and helping to translate his Spanish and broken English is his forty-year-old daughter and her husband. Mr. Ramos trembles and his voice quivers as he tries to tell the story of what happened to his wife as the two of them swam towards shore on the day of the attack.

"Maria better swimmer. Escuchamos la alarma y le dije a Maria que no se preocupara. La dije que se fuera."

"He said when they heard the alarm he told her not to worry and go ahead," his daughter translates.

Mr. Ramos pauses and looks down as tears fill his eyes. His daughter wraps her arm around his shoulders and says softly in his ear, "It's okay, Papi. Go on tell them."

"Ella estaba nadando junto a me."

"He says she was swimming right next to him."

"Luego desaparecio."

"Then she was gone," translates his daughter.

"Did you notice anything strange in the water Mr. Ramos? Anything at all?" inquires Hill.

"Cuando se sumerge vi una mancha roja junto a ella."

"He says that when she went under he looked back and saw a red shape."

Mr. Ramos struggles to continue. He spreads his arms and says, "It was more big than man. I think it shark. Pensé que me sería el próximo."

"He says he thought he was going to be next," relays his daughter.

"Then I see the lits," rambles Mr. Ramos in a vain attempt to speak English.

"Excuse me?" asks Hill leaning forward so she could hear him better.

Mr. Ramos turns and stares at his daughter with a look of frustration, "¿cómo se dice luces?"

"Luces?" she responds.

"Si las luces," says Mr. Ramos excitedly.

"Lights," answers his daughter.

"Si lights!" Mr. Ramos stammers, "Luces intermitentes, rojas y blancas, bajo el agua."

His daughter looks over at Hill and translates, "He says he saw flashing red and white lights under the water."

"He told the same thing to the police but they didn't believe him," interrupts Ramos' son-in-law.

Daily jots down what he has heard on a little pad as Hill continues to question Mr. Ramos. "Is there anything else you remember? Anything at all?"

"No, puedo creer que este muerta ella," he buries his head into his daughter's shoulder and sobs uncontrollably.

"He just can't believe she's gone," says his daughter.

Hill and Daily stand up to leave. Hill shakes the hand of the son-in-law, "We're sorry for your loss. If it's any consolation what you've told us today may help prevent this from happening to anyone else," the son-in-law nods in agreement as Mr. Ramos and his daughter continue to hug each other.

The son-in-law looks down at them and comments, "The trip to IB was our treat. They were celebrating their 42nd anniversary," his eyes begin to well up with tears.

Seeing how grief-stricken the family is Hill replies gently, "Again Sir, we're very sorry. We'll show ourselves out. Thank you." The FBI Agents quietly leave the Ramos' apartment.

After about two hours of questioning witnesses the two teams return to Halsey Field on North Island. Waiting for them at the secure hangar is the rest of the team. They all greet each other and sit around a large table.

"So, what have we found so far?" asks Bloomberg.

Cliff looks through the notes he has made and says, "Most of the witnesses we've talked to recall seeing under water flashing lights."

Dr. Hinds, who was reading a folder, snaps her head up when she hears this, "Flashing lights? Are you sure?"

"Yes all but two people said they saw them."

Hill jumps in, "Our witnesses said the same thing. One even said he saw a large man-sized object under the water but couldn't make out what it was."

Daily noticing Hinds' interest asks, "What gives Doc? You know what it is?"

"Maybe. Did anyone have any unusual marks on them?"

"The first person we spoke to did," remarks Brad, "he had large round scars on his leg where he said something grabbed him. Here I took some pictures," he hands her the digital camera.

When Dr. Hinds switches it on her eyebrows rise up. She looks at Troy and hands him the camera, "Could you put these up on the monitor?"

"Sure, give me a sec," he takes the camera and connects it to his laptop computer then begins pressing several buttons on the keyboard.

"I think I know exactly what we are dealing with and if I'm right they're not going to be easy to get rid of." The large monitor on the wall behind her comes to life and displays a large color photo of Johnny's leg covered with large round scars.

Dr. Hinds gets up and walks over to the monitor and begins pointing to the wound, "You see the jagged edges around the edge of each scar? There is only one animal that I know of that inhabits this region that can leave a mark like that."

"And what's that?" asks Cooper.

"Dosidicus Gigas," answers Hinds

Daily twists his face and says, "English Doc, English."

"The Humboldt Squid. Also known as the Jumbo Squid or as the Mexicans call it Diablo Rojo for Red Devil. They have been a problem in this area for years even before SF-20. Because of overfishing in their natural habitat and the rising temperatures of the ocean they have migrated up from the west coast of South America all the way up to Oregon, and Washington. I've even heard stories of them seen as far north as Alaska."

"If they've been a problem for that long why haven't we heard anything about them until know," asks Brad.

"Well the only real problem they have caused is that they compete with fisherman for the same fish. They have attacked humans in the past but nothing that has ever been fatal. I remember a few reports a couple of years ago of Humboldt attacking divers and fishermen in the Sea of Cortez. They were trying to drag them into deeper water."

"How big are these things?" asks Forrester.

Hinds walks over to Troy, "Can you go into the EPA database and bring up the file on Humboldt Squids?"

"I'll have it in two minutes," says Troy as he quickly types in her query.

Hinds continues, "From what I can remember they normally grow to about seven feet long, but who knows what effect SF-20 has had on them."

The Monitors image changes and it now shows the picture of a large squid with data underneath it.

Hinds turns to the monitor, "Ah, here we are. Yes I was right--about seven feet long and weighing 100 pounds. But the size of the scars on the victim suggests that they have grown much larger."

"How have the local fisherman dealt with them in the past?" asks Cooper.

"Well, some have even taken to fishing directly for the Humboldt. I hear they're very tasty," the team gives a collective giggle.

Forrester mumbles, "Ummm Calamari."

The group shares a laugh.

Dr. Hinds continues her lecture, "The main problem with these animals is that they're very intelligent, maybe even problem-solving smart, and very aggressive. Those flashing lights everyone says they saw were the animals giving off a chemical change in their skin called bioluminescence. This allows the squid to change color rapidly. They do this usually while mating or as a display of aggression. The information that we have relates to normal Humboldt, which suggests that they are only aggressive while feeding but at other times they are very passive. But as we now know SF-20 can change that behavior."

Dr. Bloomberg jumps in, "Karen, can you tell us some more of their characteristics?"

"Yes, well they grow very fast and have keen eyesight. They have ten tentacles, eight for swimming and grabbing and two longer ones for attacking prey. The tentacles are covered with large suckers. Each sucker is lined with sharp teeth that can hook into flesh. They eat by drawing their prey towards a razor sharp parrot-like beak, which can quickly shred skin right down to the bone. Oh and another thing, normal Humboldt squid travel in packs of anywhere from 100 to as many as 1200 individuals."

Everyone around the table silently looks back and forth at one another.

"So what's our plan?" asks Daily, "I mean how do we stop 1200 hungry squid from attacking more people? Do we close all of the beaches? What?"

Hinds steps forward, "I have read that many squid including Humboldt can be attracted to glowing objects. Maybe we can use the Nautilus to draw them away from shore and into some sort of net."

Cooper jumps in and says, "If this pack of squid is..."

Hinds interrupts, "a school of squid."

Cooper continues, "Okay, if this school of squid is anywhere as large as you say it could be, I don't think we could get a net big enough to catch them all and even if we could what do we do with them after that?"

Forrester looks up and says, "What about electrocution?"

"What?" replies Hinds.

"Electrocution, Listen they're already in the water right, why couldn't we rig some sort of electrified net? You know we can wait till most of the squid hit the net and then pull the switch, then bam, fried calamari."

Hinds looks at Troy, "What'd you think? Is it doable?"

Troy thinks for a moment then says, "Yes, I think it is! It'll take some time to complete with the right supplies, but I think it could be done."

Bloomberg steps toward Troy, "Great, get on it right away. The Navy personnel and supplies are at your full disposal."

"I'm on it!" Troy jumps up and hurries out of the room.

"Simon, you and Jacob help Karen outfit the Nautilus with some underwater strobes so we can attract the squids."

Hinds looks up and says, "You know I also remember reading somewhere that a scientist working out of Oregon State

University identified the mating sounds of the Humboldt. We could construct an underwater speaker to transmit that sound. If we use the mating call along with the strobes we're sure to attract the squid."

"Fantastic," responds Bloomberg.

"What about us?" asks Cliff.

"The rest of you come with me. I'm going to take to the Nautilus Simulator so you can become acquainted with its operation."

"Why? We're not driving the thing," says Daily.

"I been informed that the Nautilus' sister ship, the Stingray, is being flown here as we speak. So we'll be able to have two submersibles in the water at the same time and cover twice as much ground. So we're going to need more crew members to man the rear ports."

Brad shakes his head as they follow Bloomberg out of the room, "Man this just keeps getting better and better."

"I know what you mean partner," replies Cliff.

Through the night they work in the sub simulator learning its various functions and controls while Troy and a team of Navy engineers construct the electrified net.

It's 6:00 am the next day; overnight the second sub arrives and is outfitted with underwater strobe lights and speakers. Both subs have been loaded aboard the 900-ton research catamaran Poseidon's Son that will serve as the base of operations while they are out at sea. The team and the subs leave the naval port off of North Island and head south towards Imperial Beach. While in route Dr. Bloomberg assembles the team as he gets ready to assign members to each of the two subs. Every one arrives at the cargo bay located between the Poseidon's two hulls. The subs are attached to huge cranes ready to lift them into the ocean. This is the first time that many of the team members have seen the subs up close. Both the Nautilus and the Stingray are of the same design. The only difference is their color. The Nautilus is bright yellow with black markings and the Stingray is white with black markings. The subs are forty feet long and twenty-five feet wide.

The bow of each sub is outfitted with a large glass observation sphere. Above that are various cameras, sensors and lights as well as lateral and vertical thrusters. On each side of the subs are many control surfaces and thrusters. At the rear of the ships are two smaller observations windows on each side. At the subs stern is a large electric powered propeller. There is only one way in or out of the subs and that is a hatch located on the top near the center big enough for only one person at a time to crawl through at a time.

The team is lined up beside the two subs as Dr. Bloomberg steps in front of them holding a clip board, "Okay for the crew of the Nautilus we have Karen, Simon, Cliff and Clarence. For the Stingray we'll have Jacob, Brad, Debra and myself," he looks up from the clipboard, "this is the plan. The subs will launch about ten miles off of Imperial Beach. We'll be spaced about five miles apart from each other. Troy's on a fishing trawler retrofitted with an electrified net that will be located between us about twenty miles out. We'll use the strobes and sound devices on the mini subs to attract the squid and lead them towards the trawler, any questions?"

Cliff raises his hand and says, "How certain are you that the squid will follow?"

"We're pretty sure but just help our chances we'll be chumming the waters around the net and Troy has also set up a series of buoys strung across the search area outfitted with sonar transducers. So we have a better chance of directing the subs to the squid's location. Now it's also important to remember you must get your sub clear of the net before Troy can throw the switch, anything else?"

There is an eerie silence as everyone just looks at one another. Bloomberg looks over the team then remarks, "Alright then, grab your gear and saddle up. We'll be at the first drop point in twenty minutes. The Stingray will be going in first."

The team members all dressed in wet suits as a safety precaution head toward their subs.

Cliff stops in front of the Stingray and grabs Brad by the arm as he is about to climb aboard, "Hey partner, I wanna talk to you a sec."

Brad stops and turns around, "What's up?"

"Listen it might get a little hairy out there and I want you to do me favor and play it safe. No superhero stuff, okay? Remember you have a kid on the way and besides Pat would kill me if anything happened to you."

Brad smiles at his partner, "Don't worry about me, you just make sure YOU don't do anything stupid cause Doris would kick my ass. I'm scared of that wife of yours."

The two men nervously chuckle while they embrace each other. They step back and stare silently at each other for a moment. Then Brad with a serious look on his face slaps Cliff sharply on the arm and says "You take care of yourself, partner."

Cliff nods and replies, "You make sure you do the same."

Brad turns and climbs the ladder towards the hatch on top of the Stingray as Cliff turns and heads for the Nautilus where a similar scenario was playing out between Daily and Hill.

As Hill heads toward the Stingray Daily gently grabs her arm. She turns and the two exchange a short look of concern. He pulls her towards him and they embrace. As they do he whispers into her ear, "You better be careful, you hear me?"

She whispers back, "Oh big bear, don't worry about me. I'll be just fine." She kisses him gently on the neck and smiles then heads for the Stingray.

It's 7:00 am and the Poseidon's Son has arrived about ten miles off the coast of Imperial Beach. The Stingray is lifted up and submerged into the Pacific. The ship moves five miles south where it deposits the Nautilus II then turns east to rendezvous with the fishing trawler twenty miles out.

On board the retrofitted fishing trawler, The Captain's Hook, Troy sits in the control room monitoring a series of screens connected to the floating sonar buoys. The Stingray has descended down to a depth of 600 meters along the south eastern face of the undersea Coronado Escarpment while the Nautilus II, five miles away, skims along the Northern side of the Coronado Canyon at a depth of all little more than 500 meters. Both subs begin emitting the underwater sounds designed to mimic the squid's mating call. They are also flash their high intensity underwater strobes. In the Stingray Dr. Bloomberg is piloting the sub while Forrester monitors the sensors. Brad and Hill are positioned at the rear view ports keeping a lookout for any signs of the elusive animals. Operating the Nautilus II is Dr. Hinds with Cooper on the sensors and Cliff and Daily at the rear viewports.

After about four hours, neither sub has anything to report and the sonar buoys are silent. The search begins to seem hopeless. Dr. Bloomberg, frustrated with the failing attempt at finding the squid says over the radio, "Stingray to Nautilus over."

After a few moments, "This is the Nautilus go ahead Stingray," answers Cooper.

"Anything to report?"

"Negative. We're moving down along eastern side of Coronado Canyon. Depth 650 meters."

"Roger Nautilus. We're moving south of the Coronado Bank, 700 meters. We have only about two hours more of battery power. I don't want to push it too much. We'll stay out for another half hour then head in. Do you copy?"

"Roger Stingray. Copy that."

In the Stingray Brad, who is seated at the port side view window, is looking for anything out of the ordinary in the murky ocean. Suddenly he notices something. He begins operating the external cameras to get a better view through the dark depths.

"Hey Jacob," says Brad.

"What's up?" Forrester answers from the front of the sub.

"I've done some scuba-diving in the gulf with Cliff and we've always been surrounded by fish. But there's nothing out here. It's barren, no life at all. Is that the way it's supposed to be?"

"He's right. Come to think of it I haven't seen too many fish in the past half hour," Hill adds.

Forrester checks his instruments then says, "You two may be on to something."

"What is it Jacob?" asks Bloomberg.

"The lack of fish. It could mean we're getting close to the school. This could be their feeding grounds."

"What's the normal feeding depth of the Humboldt Squid?" asks Bloomberg.

"Around 700 meters," Forrester quickly responds.

"Maybe the mutants can go deeper. I'm taking her down to 900."

Forrester looks back at Brad and Hill who gaze at him with concern in their eyes. Bloomberg pulls back a lever and the whirling sound of the vertical thrusters fill the cabin as the sub begins to descend.

All members are silent as Forrester calls off the depth, "750…..800…..850…..875…..900 meters!"

Bloomberg pushes the lever forward and the sub stops.

"Alright people keep your eyes open," orders Bloomberg. He pushes the throttle forward slowly and the sub glides along side of an underwater canyon. The ocean at this depth is extremely dark and visibility is only about thirty meters. For a while all is silent then suddenly. There's a sound from one of the instruments at Forrester's console.

PING!……………………… PING!…………………………
PING!

"We have a contact!" Forrester shouts excitably.
PING!……………………… PING!…………………………
PING!

"Where is it?" commands Bloomberg, "What direction?"

"Below us, 70 degrees off the port side!" shouts Forrester.

Bloomberg looks back over his shoulder, "Brad do you see anything?"

"No! Not yet it's too dark. I can't see a thing."

"Okay I'm bringing her down a little deeper," says Bloomberg as he pulls back on the lever that controls the depth of the sub.

Forrester begins reading off the depth, "950…..1000…..1075….1100….1150….1200. Hold it! Stop!"
PING!………… PING!………… PING! ………… PING!

"Large contact 300 meters away about 40 degrees port and closing fast," says Forrester excitedly.

"I still can't see shit!" comments Brad.
PING!…… PING!…… PING!…… PING!…… PING!

"200 meters and closing!"
PING!… PING!… PING!… PING!… PING!… PING!

"100 meters it's on top of us!"

Brad strains to see through the port window, "I still can't ...OH MY GOD!"

BANG!

The sub rocks violently to the starboard side sending all of its crew crashing against its bulkhead.

BANG!

Another strike pushes it into the side of the underwater canyon causing its starboard wall to buckle. The lights inside the sub flicker and water begins to spray through a small leak above Hill.

"Debra, turn that valve by your feet clockwise!" shouts Forrester.

"This one?" says Hill as she points to a valve next to her foot.

"Yes, turn it clockwise!"

She begins turning the valve and the leak starts to slow down.

Bloomberg straps himself into the command chair and tells the other members to strap themselves in as well. He then looks back at Jacob, "How much damage do we have?"

Forrester checks some of his controls then he responds, "Everything seems to be working," he pauses for a second. "Wait a minute, there's some minor damage to the starboard vertical thrusters. Nothing major, but they're registering a twenty-five percent decrease in output."

"Contact the Nautilus and let them know we've made contact," orders Bloomberg.

Forrester begins turning some knobs and adjusts the underwater communication system, "Nautilus, this is Stingray do you read? Nautilus, this is Stingray come in please."

"Go ahead, Stingray," replies Cooper over the radio.

"We've made contact. Approximately one mile between the Coronado Canyon and the Bank, we're 1225 meters down. Heading north to rendezvous point."

"Roger that Stingray. Heading to rendezvous point. Meet you there, out."

Bloomberg pushes the throttle forward and the sub begins to strain.

Suddenly Brad shouts, "My God! Look at this!"

He's staring out of the rear port window with the look of horror on his face. Spread out against the port window in front of him is the massive underbody of a huge squid. In the middle of the window is a two-foot long, sharp, parrot-like beak clawing at the glass. The mouth is surrounded by ten tentacles that stretch across the entire window. The tentacles are covered in hundreds of tooth-edged suckers each struggling to maintain a grip on the sub's window. Hill and Forrester move to the back of the sub for a closer look.

Forrester after closely examining the creature says, "Jesus they're much larger than I thought they would be. It must be at least twenty feet long!"

"Isn't that about half as long as this sub?" asks Brad in a matter of fact way.

"Yes. You're right," replies Forrester.

Bloomberg who's still sitting in the command chair peers out of the main view sphere, "The commotion is attracting other's I can see them coming into view. I'm going to try and ease her up. Everybody get back in you seats!"

He pushes the lever forward and a whirling sound of the vertical thruster fills the cabin of the sub. The sub slowly climbs.

BANG!

Another squid hits the submersible right above the main viewing sphere. It grips the sub just as the first one does. Its additional weight forces the sub to pitch downward. Bloomberg pushes on the lever. The thrusters strain but the craft fails to rise.

BANG! BANG!

Two more squid attach to the sub pulling it down.

"We've got to get them off. I can't steer or surface with all this extra weight. We won't make it to the rendezvous point," shouts Bloomberg as the sub continues to sink, "What's our depth?"

Forrester checks the gauge, "1400 meters and dropping."

"What's our maximum depth?" asks Brad.

"7000 meters!" shouts Bloomberg as he continues to struggle with the controls. The sub rocks back and forth as it pitches forward and back shaking up the crew inside.

"How deep is the bottom?" asks Hill.

Forrester turns toward her, "About 9000 meters."

Hill and Brad exchange a quick glance at each other. She continues, "And how deep can these squid go?"

Forrester gives her a worried look and says, "I don't know but from the look of their size I'd say deep. Very Deep."

"Well we've got to get them off. How deep are we now?" she says nervously.

Forrester checks the gauges, "We're approaching 2200 meters and dropping fast!"

"Anybody have any ideas?" asks Bloomberg.

"What about trying to crush them against the side of the canyon?" comments Brad.

"Too dangerous. If I hit too hard I can tear a hole in the sub."

"2800 meters and still falling," shouts Forrester.

"We have to try," exclaims Hill.

Forrester taps Bloomberg on the shoulder, "She's right Kevin. It's probably the best bet we have. If anymore gab onto us we're gonna sink even faster we already passed 3000 meters."

"Alright I'll try it. I'm going to need everybody with their eyes open to help guide me," he turns toward the rear of the sub, "Brad keep your eyes peeled on those external cameras."

Brad gives him a thumbs up and adjusts his monitor.

Bloomberg begins slowly steering the sub towards the wall of the canyon.

CLANG! SCREEEECH!

The submersible scrapes the side of the canyon hard and rocks the ship to one side. The lights dim then flicker and another leak sprouts as the sub continues to sink.

CLANG!

The sub hits again. Water is now spraying into the cabin at a high rate and is beginning to accumulate inside of the sub.

"We're still dropping! 4200 meters Kevin!" yells Forrester.

Hill looking through the viewport in front of her screams, "They're all around us!"

BANG! BAM! BOOM!

Forrester, with a horrified look on his face, stares at his instruments and shouts, "Jesus, Kevin we're passing 5500 meters!"

Bloomberg struggling at the controls hollers back, "I'm trying but something is jamming the propeller!"

"6200 meters!"

Bloomberg works the controls feverously. Then finally, "I got it! I've got control back."

Brad, soaking wet and shaking, stares at the monitors connected to the sub's external cameras. Watching hundreds of the twenty-foot long squid circle the sub darting in and out hitting the ship repeatedly as if testing for weaknesses.

The hits are having an effect not only on the sub but the crewmembers as well. They're being thrown about violently and bashed around the cabin.

"We're still falling. 7100 meters! We've passed max depth!" shouts Forrester.

Suddenly the squeaking sound of bending metal resonates throughout the sub.

"Now what?" cries Hill.

"It's the hull giving way. We're too deep," says Forrester.

"Everyone hold on. I'm going to try something," states Bloomberg, "look up ahead," he points straight ahead, "that crevice over there. It's just big enough for the sub to squeeze through. I'm going to try and make for it."

"Looks too narrow," says Forrester.

"I think I could make it. Maybe we could scrape some of them off of us."

"Whatever you're going to do just do it we're still dropping!" shouts Forrester, "7400 meters!"

"Hang on I'm almost there," says Bloomberg as he struggles to maneuver the craft through the dark split in the canyon.

BANG! CRACK! SCREECH!

The sound of scraping metal echoes throughout the cabin as more water sprays in from several small cracks in the hull.

"We lost our port video camera!" yells Hill over the sound of spraying water.

"The water's starting to fill up in here!" screams Brad.

"Brad there's another pressure valve near your feet. Turn it clockwise. It should stop some of this water from rising," shouts Forrester.

The water is about two feet deep. Brad reaches down and blindly moves his hands around searching for the valve. After several seconds he finally feels it. It's a large metal knob about a foot in diameter. He grabs it with both hands and turns.

"It's stuck!"

"Here let me help," says Hill as she sloshes through the water towards him, "you take that side"

"Pull," shouts Brad as the two strain to turn the valve.

The valve makes a quarter of a turn which causes the water to slow down a bit. But the sub continues to shake and vibrate wildly as Bloomberg pushes the sub through the undersea crevice.

"It's working! One of them just let go!" shouts Brad, "Another one is losing interest. Wait a minute! Yes he's letting go too."

Bloomberg pushes the throttle all the way forward and the sub lunges forward, "We're through!" he shouts.

"Keep going they're right behind us!" yells Forrester while staring at a video monitor.

"Blow ballasts one and four"

Forrester flicks two switches on his console. There is a low-pitched booming sound, which is soon followed by a loud hissing sound.

"We're rising!" shouts Forrester, "7000 meters.....6500 meters......6000 meters!"

"Are the squid still behind us?" queries Bloomberg.

Forrester checks the sonar screen, "Yes, they're about 1000 meters behind us, still following. I think we got them hooked."

"Don't get too excited. We still have a long way to go to get to the net and that attack drained our batteries quite a bit," says Bloomberg as he adjusts his headset, "Nautilus this is Stingray come in."

"Go ahead, Stingray. We're waiting at the Captain's Hook. What's your position?" replies Hinds over the intercom.

"About five miles out. We were attacked by the squid and sustained some damage. Batteries are running low. We're heading to your position at top speed. The squid are a lot larger than we thought and extremely aggressive, about twenty feet long. They dragged us down passed max depth. We barely made it out."

"Copy that Stingray. Is everyone alright?"

Bloomberg looks back at his crew, "Just a little banged up but everybody's fine."

"Good to hear. We'll be ready here!"

"See you in a few. Nautilus out."

"Good luck," adds Hinds as she signs off.

"What's our speed?" Bloomberg asks Forrester.

"Ten knots."

"How fast can those squid swim?" asks Hill.

"Normally, around thirteen knots," replies Forrester.

"But these are not normal squid," comments Hill.

Forrester turns and looks at her with a worried expression, "You're right."

"Just about how much is a knot in miles per hours?" asks Brad.

"One knot equals about 1.2 miles per hour. Our top speed is fifteen knots so that's about seventeen miles per hour," answers Forrester.

"How far are those squid?" asks Bloomberg.

Forrester looks down at the sonar, "About 700 meters and closing."

"Okay I need to bring us up to the surface and try and outrun them for as long as I can," Bloomberg operates the controls and the sub begins to rise.

Forrester continues to monitor the sonar. Hill and Brad stay glued to their monitors and to their view windows.

They are about three miles away from the rendezvous point where the Captain's Hook and the Poseidon are waiting with a large electrified fishing net to catch and hopefully destroy the squid.

Ding ....Ding ....Ding

The sound of an alarm fills the cabin of the submersible. Bloomberg twists his head around and looks at Forrester, "Jacob? What's happening?"

"Low Battery alarm! It's almost dead."

"How much time do we have?"

"Not sure. The gauge is damaged. It's not displaying the amount of power left."

"Great," mumbles Brad.

PING!.......................... PING!...........................
PING!

"Now what?" shouts Hill.

PING!............ PING!............ PING! .... PING!

"The squid! They're gaining on us and there are more of them!"

PING!...... PING!...... PING!...... PING!...... PING!

"They're gaining fast!" shouts Forrester.

"Faster! We have to go faster!" cries Hill.

"I got it pushed all the way forward!"

PING!... PING!... PING!... PING!... PING!... PING!

Forrester staring at the sonar screen yells out, "Faster damn it! They're almost on us!"

"We're at top speed damn it!" Bloomberg shouts back.

"Thirteen knots my ass," remarks Hill as she buckles back into her seat. Brad takes notice and does the same.

PING! .. PING! .. PING! .. PING! .. PING! .. PING!

"They're on top of us!" exclaims Forrester.

BANG! BANG!

The impact throws Forrester from his chair and onto the floor of the water logged sub. Hill unbuckles herself and makes her way over to him, "Give me your hand," she says as she reaches down toward Forrester.

BANG!

Hill with her hand outstretched slams hard into the metal hull of the sub.

BANG!

Forrester and Hill are flung against the opposite side of the sub. More leaks begin to spring up all over the sub.

Brad with a severe case of whiplash holds on for dear life, "Debra! You alright?"

Hill stumbles to her feet in the knee high water, soaked from head to foot, "Yeah, I'm okay," she says while breathing heavily. She looks over at Forrester, "How about you?"

Forrester nods that he's fine and staggers to his seat.

"What's our depth?" shouts Bloomberg.

"We're still too deep, 2450 meters."

"That's better than I thought. Those last hits gave us a little push upward."

"How far are we from the net?"

"About two miles! But we're slowing. Battery's almost drained."

"We're not going to make it. Blow the remaining ballasts!"

Then Hill looks up as she hears the ballast tanks empty and Brad grips his chair as the sub quickly shoots toward the surface.

Bloomberg switches on his headset, "Nautilus this is Stingray come in!"

BANG! BANG!

The sub rocks violently to one side then to the other.

"Nautilus, come in!"

"Go ahead Stingray," replies Hinds, "how far are you out?"

"We're in trouble. Battery power is low, we're leaking water and squid are attacking. Can you get closer?"

"Will do, but we need your position."

"I'm sending up the emergency beacon. Key in on that!" Bloomberg turns to Forrester, "Jacob, launch the emergency buoy."

"Got it," says Forrester as he flicks a few switches. The sound of a metallic clamp can be heard springing open from on top of the sub. A small yellow and orange buoy attached to a cable quickly rises to the surface. As it bounces on the waves it flashes a high-intensity strobe and emits a radio signal directing the surface team to the location of the sub.

BANG!

The sub quickly rocks to the left then to the right. The crew is smashed against the metal bulkhead like rag dolls.

Bloomberg while struggling with the controls looks over his shoulder and shouts, "We can't take too much more of this. Everybody put on your re-breathers just in case we have to bail out."

Everyone struggles to strap on their re-breathers. Being about the size of a school backpack they are much less bulky than conventional scuba gear, but still tricky to put on in the cramped quarters of the mini sub.

Meanwhile on the surface the Captain's Hook, Poseidon's Son and the Nautilus II are all steaming at full speed towards the Stingray's beacon. Troy is at the bow of the Captain's Hook using a pair of binoculars to search for the floating emergency buoy. He's scanning slowly back and forth till he sees something in the distance.

"Hold it! I think I see something. Yes there it is about ten degrees starboard!" he shouts into a com link to the bridge of the ship, "contact the Nautilus and the Poseidon, we found them!"

Below the surface the battle continues as Bloomberg attempts to surface the damaged sub. Water is spraying into the vessel from numerous leaks and the squid continue to grab and shake the mini sub violently.

BANG! BANG! BANG!

"We should almost be at the surface!" shouts Bloomberg.

"300 meters but what about the net?" asks Forrester?

"They should be in position by now."

BANG! CLUNK! BAM!

"They're really tearing us apart!" cries Hill holding on to a pipe above her head.

"Jacob, what's our depth?"

"200 meters! We're rising slowly. I think they're hanging on."

"They are!" shouts Brad while he and Hill look out of the rear window.

"Oh my God they're going to pull us back down," shouts Hill as she sees more squid latch on to the sub.

"195 meters!" shouts Forrester.

Bloomberg frantically working the controls, "I'm blowing the hatch when we hit the surface! Can you tell where our ships are?"

Bang! Bang!

Forrester looks down at his instruments and frantically flicks switches, "Ah shit! Now the sonar's out," he turns to Bloomberg with a worried look, "we're swimming blind!"

"Alright then, everybody hold on." Bloomberg pushes the vertical thrusters to full power and the sub jerks and lunges upward, "Come on, damn it!" the sub jerks again, "Come on, rise!" he shouts.

"It's working," shouts Forrester, "150 meters! Almost there."

Just above them the Nautilus sits quietly on the surface. Cooper is perched on top of the sub with the main hatch open and Hinds is at the controls. Beside them is the Poseidon's Son with its crew on deck looking for signs of the damaged Stingray. About 400 meters away is the Captain's Hook with Troy and a few crewmembers on deck also looking out for the sub. Then suddenly the water near the Nautilus begins to bubble and splash as if were boiling.

Cooper points to the disturbance and shouts, "There--look there! They're coming up!"

In the middle of the rumbling sea a large white mass slowly appears covered in dozens of tentacles.

"Karen, see if you can get closer."

Hinds slowly maneuvers the craft toward the Stingray as it continues to surface. The hatch of the Stingray pops open, Forrester peers out just as a tentacle lashes out past his head. He ducks then stares at the waving arm with the look of horror on his face.

Cooper screams down into the Nautilus, "A little closer, come along side them! Cliff hand me that cable."

Cliff passes a cable up through the hatch. Cooper takes the cable, which has two large metal clamps at either end from Cliff and clamps one end to a metal ring near the hatch.

"Jacob, here--catch this line!"

He throws the cable to Forrester who then clamps the other end to the metal ring on his sub. He then pulls on the line to draw the subs closer together. By this time the entire area around the two subs is bubbling with movement. Tentacles are splashing all around them. Four large squid are still attached to the back of the Stingray and are making it difficult to stay afloat. Racing towards the two subs is two large speedboats from the Poseidon's Son each manned by three sailors. When the boats get close to the boiling water they begin to rock and sway over the sea of tentacles and squid bodies. The animals slap their arms sharply across the two boats in an attempt to knock their occupants into the water. The sailors hold on for dear life. As the boats approach the Stingray a sailor in one of them stands up with a rifle and begins firing into the water at the squid that have come too close. He hits a number of the animals causing clouds of blood to spread throughout the water. The bloody water only makes things worst as the squid go into a frenzy lashing out at everything within reach. They even rip apart several of their wounded brethren. The two subs, now tied together, and the speedboats all become victims of the increasingly turbulent ocean. One of the speedboats moves along side of the Stingray and a sailor yells to Forrester, "Quickly give me your hand. We can't stay out here much longer."

Forrester inches over the top of the sub and slides down into the waiting boat just as Hill emerges from the hatch. A large squid which has attached itself to the rear of the Stingray launches one of its deadly tentacles in Hill's direction. In an attempt to dodge the attack she slips on the hull of the sub and grabs the edge of one of the metal strobe lights just along its side leaving her feet dangling about a foot from the water. Cooper quickly climbs over from the Nautilus and onto the Stingray. He grabs the Stingray's hatch with one hand and reaches down with the other towards Hill, "Debra, give me your hand!" he shouts as she fights to maintain her grip.

The boat with Forrester, having drifted away due to the turbulent water, wrestles to inch closer toward Hill as the sailors onboard use harpoons, machetes and guns to fend off the lashing tentacles.

"Debra, take my hand," screams Cooper as he strains to reach Hill.

Suddenly another tentacle springs out of the bubbling water behind Hill and grabs her re-breather. She fights with all her might to hold on to the strobe as the animal's arms try to pull her into the water.

A second boat speeds to Hill's location just as another large tentacle uncoils from the water along side it and slaps violently down across the vessel smashing it in two, sending its occupants flying into the fierce sea.

"*Ahhhh!* Help me," yells one of the sailors treading water amongst the deadly snake like arms.

A tentacle grabs him, lifts him into the air, dangles him for a second then quickly pulls him under the water.

After seeing their comrade disappear beneath the waves the other two sailors begin swimming feverishly towards the two subs. Abruptly one of them disappears with a splash causing the other sailor to wade about while screaming in terror. A sailor from the first boat fires his gun near his downed buddy as tentacles dart in and out of the water around him. Suddenly his body rises up from the water. Forrester and the sailors on board the speedboat gasp as they realize that a huge birdlike beak has swallowed the lower half of his body.

"Help me, oh my God, help me," the sailor shouts, as he struggles to free himself from the monstrous mouth surrounded by ten wildly waving tentacles. One tentacle reaches over and grabs one of the man's arms then rips it from its socket as the sailor lets out a blood-curdling scream.

Two sailors in Forrester's boat begin firing their rifles rapidly at the beast in an attempt to dislodge the struggling victim. The squid begins thrashing about even more violently. Its beak clamps down sharply around the man's torso causing him to vomit up thick blood. It then splashes quickly back under the ocean leaving an undersea cloud of bloody water.

Cooper makes a final lunge toward Hill and grabs one of her arms and pulls. Brad appears at the top of the hatch and quickly reaches down to help Cooper pull Hill up against the strength of the squid's tentacle wrapped around her re-breather.

One of the sailor's with a rifle turns his weapon on the submerged beast holding Hill but the animal continues to hold fast. Another tentacle springs up from behind the rescue boat and wraps around another of the sailors. He lets up a scream as the tentacle crushes his rib cage then yanks his lifeless body into the sea.

As Cooper holds Hill's arm tightly Brad manages to loosen one of her re-breather's shoulder straps and the tank is quickly torn off of her back ripping her right arm backwards in an unnatural position.

"You alright?" he shouts to her as he and Cooper pull on top of the Stingray.

"I think my shoulder is dislocated. I can't move it," Hill says as her right arm dangles loosely by her side.

"You'll be alright," Brad comments as he waves at the speed boat, "We're going to lower you down to rescue boat."

He then motions to the remaining sailor to try and maneuver closer to their position as they do he and Cooper swing Hill over to the boat. She is caught and lowered safely on the boat by Forrester and the sailor.

Cooper, sitting next to Brad on top of the Nautilus yells to Brad, "We need to get out of here now! The trawler's coming around."

Brad turns to see the ship streaming towards them. He turns back to Cooper, "Hurry, jump down--I'm right behind you."

Cooper leaps into the rocking boat below.

Onboard the Captain's Hook Troy, stationed on the bridge, speaks to Bloomberg over the radio. "Get everybody off that sub. Do you hear me! We need everyone off so we can use the net!"

"We're out!" replies Bloomberg as he leaves the controls and heads up the hatch.

Troy turns toward the commander of the Captain's Hook, "Full speed ahead Captain, drop the net and charge the capacitors!"

"Yes sir!" the captain responds.

The sea around the subs is now too turbulent for the speed boat, after securing Hill, they quickly and carefully maneuver their craft away from the disturbance, all while fighting off attacking tentacles, leaving Brad and Bloomberg on top of the Stingray.

"I'll unhook the cable. We can move away on top of the Nautilus," shouts Brad as he holds on to the cable. He looks up at Bloomberg, "Go ahead climb over I got it!"

Cliff climbs up on top the Nautilus and yells to the two men, "Come on get over here quick!"

By this time even more squid are climbing onto the Stingray as well as the Nautilus, sent into a frenzy by the bloodied water and the commotion around the subs. Bloomberg struggles to make his way across the distance between the two subs holding onto the shaky cable attached to the hulls. Brad holds onto the cable as Bloomberg reaches the Nautilus. As Bloomberg steadies his footing on the Nautilus' hull a gigantic squid rises up out of the water and strikes the Stingray with two of its tentacles. The two subs buck and rock wildly to one side then the other sending Brad's body flying up into the air. Only his grip on the cable prevents him from flying off the sub and into the water. He drops hard headfirst with a sickening thud on top of the Stingray's metal skin. Dazed, Brad slides off the hull of the Stingray and into the water below. With Bloomberg secured on top of the Nautilus Cliff jumps on the cable and climbs over to the Stingray as it violently sways from side to side. Bloomberg watches him for a moment then finally slides down into the hatch of the Nautilus.

Cliff holds onto the hatch of the Stingray as he searches the bubbling water for a sign of his friend.

"Brad! Brad! Brad!" he yells.

Finally Brad surfaces, blood pouring down his face from a large gash over his right eye and begins weakly treading water near the front of the Stingray. Cliff spots him and yells, "Give me your hand! Brad, give me your hand!"

Cliff maneuvers himself to get a better angle to reach his friend but Brad is moving slowly. As the squid around him continue to lash about uncontrollably he reaches up from the water and strains to grab Cliff's hand. From behind him one of the smaller squids grabs his left arm and attempts to pull him under.

"*Ahhh!* My arm," he screams as the teeth around each of the suckers dig deep into his flesh. He fights vigorously, kicking and slapping at the beast with all his might all the while trying to claw his way to his friend's outstretched hand.

Cliff with tears in his eyes cries out to his friend, "Brad, Jesus, Brad, grab my hand."

Cliff with one hand still on the open hatch, strains to stretch out his other toward Brad. The two men stretch and strain to reach each other. Finally Cliff grabs Brad's hand and fights to pull him up onto the Stingray. The squid's tentacles around Brad's other arm tighten and rip deeper into his flesh.

"It's ripping me apart!" he yells. Let me go Cliff! Save yourself," cries Brad while he hangs like a rag doll being torn by Cliff holding one arm and the monster squid gripping the other in a grotesque game of tug of war.

"Never!" shouts Cliff as he pulls and pulls. Finally the squid releases Brad's arm tearing off a small chucks of flesh in the process. With a final pull Cliff gets his friend onto the hull of the Stingray. The two men sit up on top of the craft trying to catch their breath. Cliff looks at Brad, "You okay buddy?"

"Yeah, thanks," replies Brad breathing heavily and wincing from the gash in his head.

"You had me scared there for a sec, partner. You know what Pat would do to me if I let something happen to you?"

Brad gives a painful grin.

Cliff leans over towards him and says, "Come on, let's get you outta here."

He reaches over to help Brad up when suddenly a huge tentacle whips across him and wraps around his neck. The toothed suckers rip into his flesh. Cliff pulls at the squid's arm as blood begins to gush down his neck. Brad seeing his friend in danger yells out, "Cliff!" he jumps up and pulls at the squid's tentacle but his own injuries have left him too weak to dislodge the creature. Another tentacle lashes out and coils around Cliff's face. His legs begin kicking wildly as the creature lifts him up into the air. Cliff's muffled cries can be heard under the flesh of the monster's arms. The animal shakes him violently in the air then squeezes even tighter resulting in a nauseating cracking sound as his skull crushes under the squid's force. Cliff's arms and legs suddenly drop limp and dangle as the tentacles yank the lifeless body into the sea. Brad can only look overboard in horror as his friend's body disappears beneath the waves. By this time, the second rescue boat has made its way back over to the side of the Stingray.

Cooper motions for Brad to jump down into the boat.

"Cliff! Cliff! Cliff!" Brad continues to shout.

"He's gone!" Cooper yells as he ducks a tentacle whipping over his head.

"Cliff!" shouts Brad again.

"Brad We have to get out of here!"

"Oh my God no! No! No!"

"I'm sorry there's nothing we could do. We have to go!" Cooper shouts to the sobbing man.

Brad finally steadies himself and jumps down into the waiting craft.

The speed boat turns and jets toward the Captain's Hook. Bloomberg climbs up the hatch of the Nautilus and unlatches the cable. Dr. Hinds throttles the sub out of the way of the oncoming trawler. The Stingray bobbles on the surface still blaring the mating call and flashing its strobes just as the Captain's Hook sails around the spot. Troy signals his assistants to circle the sub and close the net. Then they fire up the generators. He waits a few minutes then throws the switch. The ocean behind the ship steams and boils as a foul stench of boiled squid hovers over the area. Slowly dead squid begin to float to the surface in the wake of the trawler to the cheers of the crew.

Meanwhile the Nautilus slowly makes its way back to the Poseidon's Son. It's lifted into the cargo bay and its crew is disembarked as are the members from the rescue boat. They all quietly gather on deck to watch the cooking squid in the net of the trawler across from them, all except Brad who remains in the ship's infirmary getting treated for deep cuts on his left arm, facial lacerations and a concussion. After dressing Brad's wounds the ship's doctor leaves him resting on a bed with his head heavily bandaged. Once alone, tears begin to pour down Brad's face. He can't believe he has just lost his best friend, a friend who risked his own life to rescue him. How can he go home without him? How is he going to explain this to Cliff's wife? What has he gotten himself into? He closes his eyes turns on his side and quietly begins to sob.

Repentance

Brad takes a deep breath and exhales the warm desert air as he sits outside the living quarters of EPA One. He leans back on a lawn chair with his arms crossed and stares blankly at the orange-brown sunset descending behind the distant mountains.

"Hey Brad!" calls Hill from behind him as she exits the building with Daily.

Brad, lost in thought, continues to stare across the darkening desert. Hill with her arm in a sling and Daily, walking closely next to her, approach him slowly as he sits motionless on the edge of the base.

"Brad, you alright?" she asks. But Brad still doesn't respond. Hill gives Daily a look of concern as the two walk up to him. Hill comes up along Brad's left while Daily approaches from the right.

"Hey Brad. You okay?" Hill asks softly while gently touching his shoulder.

Brad sits up with a startled look. He glances at Hill then at Daily then back to Hill, "Wh-what was that?"

He seems to take a moment to get his bearings then relaxes and leans back in the chair, "I'm sorry I-I kinda spaced out for a minute," he stammers as he sits up and adjusts the bandage wrapped around his forehead.

"How're you feeling?" asks Hill in a calm concerned voice. Brad hasn't been the same since the horrible death of his friend and partner Cliff. Hill can't imagine how he feels, or imagine what it would be like to lose Daily.

"I'm alright." Brad replies.

"Really? How's your head?" adds Hill.

Brad rubs his bandaged forehead, "I've been worse," he looks up at Hill, "How's your arm?"

Hill gingerly lifts her bandaged arm, "I've been worse," she says with a smile.

Brad gives Hill a brief grin as Daily touches him on his shoulder. Brad turns and looks up at Daily, "Brad, I never got the chance to tell you how much I'm sorry about what happened to Cliff."

"The same goes for me," adds Hill as she kneels beside him, "If you need anything, anything at all just let us know."

Brad flashes another brief smile, "Thanks guys, but I'll be alright. I just have to work some things out that's all."

"We understand," comments Hill.

"So, what are your plans?" asks Daily.

Brad leans back and stares back out at the sunset, "Don't know yet. The Professor's allowing me to go home. But I'm not sure what I'm going to do just yet," he sighs deeply, "I just can't believe what happened. I can't believe Cliff is gone, I just can't believe it," he looks up at Daily with tearing eyes, "you know what I mean?"

Daily clears his throat and pats Brad on the shoulder, "Yeah buddy, I know."

Brad shakes his head slowly then stares back out at the desert. Daily and Hill remain quietly at his side for a few minutes then Hill stands up and says, "Listen Brad, we're heading inside. The professor's back and we want to hear what he has to say. Want to join us?"

"Nah, I think I'll hangout here for a little while longer."

"Okay but like Clarence said if you need anything you know how to get in touch with us, okay?" She leans over and gently kisses him on the cheek.

Brad looks up at her and smiles, "I will. Thanks."

The two FBI agents leave Brad to his thoughts and head toward the EPA One hangar. As they cross the tarmac Hill turns to Daily, "Clarence I'm worried about him."

Daily after taking a quick look back at Brad comments, "You're not the only one. It's bad enough that he lost his best friend and his partner but…the way he died," Daily pauses and shakes his head for a second, "There isn't even a body to bury. Damn!"

"Clarence, that could have been any of us. It could've been me, it could've been you," she glances up at Daily, "I don't know what I would've done if that were you."

The two stop just outside of the entrance to the hangar. Daily holds Hill by her shoulders, "Don't think about it. It'll just make you crazy and we can't afford to lose it now, Deb. I have a bad feeling about all of this. It seems things are getting worse and I'm not sure we can do anything about it."

Hill gives him a worried look, "Why do you say that?"

"I don't know. It's just a feeling. All I do know is that you and I have to stay sharp both physically and mentally. We can't afford to let our emotions get in the way of our judgment."

"I know you're right, but…"

"But nothing, Deb! We have to be on point or--" he pauses and looks back at Brad, "one of us could end up like that," he looks back at Hill who is also looking at Brad.

Hill turns back to Daily, "I know what you mean," they turn to the hangar entrance, "You know what's really crazy?"

"What's that?"

"We've faced armed kidnappers, bank robbers and even terrorist and none of that frightened me. But this! Clarence this is the first time that I'm scared. I mean I'm really scared," says Hill as she stops at the entrance.

"You're scared?" says Daily excitedly, "I'd take a dozen heavily-armed terrorist over those squid any day!"

Hill looks up at him and giggles, "I never thought anything could scare you."

Daily grins, "Well, now you know. Come on, I think we better get inside," the two turn and enter the hangar.

Dr. Hinds is addressing the team members inside the conference room at the rear of the hangar as Daily and Hill enter.

"—And there's still one thing that we haven't been able to isolate yet," she says as she stands in front of a large monitor displaying the image of a dead squid.

"What's that?" asks Forrester as he adjusts his seat to make room for Hill and Daily.

Hinds picks up a remote control off of the table and presses a button. The image on the monitor changes to a collage of photos of some of the mutant animals they have encountered, "We know that SF-20 was designed as some sort of food additive to induce rapid growth, right?"

The group collectively nods their heads.

"What puzzles me is how has it been able to mutate an organism's DNA? These animals we've encountered are not just larger than normal. We're finding signs that they're becoming more intelligent. We've captured some of the ants," she presses a button on the remote and the image on the monitor changes to that of ten caged ants running through a maze, "and studied them closely," she looks up at the screen closely, "What we found was that they exhibited the beginnings of rudimentary problem-solving abilities," some of the team members mumble amongst themselves and exchange glances, "so in order to stop these outbreaks we first must learn more about SF-20."

"That's going to be difficult!" says a voice loudly from behind the group. They all spin around to see Professor Hamilton enter the conference room with a large bundle of files under his arm. He sets the files down at one end of the table then approaches Dr. Hinds, "For years they have been stonewalling us," he looks around at the team members sitting around the table, "giving us the run around," he stops next to Hinds and faces the group, "they've used their political connections to get around subpoenas. They've exploited loopholes to dodge regulations," Dr. Hinds takes a seat as Hamilton continues to speak to the group, "and now they send us on a wild goose chase."

"What do you mean Richard," asks Bloomberg.

Hamilton walks over to where Bloomberg is sitting, "While I was in New York I met with a few Gen X officials who assured me that they were working around the clock to solve this problem. They even volunteered that pile of documents over there," he points to the stack of files he'd just placed at the other end of the table. All of the members turn to glance at the pile of files, "don't get too excited," he continues, "I've already gone through most of them." He pauses as the team members refocus on him, "they're completely worthless. None of the information is of any use whatsoever," Hamilton snarls, "and they knew it!" he pulls out an empty chair from the table and angrily takes a seat," Hamilton slowly looks around the room at his team, "I believe they are deliberately trying to throw us off track," Hamilton sits up in his seat and leans toward his group, "I want to change our focus. We're getting nowhere sitting around waiting for a new incident to pop up. It's time to take the fight to the source," he pauses for a moment, "Gen X Tech!" exclaims Hamilton as he slams his fist down onto the table, "They're our new target! We've collected more than enough data and samples. Now it's time to double our efforts at finding out exactly what they did and come up with a solution to stop it."

"Richard," interrupts Hinds, "What did you find out about the SF-20 outbreaks overseas?"

Hamilton sits up in his chair and removes his glasses. He pulls a handkerchief from his breast pocket and begins cleaning the lenses as he speaks, "That was a very disturbing meeting," he puts his glasses back on.

"First of all the outbreaks in Europe, Asia and Africa have been occurring a lot more frequently than we originally thought. Soon it'll be difficult to keep them out of the media and they're no closer to a solution than we are," he nods his head slowly then leans back in his chair, "it just doesn't look good over there. Not good at all."

Hinds glances at Bloomberg as Daily and Hill exchange a similar foreboding look.

Cooper sits up in his seat, "So what do we do now, Professor?"

Hamilton clears his throat, "First I want Troy along with Agents Daily and Hill to head to our records room," he looks over at Troy. "Go over everything."

"We've done that already!" states Troy annoyingly.

"Go over it again!" Hamilton snaps causing Troy to raise his eyebrows, "Dig through all of the information we've complied on Gen X Tech. Look for any anomalies no matter how small. Look for anything out of place," he looks at all of the team members, "Listen, people, we've been fighting a losing battle. We need a break! Don't overlook anything."

"Alright, if that's what you want. We're on it, Pop!" says Troy. Hamilton snaps his head around and shoots Troy a look of annoyance. Troy cringes then says sheepishly, "I mean, Professor."

Troy heads toward the hangar's entrance with Hill and Daily following closely behind.

Hamilton moves his attention back to the group, "The rest of you head over to the lab. Pull out every sample we've ever taken and retest them. We could've missed something. Leave no stone unturned."

"We'll begin immediately," states Bloomberg as he rises from his seat and heads for the exit. Hinds, Forrester and Cooper stand up and follow. As Forrester passes Hamilton, he looks down and asks, "Hey Professor, you want to join us? We could use your expertise."

Hamilton slowly looks up at Forrester with weary eyes, "Sure, son. I'll be there shortly."

Forrester nods then continues on toward the lab leaving Hamilton alone in the conference room.

Early the next morning a black military sedan pulls up in front of Jaclyn Taylor's two-story townhouse. The marine behind the wheel steps out and opens the rear door to the vehicle. Brad steps out carrying a small bag and stares at his mother-in-law's house for a moment with sweat beading on his forehead from the anxiety of what he is about to face. After dismissing his driver he walks slowly up the path leading to the front door. Just as he is about to ring the door bell the door swings open. There in the entrance is his wife Patricia grinning from ear to ear. She's a dark-skinned slender woman with straight black hair pulled back in a ponytail. Her expression is bright and cheerful with her big brown eyes and long, curved eyelashes. As she smiles at him, her cheeks form dimples and her little nose seems to shine.

Pat launches herself into his arms smothering him in kisses all around his face and neck.

As she squeezes him Brad winces in pain, "Ahh, easy baby, easy."

Pat looks up at his bandaged head and strokes it gently, "Oh, I'm sorry, honey. Are you okay? Where else are you hurt?"

Brad raises his left arm up slowly, "Just this," he comments.

Pat holds her hand over her mouth, "Oh my God, what did they do to my baby?" she begins to sob.

Brad drops his bag on the ground and pulls her closer to him, "It's alright, baby. It's alright. I'm here now."

The two embrace one another as they exchange a long passionate kiss. Jaclyn, Pat's mother quietly appears in the doorway behind her daughter, smiling. After a few moments she says, "You two finished giving the neighborhood a free show?"

The two stop kissing but continue to hold each other as they begin to giggle like little kids.

Brad looks over at his mother-in-law and says, "Hey, Jackie. Thanks for looking after Pat for me."

"Brad now you know how I feel about you guys," she says warmly. "Now come on you two, get in here," she says as she gently pushes the couple inside and closes the door.

"The base called and said that you were on your way," explains Pat as they walk into the living room holding hands like a pair of teenage lovers, "I just couldn't wait for you to show up." They sit down together on the sofa as Jaclyn sits across from them in a large lounge chair.

Jaclyn cuts in, "I'm so glad you're finally here. The poor child kept running to the window every time a car drove by. She was making me crazy."

Brad smiles and turns to Pat, "So you really missed me huh?"

"Baby, I'm just glad you're alright," says Pat as she gently strokes the bandage on his head.

"Yeah I'm okay. I just. I mean I'm worried about," he pauses for a brief moment, "Where's Doris? How is she doing?"

Pat looks down and the room grows silent for a moment as Jaclyn quietly gets up and leaves the room. Then Pat looks up at him and says, "The military was here two nights ago with a man named Hamilton. He told us that what happened to Cliff was a matter of national security so he couldn't give us any details. All he told us was that Cliff died serving his country," she reaches over and strokes his bandaged head again, "Brad what happened out there? What's going on? They told us we couldn't even see his body."

"How did she take it?" Brad asks softly.

"Not well. Not well at all," says Pat while nodding her head, "her brother and his wife had to come by and took her home. I tried to call her a couple of times but they said she got so hysterical that they had to call a doctor and have her sedated."

Brad shakes his head and frowns, "I need to talk to her. I need to see how she's doing. Cliff would want that."

"Listen you both have been through a lot. You just got home. Why don't you go over there in the morning? Give her some time. Besides there's other things we need to talk about," Pat leans back on the sofa and rubs her stomach, "Did you forget?"

Brad stares at her for a moment then places his hand over hers and continues to rub her stomach, "No baby, I didn't forget. We're having a baby," he leans over and kisses her on the lips, "I guess you're right. Alright, I'll wait till the morning," he whispers.

Just then Jaclyn comes back into the room with an apron wrapped around her waist, "Alright, love birds I have some freshly baked peach cobbler and vanilla ice cream in the kitchen. I seem to recall someone having a sweet tooth for my cobbler," she chuckles.

Brad smiles at her then takes his wife's hand, "Come on, you know I can't resist her cobbler."

"Welcome home baby," Pat responds as the three move into the kitchen and sit around the table in front of a large hot pan of peach cobbler and a container of vanilla ice cream.

Meanwhile Troy, Hill and Daily are in the records room poring over documents relating to Gen X Tech dealings and SF-20 incidents.

"This is frustrating," exclaims Hill.

"What's the matter?" asks Daily as Troy looks up from his pile of folders.

"These records don't help us at all. Most of them are observation notes about the effects of SF-20 the rest are internal memos and reports. There's nothing about how it was developed and very little research data, that's it."

"Yeah, I've noticed the same thing over here," adds Daily, "looks like the Professor was right. They're hiding something."

"I remember when we first complained about the lack of detail in a lot of the documents they submitted," says Troy, "they pulled out every trick in the book to stop us from obtaining more information. We were even accused of violating the Uniform Trade Secrets Act and had a couple of senators come after us."

"You're kidding?" says Hill.

"Yeah they can really play hardball when they want to. But after reading through these reports again I'm starting to notice one thing that strikes me as strange," adds Troy.

"What's that?" asks Daily.

Troy continues, "Over the past five years they have been diverting huge sums of money and resources to some project named New Eden."

"Why is that strange?" asks Daily.

"It's the amount of money, manpower and funds that they are throwing at this project that I found unusual. They've been spending over two billion dollars a year, which comes to over ten billion dollars for one project," he opens one of the folders in front of him and thumbs through the pages till he comes to the one he is looking for, "here look at this," Troy opens the folder so that both Hill and Daily could see it, "they even shut down some of their most promising programs to focus on this New Eden Project."

The three slowly thumb through the folder staring at the data in amazement. Then Daily notices something, "Look they shut down research on Allevicon, their new HIV vaccine. I remember reading about that in Time magazine a few months ago. They were on the verge of a real breakthrough with that vaccine. Hell, if it's only half as good as they reported it can make them hundreds of billions of dollars."

"And they cancelled it?" says Hill as she sits back in her chair to think.

"What is this, New Eden?" Daily asks Troy.

"There's no real information on what it is. It just mentions it by name and lists costs associated with it. But I'm going to check their corporate database for more information," he slides over to his computer and starts typing.

"You have access to Gen X Tech's mainframe?" exclaims Hill, "How did you manage that?"

Troy gives her a devilish look and grins, "I just developed a new decryption algorithm that I've been dying to try out. It's not fully tested but it should work. What better way to test it than here?"

"Okay," she says, "Go ahead do your thing."

When Troy logs onto the Gen X Tech's website a large window appears asking for a user name and password, "This is where I work my magic. If this new program works we should have no problem getting in," he punches a few more keys then a red window appears over the Gen X Tech login screen. A message appears in the window.

`"Decoding Please Stand By…"`

"This may take a while so I'll just let it run," states Troy as he sits back and watches the monitor.

"Where is Gen X Tech's headquarters?" asks Hill as she paces back and forth behind Troy.

Troy looks over at her, "New York. They have an office building in Manhattan but their main headquarters are on some private island in East Hampton. "

Hill stops next to Troy crosses her arms and says, "I think it's time we paid them a visit." She pauses for a second then glances at Troy then Daily. "I mean the Professor did say bring the fight to them didn't he?"

Beep, Beep, Beep, Beep. The computer screen begins to flash red and white.

"I'm in!" shouts Troy as he sits up and begins typing.

"Wow, that was fast. You're good," says Hill.

"Remind me to keep him away from my iPhone," jokes Daily. All three chuckle as they lean over Troy to look at the computer screen. Troy is typing away as he goes deeper and deeper into the archives of the biotechnology company.

"Here we go: New Eden. Estimated cost 15.5 billion dollars and wait a minute, what the fuck is this?"

"What?" inquires Daily.

"Look here," says Troy as he points to the screen, "they claim it's a research facility in Antarctica? New Eden is being developed at the South Pole."

"Don't many companies go down there to do research?" asks Hill.

"Sure, they do research on global warming, climate change, paleontology, geological studies even ocean current studies. But this is Gen X Tech a biotech company. Why do they need a huge R & D lab in the South Pole? What could they possibly be studying down there?"

Each of the team members look at each other for an answer.

"And another thing," Troy continues as he reads the information off of the computer screen, "they started this project around the same time as the reports of SF-20 incidents began to peak and around the time we were pressuring them about its development."

"This New Eden looks very suspicious. See if you could find a more direct connection between it and SF-20," adds Hill as she stands over Troy's shoulder.

"Yeah, see what else you could dig up. We may have something," agrees Daily.

"Alright then here I go," says Troy as he begins typing at the computer again. Suddenly the screen goes blank, "What the fuck?"

Daily looks over his shoulder, "What happened?"

"My connection was cut!"

"How did that happen?" asks Daily.

"I don't know!"

Suddenly a gray window pops up on the screen containing a scrolling list of files.

Troy sits up and stares at the monitor, "Oh no you don't!"

"What's going on?" inquires Hill as Troy types frantically on the keyboard.

"A back trace."

"A what?" asks Hill.

"A back trace! Damn it! They detected my connection, shut it down and now they're using some sort of trace program to scan my system. Damn their security is good," he continues to type like a man possessed, "but I'm better," he triumphantly hits the enter key and the gray window disappears. Troy leans back and sighs with relief.

Daily pats him on the back, "I guess whatever they're hiding they don't won't anyone seeing it, good job Troy."

"Well so much for accessing their computer. At least we have something to look for. But we still have about ten boxes of files to go through so we might as well get a move on it," says Hill as she tosses one file to Daily and another one to Troy.

Daily takes out his cell phone, "This is definitely an all-nighter. Anybody want pizza?"

"Pepperoni for me," says Troy.

"Ditto," adds Hill.

"One large pie with pepperoni coming up," says Daily as he makes the call.

The three stay up most of the night poring over the files and taking notes about Gen X Tech and SF-20.

Meanwhile across town at Brad's mother-in-law's home Brad tosses and turns through out the night. Although he was happy to cuddle up with his wife the nightmares of his friend's death continue to haunt him.

"Bradley! Bradley!" Brad wakes up to a voice calling his name. He rolls over to see Pat still asleep by his side. He looks up and is startled to see a dark figure standing over him. Brad reaches for the light on his night stand and turns it on.

There in his bedroom standing over him is a beautiful woman with long jet black hair dressed in a night gown.

"Doris, Doris what are you doing here?"

"Why did you leave Cliff? He trusted you; you were supposed to be his friend. How could you leave him behind?"

"Doris no it's not like that. You don't understand," he sits up and continues to plead with her, "I'm sorry there was nothing I could do. Everything happened so fast."

"What am I going to do now, Brad? What am I going to do without Cliff? It's your fault; it's all your fault! He would never have gone if it weren't for you. Now I have nothing. You should have died, not Cliff. It should have been you!" Doris shouts.

Again he pleads, "Doris please believe me, if I could have saved Cliff I would have."

"Liar," she snarls, "you should have died. I hate you. I hate you," she shouts, "I wish you were dead."

All of a sudden Doris holds up a large butcher knife that Brad hadn't noticed before. She holds it over her head, "I hate you for living. Die!" before Brad can react she strikes down at him stabbing him deep into his chest. He falls back onto the bed with blood spraying from the wound, "Die! I want you to die!" she stabs him again over and over.

Brad looks up at her choking on his own blood. He reaches up toward her and tries to talk, "Doris no. I'm sorry," she stops, stares at him for a short moment. Brad repeats himself, "I'm so sorry. Please forgive me," she slowly raises the knife over her head and strikes down into him hard a final time.

Brad sits up quickly in his bed. Warm sweat is pouring down his face. He looks down as he rubs his hands over chest and finds only a sweat dampened t-shirt but no wounds. Brad turns and looks at Pat sleeping peacefully beside him. Still shaking from the nightmare he swings his legs over the edge of the bed and with his head in his hands quietly sobs.

It's 6:30 am, when Brad leaves the guest room and proceeds quietly downstairs. Dressed in only a t-shirt and shorts he sits on the front porch of the house with a cup of coffee. He sits there enjoying the cool morning air thinking about what he's going to say to Doris, trying his best to shake the effects of the horrible nightmare still fresh in his head. How would he comfort her? How can he make her feel that Cliff's death was not in vain? After about a half an hour he hears a voice call to him from inside the house.

"Bradley! Baby where you are?" calls Pat from the living room, "Brad you out there?"

She heads to the porch and sits down next to her husband, "Hey baby, whatcha doing out here?"

"Just thinking."

"About what?"

"Cliff."

She wraps her arm around his shoulders, "I know, baby. I know how hard it must be."

Brad slowly shakes his head, "No honey, you don't. You have no idea, Pat. Cliff died because of me."

"What do you mean?" she says with a startled look on her face.

"He was trying to save me. He put his life in danger to save mine. I'm the reason Cliff is dead."

"Oh my God! I didn't know. Now I understand what you're going through. My God Brad what do we tell Doris?"

"I don't know but I have to talk to her. I'm going over there today."

"I'll go with you baby."

"Thanks honey, but no. I need to do this myself," he stands up and kisses her on the forehead then leads her back into the house and into the kitchen.

"Well at least let me make you a nice home-cooked breakfast. It's been a while since you've had one of those," Pat begins taking out some pots and pans from the kitchen cabinet, "How about some fresh made-from-scratch banana pancakes?"

Brad sits at the kitchen table and smiles at Pat, "I love you baby, but maybe some other time. I'm not very hungry," he goes back to slowly sipping his coffee and seems to drift off into thought.

Pat walks over, kisses him on the cheek and whispers, "Don't worry baby, everything will work out. I have faith in you."

He smiles at her then kisses her on the lips, "Thank you, sweetie; I don't know what I would do without you."

The two again exchange smiles. Brad kisses her gently on the forehead then leaves the kitchen and heads back upstairs to the bedroom.

Twelve o'clock noon back at EPA One's laboratory and Professor Hamilton has just entered the lab to check the team's progress. In the lab early is Hinds and Forrester. Hamilton approaches Dr. Hinds who is studying some samples of a squid under a microscope.

"Find anything useful, Karen?"

Without looking up from the microscope she replies, "Oh, I found some things alright, but I don't know how useful they are," she looks up from the microscope and spins around on her stool to face Hamilton, "I don't know what those bastards over at Gen X were doing but it wasn't making a growth formula or a food additive that's for sure."

"Really?"

"Richard the level of genetic mutation in these samples is off the chart. They're still mutating. Based on all the data that we've recovered since this operation began I can safely say that whatever they did has caused some sort of genetic chain reaction. Take these squid for instance. They didn't just get bigger--they've evolved."

"Yes like the fire ants and the rats," adds Hamilton as he circles around to take a look at the sample under the microscope.

"Did you hear what I said? They're still evolving. Several of the squid that we've studied were at different levels of evolutional development. This is not over. It's only the beginning and I still don't know where to look for a solution."

Hamilton looking up from the microscope shakes his head, "Well, Troy and our FBI friends also found something. They dug up some inconsistencies in the Gen X records. So Hill and Daily are planning a visit to their corporate headquarters in New York. Maybe we'll get some answers then," he looks around the lab, "Have you finished going over all the samples?"

"No, I still have a lot more, want to help?"

"That's what I'm here for," he takes off his business jacket and puts on a white lab coat, then sits down next Hinds and begins examining the tissue samples under a microscope.

1:00 pm and Pat is waiting in her car outside of her mother's house with the engine running. She's waiting for Brad who's going a few blocks away to Cliff's home. Because of his head injury he agrees to let Pat drive even though the house is within walking distance. When he emerges from the house he's clean shaven and smelling of cologne, wearing a blue polo shirt and a pair of designer jeans. He now sports a smaller bandage over the wound on his head and a fresh one on his arm as he walks slowly over to the car. After the short drive over to the Johnson's residence, on West Monroe Street, Pat pulls up in front of the brown brick ranch style house and turns the engine off. Brad sits there in the passenger seat just staring at the house. He feels every muscle in his body begin to tense up. His heart starts to pound, sweat forms on his forehead, and he can't move a muscle.

Pat looks over at Brad, "You okay, Baby?" Brad doesn't respond. He just sits there motionless, "Brad honey? Baby you okay? You want me to go in with you?" He still remains frozen and does not respond. He just sits there staring at the house.

"Bradley, baby talk to me! What is it? If it's too much, I'll take you home," she shouts. Still no response. Pat takes out her keys and starts the car.

Just then Brad turns to her and grabs her arm as she turns the key in the ignition, "No, No, I'm okay. I'm okay. I'm going in now."

"You sure? You want me to go in with you?"

"I'll be alright. Just wait here," says Brad as he looks into Pat's worried eyes, "I'll be fine. I'm okay."

He leans over and kisses her on the lips then exits the car and slowly walks to the front door. Brad pauses for a moment and turns back to look at Pat sitting in the car. After seeing her reassuring smile he rings the doorbell.

After a few moments the door opens and in front of him stands a startled petite woman with short brown hair in her early forties wearing a yellow sun dress and apron. It's Doris' sister-in-law Amy Bradford.

"Brad! Oh my God, Brad. How are you? Come in, please come in," she stammers as she hurries him into the house.

As she shuts the door she calls out, "Doris! Doris!" as she leads him into the living room, "She's in the backyard with the dogs. Doris, you have a visitor!" she shouts again then turns back to Brad, "Brad, here, sit down--I'll go get her," she nervously runs off and leaves Brad standing in the living room.

As he waits Brad walks slowly around the room. He has been in this room hundreds of times but never really took the time to examine its contents. On one wall are three shelves of photos that Brad had never paid much attention to before. He walks over and carefully inspects each one of the pictures. He stops at one photo and picks it up. It's a picture of Cliff and himself on a fishing trip they went on the year before. The two friends are standing together smiling while holding a large fish between them. He begins to reminisce about the fun he and Cliff had during the trip. His mind drifts as he remembers the fish they caught, the jokes they made and the camaraderie they experienced.

Then a voice from behind him snaps Brad back into reality.

"You know he never stopped talking about that trip."

Brad still holding the photo spins around.

It's Doris; she's standing behind him wearing a denim skirt and a white blouse. She's an attractive woman standing about five seven with a shapely figure. She's thirty years old and has long jet black hair that hangs down her back all the way to her waist. She isn't wearing any makeup and her eyes look tired and glazed.

"This was best trip we ever went on. Everything was just perfect. The weather, the fish were biting," replies Brad.

Doris walks over and looks at the photo in his hand.

"I remember he came home with so much fish I told him I wasn't cleaning and cooking all of that. He just laughed," she pauses a second as if to reflect on her memories, "we ended up giving most of it away. But he was happy. He was so happy," she looks up at Brad with saddened eyes, "you made him happy. I was glad he had a friend like you," she gently takes the photo from Brad and looks down at it, "I always worried about Cliff; he could be so impulsive at times. And with the type of job the two of you had it eased my nerves to know that you had his back."

Hearing her last words turns Brad's face sour. He takes the photo from her and puts it back on the shelf then takes Doris' hand and leads her to the sofa.

As they sit down Brad rubs her hands, "Doris, I'm sorry. I'm so sorry."

Doris strokes the bandage on his forehead and gives him a brief smile as she shakes her head, "Brad, it's not your fault. It was a shock at first, but I'm a cop's wife. These things come with the territory. You wish and you pray that it doesn't happen to you. But the possibility of losing your husband is always in the back of your mind. Every time he would put on that uniform and left the house I would feel deep down that it could be the last time I would see him alive. You try your best to hide it but you're never really secure until he walks back through that door. Pat feels the same way I do we've talked about it often. We're proud of you and respect the work that you guys do but at the same time we're scared."

Brad sighs deeply then says, "But Doris this time it was different. This assignment with the government is more dangerous than anything we've ever had to deal with."

"I have to believe that if the two of you were selected to work with the government then it must be something very important."

Brad's head drops and his voice lowers, "Yeah, it's important but also dangerous. I wish I could tell you more."

"I understand. But Brad, tell me something?"

"Yes," he says as he looks up at her.

"Is this assignment necessary? Will it save lives?"

"Yes, yes it will!"

Doris sits back, "Then Cliff's death was not in vain," she pauses then looks up at the ceiling, "I admit that at first I went to pieces. I couldn't believe this was actually happening to me. I didn't want to believe it. Then I remembered how the two of you wouldn't give up on the Hernandez case. Even when the department put it in the cold case file you two continued to investigate on your spare time. I remember asking Cliff about it and he told me that someone had to care. He said those could have been our kids. He told me how you felt the same way and that the two of you promised the parents that you would solve the case no matter how long it took."

Brad nods his head in agreement, "That case really shook us up. I'll never forget the horrible look on the parents' faces, both of their young children gone without a trace. I wouldn't wish that on anyone."

"So you see Brad I'm not just learning to deal with the fact that my husband is gone but that he died for a good cause," she says with a big smile.

Brad still with a saddened look on his face looks over at her, "Doris about how he died. I have to tell you something."

"No Brad, you don't have to."

"Doris, you don't understand!"

"Brad it's okay."

"I have to explain!"

"Brad you don't have to!"

"He died because of me!" Brad shouts, "I'm responsible Doris. I'm responsible for Cliff's death," he exclaims.

Doris, startled looks at him with puzzled eyes, "What do you mean, you're responsible?"

He looks at her with tears in his eyes, "It's my fault, Doris. Cliff died saving me. He put himself in danger to save my life. I should have died out there, not him," tears begin to stream down his face, "please forgive me. I'm sorry Doris. I'm so sorry."

Doris stares at him with glassy eyes, "No, Brad. I can't blame you. The two of you were like brothers," she pulls him to her and lays his head on her shoulder.

"It was my fault I tell you. He came back for me. He didn't have to. He should have stayed but he came back for me," Brad shouts.

She sits him up and stares him straight in the eyes, "Stop it. Stop it, Brad. It's not your fault. Don't you see that's the same thing you would have done for him?"

He holds his head and sobs, "I can't go on. I can't do it anymore. I keep seeing his face just before it happened. I can't believe what happened. I can't believe he's gone."

Now Doris is crying as she holds him in her arms, "Brad, Brad. It's alright. I promise you it's alright. Listen, you have to get back in there. Make a difference. You have to make a difference for your new baby, for all of us. Cliff would want that. Don't let his death be in vain. Please do it for Cliff."

Brad now slowly beginning to regain his composure, "Doris I'm not sure if I could. I keep wondering if there was anything I could have done to help him. And the way he died, it was horrible. You have no idea."

The second the words were out of Brad's mouth, he regretted them but it was too late. He watched a terrible mixture of sadness, shock and loss upon Doris' fallen face. But to her credit, she recovered with a hard swallow and continued.

"Brad, I can only imagine what you must be going through. I'm just letting you know that I understand if you go back in."

Brad wipes the tears from his eyes and sits up, "Doris, I have to admit I've seen some unbelievable things and sometimes it scares the crap out of me. I don't know if I want to go back, especially with Pat being pregnant and all."

Doris adjusts herself on the sofa, "Brad, I know you can't talk much about what the two of you were working on but I do know it was some sort of threat against the government. I figured its some sort of anti-terrorist assignment. I just want to know…is the threat over?"

Brad gives her a very serious look, "Not by a long shot. I can tell you this. It's going to get worse and the lives of thousands of people are at risk."

Doris sits back, "It's that serious?"

"I'm afraid so," says Brads as he shakes his head.

"Then if anything that's a reason in itself to go back. It's your duty. You have to ask yourself something. What will happen if whatever is going on doesn't stop and will it affect the world your child will grow up in?" she gently strokes the bandage on his forehead as if she has just noticed it, "my God you've been through so much Brad. I know you're worried about me. I know you blame yourself. But I'm not mad at you. You and Patricia are like family to me. I know that if there was anything you could've done to save Cliff you would've. I'll be alright. I just want you to do what's right. Go ahead Brad. Make the world safe. Make it safe for all of us."

"Thanks, Doris."

"It's alright, Brad," she turns and slowly looks around the room with teary eyes, "It'll take some time to get used to not having him here, but I'll survive."

"If there's anything, anything at all I can do..."

"I know Brad, I know," says Doris as she holds his hand, "We're having a memorial service tomorrow. I know it might be a lot for you but I'd like you to be there."

"You couldn't keep me away if you wanted to."

"We're having it here, around six."

"I'll tell Pat. We'll be here."

"Thank you and thank Pat--for me she's been a doll."

"Actually she's waiting for me out front."

"Why didn't she come in?"

"She wanted to but I needed to talk to you on my own."

"I understand."

Brad takes a deep breath then stands up, "Well, I better get going."

Doris stands up along side him and gives him a hug. She then escorts him to the door. After opening the door Doris and Brad hug again.

"Remember, if there's anything you need please call us," says Brad.

"I will, Brad, I promise." Doris smiles bravely. "And don't you forget what I told you."

Brad smiles at her, "I won't."

During the drive home Brad feels much better. It's as if a huge weight had been lifted off of his shoulders. He now knows what he must do. It is very clear, clearer than it has ever been before. He'll call Professor Hamilton after the memorial service and give him the news.

The Colony

It's been two days since Cliff's memorial. Brad has taken this time to rest and deal with the loss of his friend. One thing that has helped him is spending time at home with his wife Patricia. He tries to take his mind off of Cliff's death and of the events he's witnessed while working with the INVASION team but investigating is in his blood. Brad frequently drifts off thinking about what's going on back at the base. He tells Professor Hamilton after Cliff's memorial that he would return, but that he needed sometime to be with his wife and to look after Doris. The Professor told him to take as much time as he needed.

Patricia and Brad both agreed that they needed to help Doris cope with the loss of her husband. They even decided to make her the godmother of their pending child.

Doris has her good days and her bad days but for the most part she's handling the loss of Cliff as well as can be expected. She often says, "As the wife of a cop I've tried to always be prepared because I knew that a day like this could come and now that it is here I have to try and remember that he died for a good cause. He gave his life to save others."

She now spends a lot of her time caring for her two dogs, Max and Nina. Max is a purebred seventy-pound, well-trained Boxer. He was Cliff's favorite; he had even taken the dog on several fishing trips he went on with Brad. Nina is a four-pound Chihuahua and is Doris' *"mini-me"* as the dog follows her around the house all day, eats off her plate and even sleeps next to her in bed. Now with Cliff gone, the two dogs have become Doris' sole companions helping to keep her spirits up. Doris' brother and sister-in-law come by to check up on her regularly but her dogs are always there. She says they help keep life in the house and Cliff's memory alive.

It's 10:00 pm Friday evening and the dry Arizonian heat has finally settled down to a near comfortable 93 degrees. Pat is spending the weekend with her mother while Brad relaxes at home watching the evening news. He leans back on the couch in his living room with his feet up on the coffee table and the remote in his hand. Brad has just finished off a bowl of his mother-in-law's peach cobbler and his eyes are starting to get heavy as he watches the television. All of the reports seem to sound the same after a while, the weather, local crime, budget problems in the city government, and more politics. He's about to turn the television off and go to bed when a series of local news reports catches his attention.

"This morning a young woman was reported missing from Clearview Hills. According to her parents, Amaris Watson age 22 was out jogging with her small dog Tiffany around six thirty this morning and never returned. Her car was found parked near the North 40th street entrance to Phoenix Mountains Park and her dog's leash and collar were found on a trail nearby. Police officials haven't said whether or not they have labeled the disappearance as suspicious but persons close to the case say that they are convinced that something terrible has happened to the young woman.

Also in the news several residences of Claremont Place have reported missing pets and livestock. They say this has been a problem for over a month and the police department isn't doing enough about it. Many residences believe that a rogue Cougar or Coyote is responsible. A group has begun forming armed hunting parties along the southern portion of Phoenix Mountains Park. The Chief of police has issued a warning that anyone caught armed in the park without the proper permits will be arrested.

In other related news a rancher reported finding his horse badly mutilated on his farm in Vista del Cerro. Milton Mosley said he went to check on his mare around eight o'clock this morning and found the animal half eaten in his barn. Mr. Mosley reported that the horse was fine the night before and that he heard no unusual noise during the night. He also reported that the body had a very foul acid like smell to it. Almost like strong vinegar."

Brad's eyebrows rise and his eyes open wide as he quickly sits up in shock. The reporter's words burn into his mind. He thinks to himself, *"The facts, what are the facts? There are missing people, missing pets, mutilated animals and a strong vinegar odor."* He switches off the television and heads for the kitchen and begins searching through all of the drawers for a map. After a few moments he finds one of the Phoenix area. Brad takes out a pencil from on of the drawers then spreads the map out over the kitchen table.

"Let's see the missing girl was from Clearview Hills," Brad circles the location on the map, *"the missing pets were from Claremont Place,"* he finds the spot then circles it, *"and the horse was found in Vista del Cerro,"* using the tip of the pencil Brad searches and searches. Then finally, *"Got it!"* he draws another circle. Brad steps back to look at the whole map. The marks that he made form a triangle around a large thinly wooded mountainous area known as the Phoenix Mountains Park and Reserve. The evidence is all there and is pointing to only one conclusion, *"THE ANTS ARE BACK!"* and to make matters worst they're only about *two miles from his home!*

It's 12:00 midnight at EPA One. Troy, Hill and Daily are up compiling their notes for their trip to New York to confront officials at Gen X Tech. They're sitting around a large table in the conference room. The table is covered with folders and papers as well as the remnants of the Chinese food they ordered an hour ago.

Daily leaning back in his chair thumbs through a folder he's holding in front of him, "Okay, we have Jorge Torres their director of public relations, who I might add is a little too eager to speak to us, he's called me three times already to confirm. Then we have Chad Brooks the company's CEO and founder," he looks up from the folder with a look of concern on his face, "I did some checking on this guy and he's supposed to be some kind of recluse with an IQ of over 140. No one has seen him for the past four months but I think we should try and track him down anyway," he glances back at the folder, "if that fails there's Answorth Lahey the director of research and development and there's also the COO and co-founder Lloyd Richardson. My sources say that he's almost always in New York either at the Manhattan Office or their Long Island headquarters," he closes the folder and throws it down on the table, "all we're waiting for right now is the search warrants and subpoenas and the go ahead from the Attorney General's office. We're going to need all the leverage we can get against these guys."

Troy jumps in while looking at the screen of his laptop, "I think I may have something that could help. I'm not sure if it's a lead or a wild goose chase," he closes the laptop and leans back in his chair.

"What is it?" asks Hill.

"Well this is something I've been following up on my own for a couple of days now. Remember the night I tried to break into Gen X Tech's online database system?"

"Yes," responds Hill.

"Well since then I've received a couple of encrypted emails from someone claiming to work inside Gen X Tech identifying them selves only as Mr. Black."

Hill and Daily lean in toward Troy, both with looks of surprise on their faces.

"You didn't think that was important enough to tell us sooner?" snaps Daily.

"Like I said, they were very short encrypted messages. One gave me information on how to better access unrestricted and unmonitored Gen X Tech's personnel files. I tried it but only with minimum success. Another mentioned New Eden as an item we should focus our investigation on, but we had already figured that out. And finally I got one this morning that suggested the Brazilian incident was in fact no accident and that the release of SF-20 was deliberate."

"How many messages did you get?" asks Hill.

"Just the three," replies Troy.

Daily scratching his head asks, "Any ideas as to who this informant could be?"

"No, not really. But I did send them a message informing them of our trip to New York and I'm waiting for a reply."

Daily and Hill stare at each other for a moment with eyebrows raised.

"An informant on the inside. This could be the big break the Professor was looking for," says Daily.

Hill stands up from the table, "I damn sure hope so," she turns to Troy, "Good work Troy. Keep monitoring your email and inform us right away of anymore messages."

"You got it," responds Troy.

"Good," answers Hill, "It looks like we're more than ready for New York," she says as she walks over to a counter where there's a coffee maker and pours herself a cup, "now we all know the game plan," Hill sips her coffee as she paces around the room, "first we hit the Manhattan office and speak with Mr. Brooks. He knows we're coming but has no idea that we're bringing a warrant, so that should be interesting. Then we secure their records and interview as many people as we can find that are in someway connected with the development of SF-20. At the same time, another team will be doing the same thing at their Long Island Headquarters," she puts her cup on the table and takes a seat across from Daily and Troy, "Lastly, we'll wait to be contacted by Troy's Mr. Black and see what information he has, any questions?"

Both men nod their heads no as Hill takes another sip of her coffee.

Suddenly the door to the conference room swings open violently and in rushes Brad, breathing heavily and sweating.

Hill, startled by his entrance, almost spills her coffee. She quickly rests the cup on the table then rushes over to Brad, "Brad! Are you okay? What are you doing here?"

Brad, still breathing heavily, leans over the conference table as he slowly regains his composure, "The….the….the ants! The…the damn ants are back!"

The three give each other a puzzled look as Daily gets up and offers Brad a seat, "Here buddy sit down. Catch your breath and tell us what's going on."

Brad takes the seat, catches his breath and begins to fill them in on what he has found out, "Did any of you see the evening news tonight?"

"No we've been going over our notes for the New York trip. Why?" responds Troy.

Brad glares at Troy, "I thought you have people monitoring all news broadcasts for signs of SF-20 outbreaks?"

"Yes we do down the hall in communications," explains Troy, "But they haven't reported anything out of the ordinary to us."

"Well they damn sure missed this one," says Brad irately.

"What happened, Brad?" demands Hill, "What's going on?"

Daily hands Brad a small bottle of water, "Here, drink this slowly."

"Thanks," says Brad as he opens the bottle and sips the water, "I was home watching the news and this report comes on about a missing girl and her dog near the Phoenix Mountains Park. Then they start talking about missing pets in the same area and a half eaten horse," he takes another swallow of the water, "here's the real kicker, the remains of the horse smelled like vinegar!"

Daily sighs, "Holy shit, he's right! The ants!"

"Clarence," says Brad in a solemn voice, "that's only two miles from my home. That's damn near downtown Phoenix. My wife, my family, Cliff's wife and family all live near there."

"Was there any other information in the report that can help us find the nest?" asks Troy.

"Not much, but I do remember them saying that the reports of missing pets have been going on for a while and that the residents think it's the work of a rogue mountain lion or coyote. They have armed groups planning to go into the mountains."

Hill gets up closes her eyes and holds her head, "Oh my God. This is bad if those hunters find the nest we're going to have a massacre on our hands right on the evening news," she turns to

Troy, "wake up the Professor. Fill him in on what's happening we'll need to move on this right away."

"I'm on it!" says Troy as he takes out his cell phone and dials.

"I'll head over to the living quarters and wake the team. Meet you back here in a few," shouts Daily as he runs out of the room.

Hill then turns to Brad, "We can handle it from here. You need to be home with your wife and family."

"I can't! I need to be part of this. I need to be back in," states Brad.

"Brad I don't think now is the…"

"It's alright," he cuts her off, "I spoke to Pat already and she's agreed to stay with her mother at our house. She knows this is something I have to do."

"Are you sure you're up for this?"

"I need to be a part of this. I need to," he looks away for a moment, "I need to do this for Cliff."

Hill looks down at him and pats him on the shoulder, "I understand. Come on let's get ready," she nods her head for him to follow, "I was thinking we could head over to communications and see if we can grab a copy of that broadcast you saw. There might be some other information in it we could use."

"Right!" says Brad as he follows her out of the door.

Within the hour there is a flurry of activity in the conference room. Troy has contacted Hamilton and advised him of the situation as Brad, Daily and Hill mobilize the military support team. During the next few hours they get the INVASION mobile command center equipped and prepared for an assault on the mutant ants.

While in route inside the mobile command center, Professor Hamilton stands beside a video monitor which displays a soldier dressed in a beige camouflaged uniform wearing a gas mask.

"We have some new equipment for all of you to wear during this operation. Everyone will be issued the latest light weight Kevlar coated charcoal impregnated NBC suits."

"NBC?" asks Brad.

"Yes it stands for Nuclear, Biological and Chemical. These protective suits are designed to allow troops to operate in hazardous environments during warfare. As you can see they work in conjunction with a respirator mask system. The Kevlar coating should be enough to protect you against the ant's stings while also giving you protection against the poison we'll be using on them. We've added a corrosive enzyme to the deltamethrin to make it more effective but at the same time making it more deadly to the soldiers in the area. These suits should protect you from the poison."

"Should protect us?" asserts Daily.

"Yes, should protect you Agent Daily. It's the best we could do."

"Well, I hope it's more effective than the last time," exclaims Daily.

"It should be. Like I said we've added a corrosive and the formula is forty times more powerful than the last one we used," comments Hamilton in an annoyed tone, "now let's go over our plan of action."

Hamilton switches the display to show a map of the Phoenix Mountains Park and surrounding area.

"We'll have six teams converging on the area, one team entering the park from the north at Vista del Cerro, two from the west at Sunnyslope and Skyline Heights. From the south we'll have a team at Biltmore Gates and from the east there'll be one from Camelback Estates and finally our team will be entering at Clearview Hills."

"Wow, that's a lot of ground to cover," says Hill.

"Based on the areas covered in the attacks we calculated this to be an extremely large colony. We're not taking any chances this time. We'll have the entire park surrounded."

"All right we surround the park then what?" asks Daily.

"Well according to what we've been able to gather the young woman, who lives on East Joshua Tree Lane, drove to the southern edge of Phoenix Mountains Park to jog with her dog," Hamilton traces the route on the monitor with his finger, "they went along North 40th Street into the mountains. Her car was found at the entrance to the park around 9:30 and shortly after that her dog's leash was found off the side of North 40th street about 1000 feet from her car. So I think we should start our search there," Hamilton checks his watch, "It's now about 1:30 am. We should arrive on site around 3:00. I'd like to be able to find and destroy the nest before noon. If we could wrap this up before most of the public wakes the better chance we have of keeping a lid on it," Hamilton takes a seat in front of the monitor, "I've contacted the local police and informed them that we need the park cordoned off and free of civilians."

The caravan of four Humvees, two supply trucks and the huge black tractor trailer, which serves as the team's mobile command center, rumble through city of Phoenix in the early morning hours. They drive through Clearview Hills and turn onto North 40th Street and into the park. Awaiting them at the entrance are five parked cars, three police cars and six police officers. It's now 2:40 am and the officers seem thoroughly surprised to see the military vehicles along with the command center roll into the park. The parade of vehicles comes to a halt near the patrol cars and Professor Hamilton steps out along with the rest of the team and military personnel as the officers approach cautiously.

One of the policemen with lieutenant stripes on his sleeves step forward towards Professor Hamilton. He's a narrow-eyed blonde-haired man with a big ball of chewing tobacco under his right cheek. He stands about five-feet-six with a big barrel-shaped chest and the look of a man that's used to giving orders and having them carried out without question, "Excuse me, but what the hell is going on here?"

"We're a special task force from Monthan Air Force Base in Tucson," answers Hamilton, "This area is now under military jurisdiction. You should have been notified of our arrival."

The lieutenant spits tobacco juice onto the ground in front of the Professor then wipes the brown drool from his lips with the sleeve of his shirt, "I didn't hear a thing about no army taking over down here. You just hold on a sec," The lieutenant spits again then grabs his radio from his belt, "Dispatch this is One Adam Twelve over."

"Go ahead One Adam Twelve," a voice crackles back over the radio.

"We're at the 40th Street entrance to the park and have the damn army down here! Does command have any information on this?"

"Hold on, One Adam."

After a few moments his radio squawks back to life, "Come in One Adam Twelve."

"This is One Adam, go ahead."

"Command confirms the military activity in your area. You are to give them any assistance they may need, over."

The lieutenant lowers the radio from his mouth and gives Hamilton a look of contempt then mutters, "You gotta be fucking kidding me."

"Do you copy One Adam Twelve?" repeats the dispatcher.

"Roger that dispatch," the lieutenant spits again, "Okay fella, it seems you guys are in charge. So what's going on here?"

Professor Hamilton points up the road toward the mountain, "We have an emergency situation here. We need to secure this entire area and keep all people off the mountain till we complete our operation."

"That's what we were doing when you guys showed up. We were told to close down the park and keep out any civilians. But we weren't told about no military operation. So what gives?"

"We have a dangerous situation in the park and before we send in our troops we need everyone off the mountain and out of the way."

"Well that normally wouldn't be a problem but another one of the reasons why we're out here is because we got word that a number of trigger happy hunters went up into the mountains to hunt down a cougar. We were just getting ready to go after them when you guys showed up."

"Listen, Sergeant," says Hamilton.

"It's Lieutenant!"

"Sorry, Lieutenant. What's on that mountain is one hundred times more dangerous than a cougar. We have to find those people and now!"

"You mind telling me what we're going up against that's so dangerous?"

"Lieutenant when the time is right you'll be given all the facts. But right now our priority is to secure this park and find those hunters. We already have teams securing the north, the west and the east of the park. My men will go into the park and look for the hunters from here. I need your people to cordon off all southern routes leading into the park. Under no circumstances are you to allow anyone through."

The lieutenant hesitates and gives Hamilton a look of skepticism. He turns his head to the side and spits on the ground then glances at the uniformed soldiers exiting from their vehicles behind the professor, "What part of the military did you say you were with?"

"I didn't," says Hamilton sharply.

"Listen, in all my years on the force I've never seen anything like this. I think I have the right to know what's going on."

"Listen, we don't have a lot of time. The sun will be up soon and people will be all over this place which will make our job a lot harder. All you need to know right now is that this is a matter of national security and we are here under order of the President of the United States. I have been given all assurances that I would have the full cooperation of the Phoenix Police Department. Now if there's a problem, I can get the mayor on the phone and you can discuss it with him," Hamilton pulls out his cell phone and begins to dial.

"No, you got me wrong, buddy. I'm not trying to start no trouble," he reaches over and gently grabs Hamilton's arm that's holding the cell phone. Hamilton stops dialing and puts the phone away, "It's just that there's been a lot of weird things going on in the news lately and now the military comes rolling in and nobody's talking. Hell, my job is to protect the people of this city and I feel I have just as much right to know what's going on as anybody," again he spits tobacco juice and wipes his lips.

Hamilton stares at the lieutenant for a moment with the look of understanding he then says calmly, "You know something Lieutenant you're right. Come with me," he directs the officer over to the side of the command center where the rest of the team members are standing.

"This is Lieutenant…um--" he pauses and looks back when he realizes he doesn't know the officer's name.

"Broody, Lieutenant Broody."

"Thank you. This is Lieutenant Broody. There are civilians on the mountain that we have to find ASAP. I figure the Lieutenant and his men know this area better than we do so we could use their help getting those people out of the park. They may also be helpful in finding the nest."

Broody gives Hamilton a strange look, "Nest?"

"Yes, Lieutenant. A nest," Hamilton pauses for a moment, "Lieutenant what I'm about to tell you is a matter of national security. It's also going to seem incredible but I ask that you just keep an open mind. We have reason to believe that there is a nest of mutant fire ants in this park. They are extremely dangerous and may be responsible for a number of unexplained attacks in the area."

Broody smiles then spits a large wad of tobacco on the ground, "Mutant Fire Ants, huh? You're joking?"

"No I'm afraid not."

Broody scans the faces of the other team members and notices the seriousness in their eyes, "How big are these things?"

"About a foot long."

"Holy Shit, a foot? You're serious."

"Yes I am, Lieutenant."

"You know that would explain a lot of the strange reports we've been getting around here lately you know like missing pets," responds Broody.

"I understand. Listen, Lieutenant we are going to have to work fast. We would like to find the nest before sun up."

"Right, just tell me what you want us to do?"

"First you must understand that what I have told you is not to be shared with anyone!"

"I understand."

Hamilton then takes the Lieutenant and his men to the side and puts together three groups. Each group contains six soldiers armed with M500 Combat Shotguns, two soldiers with flamethrowers, two soldiers armed with deltamethrin chemthrowers and two police officers as guides. All of the police officers are issued gas masks as added protection against the deltamethrin. As soon as the groups are formed they head up into the park.

"We can head up in that direction," states Broody as he points upward towards a group of small mountains, "I think that would be a good place for a nest to be."

"Why is that?" asks Hill as they climb together over the rocky terrain made up of small low lying bushes, medium sized trees and steep hills.

"It's an area that not many people visit. It's very rocky and isolated."

Bloomberg and Hill, both armed with shotguns, nod at each other then Hill shouts to her team, "Alright, let's move it! We're following the Lieutenant."

The elevation increases slightly as they begin making their way up the side of the mountain.

"Remember to check under every fallen tree and inside every crevice and cave and behind every boulder," reminds Bloomberg.

After the teams have moved out Professor Hamilton checks in via radio from the command center periodically, "All squads this is command. It is now zero five hundred. Is there anything to report?"

Hill responds over the radio, "This is Hill. We're a mile and a half out with nothing to report, over."

"Daily here, a mile and three quarters due north and nothing to report," reports Daily.

Brad's voice shrieks in over the air next, "Command, this is Brad, two miles and still nothing."

Hamilton comes back, "There's still nothing from the five other teams to the north, west and east sectors. We need to pick up the pace. Sunrise in one hour."

All of the squads acknowledge the message over the radio system. Lieutenant Broody takes Hill and her squad along what is known as the L.V. Yates Trail which flows up the side of a small mountain to an elevation of about 1900 feet, where there are many shrubs, cracks and crevices. He moves up ahead of the team towards a ridge that overlooks a valley on the other side of the mountain. Just before he gets to the top of the ridge four gunshots ring out across the canyon.

BAM! BAM! BAM! BAM!

Everyone in the squad drops to the ground and freezes for a moment staring in the direction of the gunfire. The soldiers in the group instinctively aim their weapons toward the ridge. Everything is silent then again gunshots.

BAM! BAM! BAM!

Shortly after that there's another series of shots and someone screams, "*Arghh!* Run Dave Run!"

Suddenly eight men with hunting rifles come running over the ridge, their frames silhouetted against the soft orange glow of the rising dawn sun. They run right into the middle of the squad and don't seem to be aware that the soldiers are even present.

Lieutenant Broody with his hand on his gun yells to the men, "Alright, hold it. Stop right there!"

The startled men stop in their tracks. It is only then that they notice that they are surrounded by armed military personnel. They're shaking and look frightened as they slowly raise their hands over their heads. Broody approaches the men cautiously with his right hand still on his holster. With his left hand he motions to them slowly.

"It's alright gentlemen. You could put your hands down."

The men still shaking lower their hands slowly.

"Are there any more of you?" he asks.

One of the men, a tall rough looking guy wearing denim overalls and carrying a doubled barrel shot gun, steps forward, "D…D… Dave is still back there," he says with a shaky voice.

"What happened? We heard shots," asks Broody.

"We found a human leg back there. I think it belongs to that missing girl. It was all chewed up and there were these big bugs all over it. They started to come after us so we shot at them. Next thing we knew they were everywhere. They came out of nowhere. They got all over Dave," the man looks at Broody with tears in his eyes, "You have to understand we couldn't save him. There were too many of them. You have to understand we tried, I swear we tried," the man continues to plead.

Broody in a very understanding voice says, "It's alright, just try and calm down. We need you to take us to where you found the woman's leg. Do you think you can do that?"

The man hesitates while his body shakes uncontrollably. Then one of the other men steps forward. He's a shorter stocky man dressed in a short sleeved plaid shirt with broad shoulders, long straight jet black hair and a wide square chin carrying a Remington 700 hunting rifle. He appears to be a Native American from one of the tribes in the area, probably Apache, "Officer, I'll show you. I'll take you there just follow me. It's right over that hill," he points to the ridge the squad was originally heading towards.

Hill and Bloomberg approach Broody and the hunters. Hill walks over to the Native American, "Excuse me sir, what's your name?"

"Govind, Govind Lightfoot, ma'am."

"Mr. Lightfoot, did you notice a large dirt mound near the insects?"

"No I can't say that I did. Everything happened so fast. I didn't really see where they were coming from. One minute there were a few crawling over this leg then the next thing we knew there were hundreds everywhere."

"Thanks," Hill takes out her radio, "Hamilton this is Hill over!"

"This is Hamilton, go ahead."

"We've come across the hunters about two miles north east of base. They report finding the remains of the girl and the ants on the other side of a nearby ridge. We are moving to investigate."

"Copy that, Agent Hill."

Hill then turns to the squad, "Okay we're moving out. Soldiers with flamethrowers and chemthrowers on point, shotguns follow. Lieutenant you and the hunters can bring up the rear. If it gets too dicey I want you to get the civilians back to our mobile command center."

"Got it," replies Broody as he pulls out his handgun.

Hill puts her hand on Govind's shoulder, "Okay, lead the way.....slowly."

"Yes ma'am."

The team gets into formation and cautiously begins their way over the ridge.   They climb over the ridge and down into the valley. About 300 feet from the top of the ridge Govind stops and freezes.

Hill slowly moves up behind him, "What is it?" she whispers.

"Over there," he points over towards some boulders near the side of the mountain, "that's where we found the leg and where Dave fell."

Hill motions to the soldiers with the chemical and flamethrowers to advance toward the boulders. They move ahead slowly with weapons at the ready with the rest of the squad close behind. When they arrive at their destination they find the area covered with blood but no sign of the ants.

Govind looks around with a perplexed look. Hill notices his uncomfortably, "What's the matter?"

"Dave."

"What about him?"

"Where is he? Where's his body?"

Hill quickly scans the area for any signs of the fallen hunter but sees nothing.

Govind responds, "Could they have carried him away?"

Hill just shakes her head and shrugs.

"Over there!" shouts Bloomberg. Everyone turns to see him pointing east off into the distance, "Looks like a mound, could be the nest!"

Up ahead is a small hill surrounded by shrubs and rocks. The team moves forward slowly. Just as they are about twenty feet from the mound Hill's radio makes a loud squawking sound. She fumbles with the volume control as Professor Hamilton's voice comes over the radio.

"Hill this is Hamilton! Come in!"

"Go ahead, Professor," she whispers.

"Have you found the nest? If we wait any longer they're going to become too active and start hunting for food."

"Yes, Professor we've found it. Hold on for location," she pauses as one of the soldiers with the GPS navigation equipment shows her their coordinates, "our position is 33 degrees 33 minutes North and 111 degrees 59 minutes West! Do you copy?"

"Got it, Hill!"

One of the soldiers walks up the mound then turns back toward the team, "I don't see anything in the hole. No movement!" he shouts.

Suddenly a loud buzzing sound can be heard coming from the east. Everyone turns and looks up into the yellow and orange sky. Against the rising sun is a dark cloud moving closer to the team. The buzzing sound gets louder and louder as the cloud descends on the team.

"What is it?" shouts Hill over the growing buzz.

"I'm not sure," replies Bloomberg. Then a look of shock comes over his face, "Holy mother of God! Run! Everybody take cover!" He shouts as he grabs Hill's arm and dives behind a boulder.

"What! What is it?" Hill asks again.

"They're ants!"

"I thought ants don't fly!"

"They must have mutated again. Everybody get down now!"

Every member dives to the ground. The soldiers equipped with the flamethrowers aim their weapons into the air and begin sending bright orange tongues of fire high into the descending cloud causing dead ants to rain down all around the group. But the swarm is too large. Soon flying ants begin diving from the sky to attack the soldiers by landing onto their backs and stinging and biting them over and over. Five flying ants land on the back of one soldier and sting him right through his NBC suit. As he twists and turns from the pain another ant flies onto his face mask and stings him in the throat. He grabs the insect and throws it to the ground. The others on his back crawl around his body stinging and biting him over and over. Finally he falls to the ground vomiting up blood and straining to catch his breath. Before long more flying ants sensing his weakened state swoop down on the soldier. In a matter of seconds he is covered with a living sheet of insects and not too long after that his twitching stops and the ants begin devouring him right before everyone's horrified eyes. Everyone is looking for cover as the area erupts into pandemonium. Soldiers can be seen stomping, waving their arms, and firing their weapons into the air. Bloomberg, Hill, Broody and Govind continue to hide behind the boulder. As they do an ant lands next to Hill who quickly stomps the insect until its dead. Bloomberg reaches down and picks it up while Hill turns and fires her shotgun over the boulder into the angry mass of insects.

Bloomberg with Govind looking over his shoulder examines the dead insect, "Fascinating," says Bloomberg as he turns the dead ant around, "look at the size and shape of the mandibles. They can bite right through our suits!"

Hill fires another shot over the boulder then drops down next to Bloomberg, "Sorry doc, I'm a little busy," she jumps up and continues firing.

Bloomberg seemingly unfazed by the commotion continues to examine the insect, "This is a soldier but it has wings similar to a queen's except that these are larger and permanent. This is what we were afraid of. Karen was right the mutations haven't stopped. They are still evolving!"

"Great! That's just great, Kevin! Watch it!" shouts Hill as she fires her shotgun at two other ants crawling toward them.

"They're everywhere," screams Govind as he stands up and fires his rifle into the swarm.

BAM! BAM! BAM!

Bloomberg yells at him, "Get down! You'll only aggravate them more. That rifle can't do any damage. You'd have better luck with a shotgun."

Govind ignores him and continues firing.

The soldiers with the chemthrowers step up and begin spraying into the air. A thick grayish chemical cloud sweeps slowly across the area. Everyone except for the hunters grabs their gas masks and struggle to put them on while defending against the attacking insects. Govind's eyes turn red and he starts to cough, wheeze and choke from the fumes.

Hill turns to Broody, "Lieutenant, take Lightfoot and the other hunters to the other side of the ridge. It's too dangerous here."

"Gotcha!" replies Broody as he grabs Govind by the arm and leads him through the cloud of flying ants. He waves to the other hunters to follow him as he runs toward the ridge. They see him and rush with their heads down in his direction.

With the deltamethrin swirling through the air the cloud of flying ants slowly begins thinning. Suddenly the ground around them starts to vibrate. Hill looks down with a look of terror, "Oh shit! I remember that feeling. We're in big trouble!"

Thousands of angry ants begin to pour out of the mound. As cracks open up all around the area.

"It's just like the forest. They're trying to surround us!" yells Hill as she watches the holes open around her.

Bloomberg yells to the soldiers with the chemthrowers, "The nest! Aim at the nest!"

The two soldiers turn and direct their weapons toward the hole at the top of the mound and begin unloading their payload all over attacking ants. The soldiers equipped with flamethrowers responding to Bloomberg's command quickly turning their weapons toward the nest without noticing that they are too close to one of the soldiers carrying the chemthrower.

Bloomberg notices the mistake and yells out to the flamethrowers to fall back, but it's too late. The flames ignite the soldiers NBC suit. Flames quickly crawl up his back and around the backpack containing the two large cylinders of deltamethrin. He rolls on the ground but the flames quickly engulf him, heating up the cylinders till they burst causing a massive explosion over the nest blowing everyone within thirty yards into the air, showering them with pieces of burnt flesh from the soldier's body. The stunned squad members gradually climb to their feet and resume lashing out at the ever-expanding wave of ants pouring from the nest.

A soldier armed with a shotgun back-pedals from the nest while firing at the ground. But the soldier ants keep advancing. Unexpectedly, a flying ant lands on the back of his neck and drives its stinger deep into the base of his skull just above the top vertebrate of the spine. His body immediately stiffens then begins to convulse uncontrollably. Bloody tears run down his face and out of his nose and ears, thick saliva foams out of his mouth, his tongue swells and turns bluish gray. His body falls to the ground shaking and twitching as ants from the nest begin to cover his body and more flying soldiers descend on him to implant their stings. With one final arch of his back the soldier gasps one last time before remaining still as the reddish brown mass of killer ants commence on dismembering his body.

As the battle continues this scene plays out over and over again until only a few squad members are left alive. Of the original twelve squad members that went over the ridge, only eight remain alive. There's two soldiers with flamethrowers, one with a chemthrower, and three armed with shotguns along with Hill and Bloomberg. The eight hunters make it safely to the other side of the ridge along with Broody and one of his officers. There are dead ants everywhere covering the entire area. But the cloud of flying ants is no longer the threat that it was a little while ago. The insects coming out of the ground hasn't slowed a bit and the team is doing everything in their power to slow down the spreading sea of ants.

Hill signals for the squad to regroup near the boulder that she and Bloomberg have been using for cover. They form a line with the chemical and flamethrowers and begin pushing the ants back toward the nest. Hill gets on her radio and calls Professor Hamilton, "We need help over here. We're under attack! Where the hell are the other teams?"

"This is Hamilton. They have your coordinates and are on their way to your location. Try and hold on."

Suddenly the ground around them starts to shake and rumble violently.

"Watch it their coming up under us!" shouts Hill as she steps carefully over the undulating ground. As antennae begin wiggling up through the ground the chemthrowers turn their chemical spray on the new threat. But no matter where the team members move the ants seem to be able to detect their location and tunnel up under them. Bloomberg yells out to the squad, "We need to fall back to the ridge till we get some help out here."

"I agree," shouts Hill, "Everybody fall back! Fall back to the top of the ridge!" She takes off and runs full tilt up the hill towards the ridge. Bloomberg and the others quickly follow. When they reach the top they turn back to behold the spectacle that sits before them, 300 square yards of a growing bubbling sea of living deadly insects. Hill looks up into the eastern sky, "It's going to be light soon we need more help."

Bloomberg checks his watch and says, "You're right! Contact Hamilton and let him know we're coming back."

Just then a voice can be heard over the radio, "Debra come in! Can you hear me Debra? This is Brad, come in Debra!"

"This is Debra, go ahead Brad."

"We were heading toward your location but ran across another entrance to the nest and a swarm of ants. We can't get to you!"

"It's okay Brad; we're falling back to the command center. Our area is overrun. We've had casualties! You should head back too. The sun is coming up and the ants are becoming more aggressive!"

"Copy that, Debra. I'll meet you back at command, out!"

Just then Hamilton cuts in on the transmission, "Attention! All teams abort! I repeat all teams abort! Reassemble at the command center ASAP!"

"Copy that! We're already in route," responds Hill.

"Heading back," reports Daily.

"Right behind you," says Brad.

It's 6:45 am when all of the squads arrive back at the command center. While they were gone four large tents had been sent up along side of the mobile center. One serves as a mobile hospital, another is a mess hall stocked with water and food. The other two tents serve as makeshift barracks for the soldiers of the INVASION team complete with showers and cots.

Even though both Brad and Hill's squads encountered hostile ants only Hill's had any casualties. Her troops stagger back into base camp battered, bloodied, bruised and shaken.

As they approach the command center Hamilton is waiting for them out front, "Take the injured to the first tent," he commands to the men as they stumble through the bush, "In the other tent is food and water!" he then turns to Hill and Bloomberg, "I need to see you two inside. This situation has taken a turn for the worst."

"What happened?" asks Hill as they walk quickly to the mobile command center.

"We've uncovered five different entrances to this nest. The two you and Brad discovered, another in the north near Vista del Cerro and two in Sunnyslope. We knew that this was a big nest but not this big!"

Bloomberg and Hill give each other a look of concern as they enter the mobile command center. Inside the briefing room Brad, Daily, Troy and the rest of the team are already there waiting for them. Hill and Bloomberg sit down just as Hamilton begins to speak, "Ladies and gentlemen, let me start by saying that this may be our greatest challenge to date. We have monitoring equipment positioned near each of the holes that you've found and the data we're getting is disturbing. For one thing, because of the time of day the ants are very active and, as most of you already know, we've found that they've mutated again. They're now more aggressive, stronger, and smarter than before. Even their venom is deadlier. We also have to contend with winged soldier ants that can sting right through our new Kevlar NBC suits. And finally we have this," he throws the memo he was holding down on the table, "Five minutes ago a swarm of ants was spotted in Granada Park near East Maryland Avenue, some were flying and some were on the ground."

"That's near the canal! There are homes near there," shouts Brad.

"I know and they've already attacked several people in the area. Phoenix P.D. is trying it's best to keep them contained. But we have more bad news. This is a very large colony. One this size needs a lot of food. They're going to start scouting. They're also agitated by our disturbance of their nest. These two factors may cause them to spread out of the park and into the populated areas of the city. We must find a way to stop them from doing that. I'm open to suggestions. I've already called for more reinforcements but we need a plan."

"Well we could rule out that air fuel bomb that's for sure," comments Daily.

Forrester looks up and says, "Why don't we just soak all of the entrances that we've found with deltamethrin? Shouldn't that kill them all?"

"Normally yes, but we've found five holes so far and now it looks like there may be one in Granada Park as well that's within the city limits. If that's true then this colony spreads out further than we thought. There could be other holes we haven't found yet. They could have tunnels all across the city and what we've been able to gather from your reports is that once they're disturbed they begin to swarm in all directions. An attack even at one location could trigger them to surface anywhere."

"Why not use pheromones or sounds like we did with the squid? We could attract the ants and guide them to an unpopulated area where we can dispose of them," says Hill.

Hamilton responds, "I thought of that and we tried it once down in Brazil a few years ago. We used the pheromones of regular fire ants but the mutants wouldn't respond to it. Now if we can get hold of a mutant queen that may be possible. The only queens we've come across were already dead for some time. We would need a live one or at least one that was freshly killed in order to extract enough pheromone to make it work."

Daily raises his hand, "How hard is it to find a queen?"

"They're usually located in a lower chamber near the center of the nest surrounded by soldiers and without knowing where all of the entrances are there is no way of determining the center of the nest. And even if we could there is no way to determine how deep it is. Furthermore once we started digging into the nest the soldiers would move the queen to a safer location."

Daily raises his hands in disbelief, "You're kidding me? What are they, the ant secret service?"

"Believe it or not that's exactly what their function is. The life of the colony depends on her survival," continues Hamilton, "they will give their lives to defend her without hesitation. And now that they've mutated again we have no idea how they will react."

Cooper stands up and says, "You know we may not like it but the way it looks to me is that we may have no choice but to launch an attack on all fronts regardless of the dangers. Yes, we will have casualties but if we do it right we can minimize them."

Hamilton approaches him, "Well Simon I'm all out of ideas so if you have a plan, the floors yours," he pats Cooper on the back and takes a seat near him.

Cooper steps forward in front of the group, "The first thing I think we should do is inform the public on what is going on. Stories have already been leaked to the press. How long do you think we can keep covering this up? Look at what's happening here. Those hunters have seen the ants so have the police. Do you think we can stop them from talking? What do we tell the family of that missing girl? We can't keep this thing a secret forever. The public has the right to know."

Forrester cuts in, "What about panic? How would we manage that?"

Cooper responds, "Which do you think would be worse, People who panic because they are frightened about a known threat or people who panic because they are surprised by some unknown threat," everyone quietly and slowly looks at one another, "Think about nine-eleven for a moment. Don't you think that if the citizens of New York were prepared for an attack that it wouldn't have been as devastating to them? All I'm saying is that they deserve to know the truth."

Hamilton looks around at the other members, "He's right, you know. We've kept this from the public far too long. I think it's time that I advise the President that our policy needs to be changed."

Cooper continues, "Thanks, Professor. Now this is what I propose; first we're going to need all of the resources that we can get our hands on. Next we'll need troops armed with chemthrowers and flamethrowers at each of the holes we have identified as well as throughout the city just in case they come up anywhere else. We'll attack the nest after we've issued an order for everyone to lock themselves indoors. When the attack begins we could have crop dusters filled with deltamethrin fly over the Phoenix Mountains Park to kill any insects that begin to swarm."

Hamilton looks at Cooper with a faint gin, "Impressive, very impressive. But what about the people that live close to the park? They'll be vulnerable to deltamethrin drifting in the wind."

"I'm aware of that. I figured that we can move the people who live on the outer edge of the park to the Phoenix Convention Center, the U.S. Airways Arena or hotels in the city's center for safety."

Hamilton stands up and pats Cooper on the back, "Good work, Simon. I think this is just the way we ought to go. I'll inform both the president and the governor of our plans. All Hell is about to break loose. This city is going to have to be placed under martial law and no one's going to like it," Hamilton heads to the door then turns back to the group, "Simon since this is your plan you are in charge. Start making all of the arrangements. Remember you have the entire military, National Guard as well as the state and local police at your disposal."

"Got it!" responds Cooper as Hamilton leaves the room.

For the next four hours plans are made to prepare the city for the upcoming battle. Hamilton contacts both the president, the governor and informs them that they can no longer keep SF-20 a secret and that the public needs to be aware of the impending danger. By 1:00 pm troops from the Arizona National Guard quietly roll into Phoenix and take up positions around the city. They are soon joined by the companies from the 4th Infantry Division out of Fort Carson in Colorado. At the Phoenix Sky Harbor International Airport where all air traffic has been grounded, several crop dusters are loaded with the poisonous deltamethrin solution. A less potent version of the chemical is used in case the toxin drifts into populated areas. Police are spread throughout the city streets in preparation of a shut down of all nonessential city traffic. The Valley Metro Bus Line is shut down as well as the Metro Light Rail system and all taxi cabs have been garaged.

By 2:00 pm the city is at a complete stand still. The emergency broadcast system is then activated. All of the city's radio and television stations begin broadcasting information about what the residence should do while marital law is in effect. Mobile loudspeakers mounted on trucks slowly drive up and down the city street rebroadcasting the emergency message for those who are not tuned into the local television or radio stations.

"Attention we interrupted regular programming to activate the emergency alert system for the greater Phoenix area because of a local emergency. Please stand by. Important information will follow.

By order of the Governor of the state of Arizona and the President of the United States beginning at 2:00 pm and until further notice the city of Phoenix is under martial law. All persons are to remain indoors. Any unauthorized vehicles or personnel found on the street will be arrested and detained by the military. All government buildings and businesses will remain closed, and all mass transit systems have been shut down. People living near the Phoenix Mountains Park will be evacuated to shelters setup around the city. These precautions are for your own protection.

And now the reason for these drastic measures, recently mutated fire ants have been discovered in the vicinity of the Phoenix Mountains Park. These insects are larger and much more dangerous than the normal fire ants native to the area. They are already responsible for a number of deaths. All preparations have been made to eradicate these monsters.

For the time being close and lock all windows and doors. Remain indoors. Bring all pets inside. Seal all chimneys and openings. Under no circumstances should you go outside. If you come in contact with these insects they will kill you.

If you spot any of these insects call 911 immediately!

Stay tuned to your local TV and radio stations for more information or log onto www.PhoenixArizona.gov."

It's now 3:00 pm and the city of Phoenix has become a ghost town. Only military and police personnel can be seen stationed at most of the intersections throughout the city. It's as if the entire city was holding its breath in anticipation of the coming attack. Squads of troops dressed in NBC suits and armed with deltamethrin stand positioned at the entrances of the ants nest in the park. The crop dusters stand armed, fueled and ready.

The INVASION Team's mobile command center has been relocated to the Phoenix Sky Harbor International Airport. Hamilton is sitting at the communications table coordinating the attack. The rest of the team is with him communicating with ground troops and monitoring various video feeds from around the city. At 3:30 pm Hamilton gives the signal to begin the assault. The teams in the park have bought with them ten foot augers and use them to start drilling near the holes so that they can pump the deltamethrin directly into the ground while other troops saturate the area around the nest entrances with the deadly chemical. A few minutes after the augers penetrate the ground the first ants begin to emerge from the nest. Soldiers equipped with chemthrowers react quickly and drown the insects in a chemical bath leaving them writhing and twisting on the ground. The soldiers with the augers begin pumping the deltamethrin into the earth near the entrances. As they do the ground underneath them starts to vibrate and rumble. Ants emerge from the ground for a brief moment then suddenly stop and withdraw. As they do flying soldier ants, coming from another location, launch a surprise attack and descend onto the troops from above. The startled soldiers react swiftly and redirect their sprays upward cutting into the swarms like hot knives cutting through ice. But the flying mass of insects is too large and soon begins overtaking the ground troops. Suddenly the crop dusters appear from the south, laying down a thick white cloud of deltamethrin over the area. The troops dive to the ground as dead ants rain down around them.

Back at the command center the team analyzes the reports from the battlefield. Hinds approaches Professor Hamilton and hands him a clipboard with their findings as she fills him in on the situation.

"It looks like Simon's plan is working. We're a half an hour into the attack and so far there have been only a few causalities and the number of ants coming out of the nest have decreased considerably."

Hamilton doesn't respond and instead just continues reading the report intently.

Hinds continues, "It looks like we'll have this one wrapped up sooner than we expected."

Hamilton slowly raises his head, sighs then says, "I hope you're right Karen. I really hope you're right. Tell all teams to continue for another fifteen minutes then report back."

Hinds gives Hamilton a puzzled look as she takes the clipboard and returns to the rest of the team monitoring the attack.

During the assault in the park the rest of the city is still eerily silent. A lone military patrol heads down West Van Buren Street towards University Park in a Humvee with six soldiers on board. They're patrolling the outskirts of the city for any signs of the ants. As they approach the corner of North 10th Avenue the sergeant sitting in the passenger seat spots something in the park.

"Slow down private, there's something going on over there," he points to two small beige colored maintenance buildings on the corner of the park. They're covered in a slow moving brownish mass of ants. "Stop here and radio in that we have contact," he orders frantically.

"Yes, sir!" responds the soldier driving as he pulls into the parking lot of a Desert Inn Motel located across from the park on the corner of West Van Buren and North 10th Avenue.

The sergeant turns to two of the soldiers sitting in the back seat, "You two grab the flamethrowers! Let's go double time!"

"Yes, sir!" The two acknowledge in unison as they dash out of the vehicle and begin strapping on the flame throwing equipment. The soldier in the driver's seat radios the command center.

"Command, this is Bravo team in sector 16. Do you copy?"

"This is command go ahead Bravo."

"We have positive contact with the intruders. Location is 33 degrees 27 minutes North, 112 degrees 5 minutes West."

"Roger that bravo, 33 degrees 27 minutes North, 112 degrees 5 minutes West. Reinforcements in route. Secure location and report any change in movement. Do you copy?"

"Roger command, securing location, out!"

The soldier joins the others in front of the Humvee and relays the message to the sergeant. The sergeant looks at his men, "Good work, private," he points to three of the soldiers, two have shotguns and another has a flamethrower, "You three head over to the opposite side of the street behind that car parked near the palms and we'll stay on this side. You see any ants leaving the park, fry them. Got that?"

"Yes sir!" They yell as they run to the opposite side of West Van Buren Street and take up position behind the abandoned vehicle.

Back at the command center the team takes the information gives it to Troy who plots the coordinates into his computer system. The display shows a satellite image of the entire city the slowly zooms into one area.

"My God that's University Park!" shouts Brad as he points to the screen, "I gotta get out there! I gotta get home!"

He turns and begins the run towards the door but Daily grabs him by the arm, "There's a team on the ground over there already and more on the way. They can handle it. Relax."

"You don't understand! That park is down the block from my house! Patricia and Doris are there with my mother-in-law alone. I need to get to them! Now!"

Hill steps forward, "What's the fastest route to your house?"

"Debra, it's too dangerous!" shouts Bloomberg.

Hill ignores the comment and looks at the determination in Brad's eyes, "Don't worry, I'm going with you Bradley."

"Then so am I," says Daily.

A voice from behind them startles the group, "You'll need more help than that!" They turn to see Professor Hamilton standing behind them, "I'm sending a squad with you. Try and evacuate as many people from that area as you can."

"Thank you, Professor," exclaims Brad as he turns back to Hill, "The quickest way is to take Interstate 10 west and exit at 144. The roads are clear so it should take no more than ten minutes."

Hill grabs a shotgun, chambers it and says, "Then let's get moving!"

"I'll get your support team ready," responds Hamilton as he picks up a radio.

A few minutes later Hamilton gives the team the go ahead, Daily grabs a flamethrower and follows Hill and Brad out of the command center. They are met by four Humvees, one M113 armed personnel carrier and three buses to transport civilians out of the danger zone. The caravan speeds off down Interstate 10 following Brad in the lead Humvee.

Meanwhile bravo team stationed at the corner of 10th and Van Buren observe that the swarm of ants is beginning to spread out from the maintenance buildings and into the street. They unleash their flamethrowers on the advancing insects in a sweeping motion killing hundreds of them in seconds. All of a sudden they feel the ground beneath them begin to rumble and shake. One of the soldiers looks down at a sewer hole along the curb near his feet. He hears a faint rustling sound and stoops down to listen more closely.

"What's wrong Corporal?" asks one of the other men as he stands behind the kneeling soldier.

"There's something down there. I can feel it. Wait a minute," he pauses for a moment, "I think I hear something."

In an instant a massive wave of angry soldier ants rushes out from the sewer and completely engulfs the soldier's body. The other two jump back in horror as he lets out a blood-curdling scream. Blood sprays in all directions from the deep lacerations inflicted by the biting insects. The sergeant and the other soldiers across the street are unable to help him. They have become trapped against the wall of the motel as hordes of ants block their escape from the parking lot. The soldiers' burn and shoot as many of the ants as they can with their backs pressed against the building's wall.

The sergeant shouts to one of the privates as he fires his shotgun over and over again, "Can you make it to the Humvee?"

"I don't think so!" the private shouts back.

The sergeant glances up across the street just in time to see the two remaining troops succumb to the mass of deadly creatures.

"Keep firing! We have to hold out!" The sergeant shouts to the other soldiers unaware that another wave of ants is descending down on them from the roof above.

At that same moment on the quiet palm tree lined North 11th Street, two women peer cautiously out of the front window of a beige and brown ranch style house. Just before the alert Brad brought Doris and her two dogs over to his house to stay with Pat and her mother. He felt having all of them together would be safer than having them alone spread across the city. Pat and her mother are the first to hear the gunshots and they slowly part the drapes in the living room to get a glimpse of what could be going on.

"Can you see anything?" whispers Doris standing behind the two holding her little dog Nina.

"No. But I'm sure it was a gunshot and I could swear I heard someone scream," says Pat in a low voice.

"I think I did too," adds Jaclyn.

Then Max, Doris' boxer, begins to bark from the back of the house. The women turn to look in the direction of the noise.

"Max no! Quiet boy!" commands Doris, but the dog continues to bark louder and louder, "Max come here boy! Come here!" the dog just continues barking.

"Let me find out what's wrong with him. It's not like him to bark like that," Doris says as she walks to the back of the house carrying Nina who's shaking in her arms. Pat and Jaclyn go back to staring out of the window. After a few moments they hear Doris' frightened voice, "Pat, Jackie! Come here quick!"

They sprint to the rear of the house and find Doris standing in front of the glass doors that exit into the backyard. She's frozen with fear squeezing poor little Nina in her arms. Max is in front of her barking and scratching at the glass doors. They look up into the backyard and fix their gaze on a horrific sight. In the backyard a carpet of mutant ants is slowly approaching the patio doors. Pat grabs Doris by the arm and pulls her into the kitchen.

"We have to make sure there are no openings they can get through," she shouts, but Doris just stands there gripped in fear, holding Nina in her arms, "Doris! Did you hear me? We need to board up the windows and doors!" Doris remains frozen silent. Pat runs over and slaps her sharply across the face, "Come on girl, I need you to get it together."

Doris shakes her head and rubs her cheek as she slowly responds, "What…what do you want me to do?"

"Look for any way they can get in and seal it up with any thing you can!" Pat shouts, "Mom you do the same. Come on we have to hurry!"

The women scurry around the house stuffing towels under doors, pushing furniture against doors and taping up windows. Pat tries calling Brad on her cell phone, "I can't get through all the circuits are down!"

Crash!

The sound of breaking glass fills the house causing the women to huddle together in the living room. Max runs toward the sound, barking frantically. Pat, with a broom in her hand, cautiously follows him to the back of the house. When she enters the patio area she stops dead in her tracks. In front of her the large glass doors leading to the backyard are shattered and flying ants start swarming in through the opening like a living cloud. She screams and runs back into the living room with the other women. Max barks and snaps at the invading threat which only angers the insects and causes them to change direction and dive down onto the unsuspecting pet. The three women cringe as they hear the animal whimper in pain. They stare at the entrance to the back of the house waiting to see what happens next. There's silence for a minute which seems like an eternity. Then suddenly an explosion of ants floods into the room. The women grab anything they can to swat the insects. They flail their arms around in an attempt to keep the bugs off of their bodies. The insects are everywhere, on the ceiling, on the walls, crawling on the floors and flying through the air. Four ants jump onto Doris' shoulders and implant their stings deep into her back. She arches her back in an unnatural position as she claws her shoulders. Doris falls to her knees as more ants jump into her hair. Nina jumps out of her arms and growls at the ants surrounding her on the floor. She is no match for the voracious insects, some almost as large as she is, but she bares her gums and growls trying in vein to protect her master. The ants quickly pounce on the little dog reducing her into a mass of quivering flesh and fur in seconds.

Pat and Jaclyn try frantically to knock the bugs from Doris' body while protecting themselves from the stinging insects. Doris begins to convulse and vomit as the venom spreads throughout her body. Bloody tears stream down her face as her muscles tense and stiffen. Pat and Jaclyn recoil in terror as Doris twists and writhes on the floor in front of them. The ants then turn their attention on the two remaining women. Jaclyn reaches for the front door and, in a panic, struggles to unlock it. Suddenly there's a loud bang and the door swings open. Jaclyn falls back against Pat as two soldiers with a battering ramp charge into the house. They grab the two women and pull them screaming from the house and into the front yard. Following them are two more soldiers with flamethrowers. They enter the living room and set the whole room ablaze.

Pat, now sitting on the front lawn and still in shock, turns and screams, "No stop! My friend is in there! Doris!" one of the soldiers grabs her and pulls her away from the burning house, "She's still in there! Get off of me. Doris!" She breaks away and dashes toward the house when a hand grabs her shoulder. She turns to see her husband and collapses into his arms.

Brad whispers into her ear, "She's gone there's nothing we could do."

With tears in her eyes she looks up at him, "My God, Brad they killed her!"

"I know baby. I know. But we've gotta move now. It's not safe here."

He hurries her into a waiting Humvee where her mother is already sitting with a military medic.

"Are you injured?" asks the medic. Pat still in a state of shock can only nod slowly. She takes a seat next to her mother and looks back out of the window at her house, ablaze and surrounded by military personnel. As they drive down the street Pat glances out of the window and notices that all around her there's commotion. Soldiers are pulling people out of their homes and putting them into waiting buses. Others are torching houses that are infected by the swarming ants. There's screaming and shouting everywhere. It's total chaos on a block that once was a part of the quiet suburbs of Phoenix, now it has become a war zone.

When the squad returns to the command center the civilians are taken to a makeshift military hospital and the INVASION team members regroup inside the command center. There they are faced with the horrible truth. The scene that just unfolded near University Park was not an isolated incident. At other parks throughout the city similar attacks have taken place. At the Phoenix Zoo, the Desert Botanical Gardens, Echo Canyon Park, and the Palmer Park in Sunnyslope thousands of ants emerged from the ground killing hundreds of soldiers and civilians. They came up through the sewers as well as hidden holes in parks and abandoned homes, before long most of the city north of the Airport was infested with the insects.

Hamilton stands in front of a map of Phoenix, "This is far worse than we could have imaged. It is actually what I feared. This colony has been here a very long time and is immense!" he points to locations on the map, "We've lost the Desert Estates, Peoria, Glendale, and Scottsdale!"

"What do you mean lost?" asks Forrester.

"They've been completely overrun by the ants. We can't even get rescue personnel into those areas to help civilians."

"My God! What do we do?" says Hill in a solemn tone.

Hamilton holds his head down and speaks in a very low tone, "I've been in contact with the President and he agrees that we've lost control of the situation here in Phoenix and has issued an executive order."

Troy stands up from his seat with the look of concern, "An executive order? What the hell does that mean, Pop? What are they going to do?"

Hamilton just stares at the team for a moment not saying a word.

Hinds sees the worried look on the professor's face, "Richard, what's going on?"

Finally Hamilton breaks his silence, "We are to relocate our operations to Andrews Air Force Base immediately. Phoenix is to be cleansed of the threat permanently."

"What exactly does that mean Professor?" inquires Daily.

Hamilton again pauses for a moment then takes a deep breath, "Like I said the President has issued an executive order. And that order is the eradication of the threat via nuclear warhead."

A collective gasp falls over the entire team. They just sit there with their mouths open and the look of disbelief in their eyes.

Hamilton continues, "If there isn't any change in our present situation for the better by 1900 hours a B2 bomber will carry out the order."

"How can they do this? What story are they going to give the public?" asks Bloomberg.

"We have family and friends here!" shouts Brad.

"This can't be happening," says Hill as Daily puts his arm around her.

"They just can't wipe out an entire American city and hope that nobody notices," exclaims Bloomberg.

"Well that's the other part," adds Hamilton as he slowly takes a seat.

"You mean there's more?" adds Bloomberg.

"Yes, I'm afraid so. While we were conducting this operation. I received information that there were several other major outbreaks of SF-20 related incidents," he picks up a folder from the table, opens it and begins to read, "In Houston Texas a swarm of mutated killer bees attacked 2000 people attending a rock concert. So far there are 1200 reported dead," Hamilton turns the page in the folder, "In Clarksburg West Virginia approximately ten thousand eagle size brown bats attacked and killed about one hundred people," he flips another page, "and in Greensboro North Carolina a flock of hawks killed a family of four," Hamilton closes the folder and drops it on the table, "I can go on. There at least five more incidents in this report."

All of the members of the team have the same stunned look on their faces. They just stare at one another in silence.

Hamilton continues, "The executive order the President issued calls for martial law throughout the entire country. He's going to make an official announcement tonight sometime after he decides the fate of Phoenix. So as you can see things have gotten worse a lot quicker than we expected. We are to leave for Andrews and run things from there. And Brad don't worry I've made arrangements for both your wife and mother-in-law to be transferred over with us."

"Thanks, Professor," says Brad.

"Our next move is to go after Gen X Tech. Debra, I need you, Daily and Brad to fly up to New York immediately and get any information you can that helps fight these outbreaks."

"I'd like to go with them Sir," says Troy.

"I don't think that's a good idea son," says Hamilton as he places his elbows on the table and rubs his weary eyes.

"In all fairness Professor we could use his help. He has already helped us establish some good leads. We could use his expertise in the field," comments Hill.

Hamilton stares at Hill then back at Troy and then back at Hill again.

Troy steps forward, "Don't do this to me, Pop. I'm not a little boy anymore. I'm one of the team remember."

Hamilton sighs, "Troy--"

"Let me go with them Professor!" demands Troy as he leans into Hamilton's face, "This is something I want to do. I need to do. You need to let me go!"

Startled by his aggressive response Hamilton pauses for a moment then mutters, "Okay, okay if that's what you want," he then turns to Hill, "he's your responsibility Debra. I mean it. Nothing better happen to my boy you understand me?" he says sternly.

"Loud and clear, sir!" replies Hill.

Troy standing up straight looks down at Hamilton and grins, "Thanks, Pop."

Hamilton pulls him close, "Just be careful out there, Troy. You're all I have and I'd like to see you again in one piece."

"Don't worry Pop. I'll be alright," Troy pats him on the arm then turns and follows Hill out of the Command Center.

Hamilton stands up, "Alright folks it's time to clear out. The remainder of the city is being evacuated as we speak. Well at least the parts we can get to. The transports are waiting on the tarmac. May God have mercy on our souls."

1800 Hours...

The team is finally in route to Andrews Air Force base outside of Washington D.C. in their EPA 747. All is quiet during the trip. In an hour for the first time in its history the country will be in a state of martial law. A major city will be destroyed and panic will surely spread throughout the nation.

1830 Hours...

As they fly over New Mexico Brad and his wife sit together with Jaclyn, Hinds, Forrester and Bloomberg in the conference room watching a monitor showing SF-20 outbreaks occurring around the world. Troy works in the lab with Cooper. Hamilton rests in his office. Hill and Daily lay together in Daily's cabin.

1900 Hours...

The team is entering Oklahoma airspace. At the same time a huge jet black bat shaped figure quietly appears over Flagstaff Arizona. It's an Air Force Northrop Grumman B-2 Spirit stealth bomber flying at over 600 miles per hour. This silent killer, invisible to radar, slowly opens its bomb bay doors as it approaches Phoenix. As it flies over the city's center the pilot signals the bombardier who waits for the right moment then releases the nuclear payload on the plague-ridden city below. The stealth plane then soars off into the sky leaving an enormous mushroom cloud in its wake.

The blast could be seen over one hundred miles away. At that same moment all the televisions across the country go blank. All radio stations go silent. The Presidential emblem appears on TV sets, warning announcements play over the radio and text messages are sent to every cell phone in the country.

It is done. In the United States of America, Martial law has been declared!

Gen X Tech

New York the proverbial city that never sleeps. This megalopolis which is, arguably the most famous city in the world, is also the heartbeat of the nation. Home to the world's largest stock exchange, one of the world's largest subway systems, and even the world's largest biotechnology company; Generation X Technologies, Incorporated.

The impact of the national martial law is even more evident here in the Big Apple than anywhere else. The once crowded Manhattan streets are now barren. The city's roadways, typically packed with bumper to bumper traffic now have an eerie emptiness, with only the occasional military vehicle on patrol. In effect this noisy and bustling city of eight million inhabitants has been reduced to an enormous ghost town. A handful of brave souls can be seen making purchases, going to work and even attending the theatre but in an infinitesimally smaller fraction than normal. Restrictions are the order of the day, with all businesses being allowed to remain open until 6 pm, and schools until 2 pm. By 9 pm, all nonessential personnel must be off streets or face arrest. Military troops can be seen patrolling the streets as army helicopters criss-cross the skyway's overhead. Air traffic in and out of the city has also been limited and many bridges and tunnels have been closed.

As an extra precaution all dogs and cats in the city have been banned. Pet owners have been instructed to turn over their pets to a holding facility on Governor's Island, an old military base, located in the middle of New York Harbor. Naturally, many pet owners protested and some even held onto their pets in spite of the law. But after several reports of even the most docile of pets turning on their masters began to surface across the country even the hold-outs began to have second thoughts.

Sitting right in the heart of Times Square and the Broadway theater district is the luxurious forty-eight story Marriott Marquis hotel. This classy hotel features hi-tech hotel rooms and suites, high-speed elevators as well as six restaurants and lounges. Located mere minutes from such famous New York Attractions as Radio City Music Hall, Rockefeller Center and Carnegie Hall this hotel has become a popular vacation spot for people visiting the Big Apple who want to explore all of its rich culture and events. But now, because of marital law, it is virtually empty.

INVASION team members Troy, Brad, Daily and Hill rest in suites reserved for them on the tenth floor. Troy's room is outfitted with computer and communications systems so that he can keep in touch with the command base at Andrews Air Force Base as well as keep the team updated on SF-20 developments. The team checked into their suites around 3:00 am and immediately went to rest before their assault on the Gen X Tech offices in Manhattan.

At 6:00 am Troy is awakened by a beeping sound coming from his laptop computer. He drunkenly fumbles around in the dark trying to turn on the lamp on the night stand. Once he manages to get the light on, he walks over to his computer while rubbing the cold out of his eyes. As he begins to focus he can finally make out a flashing message on the screen.

"Incoming Message from Mr. Black. Urgent!"

He clicks on the link and the message changes.

"Please Wait Decrypting Message..."

After a few moments the screen turns blue and the full email appears.

"We need to meet today! Face to face. 12:00 noon @ Applebee's on 42nd Street between 7th and 8th Avenues across the street from B.B. King's Blues Club. Seat reservation will be under Mr. Black. I have important information for you. Gaia's retribution has begun."

He types in his response, "Message received. Will meet @ 12 sharp."

Troy closes the email, flops down on the bed and thinks to himself, *"Gaia's retribution? I've heard that term before. I think I know who this is!"*

He goes back to the computer and begins searching the term "Gaia's retribution" on the internet. After a few seconds fifty matches display on his screen. He makes a note of the references that appear. *"Wait a minute! I heard of this guy. Dr. Maxwell Flash. The Fall of Man. Yes that's it! I have to tell the others."*

His heart is pounding as his body flushes with adrenaline. This is the first time that Troy has done anything like this. He's actually working with real investigators and now it appears that he may have solved the first of their many mysteries. The excitement is overwhelming. All of a sudden Troy no longer feels sleepy; in fact he's wide awake even after only three hours of sleep. He throws on some pants and races out of his room. Troy runs down the hall and bangs on the door to Daily's suite. No one answers. He bangs again and again. Finally a groggy voice on the other side of the door responds.

"Who? Who is it?"

"Clarence It's me Troy! It's important. Open up!"

"Hang on a sec Troy."

After a brief moment Daily opens the door. He's bare-chested and only wearing boxers. He cracks the door open slightly and stands in the opening trying to adjust his eyes to the light in the hallway.

"What's going on Troy? What happened?"In a moment of excitement Troy pushes past Daily and enters the room.

"I just got a message from Mr. Black! He wants to meet today! Can you believe that?"

As Daily stands there scratching his head Troy suddenly realizes that they are not alone in the room. He slowly turns to see Agent Hill sitting up in the bed holding a blanket up against her naked body, trying not to make eye contact. Troy is speechless; he looks back at Daily who just shrugs his shoulders.

Embarrassed Troy slowly begins heading to the door, "I think I'll leave you two alone and fill you in later. Sorry to barge in."

Hill then says, "Troy! It's alright--you might as well stay and tell us what you've found."

"You sure? I mean I could come back later, it's no problem."

"Troy!" snaps Hill.

"Alright, alright. Well…like I was saying…" He quickly collects himself and continues, "Mr. Black just contacted me and wants to meet today at a restaurant on 42nd Street."

"What?" Exclaims Daily, "that's great. Maybe we could get some helpful information before we head over to their offices."

Hill then asks, "What time is the meeting?"

"Noon."

"And the restaurant?" asks Daily.

"Applebee's."

Hill chuckles, "Odd place for a meeting."

"Well we better let the Professor know," says Daily as he picks up his cell phone, "I'll send him a text."

"Troy would you mind excusing us a sec? Now that you got us up, I'd like to get dressed." Says Hill as she gets up from the bed with the blanket wrapped around her body.

"Uh, no problem. I'm out. And don't you worry--your secret's safe with me. Mum's the word," he makes a comical gesture across his mouth as if he were zipping it shut.

"Thanks, Troy," says Daily.

Troy stops in the doorway, "I mean when you guys said that you worked closed together I had no idea it was this close!"

"Alright, Troy that's enough!" says Daily.

Troy smiles, "I have to hand it to you, Clarence. When you say you have your partner's back, you really have her back. If you know what I mean?" he gives a sly little wink as Hill laughs, demurely covering her face with one hand and holding the blanket to her lithe, voluptuous frame with the other.

Daily gives Troy a gentle push out of the door, "Alright, Troy you've had your fun. Tell Brad we'll meet downstairs in twenty minutes."

"Twenty minutes? Sure you don't want more time?"

SLAM!

Daily slams the door in Troy's face as Hill falls back on the bed laughing hysterically with her face buried in a pillow. Daily comes over to her and says, "Well the cat's out of the bag. Hello, Alaska," he throws up his arms as if defeated then climbs into bed with Hill. She wraps her arms around him and falls back with him resting on his chest. The two kiss passionately for a few moments then stop and gaze at each other tenderly.

Finally Daily asks, "How much time did I tell him?"

"Twenty minutes."

"Damn! I should have said an hour."

Hill smiles and kisses him while reaching down into Daily's boxers, "Hmm… seems like my big bear has come out of hibernation."

Daily hisses, clenching his teeth at the familiar feel of her expert touch. Brown eyes glittering with need, he pulls off his boxers with purposeful fervor as Hill throws back her blanket with equal abandon. He enters her slowly as she scratches his back and moans in sync with the rhythmic gyrations of his hips and back. The two lovers fall into an erotic trance, completely forgetting about the problems of the outside world.

Meanwhile, Troy goes to Brad's suite to fill him in on Mr. Black's message.

"This is very interesting, Troy. We have to tell Debra and Clarence."

"Uh, they already know."

"Good, what are they planning to do about it?"

"Well, Clarence is sending a message to the Professor."

"We have a lot of questions for this Mr. Black. I better go over there and coordinate things with Clarence," he gets up and begins putting on his clothes.

"Uh, maybe you should wait before you talk to him. He said we should meet downstairs in twenty minutes."

"We should all be on the same page, Troy."

"Yeah, but it's still early. Maybe he needs some time to get ready."

Brad stops getting dressed and approaches Troy, "What's going on Troy?"

Troy lowers his head sheepishly and says, "Nothing I just think we should wait a while before we go knocking on someone's door at six in the morning that's all."

"You knocked on mine," responds Brad.

"Yeah but--"

"And you had already told Clarence and Debra, right?"

"I know, but--"

"So why can't I go over there to talk to him?"

Troy just stares at Brad like a deer caught in the headlights of an on coming car.

Brad continues, "Wait a minute. Don't tell me. You caught them together, didn't you?"

"What?"

"Debra and Clarence. You saw them together didn't you?"

Troy's eyes widen even more and his eye brows rise, "You knew?"

"I suspected," says Brad as he sits on the end of his bed pulling on a pair of socks.

"Damn, I must be losing my touch. I usually pick up on things like that."

"Don't sweat it. It's my job to read people. Listen, let me get cleaned up and dressed. I'll meet you downstairs in ten minutes."

"Alright, no problem," Troy leaves and returns to his room as Brad continues to dress.

Ten minutes later, Brad and Troy meet at the first floor restaurant for breakfast. They are joined a few minutes later by Daily and Hill.

Troy sitting next to Brad and across from Hill and Daily opens up his laptop and places it on the table in front of him, "Well let me start by saying that I think I know who our mysterious Mr. Black is."

Hill with a look of excitement says, "What? You're kidding? That was fast. How did you manage that?"

Troy punches up the last email, "It was something he said in his last message," he scrolls through the message then stops and reads, "he said Gaia's retribution has begun."

Brad looking puzzled and asks, "Gaia's retribution? What does that mean?"

Troy leans back from the table. He picks up a mug of tea and sips it as he speaks, "A few years ago a geneticist by the name of Maxwell Flash wrote a controversial book about the dangers of genetic engineering. It was titled The Fall of Man. In it, he talks about how the misuse of genetic engineering could cause nature to turn on man in an attempt to re-balance itself. He calls this phenomena Gaia's retribution. Only Maxwell would use a term like that. I think he's our man."

"Gaia?" asks Daily as he eats a slice of toast.

Troy continues, "Yes, Gaia. That's the Greek goddess of earth or nature. So in effect he was talking about nature's revenge."

"Makes sense. Look at what's happening around us," responds Hill.

Troy continues, "Maxwell was trying his best to get government regulations placed on certain types of genetic engineering. Then about three years ago he stopped lecturing and publishing papers. Even his book slipped into obscurity. From what I was able to find out around the same time he was hired by a major biotech company."

"Let me guess: Gen X Tech," adds Hill.

"You got it! He was hired to head their biogenetics division," continues Troy.

Brad then inquires, "Why would a company that makes billions off of genetic technology want to hire someone who's such an opponent of the industry? It just doesn't make sense."

Troy turns to Brad and says, "It does if you look at it this way. Flash was one of the most respected geneticists in the country. His message wasn't that genetic engineering was wrong but that if over used or misused it can negatively impact the world," he takes a sip of his tea, "having someone like that working for you sends a message to the public that here is a responsible company, one that's using genetic engineering carefully and moderately."

"So he becomes the company's poster child for the responsible usage of genetic technology. If anything goes wrong, the company would be above suspicion," remarks Hill.

Daily then adds, "That still doesn't add up. Why would he even agree to work for Gen X Tech? I can't see what's in it for him. From what you're saying this Flash guy is a real rebel rouser. He doesn't sound like someone who would sell out."

Troy takes another sip of his tea and takes a deep breath, "I wondered about that myself. So I did some more digging," he hits a few keys on his laptop and a list of names appear on the screen. "Come to find out he's not the only environmental activist working for Gen X Tech. I've found about fifty others. And you'd never guess who some of the others are?"

"Who?" asks Brad.

"Chad Brooks for one!" exclaims Troy.

"Brooks? You're kidding? You mean to tell me that the CEO and founder of Gen X Tech was an environmental activist?" asks Brad.

"That's right. I checked his background. Here--look for your self." Again he types some commands on the keyboard and an article slides smoothly into place, filling the screen. He points, scanning the text, "Look here, while in college Brooks was a member of a number of environmental activist groups including Green Peace. That's when he met Lloyd Richardson. Richardson was already a member of Green Peace when Brooks came on board."

"I don't believe this! Richardson too? This is really getting weird," says Daily.

Troy nods, "That's right. And get this, they both attended rallies against cloning as well as genetic engineering."

Daily throws his hands up, "Wait a minute! You mean to tell me that these guys go from condemning biotechnology to raking in billions from it?"

"That's the way it seems," adds Troy.

"I think that's a pretty big leap. From my experience most activists are very passionate about their beliefs. They very rarely flip sides. It almost never happens. And now you're telling me that not one but three hardcore activists and at least fifty others have jumped ship. Something else is going on here," comments Hill.

Daily jumps in, "Well, one of the questions we need to ask this guy is what made him work for Gen X Tech and why is he now turning on them?"

Hill turns to Troy and asks, "When you first started getting messages from him you said he mentioned that the release of SF-20 wasn't a mistake. We need to know what that means. Why would anyone release something like that on purpose?"

Brad pauses then says, "We to know if something underhanded is going on over there at Gen X Tech. We need know if he can get us some physical proof we could use against them or at least tell us where to look when we serve them the warrant."

"You're right--we need something concrete," adds Hill.

"Hello, Agent Hill?" comes a voice from behind her. She turns to see two well-dressed men standing behind her. One is a tall man with bright blue eyes, short brown hair and a neatly-trimmed mustache and goatee. He's wearing a gray business suit with a white shirt and gray tie. The other is a short lean man with bulging eyes and oily flaxen hair. He's dressed in an expensive navy blue double breasted suit. His perfectly pressed white shirt is adorned with large gold cuff links with a matching gold tie pin. The tall man steps forward to introduce himself.

"Yes?" responds Hill.

As he displays his identification he says, "I'm Special Agent Byron Murphy out of the New York office and this is Inspector Claude Laroché from Interpol France."

Laroché bows to Hill, "Bonjour Mademoiselle."

Hill nods to the gentlemen and responds, "How can I help you?"

Murphy takes a deep breath, "Let me get right to the point, Agent Hill. We need to know what your interest is in Dr. Maxwell Flash?"

The question quiets the entire team who now focus on the two men.

"What makes you think we're interested in Dr. Flash?" answers Hill in a sly tone.

"He's on an Interpol watch list. We flagged an internet query of his name early this morning and traced it back here. After doing a little digging we found that you were running an operation out of this location. We put two and two together and here we are."

"An Interpol watch list? What is this list and why is he on it?" asks Brad.

Ignoring Brad's query Laroché looks directly at Hill, "Mademoiselle, may we please sit down?"

Hill points to a chair at an empty table across from them and says, "Be my guest. Please pull up a chair."

The two men pull chairs from the table and join the team.

Claude Laroché begins, "Monsieur Flash was on our list for his own protection. Over the past three years more than a dozen scientists have disappeared without a trace from all over the world. These are people who are the top in their fields. No ransom notes, no bodies, nothing. After the Russian physicist Dmitri Petrov and the Nigerian biologist Abubakar Oni vanished from a scientific conference in Madrid last year we started the watch list. We hoped to see if we can find out who is targeting scientists from across the globe. I was here in New York monitoring Dr. Flash when Agent Murphy informed me of your interest."

Murphy then adds, "So now you can understand why we need to know why you are investigating him. I found out that you guys are working with the EPA so I'm really curious about his connection with your operation?"

Daily sits up and says, "We're not sure yet. All we know is that he may have some leads that could help us deal with this biological mess we're in. It also appears that Gen X Tech may be involved somehow."

Murphy then asks, "Have you found anything yet that can be helpful?"

"No, but we're meeting with him this afternoon. Hopefully we'll find out something then."

"Today? That's great!" Laroché asks excitedly, "Maybe we can accompany you on the interview, no?"

"Listen this is our first time meeting him. We don't want to spook the guy," explains Hill.

"I have an idea," says Daily, "why don't we set up a wire so you could listen in on the meeting. That way we all get what we want and Flash doesn't get rattled."

Murphy nods his head in agreement, "That's fine with me," he turns to Laroché and asks, "How's that with you?"

Laroché responds, "C'est Génial! Excuse me, I mean that will do."

Murphy continues, "What time is your meeting?"

"Twelve o'clock at the Applebee's in Times Square," adds Troy.

Checking his watch Murphy says, "That's roughly five hours from now. Do you think you can be ready in time?"

Troy blushes and says with conceit, "Are you kidding? Of course we'll be ready."

Daily smiles at Troy then turns to Murphy, "You heard the man--we'll be ready! We'll meet you here at eleven and set you up."

They all stand up and shake Murphy and Laroché's hands as Murphy comments, "Thank you for your help. We'll see you then."

Laroché adds," au revoir Madame et Messieurs," he bows and the two men walk out of the restaurant.

Over the next three hours Troy works on setting up a microphone and transmitter so that their conversation can be picked up by Murphy and his French friend Laroché who will be monitoring from a van around the corner on 8th Ave. Troy decides that he will wear the microphone since he's the one that Maxwell Flash had contacted and would feel most comfortable talking to.

Around 11:45 the team heads out down the near-empty Manhattan streets. As they walk through the streets one thing that Troy notices is the unusual number of rats scurrying about in broad daylight. Almost every block they cross about five to ten of the rodents can be seen darting back and forth from under cars and in and out of sewer openings. At one point Daily almost stepped on a large brown rat as it ran under his feet. His foot snapped the tip of the animal's tail causing it to jump up and let out a loud screech. The rat turned slowly glared up at Daily for what seemed like an eternity. Daily was stunned by the deliberateness of its actions and the sense that it had advanced consciousness that included…indignation. As if reverting back to its nature, the rat squealed again and scrambled down into an entrance to the subway.

They walk three blocks to 42nd street passing the marquees of big Broadway plays and near empty cafés. They turned onto 42nd Street and walked to the restaurant Applebee's in the middle of the block. Once inside they are greeted by the maître d'.

He is a thin, nervous-looking man with dark pouches under his eyes and a wan smile. "Welcome, a table for four?"

"No, we're here to meet someone. The reservation is under Mr. Black."

The maître d' checks the reservation log book, "Oh, yes. He's already here on the upper level. Follow me."

The group follows the maître d' upstairs to the second level. Because of martial law there are very few people in the restaurant, only eight of the twenty tables have customers. The team approaches a table in front of a large window over looking 42nd street. Seated at the table with his back to them and facing the window is a tall black man with short dread locks wearing a brown suede jacket with a beige turtleneck sweater. He's sitting at the table hugging a large folder in his lap. As the team approaches he looks up nervously. All of the members take seats in front of Dr. Flash with their backs to the window. Troy is the last to be seated. He looks at the doctor and sees a tired, frightened 49-year-old who has the look of a man on the run. Even with the undercurrent of strain and stress, one can see that the hazel-eyed geneticist is both handsome and poised.

Troy reaches across the table and shakes his hand, "I'm Troy Phillip and I believe you're Dr. Maxwell Flash if I'm not mistaken."

"Very good, Mr. Phillip. Very good, indeed."

Troy continues, "Let me introduce our team. This is Special Agent Hill, Special Agent Daily and Officer Williams."

They all nod as Maxwell nods back.

Troy begins, "Well you said that you have some important information for us so here we are. You mentioned Gaia's retribution has begun. And that the release of SF-20 was no mistake. We're here for some clarification."

Maxwell slowly looks around at all of the team members then looks back at Troy, "Let me first start by telling you that the end is near. It's too late to change anything. The genie has been let out of the bottle."

"Dr. Flash why don't you start from the beginning?" asks Hill.

He looks at her briefly then back at Troy.

"Three years ago, I was approached by Chad Brooks to head his biogenetics division. He told me that he agreed with my hypothesis and believed that by using the right type of genetic engineering we could help nature reset itself. He told me he had a plan to fix the planet. He showed me some of his notes and really had me sold. But after a while I found out what his real plans were."

The waitress comes over with a basket of warm rolls and a pitcher of water, "Are you ready to order?" She is a Latina woman, slender with her hair in a ponytail. She has a defeated stoop to her shoulders and beneath the veneer of forced cheeriness; there is an undercurrent of loss and sadness.

Maxwell tells her, "Can you give us a minute more?"

"No problem. I'll be back in a moment," she walks off with a slow, almost dazed gait so unlike the unusual brisk bustle that characterizes the staff here.

Maxwell continues his story.

"I was working with a team on the creation of fast growing tropical trees. We planned to reseed the rain forests with this new variation of trees to replace the millions of acres that have been lost due to deforestation."

Troy interrupts, "Wow, that's a great idea. How far did you get?"

"Oh we were very successful but that wasn't the problem. During my research I stumbled upon a series of documents that changed everything. I have them here for you to look over," he hands over the large folder to Troy and continues.

"In these documents you'll find what I found. SF-20 was never a growth hormone or a food additive. It's a virus! A super genetically engineered virus that can rearrange DNA. That's why it's been able to spread so rapidly. Chad directly oversaw its development."

Troy with a look of surprise says, "A genetically engineered virus?"

"Yes and that's not all. The virus was released on purpose. The whole incident in Brazil was staged to divert attention away from what Gen X Tech was doing."

"I don't understand. Why would Brooks create a virus like this and release it on purpose? I don't get it?" exclaims Daily.

"It was part of his plan."

"What plan is that?" asks Brad.

"To recreate the world in his image."

"What?" shouts Hill, "what do you mean in his image?"

"Chad Brooks has been affected by his own intelligence and success. The ability to create and change life has gone to his head. He's suffering from a God complex. He really believes that only he can change the world and he's even convinced others. He feels that Homo sapiens have outlived their usefulness on this planet and we should make way for the next species of man. He calls it Provectus Homo Eximius Sapiens or Advanced Super Humans."

Troy looks puzzled, "What the Hell are you talking about?"

"Genetically engineered humans. He has a small army of them already at the main headquarters out on Long Island. They're getting ready to move to New Eden as we speak. He's even gone so far as to kidnap scientists from around the world. Some are forced to work for him while the others were abducted for their DNA. That's what he is using to create his new race of super humans that will only follow his bidding and believe me when I tell you that he has the technology to do it. He's even done some testing on himself!"

"He experimented on himself? This is crazy!" says Troy as he shakes his head in disbelief.

"This New Eden, We've heard of that before. What exactly is it?" asks Daily.

"A large biosphere in Antarctica."

"What!" exclaims Troy as the other members look at each other in amazement.

"I've heard the term biosphere before but please remind me of exactly what it means," asks Hill.

Flash explains, "A biosphere is a self-sustained closed structure. It mimics the way earth supports life. Inside it creates its own oxygen, water and food without any interference from outside. Once sealed, it is completely cut off from the outside world. The biosphere that Gen X Tech has constructed is twice the size of the experimental one built in the 90's. This one is about the size of six football fields! In it Chad, Lloyd and the rest of his followers are planning to wait out the storm they've created. According to the data I've found the structure can sustain over a hundred people for at least fifty years."

"So you mean they can stay hold up inside this thing for fifty years while the rest of the planet goes to shit?" says Daily.

"That's about the size of it," answers Flash.

Brad sitting there with a mystified look on his face says in a solemn voice, "Hold on a second let's back this up a bit. Now I may not be a scientist but there are a few things that don't make sense to me."

Flash nods and says, "Go ahead, Officer Williams."

"The thing I don't understand is why SF-20? Why affect nature like this? Won't he have the same problems if not more waiting for him when he comes out of this biosphere?"

"Well he feels that by the time he emerges, his master race will be smart enough and strong enough to overcome any threat and reclaim the earth."

Hill slams her hand down on the table, "So we have to shut this bastard down now! Stop the production of SF-20 and end this thing."

Dr. Flash takes a deep breath and looks at Hill with a sorrowful expression, "Agent Hill, I don't think you fully understand. SF-20 is already loose. It's an intelligent, evolving virus. It's designed to mutate and replicate itself exponentially. In other words, what you have witnessed is only the tip of the iceberg. Things are about to get worse in a very short period of time."

His words cut through the entire group. The look of shock could be seen on their faces as they sit there silently staring at Flash.

Hill turns to Daily then back to Flash, "What can we do?" she says in a quiet defeated voice.

"Honestly, I don't know," replies Flash.

Troy looks around and says, "I think if we all put our heads together we could come up with a solution. I'm sure Dr. Flash will help, won't you doctor?"

"As much as I can. Lately they've had me on a short leash. I have to be careful because they sometimes follow me."

"Why don't you just come with us? We'll protect you," adds Daily.

"Yeah, that's right come with us," comments Troy.

"I don't know. I have to be careful. They've even threatened my family. I'm taking a big chance even meeting with you today. The only thing that helped was martial law. It made it easier for me to slip out without them noticing."

Just then the waitress returns, and there's very little of her faux cheer remaining. "Is everyone ready now?"

Maxwell reaches across the table for a menu, "You know what after all of this, I think I could go for something light. Let me see what you have."

He picks up the menu and begins reading it as other members at the table slowly follow his lead and pick up theirs.

"I'll have a turkey club sandwich with mustard, and a coke," says Maxwell.

The waitress jots down his order and then begins collecting the rest of the orders beginning with Troy. As Troy and Hill tell the waitress what they want to eat, Daily notices something in the corner of his eye as he is reading his menu. He glances up at Dr. Flash. The doctor is focused on buttering one of the rolls that the sad waitress had brought them. Daily notices that a small red dot is slowly moving across Dr. Flash's forehead. A rush of adrenaline surges through Daily as he realizes the significance of the dot. In the very instant that his muscles flex in an attempt to lunge for the doctor, a faint sound of cracking glass could be heard from behind him and a bullet audibly whizzes past Hill's cheek with a sharp whiff of air. Before Daily can reach the doctor, a red hole the size of a quarter instantly appears on Flash's forehead and a split second later the back of his head explodes, sending chunks of brain matter, red flesh and hair all over diners sitting behind him. His head snaps backward from the force of the shot, his eyes still open, butter knife and roll still clutched in his hands. The waitress standing by his side, splattered in blood and brains, drops her pad, inhales deeply and screams at the top of her lungs. Everyone in the restaurant ducks down to the floor. Hill, Brad and Daily instinctively draw their weapons, get low and scramble to the other side of the table where Dr. Maxwell's blood has begun to pool and drip off of its surface. From their new vantage point, they peer toward the broken window to locate the assailant, gun muzzles pointed up and out. Suddenly Dr. Maxwell's convulsing body goes limp. He slowly slumps forward in his seat. His head slams face first onto the plate in front of him with a sickening thump exposing a large, gaping exit wound where the back of his head used to be.

Diners are screaming and tripping over one another as they run hysterically towards the exits. The maître d' has fled to the kitchen along with other wait staff but the waitress just stands there, alternately screaming and gulping air. Troy, practically squatting, scrambles over to the waitress and pulls her to the floor. As he covers her with his body, she calms a bit, sobbing deeply as she weeps and murmurs incoherently. Daily crawls over to his side, gun still drawn.

"Contact Agent Murphy in the Van! Tell him what's going on," he shouts.

Troy yells into the microphone in his lapel while the still shaking waitress grips his chest and cries uncontrollably, "Murphy do you hear me? There's a sniper across the street. They killed Dr. Flash. We need help now!"

A few seconds later the screech of tires could be heard from the street below and armed FBI agents could be seen exiting vans and rushing into the building across from the restaurant. Daily, Hill and Brad slowly stand up and step to the window. The three law enforcement officers look up and scan the roof of the building directly across the street. All they could see are FBI agents, police and military personnel combing the roof top.

Murphy rushes up the stairs of the restaurant with four other FBI agents, all with guns drawn. Behind them two emergency medical officers run in as well. Murphy runs over to the murder scene and stops behind Flash's body and just stares down in disbelief.

The medical officers kneel beside the still shaking waitress and pry her hands from Troy's jacket. "She'll be fine. She's just in shock. We'll run her over to St. Luke's just to be sure," one of them says as they help the young woman up.

Murphy still standing there staring at the back of Flash's head says, "What the hell happened? Why was he shot?"

Brad walks over slowly and says, "Well someone didn't want him talking and I think we all know who that someone is."

"Chad Brooks!" answers Hill as she continues to look out of the window. She turns and walks over to Brad and Murphy, "And we're going to bring that son-of-a-bitch down!"

Murphy is taken aback by the vehemence of her words but quickly recovers, "You're talking about a very powerful man who hasn't been seen in a very long time."

Hill frowns, "You heard what he is up to. I don't care what it takes--this bastard has to pay!"

One of the agents that came up with Murphy hands him a radio. Murphy listens for a minute or so then turns to Brad and Hill, "They found something across the street I think you might want to come check it out."

Daily, overhearing the comment from the window turns around, holsters his gun and says, "Damn right we want to be there. Let's get moving." Hill puts her gun away too. Daily passes Troy who is still sitting on the floor holding Dr. Flash's folder. Daily reaches down and helps Troy to his feet and dusts off his jacket. "You alright, kid?" he says in a low voice as the team heads down the stairs toward the street.

Troy replies, "I guess it'll hit me later. I've never been shot at before. I feel like I should be pissing my pants, but I'm not scared at all."

Daily pats him on the back, "Just the same, stay behind me."

"No Prob!"

Murphy leads the team across the street and into the B.B. King Night Club. From there they all take an elevator up to the fourth floor. Waiting for them are some military soldiers. These men lead them onto the roof were they find propped against the ledge of the roof a large sinister looking weapon. It's a beige-colored rifle about three feet long with a high tech scope attached.

Brad kneels down to inspect the weapon being careful not to touch it. "I know my rifles but I've never seen this type before. It's definitely a sniper rifle but it looks like its semi automatic. Most sniper rifles are blot action."

One of the soldiers who led the team to the roof steps forward and says, "Excuse me sir. But I know that model. Our army snipers use it."

Hill walks over to the young man, "Are you sure, soldier?"

"Yes ma'am. That's a M110. It's one of the newest most sophisticated sniper rifles made."

She smiles at the solider then turns to Brad, "A high powered military weapon? Who do you think has the clout to get their hands on one of those?"

"Brooks" says Brad as he stands up near the rifle, "and I bet there's no trace of the gunman."

"My men swept the whole area sir. There was no one here when we arrived," adds the soldier.

Troy stands near the ledge of the roof and looks down over 42nd Street, "What do we do now?"

"We continue with our plan," responds Hill, "we go over there this afternoon and serve them the search warrant!"

"And don't forget we're raiding their Long Island headquarters at the same time," adds Daily.

"What about what Dr. Flash said about that army of super men out there?" says Brad.

Daily looks at Brad with a surprised expression, "You really think there's an army of genetically engineered super men. I mean, is that really possible?"

Troy interrupts, "I hate to tell you this, but it is."

Everyone stops and just stares at the young man.

Troy continues in a stern voice, "That's right. It's possible and I think if Dr. Flash said that's what Brooks created then I think we better prepare for it."

"What time is your raid planned for?" asks Murphy.

"In about two hours," answers Brad.

"Well you have some time. Maybe you might want to consider bringing some reinforcements along with you. My men can clean up here. I'll inform you if there are any developments," comments Murphy.

"Thanks, your right it's better safe than sorry," says Hill, "why don't we regroup at the hotel?"

"Fine by me," says Daily as he and the others head down to the street and back to the Marriott.

Once back at the hotel they meet in Troy's suite. While there they inform Professor Hamilton of the new developments. Troy sends Dr. Flash's folder of evidence back to Andrews Air force base for analysis by Dr. Hinds and the rest of the team. Brad, Hill and Daily prepare for the raid on the Manhattan offices of Gen X Technologies, Inc. Their new plan is to go in with the assistance of Special Forces personnel out of Fort Dix. The staff at Gen X is expecting the team to arrive to conduct an interview with their director of public relations, Jorge Torres. They know nothing about the plan to seize records and information from the company's computer systems and records room.

At 2:30 pm Daily, Hill, Brad and Troy enter a Humvee in front of the Marriott. Behind them are five more Humvees carrying thirty members of the Delta Squad Green Berets. The entire caravan speeds off toward the Manhattan offices of Gen X Tech.

Located on the corner of East 56th Street and New York's posh Madison Ave is the towering ninety story high tech marble and steel monolith known as Gen X Towers, the Manhattan offices of the world's largest biotechnology company Generation X Technologies, Incorporated. It's a beautiful building that starts off wider at the base and then progressively gets smaller in a spiraling pattern as it rises up into the sky. The front entrance sits behind a rotating two story metal sculpture of the DNA double helix. It sits in the middle of a large marble pool of water surrounded by fountains that spray water towards the center of the pool. Near the base of the helix is a large steel sign that reads; GEN-X-TOWERS. At night the entire pool is lit by colored underwater lights. The building not only serves as the New York base of operations for the company, but it also houses several research labs and is the main office of Lloyd Richardson, COO and co-founder of Gen X Tech. Most of the company's sensitive research however is done at their Long Island Headquarters.

The plan the team devised is as follows: first one group, along with Troy, will advance to the building's sub level and gain access to their computer main frame. Once there they can disable the buildings security and communications systems and begin downloading any important data they can find. Another group will ascend quickly to the 60th floor were Richardson's and Torres' offices are located. Once they are on the floor they are to locate and secure the records room. A third group will remain in the lobby of the building keeping that secure and preventing anyone from leaving with sensitive information.

At around 2:50 the team arrives at Gen X Towers. Quickly Delta Squad exit their vehicles and storm the lobby, overpowering security officers and preventing them from sounding any alarms. Troy along with ten members of Delta Squad make their way down two levels to the building's main computer room. Upon exiting the elevators their group is met by four armed security officers. The officers open fire on the Squad but are easily dispatched. After entering the computer room Troy connects his laptop to the building's mainframe and initiates a shutdown of all communications systems, security cameras and alarms. He then begins downloading all information pertaining to SF-20.

After receiving the signal from Troy that the security systems are down, the second team which includes Brad, Hill and Daily as well members of Delta Squad proceeds up to the 60th floor via the building's high speed elevators. Once on the floor they rapidly subdue all of the security staff that they encounter. The team then rounds up all of the staff and herds them into a small conference room. Brad, Hill and Daily find the records room and begin packing boxes of files they believe relate to SF-20.

After about twenty minutes four members of the Delta Squad escort two well dressed gentlemen into the records room.

"Agent Hill, here are the two men you requested," announces one of the soldiers.

One of the men is a tall thin man of Hispanic origin with a receding hair line who looks to be in his mid forties. Hill recognizes him from their files as Jorge Torres, the director of public relations. The other is an older average height clean shaven Caucasian with short jet black hair and narrow set eyes. He has an air of arrogance about him as he stands there glaring at Hill and her team. She recognizes this man also; he's Lloyd Richardson, co-founder of Gen X Tech!

Hill approaches the men in a very authoritative manner, "Take a seat," she demands.

The men just stand there and stare at her.

"I said take a seat!" she demands pointing to two chairs in front of her.

The two reluctantly pull up chairs and sit down.

"What's the meaning of this? What's with all the rough stuff?" argues Jorge Torres.

"Well here's the bottom line, gentlemen. We're shutting this company down and we're demanding that you turn over all information on the engineered virus SF-20!"

Richardson snarls, "This is crazy. You don't have any authority to close us. I want to speak to my lawyers, you're violating so many of our rights you'll be lucky if they allow you to write parking tickets when we're done with you," he stands up and attempts to leave.

"Sit your ass down, mister!" yells Hill. Richardson stops in his tracks and stares at her with a look of annoyance.

"I said sit down," she shouts as she walks up to him and stares him in the eyes.

Richardson slowly returns to his seat as Hill walks around him waving the warrant in the air.

"This and the President of the United States gives me the authority mister," she stops in front of him, "I guess you haven't noticed that the country is under martial law. This is now a matter of national security."

Richardson just glares at Hill while Torres nervously glances over at Richardson.

Hill continues, "We have information that Gen X Tech created and released a dangerous virus that's responsible for hundreds of thousands of deaths."

"What?" exclaims Torres.

"You do remember the city of Phoenix, Arizona don't you?"

Torres just lowers his head and remains quiet.

"In the eyes of the government that reads as an act of terrorism; so you see, as a terrorist you have no rights."

Richardson rolls his eyes, "This is ridiculous! You'll never make any of this stick! It's already been established that the release of SF-20 was an industrial accident. We've been cleared of any wrong doing. This is all nonsense. There isn't anything that connects us with any of those tragic events."

Daily then steps forward, "Oh no? I bet that when we're finished going through all of these records and the ones we'll find at your Long Island headquarters we'll find evidence that its release was intentional. That along with Dr. Maxwell Flash's testimony is all we need."

Richardson smiles and chuckles, "Flash?" He chuckles darkly. "I don't think you'll be getting much out of him."

Hill continues with a sly grin, "Sorry to burst your bubble but he had already talked before he was killed. Looks like your gunman was too late."

"I don't know what you're talking about."

"Sure you don't," says Hill.

Torres looks up with a look of surprise, "Dr. Flash is dead?"

Brad sensing some anxiety in Torres approaches the man and stands over him, "That's right, Dead! So that's a murder charge to add along with domestic terrorism. You know what the penalty is for that during martial law?"

Torres with sweat pouring down his forehead shakes his head, "No."

"It's death!" whispers Brad into Torres' ear.

"Death?" shouts Torres with a look of terror.

"They're just trying to scare you," says Richardson.

"But I don't know anything! I don't have anything to do with any terrorism. I'm only the director of public relations for God sake. I don't know anything," Torres pleads.

Brad continues to press Torres, "Nothing at all? You mean to tell me that you had no idea that this company was behind all of the biological mutations running all over the country? You knew nothing about that at all huh?"

"I mean, all I know is…"

"Keep your fucking mouth closed, you asshole," interrupts Richardson, "Don't say another word until the company's lawyers get here."

"Oh they won't be coming. I told you terrorists have no rights," exclaims Hill nodding her head and smiling.

Torres trembling and dripping in sweat pleads to Hill, "I'm no terrorist! All I know is that they told me that my family would be saved."

"Shut up, you idiot!" shouts Richardson.

"Quiet," snaps Brad, "Go ahead. Saved from what?"

"I don't know. All I was told was to give you guys the run-around and my family would be saved with the others."

"What do you mean?" asks Daily.

"New Eden. They would send us to New Eden to be safe."

Hill with her arms crossed looks down at Torres and says, "Really? Is that where Brooks is hiding out?"

"I think so. Nobody's seen him in a while."

Richardson, steaming with anger glares at Torres with a vile expression, "You fool! They have nothing. They're grasping at straws and you're groveling like a frightened child. You're not worthy to be saved."

His final statement catches the attention of all three team members.

Richardson continues to rant on, "You have nothing! You can't prove a damn thing! You've got squat!"

Hill leans in toward him, "What we have is that you knew what SF-20 could do and made plans to save your own asses while the rest of us get eaten alive. That's what we have. But now your little plot is busted," she steps away from him, grabs a chair then sits in front of him, "so why don't you just cooperate with us and tell us how to stop the virus from spreading."

Richardson laughs, "You fools you can't stop it. You're too late. It's going keep on evolving, changing our world for the better! Very soon nature will overrun mankind and only the chosen will remain."

"This guy's fucking nuts!" states Brad.

Hill slides her chair a little closer, "You're missing one important thing in your big scheme. We have you prisoner right here, right now. You won't be able to meet up with your buddy Brooks. You get to watch all of the fireworks right here with the rest of us," says Hill with a grin.

"You think I care? It doesn't matter what happens to us as long as the Earth is saved from man's destruction."

Brad smiles and points to Torres, "You think he feels the same way?"

Torres yells, "Hell no I don't. Listen I swear to you. I don't know anything. Just that something big is going to happen and soon."

"What?" snaps Daily.

"I don't know. I swear to you I don't. But I know something is about to happen."

Richardson smirks, "You're too late. You're all too late," he points to Torres, "he doesn't know anything. It's already begun."

"Okay, I've heard enough," says Hill, "get them out of my sight!"

The four soldiers, who brought the men in walk over, grab Torres and Richardson by their arms and guide them away. While they are being led away Torres continues to cry out, "I tell you I don't know anything! I don't know anything!"

Hill turns to her team members, "We need to hurry and get these records back to the base."

"What do you think is about to happen?" asks Daily.

"I don't know but after all we've seen anything's possible," responds Hill.

Just then a soldier enters the room with a note and hands it to Brad, "Excuse me sir we have a message from Lieutenant Lopez. He's in charge of the Long Island Operation."

Brad quietly reads the note then turns to Hill and Daily, "We need to get out to Long Island now! Check this out," he hands Hill the message.

```
                        Urgent Communiqué

    Time:   15:15 EST


    From:   LT. Miguel Lopez U.S. Delta Squad 2


    To:     EPA INVASION Team


    Resistance is heavier than expected.


    Have sustained 5 casualties.


    Entrance to Gen X headquarters blocked. Island is secured but
    unable to gain entry.


    Awaiting orders.
```

"Looks like they're having some real problems out there," says Daily as he reads over her shoulder.

Hill holding the message looks at the soldier who bought it in, "How fast can we get out there?"

"Your birds are already fueled and ready, ma'am. They're waiting on the great lawn of Central Park. We could be at the site in forty-five."

"That's great. How is it that you were so prepared?" asks Hill.

"We get our orders directly from Andrews, ma'am," responds the soldier.

"Hamilton!" says Brad nodding his head. The other members smile and nod in agreement.

"Get someone to finish up here. Contact the lieutenant and let him know we're on our way," orders Hill.

"Already taken care of, ma'am," reports the soldier.

Brad Daily and Hill head downstairs pick up Troy and rush towards Central Park, filling in Troy along the way. When they arrive at the park they are greeted by three idling V-22 Ospreys packed with armed members of Delta Squad. They pile into one of the crafts and immediately liftoff and head out towards the end of Long Island were Gen X Tech has their base of operations.

The main headquarters of Gen X Tech is located about a hundred miles east of New York City in Suffolk County on a 3,300 acre private piece of land named Gardiners Island which is a small island sandwiched between two peninsulas at the eastern end of Long Island. It's six miles long, three miles wide and was owned by the same family for nearly 300 years until it was mysteriously sold to Gen X Tech. On the island they have their own airstrip, harbor and a six story 400,000 square foot building which serves as their main base of operations and primary research center. The island, the largest privately owned island in the United States, has the largest stand of white oak in the Northeast. Along with the oak there are over 1,000 acres of forest filled with swamp maple, wild cherry and birch. The island is also home to New York State's largest colony of ospreys. This is one of the few places in the world where these birds can build their nests on the ground, because there are no natural predators to the osprey on the island. It's a fact that becomes even more ironic as a large flock of the birds gracefully take off to make room for the planes carrying their namesake.

The three V-22 Ospreys hover for a moment over the Gen X Tech airfield then touch down gently next to the four army UH-60 Blackhawk helicopters the first team of Delta Squad came in on. After they touch down and lower their ramps Troy, Brad, Hill and

Daily exit along with sixty fully armed members of Delta Squad. They are met on the tarmac by Lieutenant Miguel Lopez and four soldiers from his group. As they approach Hill scans the Lieutenant and immediately notices his large attractive brown eyes and crew cut jet black hair which has an oily shine to it. This well proportioned athletic Lieutenant is thirty-years-old but carries himself with the authority of a man much older. His sleeves are rolled up revealing a tattoo on his right forearm of the Delta Force emblem which is a sword overlaid by a triangle-shaped thunderbolt. He stands about six feet and has a pleasant yet dependable air about him.

Lopez approaches Hill and salutes.

"Agent Hill?"

"Lieutenant Lopez. It's a pleasure to finally meet you. What's the situation?" asks Hill as they all walk together towards the front of the main building.

"We have the building totally surrounded. When we arrived the airfield was already empty. According to some nearby fishermen about ten planes took off from here early this morning. We secured all of the rear and side exits then stormed the main entrance. That's when we were attacked by about twenty heavily armed security personnel."

"They attacked you?"

"Yes and that's not all. These are not ordinary security guards."

"What do you mean?"

"We were only able to take down two of them after losing five of our own."

"You're kidding. I mean aren't you guys suppose to be the best?" asks Troy innocently.

Lopez shoots Troy a look of irritation then continues, "Their bodies are in that tent up ahead. When you see them you'll understand what I mean."

After a short walk from the airfield the group arrives at a makeshift command center constructed from a number of army tents. The lieutenant leads the four into one of the tents. It's a medical tent and inside lying on cots are the bodies of the two Gen X Tech security officers. Each body is in a closed black body bag.

Lopez walks over to the head of one of the bodies while the rest of the team circles around the cot. Lopez unzips the bag to reveal the body inside. Troy, Brad and Daily stare in amazement at the figure below them as Hill stands with her mouth open in a state of shock.

"You see what I mean? This is no ordinary security officer. Hell, I don't think it's even human."

Lying before them is what appears to be the body of a human male about six feet tall and weighing about two hundred plus pounds. He's bald and has grayish skin that appears to be covered in leathery scales. His body has the muscular build of a body builder, huge chest, massive arms and thick neck. There are about ten bullet holes in the man's chest and two in his forehead.

"Take a look at this," says Lopez as he pries open one of the eye lids. What is revealed is a large yellow eye with a large brown cat like pupil.

"What the hell is this?" remarks Daily.

"Incredible!" utters Troy as he studies the body with wonderment.

Lopez explains, "I had the docs do an autopsy on the other one. They say the skin is three times thicker than ours; its heart is surrounded by a strong thick bony cage that can stop a bullet, and its blood is unlike anything they have ever seen before. And I'll tell you one thing that I've witnessed myself; these things are strong and fast as hell. It took a sharp shooter using armor piercing shells and two headshots to kill this one. There's one more thing we've found. Take a look at this," he turns the head of the dead solider so that the side of his neck is completely exposed. The team looks down and observes four slits down the side of the neck.

"Looks like gills," states Troy.

Lopez looks up, "That's just what the doctors said. They said they're just like the ones found on fish."

"So these guys can live both on the land as well as underwater? Fascinating!" says Troy.

Hill sighs and scratches her head as she walks around the cot examining the body, "How many of these things did you say there were?"

"We counted about twenty, but there maybe more. They had advanced outside a short distance then retreated back inside. They were all heavily armed. This one had a minigun."

"A what?" asks Hill.

"A minigun. Probably the most powerful machine gun around, there it is over there," he points to a mass of metal on the ground near the other body. The team looks over to find a multi barreled cannon attached to a chain of large bullets.

"Jesus!" exclaims Hill.

"Yeah, one of those can mow down an entire platoon in seconds. They fire around 6000 rounds a minute! The rest of them had these," he holds up an exotic space age looking rifle about two feet long with smooth curves.

"What is that?" asks Brad.

"Same thing I wanted to know. I had to look it up to find that out." Lopez rotates the weapon around so that the team can get a better look at it, "This is a Belgian FN F2000. It's a 5.56mm high tech modular bullpup assault rifle. These things haven't even been in production that long. From what we have been able to tell those things in there are not only stronger and faster than us but they are armed with some of the most powerful and sophisticated weapons around!"

"Provectus Homo Eximius Sapiens," mutters Troy.

Hill, Daily and Brad snap their heads around and stare at him.

Troy stares back and says, "You remember what Dr. Flash said? Genetically engineered humans; he said there was a small army of them out here."

"How many men do you have, Lieutenant?" asks Hill.

"I have about forty-five men."

"And we brought along sixty," says Brad.

"So we have over a hundred men but we have no way of knowing how many of these are inside," states Hill.

"Don't forget there may be civilian workers in there as well," adds Daily.

"It's starting to get late. I'd like to wrap this up as quickly as possible. There's information in that building that we need to have access to," says Hill.

Lopez puts down the weapon and places his hands on his hips, "Well with the added troops we should be able to breach more than one entrance at the same time. That would force them to split their resources in order to defend them. That'll give us an advantage."

"Okay, let's make it happen," exclaims Hill.

"Yes ma'am," replies Lopez as he salutes and hurries out of the tent while giving orders to his men through his radio.

After about a half-hour all of the soldiers are positioned at four of the buildings entrances. At the lieutenant's signal they all cautiously move in with weapons ready. Room by room and floor by floor the soldiers move clearing each area of the building section by section.

Hill, Brad and Daily, all armed with M16's, join Lieutenant Lopez's group positioned at the main entrance. On Lopez's signal two of his men throw concussion grenades through the entrance and into the reception area of the building. Immediately, his soldiers rush into the building with weapons at the ready. They fan out along the sides of the large reception area. They move steadily, but cautiously, taking positions behind columns and seats as the ceiling lights, damaged by the concussion grenades, swing back and forth flickering and sparking, casting eerie shadows throughout the area. Three soldiers slowly approach the reception desk about fifty feet from the main entrance when suddenly two super soldiers pop up from behind the desk and begin spraying the room with automatic weapons fire. Two of Lopez's soldiers are hit immediately and fall to the floor mortally wounded as the rest of the group dives for cover. The third Special Forces soldier expertly hits the ground, rolls over and empties an entire clip of ammo into one of the super soldiers. The creature, his chest bloodied and riddled with bullet holes, leaps over the reception desk and onto the fallen soldier. He stands over him and raises his weapon to fire at point blank range. At that moment the entire squad opens fire causing the genetically altered beast's flesh to tear apart as the rounds strike his body. He stumbles backward then finally falls with a thump against the desk from which he'd jump over. The other super soldier, still behind the desk meets a similar fate as Lopez's men turn their weapons on him.

Four more of the gray skinned super soldiers appear from an exit on the left side of the reception desk and open fire on the invaders. Brad slides behind a large sofa like seat while Hill and Daily hold their ground behind two columns just inside the entrance. Lopez, kneeling behind the same seat as Brad instantly returns fire as does his men.

It takes a full hour for Delta squad to clear the Gen X Tech facility. By the time they finished twenty five of their comrades lie dead and ten more badly wounded and all together twenty three Gen X Tech super soldiers are killed. Over a hundred workers are led out of the building and flown away to a military debriefing site. Brad, Hill, Troy and Daily move in after the all clear is given. They immediately head for the building's main information center. This is a room on the sixth floor where all the records are kept and where access to the company's main frame can be found. It is a large circular room about one hundred feet across and ringed with monitors and equipment. Troy wastes no time in linking up his laptop to their system to download any important data. He searches the monitors in the room as streams of information flash on and off of the screens. Suddenly he stops at one display and shouts, "Hey check this out!"

The other members run over and lean over his shoulder for a better view.

"What'cha got Troy?" asks Daily.

"According to this Chad Brooks along with most of his staff are already at New Eden. The last of them left this morning. They're stopping off at Puerto Montt in Chile before leaving for Antarctica," he begins typing on the keyboard in front of the monitor, "It looks like they've erased most of the important stuff and took it with them. If we're going to have any chance at stopping this we're going to have to go to the South Pole."

"Great, just great!" says Brad while scratching his head.

Suddenly the sound of an alarm breaks their attention. The monitor that Troy is sitting in front of comes alive and the image of a pale-skinned man appears on the screen. He looks to be in his early fifties with long white hair and a clean shaven narrow face. He has deep set dark eyes and a big smile. The team members are startled by the image and kneel to get a better view. As they watch the image speaks and the audio is transmitted through the room's intercom system.

"Good evening! I believe I am the one you're looking for. I'm Chad Brooks but I'm afraid you're much too late. The rebirth of Earth has already begun," he smiles and then laughs, "I hope you all have enjoyed my creations. They're the first prototypes of the new Adam that will repopulate the earth. Beautiful, aren't they?"

"Is he talking about those gray-skinned hulks we just tangled with?" asks Daily.

"I think so," answers Troy.

"Yes, they're the soldiers of the future. Immune to any disease, strong and obedient," replies Brooks.

Daily jumps back from the monitor and looks around the room, "He can hear me?" he shouts.

"And see you," says Brooks, "I would like to take this time to invite you to join me."

"Join you?" states Daily.

"Not you," says Brooks as he points toward the group, "you Mr. Phillip."

Everyone stops and stares at Troy for a moment.

"Me?" asks Troy.

"Yes, why don't you join us here and witness the birth of a new world."

"How can he see and hear us?" whispers Hill.

"He must be tapped into the building's security systems," responds Troy under his breath.

"And he knows your name," adds Brad.

"Oh I know all of you Officer Williams. I know you, your wife, FBI Agents Debra Hill and Clarence Daily and even your grandfather Professor Hamilton. I know all of you."

"What do you want from me?" inquires Troy.

"Your intellect, Mr. Phillip. I've known about you for a very long time. You have an exceptional mind and would make a great addition to our new Garden of Eden."

"You have to be kidding!" says Troy.

"No, not at all. I've been trying to recruit you for years now. Haven't you heard of the Academy of New Minds?"

"That was your group?" exclaims Troy.

Hill with a look of irritation on her face steps closer to the monitor, "Alright enough of this shit! If you know us then you know we're coming after you to put a stop to all of this," she shouts, "we know where you are Brooks and we're on our way."

"I wouldn't advise that, Ms. Hill. New Eden is not just a sanctuary--it's also a fortress. If you check the records I left behind for you to find you will notice that we are very well defended. Any attempt to raid this building will be met with extreme and deadly force. We have the latest in weaponry and can repel any invaders."

Troy slides over to another monitor and begins typing. A few seconds later a list of items appears on the screen.

"Check this out," he says. The members glance over to read the list along with Troy, "he has SA-2 Guideline surface to air missiles, Stingers, Jesus he has enough military gear to repel a small army."

Brooks then says, "Besides, even if you could reach me there's nothing I could do. What has been done is irreversible. The virus is mutating own its own. It can't be stopped not even by me."

"Brooks don't you know that hundreds of thousands of people will die if we don't find a way to reverse what you've done!" says Daily.

Brooks responds, "For hundreds of years man has exterminated species, polluted the water, indiscriminately chopped down the planet's precious rain forests and poisoned the air. How many species do you think were killed by man? Don't you think it's nature's turn to flourish?" he snorts condescendingly, "a hundred thousand? Really, you have such a small mind, Agent Daily. I'm hoping that billions are destroyed in order that Earth will have a chance!"

Daily's eyes widen, "He's a fucking lunatic!"

"Who the hell are you to decide the fate of earth?" shouts Hill.

"Why not me? I have been given a sign that it is my destiny to save this world, to give it another chance, to rebuild it, to reshape it."

"To reshape it how, in your image?" asks Hill.

Brooks smiles, "Why not. I have the means and the intellect. Why shouldn't I decide the direction for this planet?"

"You're crazy. You're fucking crazy," shouts Daily.

Brooks' eyes narrow as he glares back at the team, "Am I? I will tell you this; you have only a few days left of earth as you now know it. So enjoy it while you can."

"What is about to happen?" demands Hill.

"It has already begun and soon it will all be over. Goodbye, ladies and gentlemen. You've been warned."

The monitor goes blank and the room grows silent. The team members quietly stand there is a state of shock for what seems like an eternity. Suddenly Lopez bursts into the room out of breath and shattering the silence. Everyone spins around and stares at the hyperventilating soldier.

After pausing for a moment to catch his breath Lopez responds, "Excuse me, but I have orders to evac you back to Andrews immediately!"

"What's going on?" asks Daily.

"We haven't finished downloading the data off the main frame," comments Troy.

Lopez remarks, "I'm sorry, sir. I have my orders. This is an emergency situation. There's been a series of events across the country. New York has been deemed too dangerous at the moment. You are to accompany us back to Andrews. My men will remain here and continue the download. Now I must ask you to follow me now, your plane is waiting."

The team members stop what they are doing and quickly follow the lieutenant along with four other soldiers out of the building and onto the airfield where their V-22 Osprey is waiting with engines running.

During the flight each member is quietly immersed in their own thoughts, thoughts about their fate and the fate of the rest of the planet, thoughts about survival. Eventually all of their thoughts arrive at the same two questions: what is about to happen next and can they prevent it?

The Birds
and the Bees

It's two days after the raid on Gen X Tech. The team has been pulled back to Andrews Air force base as the nation erupts into chaos. During this time packs of cat-sized rats invade New York City. Hordes of the creatures sweep into apartment buildings attacking and killing hundreds of people across the city. Huge colonies of mutated Brown Bats swooped down on the residents of Santé Fe, New Mexico, spreading a new and deadlier strain of rabies. Hundreds of Ravens attack and kill several hikers in Wyoming's Yellowstone National Park. In Florida after a temporary lifting of martial law, thousands of oversized seagulls descended upon Disneyland vacationers, sending hundreds to area hospitals. There was even another attack of Humboldt Squids off the shores of California's Muir Beach and in Alabama a swarm of golf ball sized mutated killer bees form a thick black mile wide cloud over Tuscaloosa.

To make matters worst, the radio and television stations are jammed with religious fanatics claiming that this is Armageddon or God's wrath for man's spoiling of the planet. They even read bible verses over the air to validate that these events were prophesied and that the End of Days is here.

Panic spreads as scattered reports of looting and rioting come in from all over the country. The armed forces are spread thin and can barely keep the peace. The news from the rest of the world is just as grim. Most of Europe is now in flames as hysteria sweeps across the continent. There is unrest throughout Asia, and most of Africa as herds of mutant beasts stampede through the cities injuring and killing hundreds of thousands. The news from around the globe only helps feed the fears of an already frightened nation. In a desperate move to calm tensions, the President orders a complete media blackout. All news concerning SF-20 events must first be cleared through the government.

It's now five o'clock in the morning and Troy is hurrying down the corridor of the INVASION team dormitories on his way to Professor Hamilton's room. Troy's heart pounds as he recalls the haggard tone of his grandfather's voice during the early morning phone call. He thinks to himself, *"This isn't good. I don't like Pop's tone. He seems almost frightened. I've never heard him sound so vulnerable before,"* Troy turns the final corner then approaches Hamilton's room. He pauses for a moment then knocks on the door.

"Come in," shouts Hamilton from the other side, "it's open!"

As Troy enters the room he notices that all the lights are out except for a lamp on Hamilton's desk. His grandfather is sitting there reading some papers with his glasses hanging on the tip of his nose.

"What's going on, Pop?"

Hamilton looks up over the rim of his glasses and gives Troy the usual look of annoyance he has every time the youngster uses the term Pop. He takes a deep breath, "Come over here and sit down, son," he says as he points to a chair in front of his desk.

"Can we turn some lights on in here? How can you sit in the dark?" complains Troy as he takes a seat.

"The lights are fine, Troy," Hamilton shuffles through some of the papers on his desk then pulls out one of them and lays it down in front of him on the desk, "things are beginning to spiral out of control Troy, and I wanted to talk to you first before I address the rest of the team."

Troy noticing the worried look on Hamilton's face asks, "What's up? What's going on?"

Hamilton picks up the paper from his desk, "Since your visit to New York I've received information that two former Gen X Tech scientists are willing to help us find a solution to halt the effects of SF-20."

Troy sits up in his seat, "That's great!"

Hamilton holds up one of his hands, "Hold on a second. Don't get too excited. There are a few wrinkles."

"Okay, what's the catch?"

"Both of the scientists are in areas that are hard to reach," he reads from the sheet of paper, "one of the scientists is a Dr. Sylvia Barnes a biologist. She's in Birmingham, Alabama right the path of the largest swarm of killer bees ever recorded. The other is Dr. Hyun-Ki Kang a Geneticist. He and his pregnant wife are trapped at his home in Orlando, Florida where there's an onslaught of killer birds."

"Jesus!"

"We could really use their help. So I'm going to send two teams out to bring them back."

"How can I help?"

Hamilton puts the paper down and slowly takes off his glasses. He rubs the bridge of his nose as he takes a deep breath, "Well, son, that's why I called you here," Hamilton leans forward with his arms crossed on the desk, "after you left for New York I started thinking how much of a man you've become," Hamilton leans back in his seat, "you see, I may not be here to see this through Troy."

Troy with a saddened expression, "Pop, you know I hate when you talk like that."

"Listen son, it's okay. I've lived a long and fruitful life. Old age is finally catching up with me. Don't know how long my heart can take it."

Troy's face continues to grow grim as Hamilton continues, "What I'm saying is that I'm counting on you to take charge when the time is right," Troy looks up at him, "do you understand me, son?"

"Yes Pop," he pauses, "I understand."

"It's part of life Troy. We must be strong but we must always be aware of our mortality if we are to survive."

"Yes, sir."

"Now I want you to get the team assembled. We have work to do."

Troy stands up, as does Hamilton, who comes from behind the desk and approaches Troy, "Come here," says Hamilton as he holds his arms open.

Troy walks over to his grandfather and embraces him. As the two men hug each other Hamilton whispers in Troy's ear, "I love you, son. Remember that."

"I love you too, Pop," replies Troy as his eyes well up with tears.

As Troy leaves Hamilton's room he can for the first time comprehend how much of a toll this disaster has taken on his grandfather. This is the man that he's looked up to for strength and guidance. He was almost immortal, indestructible in Troy's eyes but now as Troy walks down the hall he slowly realizes that his grandfather, Professor Richard Hamilton, has become nothing more than a frail old man. A man facing the end of his time on this earth and he's relying on Troy to take his place. He stops and looks back at the Professor's room. A chill sweeps down Troy's spine as he wonders to himself, *Am I really ready for this responsibility?"*

Meanwhile on the other side on the building Hill is also up early. She's on her knees in the bathroom hugging the toilet bowl. This is the fourth time in as many days that she has awakened to extreme nausea and stomach cramps. She briefly mentioned it to Daily one day and he chastised her for not taking care of herself. Hill knows how overprotective he can be and how much he cares for her. She also knows that her poor health could become a distraction for him so she never mentioned the nausea again. Since this whole business began her eating habits have been off and Hill knows that once she's into a case she has to be careful and not neglect herself.

Once a few years ago she was so obsessed with catching a serial killer that she went almost two weeks without sleeping and she barely ate. It was Daily that finally snapped her out of it and that only happened after she fell unconscious during a stakeout. The doctors said she was suffering from low blood sugar and slight malnutrition. From that point on anytime they're on a big case Daily gets on her case reminding her to eat properly and to get lots of rest. But with the magnitude of this case and the pressure placed on the both of them, he hasn't had the time to nag her about her health. So Hill kneels there with her head in the bowl, heaving her guts out till it hurts. After about ten minutes she falls back against the bathroom wall, sweating from her forehead and holding her aching stomach trying desperately to catch her breath. She sits there for awhile on the bathroom floor resting and soon after crawls back into bed and falls asleep.

An hour later there's a knock at her door. When Hill answers it she finds Dr. Hinds standing there with a big bright smile.

"Morning, Deb. I thought we'd catch some breakfast together. The professor wants to meet with us at eight."

"Thanks, I'm glad you came by. I'm so tired I could have slept all day. I had just laid down for a few minutes and dosed off," she steps to the side, "come on in."

Hinds walks in and sits on the end of the bed as Hill sits next to her.

"Jesus Deb, you look like shit!" states Hinds.

"Yeah I know…haven't been sleeping too well lately."

"Really? Is everything alright?"

"I don't know. I've been throwing up, I have constant headaches and been really tired."

"Sounds like fatigue. I tell you what. Before the meeting we'll stop by my lab and I'll run a couple of tests."

"You can't tell Clarence! It'll just worry him."

"Don't worry, it'll be between us girls. Go ahead--get dressed so we have time to get to the lab. All I need is a few samples of blood. It shouldn't take more than a minute."

Hill smiles, "Thanks, Karen," she takes off her shirt and bra and heads to the bathroom. Hinds continues to sit on the bed near the bathroom door.

"So, how are things going between you two?" she asks.

"Things are great considering what we've been going through. We really haven't had a chance to catch our breath and analyze our relationship. We've just been going with the flow," says Hill from within the bathroom while she washes her face, "You're not going to believe this but when we were in New York, Troy walked in on us."

Hinds gets up from the bed and walks over to the open bathroom door. She stands in the entrance while Hill with her back to Hinds continues to wash up at the sink. Hinds then adds, "Troy walked in on you? How the Hell did that happen?"

"Our schedule has been so hectic that we try to steal some time alone whenever we can. So that night I stayed in Clarence's room. Well, Troy bangs on the door early in the morning then bursts in and sees me laying there."

Hinds Smiles, "Wow! So the cat is out of the bag, huh?"

"Yeah, I guess so."

"How do you feel about that?"

Hill stops washing for a moment and turns to face Hinds while water is still dripping down her nude body, "To tell you the truth, not bad. I mean it was kind of a relief not to hide my feelings around everyone. And you know something, Karen?"

"What's that?"

"I think I really do love that man."

"I told you," says Hinds with a grin.

"Yeah, you did," she says as she grabs a towel from off of the bathroom rack and begins drying herself off.

The two woman laugh as Hill goes back to getting ready for the meeting. After they leave Hill's quarters they head to the lab where Hinds draws two tubes of blood from Hill. She leaves the samples for her assistants with testing instructions attached then the two leave the lab and head across the airfield towards the cafeteria where the meeting is to take place.

Hinds says to Hill as they walk, "They should have the results sometime later today. It's probably nothing but it's better to be safe than sorry."

"I know, you're right. Thanks again, Karen. You know I never did get a chance to thank you for something else."

"What was that?"

"For pushing me to take the first step with Clarence. If I hadn't neither one of us would have let the other know how we really felt. I'm glad I did it. Thanks."

"Love, it's the one thing that separates us from all of the other creatures on this planet. It's just as important as breathing and the opposable thumb," Hinds holds her hands up and wiggles her thumbs as the two women giggle, "we need love to survive, Debra. It's what makes us human and I think during this time of crisis we're going to need love even more than ever. It's maybe the only thing we'll have left to hold on to."

Hinds stops, holds Hill by her arms and smiles, "Listen to me, Deb. Remember when I told you things were going to get bad?"

Hill nods.

"Well, look around sister. It's happening. Hold on to that man of yours, you hear me? You hold on tight."

"I understand, Karen. Believe me, I understand."

"Now let's hurry up and get to the mess hall before the guys eat all the food."

The two women share a brief chuckle then continue on to the cafeteria.

When they arrive the rest of the team is already there seated, eating and conversing with one another. Also present is Professor Hamilton. He's sitting among the others quietly eating a breakfast of bacon and eggs. For the first time in a while Hill really studies his face. She's shocked at how much he seems to have aged. The lines in his face seemed broader than usual and the bags under his eyes appear more pronounced. There even seems to be more gray in his hair than before. He looks tired, worn and haggard. She knows the enormous pressure that he is under and wonders how he must be handling it. A sense of sadness comes over her like a dark cloud as she watches this once strong man appear to be humbled by events beyond his control. She follows Hinds over to the buffet table and wonders to herself what kind of future do any of them have with the way the world is unraveling around them.

Hill and Hinds grab their trays and place a few breakfast items on their plates then join the other members at the table. Hill looks across the table and spots Daily laughing with Troy. As she sits next to Hinds and eats her food, she can't help but to stare at Daily. For all of these years the man of her dreams was right in front of her. She only needed to open her eyes. When Daily turns towards her and catches her staring he winks at her and grows a wide smile across his face. She winks back with a smile of her own.

After acknowledging the arrival of the two women Professor Hamilton taps his glass with a spoon then stands up and says, "Can I have your attention please?"

Everyone quiets down and turns their attention towards Hamilton.

"I know things have been looking grim ladies and gentlemen, and I wish I had some good news to finally tell you. But unfortunately,   I don't. As some of you already know we've been going over all of the data from New York, including the information we got from the late Dr. Flash and it doesn't look good."

"What do you mean, doc?" says Daily.

"According to Dr. Flash's notes, SF-20 is a super virus able to infect just about any living thing and it is still evolving," a low rumble of voices could be heard from the team. "With each evolutionary level it reaches it seems to be able to infect more types of organisms. So far it has the greatest influence on insects but from what we've learned it may soon be able to infect plant life and maybe even humans."

A collective gasp comes from the entire group.

"We do have some promising news. There are two scientists that were part of the Gen X Tech's biogenetics division that have offered to help us. They may have information that can help in putting a stop to this infestation."

Hinds raises her hand.

"Yes Karen?"

"Richard, when can we expect these scientists?"

Hamilton takes off his glasses, folds them close and places them down on the table, "Well that's the problem. We have to go get them. One is in Alabama and the other is in Florida. Two very dangerous hotspots," Hamilton slowly sits down, "people this may be our last hope. The situation has already gone from bad to worse. Along with the outbreaks across the country there have also been increased reports of infectious diseases caused by animal attacks."

"What types of diseases?" asks Forrester.

"There have been reports of wide spread outbreaks of malaria, avian flu, yellow fever and even a new deadlier form of rabies!"

"Oh my God," declares Hill.

"What about going after Brooks at New Eden?" states Brad.

"The armed forces are already spread thin but I was told that the President has sent a small task force to Antarctica to bring Brooks back alive."

"Alive? They should just level the place," says Cooper.

"Based on our Intel there maybe innocent workers and kidnapped scientists at New Eden. So leveling the place as you put it Simon would not be advisable. Chad Brooks is the only one who knows exactly how this virus was created so he is really the only person that can stop this madness."

"What makes you think that he'll cooperate? He's the one responsible for all this!" adds Hill.

"I know he won't cooperate. But I also know that we're still under martial law and American citizens are dying. The President had to do something. The commander of the task force has orders to extract the information from him by any means necessary."

Again the group gasps and whispers amongst themselves.

Hamilton continues, "But our mission is to get those scientists back here safe and sound and begin working on a solution. If we fail then our world as we know it is over. I wish I could be more optimistic but that's where we stand. So all I can do is wish you the best of luck. You ship out in an hour. God speed."

Hamilton raises his glass of orange juice as if to give a toast and the rest of the team follows and raise their glasses up then drink together.

After about a half an hour the team members head for the hangers and prepare to fly out to their destinations. They all head out onto the tarmac towards two C-130 transport planes. Bloomberg, Forrester, Cooper and Troy head to one and Hill,

Daily, Hinds and Brad head to the other. At around nine o'clock the two planes lift off in two different directions. One turns southwest in route to Birmingham, Alabama and the other speeds south on its way to Florida.

After two and a half hours the first plane touches down at Maxwell Air force Base just outside of Montgomery, Alabama. When Troy, Cooper, Bloomberg and Forrester step out of the plane they are met by a tall blonde muscular man with piercing blue eyes and a large scar on his face running from his right eye down his right cheek and ending at the bottom of his jaw. It's an old wound with thick scar tissue which gives him a mean and rugged look. He hurries up to greet the team and salutes as they exit the aircraft. Bloomberg and the others salute back.

"Morning, sirs! Welcome to Alabama. I'm Lieutenant Greene of the 75th Army Ranger Regiment. I have orders to escort you to Birmingham immediately!" reports Greene as he leads them toward a group of four Humvees parked nearby.

"How long will it take us to get there?" asks Bloomberg.

"About an hour sir, but we have to move quickly. The last report we had said that mutant bees were just outside of the city and that was over an hour ago."

"Do you have any idea where Dr. Barnes is?" asks Forrester.

"She's waiting for us at the Samford University Conservatory with some local law enforcement."

The entire group piles into one of the waiting Humvees and they speed off heading north towards Birmingham, Alabama. Along the way Troy takes the opportunity to get some information about the attacking bees.

"Lieutenant, just how bad is the infestation?" Troy asks.

Greene gives Troy a look of a frightened man, "I've been a soldier for a long time and seen a lot of action. Iraq, Afghanistan, Somalia, you name it. I'm a fighting man. It's in my blood. There's not much that fazes me. But what I've seen in the past two days has scared me shitless! These things are huge! Some of them about the size of a baseball and they're vicious. The other day I saw a man stung so many times that his whole body turned blood red and he started foaming at the mouth and bleeding from every part of his body, even his eyes. He just started to shake all over the place and the next thing you know he was dead."

"About how many dead bees do you think there was around him when he died?" queries Troy.

"What?"

"When the man died, how many dead bees were around his body?"

"None. I told you they stung him to death and then flew off"

"Jesus!"

"What is it Troy?" asks Cooper.

"This is just what I was afraid of. It's just like the professor was saying."

"What? What's going on," asks Forrester.

"These bees, they've evolved and in a way that is going to make it even harder to get rid of them."

"Explain," says Bloomberg in a serious tone.

Troy sits up in his seat, "You see when a normal bee stings someone the entire stinger, which is attached to a muscular sack of venom, is ripped out of the bee's body and the insect dies within minutes. These mutants keep their stinger which allows them to sting over and over again making them even more lethal. It's bad enough that they're larger than normal and produce a much more toxic venom."

"Damn this is a fucking nightmare," comments Cooper. He turns to Greene, "Lieutenant, how have you and your men been able to deal with the bees?" asks Cooper.

"The only thing that works for a while is flamethrowers. But if you stand in one place burning them for too long it only makes them madder and eventually they'll get to you. They're smart too. Once you start waving that flame in the air they'll send out a group to distract you while two other another swarms attack from your flanks. You have to have your head on a swivel when you deal with these bugs," remarks Greene.

The four team members each give the soldier a look of concern, then sit back in their seats quietly for the remainder of the trip.

After about an hour they arrive at the gates of Samford University. This private Southern Baptist Convention affiliated university is located in a suburb of Birmingham called Homewood. Dr. Sylvia Barnes has worked there as a researcher in the biological and environmental sciences department for eight years before being hired by Gen X Tech. Founded in 1841, the one hundred and eighty acre campus still maintains much of its old world architectural style and charm with tall steeples and high vaulted ceilings.

The team's Humvees turn off of the main highway and make a right onto a narrow two lane road surrounded by well groomed lawns and perfectly pruned trees. Lieutenant Greene leans over towards Troy and points up ahead of them.

"This is Montague Drive, it'll take us right up to the conservatory. That's where Dr. Barnes is waiting for us."

"When was the last time you were in contact with her?" asks Troy.

"About a half-hour before you touched down. We've been having some trouble with the phone lines lately and Dr. Barnes doesn't have her cell phone with her."

"What about the law enforcement personnel you said was with her. Is there any way to get in contact with them?" adds Bloomberg.

"We've tried but for some reason the police department has been unable to establish communications with them either."

As the caravan of Humvees speed around the last turn on the drive they slow down and stop as their occupants gasp at the sight before them. About one hundred feet ahead on the right hand side at the top of a gradual grade in the road sits the large glass covered conservatory which is attached to the William Self Propst Hall, a 300-foot long three-story colonial style building which is home to the college's Biological and Environmental Sciences Department, the Physics Department, as well as the Chemistry and Biochemistry Departments. This large red and beige brick building is adorned with rows of colonial style windows down its entire length. The main entrance in the middle of the building is marked by four two story roman style columns giving the building more of a court house look than that of an academic building. As for the conservatory, which is essentially a hundred foot long two story green house, it is completely covered in thick glass. It is this structure, which is closest to them, that can barely be seen through the thick undulating mass of mutant killer bees! The whole top of the hill is one huge living cloud of bees. Troy rolls his window down to get a better look at the swarm. As soon as he sticks his head out of the window he notices the deafening sound. It's a low-pitched roar, like a lengthy, steady rumble of thunder that doesn't end. The bees swirl around the building almost as if they knew where the team was heading. Troy pulls his head back inside and rolls up the window tight. He then looks nervously at Bloomberg who then looks at Greene.

"What do we do now?" asks Bloomberg.

Greene doesn't answer; he just picks up his radio and calls the other vehicles.

"Everybody gear up. We're going through in five."

"What does that mean?" asks Forrester with a sound of discomfort in his voice.

"My men are putting on protective clothing and flamethrowers. They'll take point and clear the way for us. We move out in five minutes. In the meantime grab those bags from under your seats."

Each of the team members, including Greene, begins pulling large duffle bags from under their seats.

"Each bag has some protective gear in it. Put it on, we need to be ready when we get up to the door."

After a few minutes all of the soldiers and INVASION members, are dressed in what looks like thick hazmat outfits. Six of the soldiers exit from the Humvees. These men have flamethrowers strapped to their backs and walk slowly up the road towards the conservatory. The Humvees including the one with the INVASION team drive slowly behind them. As they approach the swarm, the bees begin to take notice and many begin flying around the soldiers and the vehicles as if to investigate their actions. Greene is in constant communication with the men walking in front via radio.

"Take is easy gentlemen. Don't fire yet. They're only curious. No sense in provoking them. Head for that side door," he commands.

"Roger!" responds a voice over the radio.

The six soldiers form a semi-circle around the side door leading into the conservatory. The Humvee with the INVASION team pulls up as close to the door as possible.

"On my mark we all are going to make our way to that door," Greene shouts through the hood of his protective suit, "do you understand?"

The team members shake their heads that they do. Greene turns his radio back on.

"Okay boys, let them have it!"

The six soldiers protecting the entrance to the conservatory turn on their flamethrowers and begin sweeping their flames back and forth creating a kind of bubble within the cloud of bees. The swarm instantly reacts to the attack as waves of angry insects fly head on into the deadly flames. Just then Greene swings open door on the right side of the Humvee.

"MOVE! MOVE! MOVE!" he shouts as he waves the team out of the vehicle. First Troy then Bloomberg and then the rest pile out and sprint to the door as Greene follows. Other troops, from the remaining Humvees, armed with M-16 rifles and flamethrowers burst from their vehicles and follow. Troy is the first to the door. He grabs the knob, turns and pushes, but it won't budge.

"It's locked! I can't get it open!" he shouts with a hint of panic in his voice as he shoos away some bees that have made it through the wall of fire and begin to swirl around his head.

"Look out! Let me at it!" says Greene. He runs up and delivers a mean kick to the door near the knob.

Bang!

The door swings open and the team along with the soldiers hurries in. Greene stands by to make sure everyone is safely inside and then slams the door shut.

Once inside, they all begin swatting and stomping any bees that have followed them in.

"What about your men?" shouts Cooper.

"They're alright! They'll wait for us inside the Humvees"

Cooper looks out through one of the conservatory's windows and sees the soldiers turning off their flames and retreating inside of the vehicles.

"Is everybody okay?" asks Greene as he squashes a bee against the wall with the butt of his rifle. He looks around and everyone nods their heads positively in response to his query.

"Okay then, let's go find your doctor friend."

As the team removes their head gear Greene looks around surveying his surroundings. They're inside of the one hundred foot long greenhouse filled with hundreds of hybrid plants used by the university students in their experiments. The air inside is hot, clammy and humid making it difficult to breathe through the thick smell of damp foliage. Normally during this time of the day the inside of the conservatory would be brightly lit by the sun's rays shining through its walls of glass. But today it is dark. All that can be seen through the glass walls is a moving brownish mass of bees, clinging to the outside of the building. The only sounds are the loud hum from the bees outside. Greene spots a door on the side of the conservatory that attaches to the William Self Propst Hall.

"There's the exit!" he says as he points to the door, "Let's move out! Come on!"

Everyone quickly moves toward the door when all of a sudden it swings open. In the entrance stands a police officer with his gun drawn and pointing at the group. The soldiers with the INVASION team instinctively kneel and aim their weapons.

"Hold it! Hold your fire!" shouts Greene as he waves to his men. He then turns his attention to the officer in the doorway. The man looks to be in his late twenties, there's a deep gash across his forehead and his uniform is torn and bloody. He's shaking from fear with his arms fully extended and both hands tightly holding his pistol.

"Who-who are you?" he stutters.

Greene steps forward slowly, "I'm Lieutenant Greene of the United States Army," he then turns and points to Troy, "and these guys are from the EPA. They're here for Dr. Barnes," he extends his hand out towards the officer and waves it downward, "now why don't you lower your weapon before somebody gets hurt," the officer slowly lowers his gun but holds it at his side, "we need to find Dr. Barnes. You know where she is? We've been trying to contact her."

"The phones are out," the officer says with a shaky voice.

"Alright son, now I know your scared --Hell we all are-- but I need you to holster that sidearm of yours. You're making my guys nervous. We're all on the same side."

The officer looks down at his gun then slowly holsters it. Once they see that his weapon is secured the rangers relax, lower their weapons and stand up.

"Now can you take us to Dr. Barnes?" asks Greene.

"Yeah, they're all hold up in the conference room. I heard a sound in here. I thought the bees got in. Come, come on follow me."

He turns and leads the group down a long dark hallway. Only a few of the lights are working and all of the windows have been boarded up. They walk down to the end of the hallway and into a large room with double doors. Inside the room are about twenty people. Some of them have bruises and cuts. All of them look frightened and bewildered or just in a state of shock. To one side of the room on the floor lies another officer who appears to be badly injured and unconscious. One side of his face is swollen and red. His shirt is ripped open, revealing his bare chest with two open gashes just over his heart. There is a thick black fluid oozing out of the wounds that two women kneeling beside him are trying to clean off. As the soldiers enter the room cries of relief can be heard throughout the crowd, someone even yells out, "Thank God the army's here. We're saved!"

Greene steps forward and announces to the crowd, "We're looking for Dr. Barnes. Is she in here?"

One of the women kneeling beside the unconscious officer slowly stands up and steps forward.

"I'm Sylvia Barnes."

Greene raises an eyebrow slightly at the sight of the beautiful woman before him. She's not what he expected to see. Definitely not his idea of what a scientist should look like. She's nothing short of stunning, a petite African American woman with a slender build standing just a little over five feet tall and wearing a white lab coat with a short blue skirt. She has the look of a model with her smooth creamy unblemished skin, slim yet curvy legs, small button nose and full luscious lips. Greene stares at Dr. Barnes for a moment temporarily stunned by the presence of such beauty amongst all this chaos.

He's not the only one taken back by her attractiveness. Troy stepping along side of Greene just stares with his mouth open as if he were in a trance. Dr. Barnes slowly steps forward and walks right up to him and extends her hand.

"You must be Professor Hamilton's grandson Troy. It's an honor to finally meet you," she says as she shakes his hand, "I've heard a lot about you."

Troy still mesmerized by her beauty stubbles through his words, "I'm I mean it's a pleasure to meet you too. Um wait, what do you mean you've heard about me? From whom? Where?"

Barnes smiles, "From a mutual acquaintance, Chad Brooks, you know he's a big fan of yours."

"That maniac is no friend of mine," Troy snarls.

"Forgive me. What I meant was he's an admirer of yours. During our meetings he even talked about hiring you to be on his staff. But he knew your grandfather would never approve. I heard he even put together some scheme to trick you into working with him."

"The Academy of New Minds," mumbles Troy as he shakes his head.

"Yeah, I see his scheme wasn't convincing," comments Barnes, "guess you were just too smart," she smiles.

Suddenly Greene interrupts, "Excuse me but you two can play '*get acquainted*' another time. Right now my orders are to get you out of here. Are you ready to go Doctor?"

"Yes, but I need to bring my research. Since I've been locked in here I've had time to study these insects. I have some samples and notes over there in those boxes," she points to four large cardboard boxes sitting on the floor near the wounded officer.

"Great, is that it?"

"Yes, that's it. Tell me something just how do you plan on getting all of us out of here?"

"Us? Ma'am I have orders to bring you and you only. We'll send back some personnel for the others."

"No, no that's unacceptable! There are over twenty people in here and some of them are badly hurt. They may not last that long. You have to help them. It's your duty!"

"Ma'am, they'll be safe as long as they remain inside. The bees will soon move off and we'll be able to send people in to evac them out."

Barnes with a look of frustration on her face pleads with Greene, "No, you don't understand! These are not just overgrown bees. These are mutations. They don't just attack when provoked they attack for a reason."

Troy pulls her gently by the arm, "What do you mean?"

"Not all of these bees are the same. Some of them, the larger ones, sting not to kill but to paralyze. Then they inject parasitic larvae into their victims."

Bloomberg with a look of shock on his face says, "What?"

"Yes, and then the larvae eat the victim from the inside out. That's why they're hovering around outside. They need us as hosts!"

"Jesus!" says Troy.

"Believe me Ma'am, I would if I could. But our vehicles don't have room for all of these people and my orders are very clear. And with all due respect Ma'am my duty is to my country and commander and chief and I intend to follow his orders to the letter," Greene then points to two of his men, "Dusty, Jones, grab her stuff--we're outta here."

The two soldiers quickly sling their weapons over their shoulders and grab the four boxes on the floor and head back to the conservatory.

Dr. Barnes steps in front of Greene, "Wait a minute, officer!"

"It's Lieutenant, Ma'am."

"Lieutenant, Can you at least take the ones that are injured? That would be the humane thing to do," she says with an acid tone.

Greene looks around the room, "How many are you talking about?"

Barnes points to the wounded officer on the floor, "Well we have the policeman here," she then looks across the room and points to a group of injured people also sitting on the floor, "and five others over there."

"Six? Listen, I understand what you're saying but I don't think we can bring back six!"

Just then Cooper steps forward, "I'll stay!"

"What?" says Greene.

"I said I'll stay behind to make room for the ones that are hurt," continues Cooper, "I mean while I'm here I could help them fortify the building till you come back with transportation."

Bloomberg pats Cooper on the back and whispers to him, "Are you sure about this, Simon?"

"It's no problem Kevin, trust me. We have to do something. She's right we can't just leave them here."

"We'll stay with him Sir," comes a voice from behind Greene. When he turns to address the speaker he sees five of his own men volunteering to remain behind.

Greene grins and shakes his head, "Alright then, Davis go back to the Humvees and grab a flamethrower, a radio and some smoke grenades. That should hold you till we get back."

"Yes, sir!" the soldier salutes then runs off for the equipment.

Greene turns back to Dr. Barnes, "Happy now?"

"Yes, thank you Lieutenant," says Barnes with a smile.

Greene then puts his hands on his hips and shouts, "Okay, it's time to rock and roll," he points to Bloomberg and Forrester, "Grab some of the wounded and help them to the conservatory. Come on, all I want to see is assholes and elbows. Let's move it!"

With new found urgency the soldiers and INVASION team members quickly ferry the injured people back to the conservatory. Once there they formulate a plan to get the injured into the vehicles without being attacked by the bees. A couple of the soldiers bring in heavy blankets from the Humvees. The plan is to cover the victims with the blankets and quickly rush them into the waiting vehicles. Soldiers with flamethrowers surround the entrance from the conservatory then unleash a wall of fire up into the air causing it to rain burning bees all around them. When it seems there is enough clearing the soldiers sprint the covered victims out.

It takes some time, but all of the six injured people along with the INVASION team, remaining soldiers and Dr. Barnes make it into the Humvees without too much trouble. The bees, however, have become even more aggressive than ever. They dive down onto the Humvees, hurling their bodies against the vehicles so hard that they begin to rock back and forth. Greene noticing the intensity of the attack orders the drivers to move out.

They begin to drive away from the conservatory very slowly. But with so many bees flying around the drivers could barely see in front of them. The swarm has become so thick that it is has become difficult to tell whether it's day or night. Finally the Humvees are forced to stop. The driver of the lead vehicle, the one in which Lieutenant Greene is in, reports that he can no longer see the road.

"Did you try using the GPS?" asks Greene.

"I'm using it now, sir. But I still can't tell if I'm heading off the road or not. It's going to be very slow going like this. The other drivers are having the same problems", he reports, "I can't even use the windshield wipers and the bees are clogging the ventilation ports," he looks back at Greene and lowers his voice, "we'll lose air in a few minutes if we don't get them off sir."

"Keep going. Maybe the further away from the conservatory we get the easier it'll be."

"Okay, sir," says the soldier as he turns around and continues driving ahead.

From one of the conservatory windows Cooper along with one of the soldiers watch the slow-moving vehicles crawl down the road.

"They'll never make it at that rate," he states, "It's almost like the entire swarm is following them. We have to do something to draw them away," he pauses for a minute then he says, "I know what we can do."

"What's your plan, sir?" asks the soldier.

"Just follow me," says Cooper as he heads back to the conference room.

Meanwhile in the lead vehicle the occupants are suffering from rising heat and the lack of oxygen. The other Humvees are experiencing the same conditions making their journey even more perilous. Suddenly Greene's radio springs to life.

"Lieutenant! Lieutenant! This is Cooper do you read me?"

Greene grabs the radio, "Yes Cooper, what is it?"

"I'm going to try something to drive the bees away from you. Get ready to peel out of here."

"Don't do anything foolish, son. We should be okay once we get to the interstate."

"That's too far. You may not make it. Listen I'm already in position. Two of your men are helping me. Just be ready."

Greene, Troy, Bloomberg and Dr. Barnes turn around and strain to see out of the back of the Humvee. Then barely visible through the cloud of bees is Cooper and two of the soldiers dressed in their protective clothing. One of them has a flamethrower and the other two are holding sticks with cloth wrapped around the end forming torches. The soldier with the flamethrower ignites the torches and they all begin approaching the Humvees. As they get closer the bees change direction and head for the three men. The one with the flamethrower frantically sprays the flames from side to side. The other two men, one of which is Cooper, flail their torches wildly around their heads trying to beat off the bees.

"Lieutenant, we're free!" cries the driver.

"Step on it and tell the others to do the same."

"Yes sir!"

"What about Simon?" shouts Forrester.

"He knew what he was doing Jacob. He did it for us," says Bloomberg in a somber tone.

Just then they all feel the lurch of the Humvee picking up speed and soon they lose sight of their comrade on the road behind them.

As Cooper sees the Humvees speed off he begins to wonder if this was such a good plan. He and the soldiers had walked a lot further away from the conservatory than he realized and now getting back was near impossible. The swarm has completely engulfed the three men. Cooper is feeling disoriented within the swarm and the bee's stingers are beginning to make their way through his gear. He can't even see five feet in front of him. Walking through the swarm is like walking in a blizzard at night. Soon he realizes that he has lost sight of the two soldiers he came out with and he's not sure what direction the conservatory is in. His breathing begins to increase as fear sets in. Slowly he inches along hoping to be going in the right direction. As he slowly makes his way back to the conservatory he suddenly trips over something in the road and falls face first hard onto the pavement. *It's the body of one of the other soldiers!* The corpse lay stiff on the ground as the bees continue to sting it. Cooper then notices that his own facemask has ripped open when he fell. In a panic he grabs at the opening managing only to tear it more. Bees instantly rush into his headgear, stinging him all about the face and neck. Cooper can't breathe, he can't even scream. Every time he opens his mouth the bees rush in choking him even more. He tries spitting out the insects but is stung both on the inside as well as the outside of his mouth. His tongue begins to swell; his throat closes up as his airways bulge from the venom. He rolls around on the ground holding his throat and gasping for air. Without thinking he rips off his headgear to take a breath. Instantly hundreds of bees attack him stinging him about the face and neck. One bee plants a stinger deep into his throat and another stings him right in his left eye, which sends daggers of pain straight through his brain. He grabs the insect and crushes it in his hand. The pain is unbearable. The veins in his neck and face turn blue and swell, his body begins twitching and jerking. As his muscles stiffen, dark venom laced with blood oozes out of his ears and nose. Another sharp pain rips through his lower back causing him to arch violently. He falls to the ground, paralyzed by the venom racing through his body. But he can still feel. He can still feel the acid-like pain tearing his body apart. Then he notices a new sensation, a flesh ripping feeling starting from his lower back and snaking its way throughout his entire body. Horror sets in as he begins to realize the source of the new pain, the parasitic larvae. They're eating through his body and even in his frozen state he can feel them devour his insides. His eyes widen as black vomit leaks from his swollen lips. His body jerks violently a few more times before finally remaining still.

During the flight down to Florida, Daily and Hill sit cuddled up under one another. He wraps his arm around her shoulders as she rests her head on his chest. The two take a quick nap together for most of the two-hour trip and wakeup about a half hour before they are to land. Daily turns to Hill and with a twinkle in his eye kisses her on the forehead. She looks up at him and smiles.

"What's on your mind, Big Bear?" she says softly.

"I was just, um, j-just thinking," he stutters with a nervous look on his face.

"Thinking about what?" inquires Hill as she sits up in her seat. She turns her body so that she can face him. "What's up Clarence? What's the matter?"

"I was wondering what's going to happen to us."

"What do you mean?" asks Hill with a puzzled frown, "We should be alright. I mean the military is escorting us…"

"That's not what I mean, Debra," Daily interrupts with a tone of annoyance, "I mean us! You! Me! Us! I was just thinking about us."

The two stare at each other silently for a moment. Then Hill responds calmly, "I see."

"Yeah, I was thinking that when all of this is over, what's going to happen to us?" Daily continues.

"Clarence, I don't know what to tell you," Hill pleads as she rubs his shoulder. "Everything around us is going crazy. I just don't know what to think. We don't know how any of this is going to end. I just feel so…"

"Do you love me?" Daily blurts out abruptly.

Caught off guard by the sudden question Hill sits frozen for a moment staring at Daily with her mouth wide open.

"Do you love me?" Daily repeats softly.

"I...I-I mean...I-," Hill stammers, "I think I d-"

Daily reaches over and grabs Hill by the shoulders, and kisses her on the lips. They kiss passionately for a moment, then Hill sits back and gazes into Daily's eyes, "Yes, yes. Of course I love you. I told you before how I felt," she reaches over, wraps her arms around him and kisses him again. "Oh God, you have no idea how much I love you, Clarence. But we talked about this. You know what the bureau's policy is on fraternizing."

"I was kind of thinking the bureau can't do anything if we were a legal couple."

Hill sits up with a look of excitement on her face and stares at Daily closely, "What, what are you saying? Clarence, are you saying what I think you're saying?"

"Why not? I'm tired of hiding my feelings for you and sneaking around to make love. Why shouldn't people know we want to be together? If the bureau doesn't like it, fuck 'em!"

Hill smiles, "This means a lot to you, doesn't it?"

Daily looks at Hill with a serious look on his face, "Doesn't it mean a lot to you?"

She cups his hand inside of hers, "Yes, it does. But think about what we'd be getting ourselves into Clarence? Look at what's going on around us. The world is falling apart right in front of our eyes," Hill looks up at Daily with tears welling up in her eyes, "It scares the Hell out of me."

Daily holds her close to his chest, "That's even more of a reason for us to be together."

As she hugs Daily Hill closes her eyes and thinks to herself, *"Why am I so scared? This is the man I want to be with. So why am I hesitating?"* as Daily squeezes her tighter she smiles to herself, *"Ahh I like that. He feels so strong. He always knows how to make me feel safe. Clarence is right--this is what we both need."*

After a few moments Daily releases Hill. He cups her face in his hands and stares into her eyes with a wide smile, "Debra?"

"Yes, Clarence?"

"I need to ask you something."

"Yes?"

"I'm not sure how to put this but…would you…," Daily pauses for a moment.

"What? What is it?"

"What I'm trying to ask you is…," he pauses again.

"Clarence!"

"Would you marry me?" Daily blurts.

Hill's eyes widen in their sockets, "What?"

Daily takes a deep breath, "There, I said it. You heard me. I want you to be my wife," he says while still cradling her blushing cheeks.

"But, how…when…I mean…I…Oh my God, Clarence," Hill stammers as tears begin to flow down her face, "What am I saying? Of course. Yes, yes. Oh my God! Are you kidding me? In a heartbeat," she says while hyperventilating, "I can't believe you just asked me that. How are we going to do this? When? Oh my God, I think I'm going to faint," Hill wipes beads of sweat from her forehead as she falls back in her seat while attempting to catch her breath.

Daily laughs then reaches over and kisses her again, "Relax. We have a lot of time to figure it all out. When all of this nonsense is over, we'll make our plans."

"Oh, Clarence!" she grabs him and the two kiss and hug each other till they are ready to land.

The C-130 lands at the Central Florida Regional Airport at Seminole, Florida. Waiting for Daily, Hill, Brad and Hinds is Lieutenant Lopez. As they exit the plane he walks up and salutes them.

"Welcome to Florida," he says as the team members salute back.

"It's good to see you again, Lieutenant," says Hill.

"This is not as bad as I thought it would be," says Daily as he looks around the area and up into the sky, "They made it seem like the birds had taken over down here."

"You haven't seen anything. We're fifty miles north of where the problem is, down near Walt Disney World," replies Lopez.

"How bad is it?" asks Brad as the team follows Lopez to waiting Humvees.

"The whole area is in terrible shape. In some places there are bodies everywhere. That's why you had to land here instead of Orlando International. They've already downed two planes over there."

"What?" exclaims Hinds.

"Yeah, two commercial planes. One on take off and the other on landing, there were so many birds in the air that they got sucked into the planes engines and caused a flame out. Both planes went down with no survivors."

The team members stop near the waiting Humvee in a state of shock.

"It's going to take us about an hour to get to this doctor's house so we better get going. The birds have taken over most of the state south of Orlando and are slowly moving this way."

They all pile into the vehicle and speed off with two other Humvees in tow. They travel quickly down the Spessard L. Holland East west expressway towards the suburb of Williamsburg. The expressway is eerily empty. For miles they are the only vehicles on the road. They see no signs of human life. But in the sky above them are thousands of birds of all types circling slowly over head. There are so many that it makes the cloudless sunny day appear overcast. Alongside the road are more birds, just sitting and watching them as they speed by. Occasionally they see a human body along the road being taken apart by buzzards.

After almost an hour they exit the expressway onto Orangewood Boulevard and slow down to almost a crawl.

Daily notices the speed decrease and leans forward from the back seat to talk to Lopez.

"What's up? Are we close?"

"Yeah, but look ahead we have trouble. We have to make it through that," he points down the road in front of them.

Daily looks up through the windshield and can't believe his eyes. Down the full length of the boulevard are thousands of crows just sitting quietly in the street blocking their path.

"What do we do?" he asks.

"We have no choice. We have to go through."

He signals the driver and they pull off at a very low speed. The birds seeing the vehicle approach slowly move out of its way.

They're everywhere, on cars, rooftops, and telephone poles. They just sit there and watch as if daring the team to run over one of their kind.

"This is crazy! We'll never get there at this pace," complains Daily.

Lopez turns to the driver, "Pick it up a little--maybe they'll get the message."

The driver begins to speed up which causes the birds to move a little faster to get out of the way. One bird doesn't move fast enough and gets run over by the Humvee. As it is hit the animal lets out a loud screech. Suddenly every bird around them lifts into the air and begin swirling around the three vehicles.

"Alright, that does it! Step on it, Jackson!" yells Lopez at his driver.

Their Humvee takes off down the road and the other two follow quickly, speeding down Orangewood Boulevard at almost sixty-five miles an hour. They're driving almost blind through the thick cloud of angry birds that continuously fly in front of the vehicles, smashing into the windows and causing them to swerve out of control. All of the drivers fight fiercely to stay on the road.

The Humvees are ready to make a right turn onto Parkview Point Drive when out of nowhere a huge gasoline tanker plows into the middle Humvee. The two vehicles instantly burst into flames. The trailing Humvee almost hits the wreckage and swerves violently out of the way to avoid them. The two remaining Humvees stop for a moment near the burning wreck to look for survivors but it is soon clear that no one could have survived the explosion. So with the birds continuing to attack they speed off towards the doctor's home.

They drive down Peach Grove Lane towards the last house at the end of the Cul-de-sac. The two vehicles, both surrounded by a swirling twister of deadly birds, drive up onto the lawn and everyone jumps out with their heads down and run to the front door of the small white ranch house. Lopez pounds on the door as the other soldiers and the INVASION team members attempt to beat off the attacking birds. Two soldiers open fire with their M-16 rifles and manage to kill many of the attacking avian but there are too many. A large black crow dives onto one soldier's back and sinks its talons deep into his shoulders. He reaches up to grab the fowl only to have another one fly by and slash him across the face. As he falls to the ground dozens of more birds swoop down and attack him. Brad and another soldier grab one of his legs but when they drag him closer to the side of the house they realize it's too late. He had been gored to death in only a minute!

Lopez pounds on the door, "This is the United States Army Doctor, open up! We're here to help you!"

There's no answer.

"Doctor, open the door!" Lopez continues.

Finally the door opens and the team rushes in while trying to keep the birds from following. When the door slams shut they all look back at a small shaking Asian man in his early forties wearing brown-rimmed glasses, a beige polo shirt and jeans. His face and arms are scratched and scarred and his shirt is ripped.

"Dr. Kang?" asks Hill while breathing heavily.

"Yes, I thought you'd never come. My wife and I were getting worried."

"Are you ready to leave? We can't stay here long," asks Hill.

"Yes I have all my things in my van. My wife and I were getting ready to chance making it out on our own. I think she's going into labor! She isn't due for another month but I think all of this excitement and stress has been too much for her."

"Jesus! Where is she?" shouts Daily.

"Waiting for me in the garage."

Kang leads the team through his home and into the connecting two-car garage. In there they find a blue minivan with Kang's wife sitting in the back hyperventilating. Hill runs over and slides open the side door to the van.

"Are you all right, Ma'am?" she asks.

"Yes, yes I think so," she says in between ragged breaths.

"How far along are you?"

"I'm not supposed to be due till next month. I'm having contractions about every five minutes," she says while again breathing heavily.

"Alright try and relax we're going to get you out of here."

Hill turns to Daily, "I don't think we should try and move her."

"I agree. You sit with her and I'll drive the van."

"Good," says Hill then she turns to Lopez, "Lieutenant we're taking the van. You and your men get back to the Humvees and we'll follow."

"Right!" shouts Lopez as he and his men hurry back through the house. Dr. Kang gets into the back of the van with his wife after handing the keys to Daily. Hill jumps in next to Daily.

Dr. Kang leans forward and tells Daily, "You have to press the button on the visor to open the garage."

Daily presses the button and the garage door swings open. Instantly waves of birds roar into the garage. Daily starts up the van and lurches it forward. He could barely see out of the window and tries his best to follow Lopez.

They speed back up the way they came in, passing the burning tanker and up towards the expressway.

"Ahhh!" cries Mrs. Kang as she holds her stomach, "I think, I think the baby's coming!"

Hill staring into the back seat reaches over and gently rubs the woman's stomach, "Don't worry," she says in calm and soothing voice, "You'll be just fine," she then turns to Daily, "Clarence we have to move it!"

Daily without taking his eyes off the road shouts back, "I know!"

"I mean it!"

"I know, I know. I'm going as fast as I can!"

As they speed down the expressway birds of every type, like miniature kamikazes, smash head-on into their windshield. Several times Daily has to swerve in an attempt to minimize their impacts. He strains to keep track of Lopez up ahead through the heavily fractured windshield.

"If we get any more hits the windshield is going to go," he shouts to Hill, "Without it we're done!"

Hill looks over the mangled windshield. Cracks are spread from end-to-end along with three small holes stained with the blood of the birds that caused them. She unholsters her sidearm and aims through the hole in the windshield nearest her, "Just step on it--I'll keep them off of us!"

Two large black birds come swooping down on an intercept course with the van. Hill aims and fires.

Bam! Bam! Bam!

She misses.

Bam! Bam!

Finally a hit.

Bam! Bam! Bam!

Another hit.

Hill wipes the sweat from her brow then turns and takes a peak in the back seat, "You all right?"

Dr. Kang and his wife nod their heads yes while holding each other tightly.

Hill turns back to the road and aims again as Daily speeds and swerves wildly in an attempt to avoid debris littering the street.

Suddenly Daily shouts, "Up there at two o'clock!"

Hill aims up and to the right then fires hitting the bird on the third shot.

"Look out over there," shouts Dr. Kang as he lunges forward pointing to the left.

Three birds are beginning their dive. Hill takes aim.

Bam!

Click! Click!

"Shit! I'm out of ammo!" she fumbles through her pockets for another clip just as the trio of birds ram the windshield sending shards of glass flying into all of their faces. Daily, blinded by glass swerves the van violently back and forth.

"You alright?" shouts Hill as she slaps a new clip of ammo into her weapon.

Daily regaining control of the van turns to her with a bloody face covered with small pieces of glass, "I'll live," he responds. He squints his eyes as he looks up ahead, "this must be the off ramp, I see Lopez turning off up ahead," he steps on the gas to try and catch up with the Humvees.

Unexpectedly, two more birds hit the windshield. The impact again sends sharp glass flying through the van. One of the birds flies completely through the windshield and right into Hill's lap. It's a large black crow. The animal viciously claws at Hill as its violently flapping wings continually smack Daily in the face making it even more difficult to steer. Both he and Hill battle the crazed bird in the front of the van as Dr. Kang and his wife look on in terror from the rear. The van still traveling at a high rate of speed careens from one side of the road to the other as Daily, partially blinded by glass, fights to steer straight with wings slapping him in his face.

Hill, her face now covered in claw marks, is finally able to grab the bird by its neck. It uses its sharp beak to dig deep into her hand in an attempt to free itself. She endures the pain long enough to lift up her Glock. She aims at the bird's small head and fires taking its head completely off. The animal's headless body drops to the floor of the van between Hill's feet, its neck spurting blood.

Daily wipes some blood off of his face with the back of his hand as he glances over at Hill, "You okay?"

Hill shaking and still holding the smoking gun turns to him slowly, "Let's just get the hell--" suddenly an image catches her attention. Unknown to Daily, a huge seagull is zooming in toward the driver's side window. It's coming in like a missile right at Daily, "Clarence!" she screams, her eyes wide with terror. But it's too late the creature rams right through the window and into Daily, its beak slashing across his left cheek. The van rocks violently to the right. Daily tries to compensate by turning the steering wheel to the left causing the van to flip over the guard rail of the road and tumble down an embankment. It finally lands on its hood at the bottom of the hill.

"The van! It's crashed, sir!" yells the driver of Lopez's Humvee as he glances up into the rear view mirror.

The lieutenant quickly turns around looks out of the back window, "Damn it!" he shouts as he sees the overturned vehicle.

Brad in the back seat turns and peers through the rear window, "Hurry up--turn this shit around! We have to get back there!"

The two Humvees circle around and head back to the crash, all while constantly being attacked by the thickening cloud of killer birds.

Back at the van all is quiet except for the low-pitched moans coming from the stunned occupants. The four survivors slowly begin to stir in the upside-down vehicle. Their moans grow in intensity mainly from Dr. Kang's wife. Quickly, her moans turn into cries for help, "My baby! Help me! Somebody help me!"

Dr. Kang slowly climbs from the rear of the van, where he was thrown during the crash, to his wife's side. He hugs her with one arm and rubs her stomach with the other, "I'm here, honey. I'm here," he comforts her.

Dr. Kang looks up front and sees both Daily and Hill slowly pull themselves free of some of the wreckage.

Hill crawls over to Kang, "How is she doing?"

"Fine, I think. I don't know. We need to get her out of here. We have to get out!" he says, his voice shrill with panic.

Hill looks out of the windows of the van and sees that the circling winged menace outside of the van has not left, "We can't take her out there--it's still too dangerous."

Daily peering out of another window shouts, "I see them! Up there on the road it's Lopez. Get them ready!"

The two Humvees pull at the point where the van flipped over the railing. The doors fly open and Hinds, Brad, Lopez and the soldiers pile out and race down the hill. At the bottom they form a ring around the van and fire their weapons into the air killing many of the attacking birds. Hinds and Lopez reach into the van and help Dr. Kang and his wife out of the vehicle and up the hill into one of the waiting Humvees.

Lopez shouts out the driver, "Move it! Get them back to the base ASAP!"

"Yes sir!" The soldier replies as he speeds off down the road.

Lopez then turns back around and heads back down the embankment while ducking and dodging the aerial attack. "Come on, let's get them out of here!" He yells at Brad and one remaining soldier.

Daily and Hill, both weakened and injured from the crash, struggle to exit the van. Just as they are helped to their feet, a huge cloud of birds immediately descends upon them, making it difficult to get to the Humvee.

"Get them off of me!" shouts Hill as she wails her arms at several birds that are circling around her clawing and pecking with each pass.

Daily grabs one of the birds off of Hill's back and rips its wings off with his bare hands. Another flies straight into his face but Daily grabs the bird by its neck and squeezes with all his might, "I've had enough of you," he shouts as he releases his grip and lets the animal drop heavily to the ground.

"Come on everybody, get up the hill to the Humvees!" yells Lopez.

"Debra!" shouts Daily as he looks around for her. He turns and spots her on the ground and reaches down to help her up, "Come on. Can you make it?"

"Yeah, I'm good," she stutters while breathing heavily. She gets up and managers to jog up toward the waiting vehicle.

"Keep going, Deb. I'm right behind you," says Daily.

As they near the Humvee a large seagull swoops down out of the sky and lands on Daily's shoulder. The bird opens its beak and rips a huge chunk of flesh out of his neck. Another soars in and digs its claws into his face as a third bites him on the back of his left leg causing him to fall to the ground.

Hill reaches the Humvee and staggers to the side door, "Thank God," she pants, nearly out of breath from the climb up the hill. "We made it," she sighs, turning to address Daily. Bewildered, she whirls about to look behind her and her breath catches in her throat at the sight of Daily, sprawled on the ground halfway down the embankment. He's on his back holding his throat as blood sprays up into the air from the wound. Dozens of killer birds hover above him diving down and pecking at his mortally injured body. A few of the birds land on his chest and claw at his arms and face.

"Clarence! Clarence! No!" she shouts and she begins to run back to him. A strong arm hooks about her waist yanking her into the back of the Humvee, "Get off of me! Let me go! Get the hell off me! Their killing him!" she screams as she pulls at Lopez's arm.

He pushes her firmly against the seat, grabs her by the shoulders and shakes her to get her attention, "We'll get him! We'll get him! Just stay put!" Lopez releases her then climbs back out into the deadly cloud of birds. Daily is on his feet, but just barely, his arm around Brad's shoulder as he limps along, bloodied head hanging low. As they stumble back to the Humvee. Lopez rushes up, grabs Daily's other arm and both he and Brad usher Daily quickly back to the vehicle.

Hill sobs at the sight of him, dazed and pressing a hand to his ravaged neck.

As they speed off down the road Hill, with Daily lying across her lap, presses a large piece of gauze on the open wound. He begins to make gurgling sounds as the gaping hole in his neck continues to spray blood from a severed artery. Hill, covered completely in Daily's blood, is determined to save her partner. "Faster! Drive faster damn it!" She screams.

"We're going as fast as we can," shouts Lopez. He turns around from the front seat, "How's he doing?"

Hill looks up with teary eyes, "Not good."

"Won't be long now, we're almost there," says Lopez.

Hill cradles Daily's head in her arms as he lies there quietly with his eyes open, "Stay with me! You hear me? Stay with me!" his eyes begin to close slowly, "No! Clarence! Stay with me!"

Daily strains to open his eyes and tries to speak but all that comes out is a murmur as blood drools out from his lips instead of words.

"No, no don't talk baby. Don't talk. Everything's going to be alright," Hill whispers as she gently rocks him on her lap, "Just try and relax," she pleads as tears well up in her eyes. She pushes down harder on the gauze covering his wound.

Daily reaches up with a bloody hand and gently touches her face. He coughs causing more blood to squirt from between Hill's fingers covering his wound. She tries desperately to keep the pressure on Daily's neck but blood continues to leak out uncontrollably as his eyes slowly begin to close.

"No, No, God damn it. Stay with me!" she yells, "Open your eyes, look at me Clarence, look at me!"

Daily struggles to reopen his eyes. He looks up at Hill and silently mouths the words, "I LOVE YOU," then coughs up more blood, jerks and falls still.

"*Noooooooooo!* You can't leave me now! *Noooooooo!*" Hill screams.

Just then the Humvee pulls along side of the waiting C-130. Three paramedics pull Daily from the vehicle and onto a gurney.

Hinds, waiting outside of the plane, runs over, puts her arms around Hill and hugs her tightly. She then leads Hill quickly onto the plane. The paramedics bandage Daily's neck and apply an IV to his arm as they quickly carry him on board.

Once on the plane the pilot immediately begins to taxi onto the runway.

Lopez comes over to Hill who is sitting across from Daily, "Strap in, we need to take off right away. Those birds followed us all the way up here! They just started attacking the airport!"

Hill looks through the plane's window and sees flocks of birds of all types diving down on runway workers and other personnel.

Lopez continues, "We need to get ahead of them before they get stuck in our engines."

Hill doesn't answer she just stares across the aisle at Daily as the paramedics work tirelessly to save his life.

"Don't worry, he's in good hands," says Hinds in a reassuring voice but Hill doesn't respond, she just stares into space.

After a few minutes the plane levels off and the all-clear sign is given. Further up in the front of the aircraft Hill can hear the sound of a baby crying. She hears the voice of Dr. Kang shouting jubilantly, "It's a boy! Lein, it's a boy!" She can hear all this but it doesn't register. The only thing she can think about is Daily. Hill bends her head and leans on Hinds' shoulder with tears flowing down her scarred face. Hinds puts her arm around Hill and pats her friend's head gently. Hill then whispers to Hinds, "He told me he wanted to marry me."

"What?" exclaims Hinds.

"Clarence, he finally asked me to marry him."

Hinds feels her own eyes begin to well up with tears as she searches for reassuring words for her friend in pain. But she can't seem to find the right thing to say. All she can do is hold Hill tighter and wipe the tears from her eyes.

Lieutenant Lopez and Brad, both with sadden faces, join the two women and take seats next to them.

They all sit and watch the paramedics work feverishly over Daily for twenty straight minutes. Then finally they stop and one of them stands up and slowly turns to Hill and Hinds. He steps forward as Hill stands up.

"We're sorry, ma'am," he begins as he removes his rubber gloves, "We did all that we could. His wounds were just too deep and he lost too much blood."

Hinds stands up and hugs Hill who still doesn't react. She just stands there staring at his lifeless body as if in a trance. She's thinks to herself, *"This can't be happening. I must be dreaming. Clarence can't be dead. We're going to get married."*

"Agent Hill? Are you all right? Agent Hill?" asks Lopez.
"Clarence and I are in love. We're going to be together."
"Agent Hill? Are you all right?"

She doesn't hear a thing. Her only thoughts are of sadness and despair. She thinks about what will happen to her now that Daily is gone, *"What I am I going to do now? What I am I going to do without Clarence? How can I go on? I need him. Oh my God I need him. What am I going to do?"*

The Fall of Man

The C-130 touches down at Andrews Air force Base early in the evening. Waiting on the tarmac is Brad's wife Patricia along with Troy, Dr. Bloomberg, and Professor Hamilton. They stand and watch silently as the plane pulls up in front of them. The cargo bay of the C-130 opens and the covered body of Clarence Daily is slowly carried out, closely followed by Hill, Brad and Dr. Hinds.

Pat runs up and jumps into Brad's arms hugging and kissing him all over his face, "Oh baby, I was so worried about you. Are you okay?"

Brad, still holding his wife, says softly, "I'm alright, baby. I just want to relax and take a shower."

Pat strokes the side of his face, "I understand, honey." The two walk silently together toward the dormitories just as Bloomberg walks over and hugs Hinds.

Hill limps down the cargo ramp, her hand wrapped in bandages and the lacerations on her face cleaned up. She is greeted by Troy and Professor Hamilton. Hamilton wraps his arms around her as she buries her face into his chest. He whispers into her ear, "I am so very sorry, Agent Hill. Please believe me when I tell you how sorry I am. I wish there was something I could say to make all of this make sense, but there isn't. We lost two very valuable people today. I just pray that it was worth it."

"Thank you professor, thank you," says Hill with tears in her eyes. Suddenly she backs away from Hamilton with a confused look, "Wait a minute, what do you mean 'two'?"

Troy walks up behind her and touches her gently on the shoulder, "Simon. We lost Simon today. He sacrificed himself to save the rest of us."

Hill gasps, putting a hand over her mouth, "Oh my God! I had no idea."

She turns back to Hamilton, "Please, please tell me they got that bastard! Tell me they got Brooks! I wanna be there we they bring him in."

Hamilton glances down at the floor for a moment, "Debra, I'm sorry but no, they didn't."

"What? What happened? I thought the president was sending a task force or something down to that fortress, New Eden."

"And that is exactly what it turned out to be--a fortress!" responds Hamilton.

"What'd you mean?"

"All I know is that we lost the entire Special Forces task force that went down there."

"How in the Hell did that happen?" exclaims Hill.

Troy answers, "Remember what Chad said when we were at the Gen X Tech headquarters? Remember the list of weapons we found? Now we know what they were for. He knew someone would come after him and he was prepared."

"This is insane! This is all insane! Now what are we going to do?"

"All we can do. Hopefully now with the added help of Barnes and Kang we can find a solution," says Hamilton.

Hill looks at him straight in the eyes and snarls, "And what happens if we can't?"

Hamilton takes a deep breath, raises his eyebrows, lowers his head then just slowly turns and walks away.

Troy stands beside Hill and says to her in a low tone, "I'm worried about him, you know. He's taking on way too much."

"We all have, Troy," Hill snaps, "I think we all have."

She walks off slowly towards the dorms, leaving Troy standing alone on the tarmac.

Once in her room Hill picks up a picture of Daily that she had on her nightstand then falls back onto the bed holding it against her chest. She lies there sobbing uncontrollably thinking about what life would have been like had Daily lived and they were able to get married. She lies there daydreaming then slowly drifts into a fitful sleep for the next two hours.

Around eight o'clock Hill is awakened by a sharp knock at the door. She sits up wipes her face and slowly walks over to answer it only to find Dr. Hinds waiting at the entrance with a saddened face. Without saying a word, Hill opens the door wider and steps aside allowing Hinds to enter. The two women sit on the bed just like they had done not too long before but the mood this time is a somber one.

"How're you holding up, kid?" asks Hinds.

"I don't know. Part of me wants to say the hell with all of this shit. Another part says let's stay and see it through because that's what Clarence would have wanted. Hell, I couldn't go home even if I wanted to--they nuked the whole city! This is a nightmare, a goddamn nightmare!"

"I can't imagine the pain that you're going through Deb, but I can tell you this. You do have something to fight for."

"I don't care anymore, Karen. 'Something to fight for?' Are you blind? Look at what's happening around you! We've lost! It's over! Nothing matters anymore!" she picks up a pillow and hugs it tightly.

"What about Clarence? What about his memory?"

"What's the point? He's not here to enjoy any victories, so what's the point?" shouts Hill as she falls back onto the bed with her hands on her face.

Hinds leans over and says softly, "What about for your child?"

"What the Hell are you talking about?"

"The baby you're having, Deb. What about that?"

Hill removes her hands from her face and quickly stares at Hinds, "What? What did you say?"

"You're pregnant, Debra. It's still very early but yeah, you're pregnant. That's part of the reason you've been sick. You're stressed and overworked while your body is trying to go through some hormonal changes. The bottom line is that you're having Clarence's baby. So you see you do have something to fight for. His memory can live on in your child."

Hill sits back up, tears are pouring from her eyes. A smile slowly spreads across her face, "Are you kidding me? I mean, I can't believe it. Oh my God, are you serious? I'm having his baby?"

Hinds, her eyes welling up with tears, smiles as she caresses Hill's face, "Yeah girl, you're going to be a mommy and you know what? You're going to be just fine."

Hill hugs Hinds and says, "Thank you. Thank you for being such a good friend. I'm going to be a mother? I can't believe this."

"Listen, it's going to be alright, come by my lab later and I'll hook you up with some vitamins. We have to keep you healthy girl," the two women laugh and hug again. Then Hinds stands up, "Well I just wanted to check up on you and give you the good news. I have to get back to the lab. I'm working with Kang and Barnes on trying to find a way to slow down SF-20. So far it looks like we maybe close to something."

"Well, good luck."

"Thanks, I'll see you later."

As Hinds begins to walk out Hill calls to her, "Karen."

"Yes."

"Thanks again, for everything."

"Don't sweat it. Like I said you'll be alright."

After Hinds leaves Hill lays back down on her bed staring at Daily's picture. As she lays there she thinks out loud, "You hear that Big Bear? You're going to be a poppa," she closes her eyes and presses his picture close to her chest and smiles.

Meanwhile back at the lab, Hamilton and Troy have just arrived to get an update on the scientist's work. In the lab working together is Bloomberg, Forrester, Kang and Barnes. Kang is trying to explain a complicated behavioral analysis while Bloomberg and Forrester listen attentively. They are also comparing various geographical areas and their respective plagues as they attempt to hash out an offensive game plan. Barnes sits alone quietly analyzing some samples under a microscope. The small group is focused and diligent, but the sharp tension that comes with stress hangs in the air. Hamilton walks up to Bloomberg and asks, "So how's it going, Kevin?"

"Richard, I wish I had more results but I will say that we're close. Thanks to Hyun-Ki and Sylvia we've been able to isolate the virus. We're working on a vaccine that should prevent it from affecting humans. Apparently Chad already has such vaccine. Both Sylvia and Hyun-Ki said they saw him inoculating people that were loyal to him. We're trying to work off of some of the research they were able to smuggle out before they left Gen X Tech."

"At least it's a start. Where's Karen?" says Hamilton as he looks around the lab.

"Oh, she's checking up on Debra."

"Good. That reminds me I need to check on her myself."

While the two men continue their conversation Troy walks over to Barnes who is still busy studying a specimen under a microscope on the other side of the room.

"So how's it going, Dr. Barnes?"

Without looking up from the microscope Barnes replies, "It's Sylvia."

"Excuse me?"

She turns away from the microscope and looks straight into Troy's eyes, "My name. It's Sylvia. Dr. Barnes is what my students call me. Just call me Sylvia," she says with a smile.

Troy flashes a wide grin across his face, "Okay, Sylvia. How are things going down here?"

"Pretty good for the most part. I think we're close to being able to at least protect ourselves from the effects of SF-20. But we're nowhere near close to finding a way to stop it."

Troy with his hands in his pockets leans his back against the table Barnes is working on and says, "So tell me something Doc--I mean, Sylvia. How does a beautiful woman like you end up in a career like this? I mean, you look like you should be a model or something," he chuckles.

Barnes again looks up from the microscope this time with a frown. "What, instead of a geek with thick glasses?"

"No, no, don't get me wrong! I mean you're just so…I don't know, different than all of the other female scientists I've been around that's all."

"Please tell me you're not one of those guys who has a problem with a woman who has both brains and good looks."

"Oh hell no--I love it. If you ask me, it makes you even more attractive."

"Oh, really?" Barnes says with a smirk.

"Really! If there were more women like you I would've settled down a long time ago. You have to admit, women like you aren't that common."

"Neither are cute twenty-five year olds who can construct their own particle accelerator from scratch."

"You know about that?"

"And the fact that you hold over thirty patents."

"Wow, you really did your homework. Wait a minute, did you say I was cute?"

"Maybe," Barnes says with a smile as she turns back to her microscope.

As Troy blushes Barnes looks up and giggles.

Then she says, "Why do you think Brooks was so interested in you? You're a well-known certified genius, Troy. He wanted to either persuade you to join him or add your DNA to those super humans he wants to create."

"You're kidding? How do you know all this?"

"Let's just say that there was a time that Chad and I were more than just colleagues."

Troy's face grows gloom, "Oh, it's like that," he says softly.

Sensing his discomfort, Barnes quickly adds, "Oh no, that chapter's been dead for a long time. I despise that man now. I don't want anything to do with him."

"Oh, really?" says Troy softly.

"Yes really. Besides I kind of have a thing for intelligent young men bent on saving the world."

Troy smiles and asks, "You do, huh? How young?"

"Buy me dinner and maybe you'll find out."

"We're on a military base under marshal law. How I'm I going to do that?"

Barnes gives him a flirty smile, "You're the genius. You figure it out."

"Are you messing with me?"

"What's the matter? Don't tell me you're intimidated by older women?"

"What? Okay, be ready by ten. I'll show you who's intimidated."

She gives him a devilish smile then turns back to the microscope as Troy leaves the lab. Upon leaving he struts past Hamilton, Bloomberg, Forrester and Kang who are still engrossed in conversation with his chest out and a big smile on his face. The four older men stop and stare at him as he passes by. Then they look back at Barnes who gives them a guilty smile then turns and continues her work.

Hamilton looks at Bloomberg and asks, "What's that all about?"

"Has it been that long, Richard?" says Bloomberg.

"What?"

"You don't remember that look?"

Hamilton just stares at him with a curious look on his face.

"Love, Rich, that's the look of love, you old dog. You need to get out more."

"Love? What? They just met! That's my grandson and she's at least ten years older than him," he begins to head toward Barnes, "I'm going to have a talk with her."

Forrester steps in front of Hamilton and puts his hands on his chest, "Breathe Professor, breathe. Let them be. They need this."

"Hell, we all do," adds Bloomberg, "It's times like this that help people see what's really worth fighting for. Look at Debra and Clarence."

"Your friends are right, Professor. Love is one of those things that defines us as human. It's important that we remember that," adds Kang.

Hamilton pauses for a moment then sighs, "Yeah, I guess you're right. I guess it can't hurt."

Bloomberg continues, "You have to let go, Rich. He's not a little boy anymore, he's a grown man. Let them be. Hell, at least he has good taste in women."

At that moment all four of the men turn and look at Barnes who sits up from the microscope, turns and catches them staring at her, she frowns; shakes hear head mumbling, "Men," then goes back to work. They all turn back around and smile at one another.

"Yeah that's my boy all right," states Hamilton with a big grin on his face as the others laugh.

In another part of the dormitory Brad and his wife Patricia are on their way to visit Hill. As they walk down the corridor leading to Hill's room Pat asks Brad, "Don't you think it's too early? Maybe we should give her more time."

"After losing Cliff, Doris, Simon and now Clarence I don't know how much time any of us have. I think she could use all the support we can give her."

They approach Hill's door and knock. When she answers her face lights up like a candle.

"Brad, Pat! Come in, come in, please."

"I hope we're not intruding," says Pat apologetically.

"No, no, not at all," she says as she ushers them in and directs them to seats in the small room, "Can I get you something? All I have is juice and water."

"No, nothing for me," says Brad.

"No honey, I'm good," replies Pat.

"We just came by to offer our deepest condolences," says Brad, "I know the two of you were more than just partners."

"You knew?" says Hill in a surprised voice.

"Yeah I suspected for a while and then Troy told me he walked in on you guys in New York.

Hill laughs, "Yeah, that was kind of embarrassing."

Brad smiling says, "I know. I think Troy was more embarrassed than you guys," he pauses. "But, Debra?"

"Yes, Brad?"

"Clarence told me something before the last mission that I think you should know."

"What is it?"

"He told me that he was going to propose to you."

Hill giggles like a young school girl and says, "Brad, he did."

"Really?" says Brad surprised as he and Pat both smile.

"Yes, on the way to Florida. He proposed on the plane."

"Oh my God," says Pat.

"And that's not all. I just found out that I'm pregnant," adds Hill.

The two visitors are stunned they just sit for a moment not knowing how to respond.

Finally Pat utters, "Debra! You're pregnant?"

"Yes, I am."

"Oh my God that's great," she runs over and the two women hug each other, "You know what this means don't you?"

"No, what?"

"We'll have big bellies together!" the two women laugh and hug each other again.

Brad walks over to Hill, "Congratulations, Debra." He puts a hand on her shoulder. "And if you need anything --anything at all-- please don't hesitate to ask."

"Thank you. Thank you both. Believe it or not, after all that's happened you guys are the only real family I have now."

"We feel the same way Debra," says Pat, "Oh, and the Professor wanted to let you know that he is planning a funeral service right here on base tomorrow for Clarence and Simon."

"Great. I have to thank him. I know he's been under a lot of stress."

"You don't know the half of it Debra," says Brad.

"What do you mean?"

"Have you turned on the television since you've been back?"

"No, I thought there was a media black out"

"Some private groups have taken control of a number of television and radio stations. They've been broadcasting around the clock, documenting what is really going on and it's hell out there Debra."

"Jesus, it's gotten that bad?"

"You saw how terrible it was in Florida? Well, it's worse now. The only safe places are a few military bases and even some of those have been overrun," Brad notices the concern in Hill's eyes, "I don't want to worry you. From what I hear, we're still pretty safe here. I just thought you should know that outside there's very little left to go back to."

"I understand. Thank you Brad, for everything."

"No problem," he takes Pat by the hand, "Well we better get going and let you get some rest," he turns back as they head toward the door, "Don't forget: just call us if you need anything."

"I will, I promise," says Hill as she blows a kiss to them as they leave.

Curious about what Brad said she walks over to her bed sits down and grabs the remote control off of the night stand. Hill turns on the television monitor and dims the room lights then leans back on some pillows on the bed.

When the TV comes on there's nothing but static displaying on the screen. She clicks through several channels but they all seem to be the same way. Finally she gets to one station that has low audio with so much static she can't seem to make out what they are saying. Then another station has some fuzzy video but no audio at all. Hill continues through the remaining channels until at last discovers a clear station complete with clear audio and video. It looks like some sort of low-budget news broadcast. There's a man dressed in a T-shirt sitting at a table with a screen behind him showing images of outbreaks of SF-20 around the world. She turns up the volume to hear what he is saying.

"To all those tuning in for the first time, welcome to the People's Broadcast. The U.S. government has been powerless to help us as wild beasts roam the streets. They don't want you to see what's really happening and they refuse to keep the airwaves open but we will stay on as long as we can to keep you posted on the latest developments.

Most of the worst news comes from the southern states. Those killer ants that invaded Arizona have now spread throughout New Mexico and Texas. There have also been reports of killer bees in those areas as well. We warn you to stay clear of those states.

We have reports coming in from Louisiana, Mississippi, and Arkansas that a fast-growing vine has been spotted all over those states. It looks similar to ivy but has long thorns and large leaves with purple colored pods. This plant is extremely dangerous. It can move quickly and has attacked hundreds of people. Its thorns are poisonous and its tendrils can pop out and grab you. It reacts to both sound and body heat. If you see this plant stay clear. It will kill you.

Florida has been completely overrun by birds, rats and all kinds of mutated insects. Stay completely away from Florida!"

Other states to stay away from are California, Oregon, Nebraska, both North and South Carolina and Virginia.

Also there have been reports of outbreaks of a new form of rabies throughout the nation that is being transmitted by people bitten by mutated mammals. Large groups of infected people have been seen roaming many cities attacking anyone in their path. If you see anyone acting erratically with dark red eyes and foaming from the mouth run! This person is infected and will attack and kill you. There is no cure for this new form of rabies. It is transmitted by the carrier biting their victim and infecting their blood. After that in less than twenty-four hours, symptoms begin to develop. It appears that some of the infected die within forty-eight hours but others become carriers and live a little longer.

The President has not been able to be reached concerning these events. We will try our best to keep this broadcast on the air to keep you informed.

To all those tuning in for the first time welcome to the people's broadcast. The U.S. government has been powerless..."

CLICK!

Hill turns off the monitor as the apparently taped broadcast begins to repeat itself. She sits there in shock and horror.

"Is this it?" she wonders to herself, "Is this the end of the world?"

Hill rubs her tummy as she looks down at her stomach, "Don't worry, little one. Mommy will protect you," she turns off the lights and falls asleep in the bed dreaming about becoming a mother in an uncertain world.

It's ten o'clock and Troy is sitting in a remote corner of the cafeteria waiting for Dr. Barnes to arrive. He has a handful of dandelions and a bottle of sparkling cider. Troy's dressed in neatly-pressed beige slacks and a brown short-sleeved designer shirt with an open collar. He's wearing a gold earring in his left ear and a matching gold chain around his neck that holds a small oval locket. There's only a few other people in the cafeteria at this hour and Troy taps his hands on the table as he nervously awaits Dr. Barnes. After waiting for about ten minutes he sees an image of beauty enter the room. It's Barnes and she looks even more stunning than ever. She stops at the entrance and looks around till she spots Troy then smiles and walks slowly towards his table. Troy is frozen in his seat as if paralyzed. He sits there mesmerized by her beauty. As Barnes approaches, he scans her entire body. Her hair is fashionably styled with a wavy lock hanging down over her right eye. Her makeup is subtle yet flawless. She's wearing a low cut red blouse that accentuates her perfectly shaped breasts and a closely fitting black skirt that shows off the curves of her hips and rear. The skirt stops at her mid thigh which allows her to display her slender shapely legs. She walks as if she's a runway model, carefully placing one foot in front of the other showing off her black pumps with three inch heels. Barnes stops at the table and gazes down at Troy who still hasn't moved or said a word.

"And I thought you were a gentleman," she says sarcastically with a smirk, "You just going to sit there?"

Troy snaps out of his trance and jumps up from his seat, "Oh! Oh, of course," he runs around the table and grabs the chair in front of her and pulls it back for Barnes to sit on, "I'm-I'm so sorry," he stutters as he holds the back of her seat.

Once she is seated he returns nervously to his own seat.

"Sorry about that," he reaches across the table and hands her the dandelions, "these are for you. They're not roses but they're all I can get in a pinch."

"Aw, Taraxacum Officinale, thank you, that was sweet," she takes the flowers and demurely inhales their scent before placing them daintily down on the table, "So what's for dinner?"

Troy waves to one of the cafeteria workers who quickly wheels over a cart with two covered trays. He places the trays in front of both Barnes and Troy then removes the covers to reveal the meal beneath. There's steamed lobster tails, pasta covered in a cheesy sauce and sautéed vegetables.

"Wow, you really pulled out all the stops. How did you manage all this?" asks Barnes.

"My secret. Let's just say I have my connections," he says as he smiles and opens the sparkling cider to pour them both a drink.

"I'm impressed all this chaos in the world and you still find the time to be romantic. Not bad."

"Look who's talking. Since when do scientists pack away fashion outfits on their way to a military base?"

"You never know who you might meet."

Troy smiles, "I guess you're right," Troy leans across the table, "to tell you the truth the head cook is a friend of mine. He owed me a favor. The lobster really belongs to the base commander. We figured he's probably too busy to realize they're missing."

Barnes laughs as she sips her cider, "My my, Troy I see you have a little bad boy in you."

Troy blushes, "Just a little."

As they eat the two continue to get to know each other through conversation. At one point Barnes notices the locket around Troy's neck and reaches across the table to touch it. "That's an interesting necklace you have there. Is it a picture locket?"

"Yes, there're pictures of my mom and dad. I lost them both and this keeps them close to me."

"Oh I'm sorry. I didn't know."

"That's why my grandfather and I are so close. He always said that he loved my father like a son. He took it pretty hard when he died and then when my mom passed away he lost his only child on top of that. That's why he's so overprotective."

"You're a lucky guy."

"Why do you say that?"

"At least you still have your grandfather. I lost both of my parents too. But I didn't have any other family. I guess that's one of the reasons why I work so hard. It's all I have," Barnes grows quiet, "It's been hard for me to let anyone get close. I guess I was always afraid of losing them too."

Troy reaches across the table and softly touches her hand, "So why me? Why are you letting me get close?"

Barnes now with teary eyes looks up at him, "Look around, Troy. The world is coming apart. If I'm going to die I'd rather not be alone."

"Who says we're going to die?"

"Troy, really. Do you really think we can change all of this?"

"I don't know, Sylvia. But I'm willing to try."

For the next hour the two continue their meal while they joke and exchange stories about one another's past. Finally around 11:15 pm, an alarm sounds throughout the base followed by an announcement over the PA system.

"Attention! All sentries report to your posts! Base perimeter has been breached. This is a code red condition. This is not a drill. Repeat. This is not a drill. The base is now on full red alert. All non military personnel report to the dormitories immediately."

Troy and Barnes sit stunned as dozens of armed soldiers run through the cafeteria. Barnes flinches and grips Troy's hand as she hears gunfire followed by an explosion from outside of the building.

She looks nervously over at Troy, "What's happening?"

"I'm not sure."

Just then Lieutenant Lopez runs up to them with five other soldiers. They are all dressed in body armor and are heavily armed.

"Troy! Dr. Barnes! Are you okay?"

"Miguel, what's going on?" asks Troy.

"I need you two to follow me, NOW!"

Troy and Barnes get up and follow Lopez out of the cafeteria. Lopez and the soldiers are almost jogging, making it difficult for Barnes in her high heels to keep up. Finally she nearly stumbles as she kicks off her shoes, picks them up and continues in her bare feet. Troy holds her tightly by the elbow to help her along. As they exit the building they see that the entire base has erupted into a state of pure pandemonium. There are soldiers running everywhere and shouting orders. In the distance, gunfire and explosions could be heard and flashes from grenade blasts can be seen coming from behind several buildings. Overhead helicopters buzz back and forth and alarms are going off all over the place.

In a distance Lopez notices a group of figures running in the shadows coming towards them from left. He stops and signals his men.

"Troy, Dr. Barnes get behind us!" he shouts with a wild look in his eyes.

Not knowing what is going on, they obey his command and run behind them. Barnes holds Troy tight as the scene in front of them unfolds. The five soldiers along with Lieutenant Lopez form a line in front of Troy and Barnes. They get down on one knee and aim their M-16 machine guns at the approaching crowd. As the figures emerge from the shadows Troy and Barnes can finally see clearly what the soldiers are aiming at. About fifty individuals are racing towards them, all foaming at the mouth and growling like animals. Their clothes are torn and many of them have scars across their faces and bodies. Their movements are unnatural and more ape-like than human. Their eyes have a dark bloody red glow.

"Ready, men? Fire!"

As Lopez gives the order, he and his men begin picking off the advancing horde. Many of the attackers get back up after being hit and must be shot again. At about fifty yards away some are still coming. At twenty-five yards a few are still alive. Finally at ten yards the last one finally falls.

Lopez turns to Troy and Barnes, "Let's go, quickly!" he motions to them to begin running again and follow without question.

As they run Troy asks Lopez again, "Miguel, Miguel, what the hell's going on?"

"The Professor sent me to get you. We're leaving!"

"Leaving? To go where?" asks Barnes struggling to keep up with them in her now swollen bare feet.

"I don't know, but as you can see the base is under attack!"

Troy and Barnes give each other a puzzled look but no one says another word as they run towards a hangar in a restricted area at the far end of the base. The hangar doors are closed but there is a team of a ten soldiers with heavy machine guns behind sandbags camped in front guarding the building. Lopez and the others run past them and enter the hangar. Once inside they are greeted by the rest of the INVASION team, Hill, Dr. Kang with his wife and child, Brad with his wife and mother-in-law and several soldiers a few of whom look to be dressed as pilots. They all have frightened and confused looks on their faces as they push and shove each other in a hurried attempt to board a large plane inside the hangar. It's a 747 painted white and blue with an emblem on its side. Troy has seen this plane before. As he approaches holding Barnes' hand he gets a better view of the plane and realizes what it is. It's Air Force One!

He looks back at Forrester, "You're kidding? You mean to tell me we're taking the President's plane?"

"You haven't heard?" answers Forrester.

"Heard what?" responds Troy.

"About the President. He-He's dead along with most of his staff."

"What?" yells Troy.

"It happened about an hour ago." says a voice from behind him. Troy turns and sees his grandfather approaching him looking worst than ever and breathing heavily.

"Pop! You okay?" Troy says as he runs to his side to help him up the stairs to the plane.

"Yes, yes, I'm fine. I just haven't had to move that fast in a long time," he pauses for a moment to catch his breath, "the entire DC area is swarming with infected humans," he continues as they make their way into the plane.

"Infected, by what?" asks Barnes, following close behind.

"A new strain of rabies that's been spreading across the country. Half of the people it infects die within twenty-four hours and the other half become carriers and turn into some sort of crazed animal, going after anyone who's not infected," interrupts Forrester.

As Hamilton reaches the top of the stairs he stops and says, "The bottom line is that the government has collapsed and we have to leave before we're overrun," he then turns to one of the pilots, "Takeoff as soon as everyone is onboard!"

"Yes sir but have you figured out where we're going?"

"Not a clue," says Hamilton, "I'm still working on it. Just get us in the air."

The pilot smirks, "Yes sir. I guess anywhere is better than here."

Once onboard Lopez radios the soldiers guarding the hangar to open the doors and get onboard. Then Air Force One slowly taxis out onto the tarmac. From their windows on board the group can see that the base is now aflame. Fighting and explosions are going on all around them. Even alongside the runway soldiers could be seen shooting infected humans as well as infected humans attacking and killing some of the soldiers. It's complete bedlam. The pilot throttles the plane's engines causing the craft to roar down the runway.

Once airborne, Troy and Barnes find Professor Hamilton in the plane's briefing room. He's there with Hill, Brad, Forrester, Hinds, Bloomberg, Lopez and one of the pilots. They are discussing possible locations in which to land. On the wall of the briefing room is a large monitor displaying events from around the world. The sound is muted but from the images it's clear that things have gotten completely out of control.

Hinds, reading some information off of a sheet of paper says, "Based on our reports the virus is already beginning to affect humans. We haven't had time to test our vaccine but we are very certain that it'll work. We bought as much of it with us as we could. I'd like to start administering it to everyone on board as soon as possible."

"Alright, Karen, why don't you and Kevin head to the infirmary and get started," says Hamilton.

"Right," says Bloomberg who gets up and leaves with Hinds.

Hamilton turns to Lopez, "Now Lieutenant, have you found a place for us to land?"

Lopez points to the pilot sitting across from him, "Well thanks to Captain Matthews here I think so."

Everyone turns their attention to the pilot.

Matthews sits up in his seat, "Well we're heading for the Ramey Coast Guard facility in Puerto Rico. It's almost completely deserted but we contacted a small group of workers still there and they agreed to help us refuel and stock up on supplies."

"What happens after that?" asks Barnes.

"Excuse me?" responds Hamilton.

"Where do we go from there? I doubt that we'll be able to stay there too long. What do we do next?"

Troy then jumps in, "She's right, you know. Look at what just happened at one of our most secure bases."

Everyone around the table gives each other a look of concern.

"You make a good point but we'll have time to figure that out when we land," answers Hamilton, "If anyone has any recommendations before that time please feel free to let us know. Until then gather everyone on board and get them to Dr. Hinds for vaccination," he stands up and looks over everyone in the room, "I know this has been hard but in the meantime try and get some rest," he sighs deeply, turns and stumbles as he is about to leave the room.

Troy catches him by the arm, "You okay, Pop?"

Hamilton looks up at Troy with weakened eyes, "I think I'd better take my own advice. I'm going to lie down for a while, Son. Let me know if there are any important changes."

"You want me come with you?" asks Troy.

"No, no, I'm fine--I can make it," he walks slowly out of the door and down the corridor.

Everyone else goes to either their assigned cabin or to the infirmary. By the time they land in Puerto Rico, three hours later, everyone on board has been vaccinated and well-rested. By 4:30 am they wait for the plane to be refueled as a number of soldiers deploy around the plane to protect it. So far the base is quiet and dark.

Lopez and another group of soldiers head to the abandoned base's armory and mess hall to load up with weapons and provisions. The Puerto Rican base, located in Aguadilla on the northwestern tip of the island, is partially covered with the deadly vines that have been spreading around the world so everyone has to be careful where they step. Soldiers carry flamethrowers to clear large sections of the dangerous plant from around the base.

It's 6:30 am when Bloomberg finds Troy, Brad and Lopez sitting in the briefing room. Troy is working at the computer and the others are around him watching the screen.

"What'cha guys up to?" inquires Bloomberg.

"I think we found a safe place to settle down at," says Troy without looking up from the computer.

"Really where?"

"I'm not sure you're going to like it," adds Brad.

"Why, where is this place you're talking about?" presses Bloomberg.

Troy looks up and motions for him to look at the computer monitor. Bloomberg walks over and looks down at the screen. Displayed in front of him is a satellite image of a huge complex surrounded by snow.

"What's this?" he asks.

"New Eden," says Troy.

"You must be kidding. We couldn't get within a hundred miles of that place and why would you want to go there in the first place?"

"Kevin, think about it--this place was built as a safe haven to ride out this storm that Brooks created. It's the only place on Earth we can truly be safe," responds Troy.

"Did you forget what happened to the task force that was sent down there?"

"I didn't forget. That's why I came up with a plan," comments Troy with a smirk.

"Troy!" says Bloomberg sarcastically.

"Trust me. Just sit down for a sec and listen."

Bloomberg reluctantly takes a seat as Troy begins to spell out his plan of action.

"I know that the base is ringed with anti aircraft weapons and the land around the facility is mined. And based on the data we retrieved for Gen X Tech everything is controlled by a central computer. If I can gain access to that system I could deactivate all of their defenses without them ever knowing."

"And how do you plan on accomplishing that?" asks Bloomberg.

"Kevin, we're on Air Force One. Its computers are filled with all kinds of top-secret information and we have connections to dozens of satellite uplinks. So here is my plan. First I'm going to hack into the Gen X Tech Communications Satellite. Based on our information we should be able to use it to remotely control New Eden's main computer system. Once I gain control I should be able to use it to power down all of their defensive systems. The next step is harder because once we land we still have to gain entry and I'm betting he has some of those super soldiers we saw in New York down there. But I have a plan for that too. I've analyzed the data we brought back from our raid on their headquarters and I think I found a weakness. It's they're auditory system. You see it's enhanced allowing them to have the hearing sensitivity of a dog."

"Okay, you got my attention. How is that a weakness?" asks Bloomberg.

"Because their hearing is so sensitive I'm going to use a technology called infrasound which is low frequency sound well below human hearing. At high volumes a frequency between seven and twenty hertz can affect the human central nervous system enough to cause disorientation or even unconsciousness. If I can put together a sonic grenade that uses this technology we should be able to emit a pitch that can disable those super soldiers long enough for our guys to take them out."

"How sure are you that this could work?"

"I've been working on something similar for a few years now as a form of non-lethal weapon for crowd control."

Bloomberg smirks, "So let me get this right. Your plan is to hack their satellite, take control of their computer systems and make a super sound device to stun their soldiers."

Troy smiles, "Yeah. Great, don't you think?"

"Listen I know you're a boy genius but don't you think this plan has way too many uncertainties. Hacking a satellite is not as easy as hacking into someone's home computer and as for creating a sonic grenade. I've never even heard of such a weapon."

"That's because no one has invented it yet," adds Troy.

"And you will?"

"Like I said, half the work is already done, and as for hacking into their satellite you're again forgetting we're on Air Force One. From here I can access the satellite uplinks and computers of the NSA, the CIA, even the Pentagon. I'll use all of that computing power to help me. I think I could blind them long enough for us to land at the Amundsen-Scott U.S. Antarctic research station. It's about 900 miles from New Eden. The pilots say we could have enough fuel to make it if we stop at the Palmer Research Station first. We could stage our attack from there. I already called them on a secure SAT line. So they're ready and excepting us"

"You what?"

"It's our only hope."

"I don't know."

"Look around you Kevin! What choice do we have? You tell me--what other options do we have?"

Bloomberg sighs and pauses for a second. He looks around the room at the other faces then gathers himself and says, "Alright, I guess you're right. We don't have much to lose. So how can we--"

Suddenly Hinds bursts into the briefing room with tears streaming down her face, "Troy! Kevin! It's Richard. Come, come now!"

She races out of the room closely followed by the rest of the team. They run down the hall of the plane and into what would normally be the presidential suite. On the bed is Professor Hamilton. He's lying there with all of his clothes on clutching a bible. Troy walks over to his side and looks down at him and gently touches his forehead.

Hinds, still sobbing, says through a trembling voice, "I came in to check up on him and found him lying there like that, he's been dead for a while but it looks like he went peacefully in his sleep. I'm so sorry, Troy."

Troy says nothing. He merely looks down at his grandfather with a blank look on his face. A few moments later Hill as well as other team members begin to trickle into the room as word spreads throughout the plane that the professor has died. Barnes walks along side of Troy and hugs him with tears in her eyes. They all surround the bed looking down at their fallen leader.

Bloomberg looks across at Troy, "That does it. I think enough people have died. It's time to put an end to this!"

Troy slowly looks up at him.

"We're going with your plan, son. We're going to make it work and we're taking the professor with us. We'll bury him when we reach our new destination."

"And where is that?" asks Hill.

"New Eden. Pack up 'cause we leave in an hour," says Bloomberg as he storms out of the room.

Everyone silently stares at Troy as he kneels by the Professor's side. They stand there wondering what will happen next. They wonder what their journey to the South Pole fortress will bring and they question whether or not it will bring an end to this incredible nightmare.

New Eden

While flying over Venezuela in Air Force One the INVASION team, along with soldiers, scientists and friends picked up along the way, take a moment of silence to memorialize the life of Professor Richard Hamilton. After the ceremony, the professor's body is placed in a refrigerated section in the cargo bay. Troy retires to his cabin with Barnes at the rear of the plane. Ever since they took off from Puerto Rico she has remained by his side. The two have become very fond of one another over the short period of time they have been together. As Troy quietly lies down on his bed, Barnes rests next to him with her head on his chest, he says nothing as he stares at the ceiling thinking about what his life will be like without his grandfather. He thinks about what life will be like with Barnes. He wonders about life in a world gone crazy, crazy with killer plants and mutant insects. What will life be like in a world that is the result of one man's ego, one man's quest to become a god?

For the next hour the two just hold each other without uttering a word. Troy thinks about how lucky he is to have met Barnes. He thinks about how lucky he is to have met someone that he can really spend his life with. But how can he have a life with her with Brooks still alive? How can he start a family and be happy when the man who changed the entire world and sent it into hell is still out there, running free? He must do something about. It's up to him now to lead the team. A feeling of euphoria sweeps over him as he looks down at Barnes, who has fallen asleep on his chest. He gently strokes her hair and realizes what he must do.

"I must stop Chad Brooks. No matter what it takes!" he thinks to himself.

Barnes awakens as Troy caresses her hair. She looks up at him with her big beautiful eyes and smiles.

"How're you feeling, Baby?" she says softly.

"I'm alright."

"You sure?"

"Yeah, I'm sure. I have to stop him, you know."

"What do you mean?"

"Chad. I have to stop him and I think I'm the only one who can."

"I understand. After everything that's happened, believe me I understand. But do you think you're up to it? I mean after your grandfather, don't you think…."

"No," he says sharply as he sits up, "It's now or never. Especially because of my grandfather, I watched him spend the last years of his life trying to undo what that bastard created. It's up to me to finish what he started! I just need you to understand that."

"Don't worry about me, Troy. You have my support."

He lies back down and pulls her over so that her entire body is resting on his. Troy tilts up her chin, holding her face and looking into her eyes, "You know, you're like an angel to me. How did I ever end up with you?"

"This was meant to be. I can feel it," she says softly.

He kisses her gently on soft, full lips then pauses to look into those lovely eyes of hers, tender with affection. She closes her eyes, inclining her head as he leans in and kisses her again, feeling her lips smile contentedly beneath his. Wrapping his arms around her, he pulls her closer, tighter, kissing her with greater passionate force. Button by button, Barnes gently undoes Troy's shirt, planting a series of small, moist kisses down his chest at the same time. Completely turned on, Troy responds by rolling her over and climbing on top of the petite beauty. Buttons fly as he bodily rips her blouse open and off of her creamy shoulders. With lust-laden haste, he undoes her bra with feverish fingers. She looks up at him, face contorted with need, and whispers, "Take me, Troy. I want you. I want you, now."

He moans, lowering himself onto her and kissing her neck. Barnes closes her eyes and her breath grows hotter and faster against his face as her desire increases. The two make passionate love to one another then fall asleep in one another's embrace.

At around 10:00 am Troy wakes up and is careful not to awaken Barnes. He quietly gets dressed and heads to the briefing room where most of his equipment has been set up. It'll take about ten hours to reach the Palmer Research Station on Antarctica and he needs to have control of the satellite way before then. He also needs time to work on the infrasonic grenade he proposed. For the next three hours he works at his computers routing and rerouting signals through ground based transmitters. Once the satellite is located he begins work on breaking its security system. This takes another hour. While he works other members of the INVASION team trickle in and out of the briefing room to check up on him. But he is like a man possessed. It's as if he doesn't even notice that anyone's around, he sits there glaring at the terminal with his fingers flying across the keyboard. He doesn't look up or even acknowledge their existence. He's become completely immersed in his work. The only time that he snaps out of it is when Barnes joins him around 3:00 pm. She brings him some food and a cup of tea then sits by his side while he works. At about 3:30 he sits back in his chair and exhales, "I'm in!"

Barnes, who has been resting her head on the desk next to him quickly looks up. "What is it, baby?"

"I'm in. I'm finally in!" says Troy triumphantly.

"You have control?"

"No, not fully, but I have broken through their security system. I can now access the satellite imaging system."

"What's that?"

"It'll allow us to see what the satellite sees."

Troy begins tapping a few keys on the keyboard and the image on the screen changes to show a satellite image of the west coast of South America just as Bloomberg enters the room.

"Oh shit! Fuck, no!" shouts Troy.

"What's going on?" asks Bloomberg as he and Barnes quickly lean over to take a look at the computer screen.

Troy try's to explain as he continues to type, "This is an image from the Gen X Tech SAT. Right now, it's over Peru."

Bloomberg gives Troy a puzzled look, "That's great! You got control."

"No, not full control. We're just viewing what the satellite sees."

"But that's still great. That means you're close to gaining full control."

Troy ignores him and continues to type away like mad.

Barnes asks, "What's wrong, baby?"

"We're flying right over the heart of Brazil," shouts Troy as he continues to hammer away at the keyboard.

"So what's the problem?" queries Bloomberg.

"That satellite! It's moving in an easterly direction! If it passes over us…"

"My God, you're right!" answers Bloomberg now with a sound of concern in his voice.

"What? What's going on, what's the problem?" cries Barnes frantically as she desperately tries to figure out the two men's cryptic conversation.

Finally Bloomberg turns to her to explain, "If their satellite passes over us they'll be able to spot us coming. That'll kill our element of surprise."

"Troy can you get control before it reaches us?" she asks.

"I'm working on it! We're about 500 miles from the edge of their visual scope. We have about twenty minutes before the edge of that scope crosses over us. I'm trying to redirect the satellite north. Not enough for them to detect it but enough for the scope to pass above us. Kevin if you can get the pilot to speed up that would help!"

"Got'cha," responds Bloomberg as he picks up the intercom and contacts the pilot.

While the pilot pushes the plane to its maximum speed of 650 mile per hour Troy finally gains access to the satellite's controls and gently guides it up above their path. Once the plane is in the clear he sits back in his chair and wipes the sweat from his forehead.

"You did it! Troy we're clear!" says Bloomberg standing over his shoulder looking down at the computer screen.

"I knew you could do it," whispers Barnes as she kisses him on the cheek.

"One down, two to go," says Troy as he stretches his arms.

Bloomberg pats him on the shoulder, "You did good son. You did real good. Your grandfather would be proud of you," he pats him again and walks out of the briefing room.

"Now what?" asks Barnes.

"Now, I have to make an infrasonic grenade. Wanna help?"

"I guess so--if I knew what it was."

"It's a sonic weapon that uses low frequency sound to disable its victims."

"How low a frequency are we talking about?"

"Below twenty hertz."

"You know I remember reading something about how extreme low frequencies could have a physical effect on people. There was an incident a few years ago where a theater full of people became nauseous from the low frequency sound played during a horror movie."

"You're right; you see at around twenty hertz it can cause loss of muscle coordination and equilibrium control. At ten hertz there's neurological interference and at seven hertz you get spasms, nausea and finally unconsciousness. At high enough volumes it can even cause organ damage."

"Wow!"

"Yeah and the other great thing about this weapon is that because it is low frequency it can even have an effect through walls."

"But what about the people using it? Won't they be just as vulnerable?"

"I've thought of that! We're going to have to develop some sort of active noise cancellation system."

"Active noise cancellation?"

"It's a system that emits a sound wave at the same amplitude as the sound we want to cancel but with an inverted phase," Troy uses his hands to show how the two sound waves will converge with one another, "When the sound waves combine they cancel each other out."

"And you think you can make all of this work before we land?"

Troy smirks and gives her a cocky look, "What do you think?"

"I'm serious Troy! We have only about five hours before we reach Palmer. Do you really think you could have both of these things working by then?"

"Most of the work of the infrasonic grenade and the active noise cancellation system I've already done. I worked on some prototypes a few years ago. The only problem that I'll have is finding the parts to construct the weapons onboard. I may have to wait till we get to Palmer to complete the systems."

"You sure sound very confident about this."

"Sylvia, I haven't been more sure of anything in my life. With all that's happened I just feel driven. Like there's nothing I can't do. I just need you to trust me."

"I do, Troy. I do trust you," She leans over and plants a wet kiss on his lips then stares into his eyes, "I'm here for you and I'll help anyway I can."

"Thanks." He kisses her back then sits up, "first thing we have to do is get the team together. We're going to need their help. Call Karen and Jacob while I put together a parts list."

For the next three hours the team works on constructing the infrasonic grenade and ear plugs that use Troy's noise cancelling technology. They are able to cannibalize some equipment found in the cargo hold of Air Force One to complete three full grenades and four pairs of ear plugs. The grenades are metal cylinders about a foot long and three inches wide. Each is covered with eight one inch holes that hold the sound emitters. On the top of each device is a knob that acts as a trigger that when switched on activates a five second timer. When the timer reaches zero the weapon emits a 175 decibel two second infrasonic burst that has an effective radius of about fifty yards. With the limited power source they were able to find they would be able to use each grenade only once.

When they are finished Troy and the others step back and admire their handy work. Forrester looks over at Troy and asks, "I don't mean to be the messenger of doom but how do we test this stuff?"

"We won't be able to. We're just going to have to go on faith," says Troy.

Everyone just quietly looks at one another.

Troy continues, "We have about two hours till we land at Palmer. So I suggest we all get some rest. When we land we'll plan the next step in our operation which is the assault of New Eden."

Again they all nervously stare at one another then slowly without a word walk out and head to their cabins. Barnes stays behind and hugs Troy.

"I'm proud of you. You've really taken charge. They have a lot of trust in you."

"I just hope I don't let them down, Jacob was right we should test the equipment. If it doesn't work we're all dead"

"Shhh, take it easy. It'll work. I have faith in you"

He smiles at her as she kisses him on the cheek and says, "Now come on and follow your own advice and get some rest."

"You go ahead; I'll catch up with you. I want to check up on Brad and Miguel before we land."

"Alright baby, don't be too long," says Barnes as she walks off toward their cabin. Troy heads up to the upper deck where Brad and Lopez are making plans for their arrival at Palmer.

"How's it going guys?" asks Troy.

"Well we have some good news and some bad news," says Brad.

"Alright, give it to me straight. I can take it."

Lopez begins, "On the good side we were able to contact a small group of Special Forces and Navy Seal troops. We told them our plans and they've already made it to Palmer. They're waiting to assist us. So including the men we have on board we should be going in with about fifty troops."

"That's great! So what's the bad news?"

Brad looks at him and frowns, "The weather. We have a large polar cyclone coming in with winds up around thirty to thirty-five miles per hour. It was just reported over the Davis Australian Base and it appears to be heading right at New Eden."

"How long before it gets there?" asks Troy.

Brad and Lopez exchange glances at one another then Brad says, "At around the same time we plan to attack, 0600."

Troy slumps back in his seat, "Shit! That's damn going to make things harder."

"We can wait out the storm. Attack when it's over," adds Lopez.

"I want to get this guy. I want to get him now!" says Troy.

As they talk Bloomberg walks up the stairs and joins the meeting, "Gentlemen."

"Hey Kevin," says Brad.

"So how's our operation going?" asks Bloomberg.

"Well we'll be ready on time. But we ran into a glitch," explains Troy.

"What type of glitch?"

Brad hands Bloomberg the weather reports, "A huge storm is rolling in and will hit New Eden around the same time that we plan to attack."

Bloomberg says nothing. He just looks over the reports then slowly looks up at Troy, "I know you want to go don't you?" he asks.

"You know I do, but..."

"Then go!" he says sharply.

Brad and Lopez snap their heads up and stare at Bloomberg in amazement.

"What? With the storm coming?" asks Troy.

"Why not? They know the storm is coming too. They won't be expecting an attack during a Polar Cyclone."

Troy sits forward with a twinkle in his eyes, "You know you're right! We'll have the element of surprise on our side."

"It's going to make this mission even more dangerous than it already is," explains Lopez.

Troy stares at him intently, "Listen the odds were already against us now with the storm they just got a little better. So you in or what?"

Lopez looks at Brad then at Bloomberg and finally at Troy, "Yeah, I'm in."

"Count me in, too," adds Brad.

"Great, Miguel contact your men on the ground and fill them in on our plans. Tell them to gear up for some harsh weather. We'll move up our planned attack to try and reach New Eden just before the storm hits."

"I'm on it," says Lopez as he rushes to the communications room.

At about 9:00 pm Air Force One lands at the Palmer station and taxies into one of their hangers. Hinds heads to Hill's cabin and knocks on her door. When Hill finally opens the door the doctor is startled by what she sees. Hill is sweaty and breathing erratically. She looks very tired and weak.

"My God Debra! Are you alright?"

She walks into Hill's cabin and makes her lie down on her bed.

"I'm ok. It's just this damn nausea. It hits me hard once in a while. Can you give me anything for it?"

"I'll see what I can do. But you need to rest."

"No I need to be on this mission," says Hill in a weakened tone of voice. She tries to get up and Hinds gently pushes her back down.

"You're not going anywhere in your condition. Doctor's orders," she snaps.

"You don't understand I need to be on this mission, for Clarence, Karen. I need to do this for Clarence, please."

Hinds pauses for a second and looks down at Hill. She sees the anguish in her friend's eyes and hears the pain in her voice.

"Okay, okay, I'll give you something light that will keep you up through the mission. But after that it's back to bed. Do you understand?"

"Thank you. Thank you so much, Karen."

"Now let's get you cleaned up."

She helps Hill out of bed and leads her to the bathroom.

In another part of the plane Brad is getting ready to leave for the mission to attack New Eden. He stands in front of a mirror buckling his bullet-proof vest.

His wife, Pat, sitting behind him on the bed is not happy, "You can get killed out there!" she screams, "What would I do then? What will I tell our child?"

"You'll tell them that their father died trying to make the world livable again, for them," as he turns to her she stands up and he holds her tight. "Listen, baby. I know the risks, but how can I sit back and watch others put their lives on the line for our family and not help? Think about what we've lost, who we've lost. Think about Cliff and Doris."

She lowers her eyes at the sound of her friend's names.

Brad continues with his voice lowered, "I have to do this. If for nothing else, for us," the two stare into each others eyes for a moment, and then kiss each other passionately on the lips.

At 11:00 pm Troy, Hill, Brad, and Lopez leave the plane and head for the operations building at the station. They are on their way to meet the head of the U.S. Palmer Research Station, an Ecologist by the name of Dr. Benjamin Gates.

Gates is a short stout man in his late fifties with dark brown eyes and a full head of oily white hair with a beard, mustache and bushy eyebrows to match. His face has an old, worn yet pleasant, friendly look about it. One can see the age in his face, full of deep lines and wrinkles, particularly around his eyes. He has been in charge of the Palmer Station for the last fifteen years overseeing research on the effects global warming has had on the Antarctic environment.

As the team enters the operations building they find Gates sitting at a console near a large wooden table in the communications room. He's wearing a headset with a microphone attached and appears to be listening to someone on the other end. When they enter, Gates turns and gestures for them to take seats around the table behind him. As they do so he continues his conversation on the radio.

"My God! You mean it's that bad? Well what about Mexico?"

He pauses for a moment to listen to the response on the other end then sighs, "And Australia--you hear anything about Australia? It's got to be safe there."

The answer he receives from the other side causes his face to sour. He slowly strokes his white hair as his voice lowers. "So what are you going to do?" There's another pause as they respond, "Well good luck and God speed."

Gates switches off the radio, removes the headset and sits there still with his elbows on the table and his face in his hands seemingly unaware of the others in the room.

Troy leans across the table towards Gates, "Excuse me, sir is everything alright?"

Gates quickly looks up from his hands and turns around as if just realizing that there are other people in the room with him.

"Sorry," he says, "It's still hard for me to digest how the whole world has gone to Hell in such a short period of time. I just can't believe it. It's like a nightmare."

"We understand--believe me, we understand," says Brad in a reassuring voice.

"If you don't mind my asking, what happened in Mexico and Australia?" asks Hill.

Gates looks up at her tired face and pauses for a moment as if to collect his thoughts. Then he leans back in his chair, throws his hands into the air and says, "Uh, forgive my manners. I never introduced myself. I'm Dr. Benjamin Gates," he says as he gets up and rounds the table to shake their hands. When he approaches Hill she stands up, shakes his hand and repeats the question, "Yes Doctor, your assistants told us who you are. But I need to know, what's the latest update on the mutations? We haven't heard much in the past few hours."

Gates looks at Hill then at the others, he takes a deep breath then returns to his seat, "South America is gone and so is Australia and most of Africa," he states in a very solemn voice.

"What do you mean, 'gone,'" asks Hill.

"They've been either covered by man eating plants or are crawling with all sorts of dangerous mutant animals and infected humans, take your pick. As of five hours ago there are no more governments operating, the world is in complete chaos."

The team members exchange frightened glances with one another as Gates continues, "That was my assistant I was talking to when you arrived. He's trapped in what used to be Johannesburg, South Africa. The place is crawling with berserkers."

"Berserkers?" asks Lopez.

"Yeah, berserkers, that's what they've started calling the ones infected with that new strain of rabies. The ones that don't die from it run around trying to eat everyone else. That's how the damn thing is spreading so fast. It only takes one bite."

"Jesus," sighs Brad.

"For now it seems that this is the only continent that's safe from the effects of the mutations. I've been in touch with several of the other research facilities on the continent and they all report that they're receiving survivors. Not many but there are survivors making their way down here. The only problem is that these bases aren't equipped to sustain large populations over an extended period of time. This is usually the time of year that most of us receive new supplies."

"How long can they hold out?" asks Troy.

"Most of them are already overcrowded and may be facing starvation within a month."

"Shit, this is worse than we thought," exclaims Brad.

"I feel helpless. There's nothing that we can do," states Gates, "I mean we have the second largest station on the continent and we only have enough provisions to last us about two months if we're careful."

Troy sits up in his seat and leans toward Gates, "There is a solution."

"You mean that plan of yours to attack New Eden?"

Troy sits up with a look of surprise of his face.

"Your Lieutenant Lopez filled me in on the details."

Troy takes a quick glance over at Lopez.

Gates continues, "What do you think that's going to accomplish? Even if you do get in and take control, we're still going to starve."

"Dr. Gates, just how much do you know about New Eden?"

"Not much. I know it's a facility run by Gen X Tech. I know they built the damn thing in record time using a lot of hi-tech prefab materials. I know that it's enormous. But that's about it."

"Do you know what they are supposed to be researching?" asks Troy.

"No, I never really thought about it. I do remember wondering why a biotech company was doing research down here. But I never really thought about it, why?"

Hill leans across the table, "Dr. Gates, Gen X Tech is responsible for the mass mutations we're experiencing."

"What! Are you sure?" asks Gates.

"Dr. Gates we've been fighting these things for some time now. I think we have all the evidence we need," adds Brad.

"New Eden is a biosphere, Dr. Gates," says Troy.

"A biosphere?" responds Gates.

"It was designed to keep its occupants safe during all of this madness," adds Troy.

"You mean to tell me that all of this was done deliberately, that not only did they cause mutations but that they knew it would go this far?" Gates says in an angry tone of voice.

"That's exactly what I'm telling you. They have the resources we need to survive and I plan to get them."

"If what you say is true then I have no choice but to do whatever it takes to bring them down. You have my complete support--whatever you need, just ask."

Troy takes a deep breath and says, "Well what we need is to be outside of New Eden by 5:00 am just ahead of the storm. We want to use the storm for cover."

"That's going to be very risky. From the data that I've seen this storm is a monster."

Brad jumps in, "Well that's why we're here. This is your neck of the woods. So we're going to need your advice for the best course of action to take."

Gates' eyes light up like a candle, "Wait a minute I have an idea that may work but we'll have to work fast. A few years ago we were lucky to get two thirty-five ton Kharkovchanka snow tractors from our Russian friends."

"What are those?" asks Hill.

"I think it's better if I show you. Follow me," says Gates as he stands up from the table.

Dr. Gates leads the team out of the operations building and across the field to a three story concrete bunker. When they enter the large building they find that it is in fact a reinforced garage filled with all sorts of all-terrain vehicles. But the most impressive of all of them are two massive trucks mounted on wide tank like treads. Each one of these behemoths is over thirty feet long and fourteen feet wide. They are painted bright-red and have high intensity flood lights attached to the front, sides and rear. The team members slowly walk the length of the rectangular trucks, looking them over in awe of their enormous size.

Gates walks up to one of the vehicles and says, "These were used by the ruskies during their South Pole expeditions in the 1960's. Each one has a 520 horse power V-12 diesel engine and can carry over twenty men."

"These are great but we're over 3000 miles from New Eden. There's no way we could cover that distance in the amount of time we have," explains Troy.

Gates waves his hands at Troy and says, "Relax, I'm not finished with the tour."

He walks over to the garage doors and flicks a switch. Slowly the forty foot long metal doors roll upward revealing the snow lined airfield. Across the field are four large aircraft hangers one of which is where Air Force One is parked. Gates points to the other three.

"You see those three hangars over there? In two of them we have a pair of C-17's. They're big enough to carry these babies. And the other has a C-130 that can carry your troops. With those we can airlift you in and set you down right on their door step. Only problem is, the drop will have to be planned precisely because of the distance we have to cover. These planes have a range of about 2500 miles so will have to land at the U.S. Amundsen-Scott base at the pole to refuel. It's another 900 miles from there. I'll have to research the geography of the area around New Eden to find a flat level place to set down."

Troy smiles, "This is great when we land at Amundsen I could use our SAT uplink to disable their defensive grid and blind their radar and satellite systems just before we take off. We need to get on this right away with a little luck this will work."

"We're going to need a lot more than luck on this mission," says Lopez.

"You got that right," agrees Hill.

Gates steps back inside and closes the door, "It's settled then. I'll tell my crews to get all of the vehicles fueled and ready to go and my technicians are at your disposal. It shouldn't take more than an hour or two to get the planes prepped. I'll also get on a secure line to Amundsen and bring them up to speed."

Troy takes a look at his team members and says, "Alright, folks! Let's move like we have a purpose! We have two hours to get ready. Miguel, get your men suited and ready."

"I'm on it," states Lopez as he dashes off.

For the next hour workers fuel and ready the planes and trucks for the assault. Lopez gathers all of the troops and makes sure they are equipped with polar gear and weapons. Gates finds a location five miles from New Eden just behind a small mountain range, for them to land and begin their ground assault from.

At around 1:00 am the two C-17's slowly taxi onto the runway. These mammoth 175 foot long planes have a range of over 2500 miles and can fly over 500 miles per hour. They have a wingspan of 175 feet coupled with four powerful Pratt and Whitney turbofans giving them enough lifting power to carry a payload of over 170,000 pounds. They rumble down the runway and gracefully lift into the evening sky with the Lockheed C-130 Hercules filled with fifty fighting men with Lopez, Hill, Brad, and Troy, following close behind. For the next three hours they fly low over the Antarctic terrain towards the Amundsen-Scott South Pole Station. This is the southernmost continually inhabited place on the planet. It's named after Ronald Amundsen and Robert F. Scott, both of whom reached the South Pole in 1911. The station is located only 330 feet from the actual geographic South Pole.

It's 3:30 am and the winds have picked up to around fifteen miles an hour swirling thick blankets of snow around the Amundsen Station, bringing visibility down to less than a mile. Several members of their refueling crew wait beside the runway looking skyward for the approaching planes from Palmer.

The planes are about ten miles away but onboard the ride has been a bumpy one. The turbulence has picked up making it difficult to handle the planes and keep them stable. During the trip Lopez while onboard the C-130 uses this time to acquaint INVASION team members Brad, Hill, and Troy with the weapons and survival gear they will be using. The three are seated alongside the heavily trained soldiers of the U.S. army and navy Special Forces. Everyone is wearing white NBC cold weather suits with body armor vests, Kevlar helmets with built in radio headsets, and wrist mounted GPS systems.

Lopez stands in front of the three holding a three foot long beige colored automatic rifle with a 16" barrel. The weapon also sports an extra wide mouthed shorter barrel on the bottom. He unfolds the butt of the weapon and locks it into place.

He gives Hill a wink and says, "Alright people, allow me to introduce you to SOCOM's Mark-17 Special Forces Combat Assault Rifle with a forty millimeter grenade launcher. This baby fires standard 7.62 NATO ammo at a rate of 600 rounds per minute," he turns the weapon over, "It has a thirty round clip and a fully adjustable butt stock," he turns the weapon on its side displaying a black switch above the trigger, "You see this switch? You turn it here for single fire turn it to this position for semi automatic and the last position is fully automatic. And this switch here," while pointing to another switch near the rear of the rifle, "is the safety. Everyone got that?"

They all nod their heads yes except for Troy. Of the three he is the only member who is not in law enforcement and has never fired a gun or even handled one for that matter. When Lopez hands him one of the weapons a surge of adrenaline rips through his body along with a slight feeling of apprehension. He cautiously looks over the rifle then looks up at Lopez and asks, "What's this for?" pointing to the large secondary barrel at the bottom of the gun. It even has its own trigger and safety switch.

"That's the forty millimeter grenade launcher I was telling you about. You just switch off the safety here, aim up at a forty-five degree angle and fire."

Troy looks up with a wide grin across his face, "Nice!"

Brad and Hill turn and watch Troy look over the weapon like a child examines a new toy at Christmas. They turn to each other and shake their heads and smile.

Lopez continues to explain all the other functions of the weapon. Then he explains how to use some of the other weapons and equipment they've been issued like the M67 fragmentation grenades, the nine millimeter M9 hand pistols and infrared goggles. Along with their standard gear the soldiers also have with them Troy is also carrying the three untested infrasonic grenades.

Lopez then begins to explain the dangers of exposure, "Now I need you all to pay close attention to this. It could mean your life or death. We're going to be exposed to temperatures well below freezing with strong winds that will make it seem ten to twenty degrees colder than it really is. The danger of frost bite is very real. So under no circumstances are you to remove your hood, goggles or gloves until we're inside. You skin will freeze in two minutes if exposed. This is a dangerous environment and it can kill you before we even get a chance to fight. So remember my warnings. If you do get frost bitten wrap the area and get to a medic. No matter what you do, don't try to not warm the area up. It'll only make the damage worse. Everyone got that?" The team members each look at each other and give Lopez the thumbs up.

4:00 am and the planes finally emerge from the snowy dark sky over the Amundsen Station their wings dipping wildly as the pilots fight to keep them level in the strong winds. They taxi quickly to a staging area as the refueling crew races to fuel and deice the planes. While on the ground Troy waits for the signal that the refueling is over and then activates the SAT uplink to gain control of the Gen X Tech satellite. He initiates a command to deactivate New Eden's defensive grid as the planes once again roar down the runway toward their destination. Lopez comes back from talking to the pilots and gives Troy, Brad and Hill a mission update.

"We've run into a little problem!" he yells over the sound of the engines.

"What's wrong?" asks Troy.

"We got into Amundsen a little late and then it took us longer than planned to refuel and get back into the air. And now we're beginning to hit headwinds from the storm. It's going to be rough the rest of the way."

"What's our ETA?" asks Brad.

"Around 0545 hours if we're lucky," responds Lopez.

"Shit! The storm is going to be right on top of us!" exclaims Troy.

"Yep. It's about to get dicey," says Lopez as he takes a seat next to Troy and straps himself in.

At 6:00 am the three planes land hard on a glacier five miles from New Eden. It's pitch-black dark with blinding snow blown about by strong thirty-five mph winds, and the temperature has dropped to fifteen degrees making it feel more like negative twenty seven. Once on the ground the strike team struggles to get their gear unloaded and prepped for the five mile run to New Eden. Although they have dressed in the latest hi-tech winter gear the soldiers still find it hard the maneuver in this inhospitable climate. As the planes take off and head back to Amundsen they all board the two massive Kharkovchanka snow tractors and begin their slow trek through the snow that will bring them right up to the New Eden facility.

The storm is really picking up now causing a complete zero visibility whiteout. The snow tractor drivers are forced to operate the vehicles entirely by GPS and radar. After about a half an hour they reach 80° South 90° East, the outer perimeter of New Eden.

Even in this blinding snow storm they can make out the unbelievable size of the facility. It's shaped like a domed football stadium measuring 1600 feet long, 700 feet wide and 100 feet high. The building is all white and its perimeter is ringed by lights shining on its exterior. There are only a few windows visible high up on the structure, but they seemed to be closed shut. The snow tractors are about one hundred feet away and from there they still cannot make out any doors on the facility.

"We're going to have to get closer," says Troy while leaning over the driver in the lead vehicle.

"What about the mines? I thought you said the place might be mined?" says Lopez.

"All of their defense systems were controlled through the same network. When I disabled them I planted a computer virus in their system that will keep them offline. It should be safe to get closer."

"Should be?" says Lopez with a hint of sarcasm.

Troy shrugs his shoulders and says, "Well, we can't go back now. I say let's go for it."

Lopez taps the driver's shoulder, "Bring us alongside the building but take it slow."

"Yes sir," responds the soldier as he releases the braking mechanism and throttles the engine. The behemoth lurches then rumbles forward followed by the second vehicle. They travel 800 feet down the length of the massive building looking for an entrance but instead see nothing but a smooth white surface. Lopez, sitting beside the driver of the lead vehicle, keeps his eyes glued to all of the monitoring equipment.

He reads off the climate data for Troy as they drive along the side of New Eden, "Wind speed thirty-five mph, temperature has dropped another five degrees! Wind chill down to negative thirty-five! It's getting dangerous out there. If we don't find an entrance soon we're screwed!"

"There has to be a way in. Stay on course, keep moving along the perimeter," orders Troy.

"Yes sir!" responds the driver.

After they travel another 300 feet Lopez, while staring at one of the monitors, shouts, "I think I've found something!"

Troy and the others run over and lean in to get a closer look at the screen.

"It's a door! A big door. Probably a loading dock," reports Lopez.

The driver hits a switch over his head which turns on extra bright flood lights mounted on the top of the tractor. He then manipulates a joystick on his console that controls the direction the outside lights are pointed. As the team members squint their eyes to see through the storm, Lopez directs the driver to where he should point the lights. Finally they all can see the door, a large metal door about ten feet high and twenty feet wide.

Lopez turns to Troy, "Well, I guess this is where we get off."

"You're right this is it. Contact the other truck and get the men ready. We move out in fifteen minutes," says Troy with an unusual sense of authority.

Lopez stands up and looks into the rear of the tractor where his men are seated, "Alright you heard the man let's move it people! Double time!"

In an instant all of the men, about twenty-five of them jump up and begin bundling up and checking their gear. Lopez returns to the com and picks up the radio, "Badger two this is Badger one."

"Go ahead Bader one," responds the voice over the radio.

"Found a hole. Ready to commence operation in fifteen, over."

"Roger Badger one commencing operation in fifteen, out!"

Fifteen minutes later the men open the heavy hermetically sealed side doors of the two huge vehicles and jump down into the deep Antarctic snow. Fifty soldiers plus Lopez, Troy, Brad and Hill, the only woman on the mission, slowly approach the large metallic doors of New Eden. They all find it difficult to walk the twenty feet from the tractors to the side of the building while fighting the thirty-five mile per hour winds and blinding snow.

Two soldiers kneel in front of the door and place thermite charges on its surface then back away. The resulting explosion cuts a hole in the door eight feet high and four feet wide. Two soldiers, with weapons at the ready quickly enter the structure. After they give the all clear signal the rest of the strike team rush in.

Once inside they find that Lopez's assessment was right. They are in a large dimly lit storage area with hundreds of crates stacked up to the top of its ten foot ceiling forming huge columns of boxes.

"It's like a maze in here," states Lopez, "I think we should split up."

"Good idea," comments Troy.

Lopez stands in front of the men, "Troy, you come with me. We'll scout this way with the men from Badger one," he says as he points to the left, "Brad, you and Debra take the other half of the troops and head in that direction," Lopez orders while pointing to the right, "Remember to keep your com link open. Don't worry, it's on a secure scrambled channel so they shouldn't be able to pick it up."

Brad, nods to Lopez then turns and waves his men over to one side and proceeds down one of the corridors created by the stacked crates. Lopez and Troy turn and direct the remaining troops to follow them in the other direction.

It takes a full twenty minutes for each of the squads to cautiously snake their way through the labyrinth of crates and containers to the exits at opposite ends of the storage area. Both squads place their thermite charges and blast their way into the interior of New Eden.

Lopez's squad proceeds down a long dark hallway at the end of which is another large heavy metal door. They prepare to use another thermite charge to blast open the door. Brad's squad finds themselves in a long white sterile brightly lit hallway about fifty feet long. Upon reaching the end of the hall they find themselves in what appears to be a laboratory area. There are halls lined with labs each with large viewing windows. There are still no signs of any inhabitants. All of the labs are empty and the halls are quiet. Brad, with Hill at his side, motions for three of his men to take point. The soldiers move slowly through one of the halls with their weapons at the ready, checking each lab as they pass.

Suddenly a young man dressed in a white doctor's lab coat emerges from a lab up ahead reading off of a clipboard as he comes through the door. The soldiers instinctively crouch down and aim their weapons at him. At that instant the young man looks up and notices that the end of the hall is full of heavy armed soldiers. A look of terror sweeps across his face.

"United States Army stay where you are!" yells one of the soldiers.

He holds his hands up and begins back peddling slowly.

"I said freeze!" shouts the soldier again.

The man continues to back up then slaps a red button on the wall next to him. Alarms instantly ring through out the base. The man turns and runs down the hall.

"Orders sir?" requests the lead soldier as he aims at the running man.

"Drop em," shouts Brad.

Bam! Bam!

Two shots from the rifle of the highly trained Special Forces soldier rip through the man's back, both along the spinal cord, killing him instantly. He falls flat on his face, twitches once then lies still.

"Alright, now they know we're here. No need to keep creeping around. Let's move it!" shouts Brad as he and the other members of his squad raise their weapons and quickly advance through the facility.

At the other end of the base as the alarms sound, Lopez and Troy have entered into a huge room filled with large trees and thick vegetation.

"You hear that, boys? Stay sharp. Safeties off!" snaps Lopez.

The climate inside is hot and humid and up on the ceiling hangs massive ultraviolet lamps flooding the room with artificial sunlight. Troy, Lopez and the other soldiers undo some of their gear due to the heat. Troy looks up and around in amazement. The room is massive maybe about 20,000 square feet across. Before him are what appears to be apple trees but the sizes of the apples are enormous. Many of them are about the size of a grapefruit. Nearby are watermelon-sized oranges and three foot long bananas and cabbage about the size of a basketball.

"This is amazing. It's an artificially made tropical biome. The amount of food in here can feed hundreds for years," says Troy as he walks through the indoor forest in awe unaware of the danger around him. A hand reaches out from behind him and violently jerks him to the ground. He hits the ground hard and turns to face the assailant. It's Lopez; he's kneeling beside Troy behind a large tree with his finger on his lips, signaling for him to remain quiet. Troy glances behind Lopez and sees that all of the Special Forces troops are also crouched down behind foliage and have their weapons raised and ready. Suddenly he feels foolish, like he is out of his league. It finally hits him that he is a novice among pros in the deadliest of games.

"Over there behind those trees. There's movement," whispers Lopez, "No matter what stay down. Take your safety off and only fire if you're in trouble. Let us handle these guys."

He motions for Troy to stay put as he and the others slowly spread out and advance towards the position Lopez pointed out. As two soldiers move from one bush to another a huge six foot tall pale skinned bald headed man jumps in front of them. He's wearing brown overalls and combat boots and moves unbelievably fast for a man of his size. So quick in fact that it startles the two soldiers. They freeze for an instant and that brief hesitation causes them their lives. The man snatches the nearest soldier by the neck and squeezes, crushing his trachea, esophagus and spine all in one swift motion. The soldier's head slumps to one side as blood and mucus drip from his mouth, nose and eyes. The super soldier then with a simple flick of his wrist tosses the soldier's body to the side. The second soldier raises his rifle and fires at point blank range straight into the chest of the aggressor.

Bam! Bam! Bam! Bam!

Four rounds hit dead center in his chest spraying blood everywhere and causing a large wound. The super soldier, stumbles back two steps then suddenly lunges forward at the soldier knocking him to the ground. He then snatches the soldier's weapon and snaps it in two as if it were a twig. The mutant then reaches down and picks up the soldier and holds him over his head. At that instant Lopez gives the order to fire. The entire squad opens up on the intruder. Bullets can be seen tearing through his body. But it's too late; the monster crashes the soldier's back sharply down onto his knee cracking his spine with a sickening crunch before finally falling to the ground beside his two victims, his body riddled with bullets.

The squad runs up to the bodies and looks them over with a sense of trepidation.

One soldier shouts, "What the fuck is this? Did you see how many rounds it took to bring him down? Holy shit!"

Lopez waves Troy over to the scene. When Troy joins him he notices Lopez's face shows signs of concern, "Are you sure those grenades of yours are gonna work?"

"Positive," says Troy with a shaky voice as he looks down at the bodies of the super soldier and the two men he just killed.

"They better, cause if they don't and we meet any more of these guys, we're fucked!"

"Lieutenant, hostiles at two o'clock," shouts another soldier.

Lopez raises a clenched fist in the air and immediately all of the soldiers drop to the ground and aim their weapons at a clearing up ahead.

Troy looks up to see what the soldiers are aiming at. Up ahead, ten armed super soldiers step into the clearing. They detect the squad and immediately spread out and open fire. Lopez gives the command and the Special Forces troops return fire from their positions. The fire fight is fierce with several of Lopez's men sustaining injuries. Lopez and Troy duck behind a large boulder. Troy is sitting with his back to the stone as Lopez stands and empties a clip at the approaching enemy. He slides down to the ground next to Troy to change the clip to his rifle.

"We're getting pulverized! Six of my men are down already and three are wounded. We only dropped one of them and they're still coming. If you're going to use your toy now would be a good time!"

Troy fumbles through his backpack and pulls out one of his infrasonic grenades. With his shaking hands he turns the knob on the top. When he releases it he can hear the ticking sound of the five second counter. Troy stands up behind the boulder and throws the device with all of his might. The cylinder tumbles through the air and lands in front of one of the super soldiers. The giant looks down at the weapon with indifference just as the timer goes off.

BOOM!

A loud low-pitched boom rocks the entire area knocking everyone to the ground. Some of Lopez' men grab their heads and cry out in pain. Troy and Lopez hold their heads as a knife like pain shoots through their skulls even through the noise-cancelling ear plugs the both of them are wearing. The pain is quick and is gone just as fast as it came. Troy stands up from behind the boulder with his nose bleeding and his ears ringing. He looks out at the clearing up ahead. On the ground are the bodies of the super soldiers, their chests ripped open and blood running out of their eyes, noses and mouths. The weapon worked! Lopez and the other soldiers all begin to rise and when they realize what has happened they all begin to cheer.

"Son of a bitch! The damn thing worked!" exclaims Lopez as he pats Troy on the back, "The damn thing worked!"

Troy gives a small grin as Lopez assembles the remaining troops and gives the signal to move out through the artificial forest in the direction the super soldiers came from.

Meanwhile back at the other end of New Eden Brad and Hill have found a stairwell and moved up a level. They reach a locked steel door labeled 'HUMAN HABITANT RESTRICTED ACCESS'.

"Get ready for resistance boys!" says Brad, "go ahead blow the door," he commands.

A soldier steps forward and places small C-4 explosive charges around the edge of the door and steps back.

KA-BOOM!

The explosion rips the door off of its hinges. As they step through the exit they see what appears to be a large living room. It's a huge circular area filled with couches, a small round bar in the center, and what appears to be a kitchen off to one side. There are several hallways that branch out into what looks like living quarters around the perimeter of the room. Inside there are several people huddled like frightened children behind the couches.

"United States Army! Keep your hands where we can see them and stand up slowly!" shouts Brad as he and the rest of the squad pours into the room with their weapons raised and ready. Hands nervously begin to rise up from behind the couches and soon after that the people hiding there begin slowly standing up.

"We're prisoners. We've been held against our will," says a man with a deep Russian accent, holding his hands straight up in the air.

Hill steps toward the man, "What's your name, sir?"

"Dmitri, Dmitri Petrov."

She turns to Brad, "My God, these are the kidnapped scientists!" states Hill as she turns back to the frightened man with his hands raised, "It's alright, sir. You can put your hands down now," she looks around the room at the other people huddled together, "You can all put your hands down. We're here to help you."

Brad comes over and talks to Dmitri, "Doctor, do you have any idea where Chad Brooks is?"

"He's usually in the incubation chamber in sector ten. Here I'll show you where it is on the online schematics. You can use them to find your way around just punch in access code 3389 then follow the on screen instructions," he walks over to a wall-mounted monitor and punches in the code. The monitor comes alive and displays a layout of the entire facility, "you see here we are and here is the incubation chamber. But I must warn you it's heavily guarded."

Brad turns on his com link, "Miguel, come in."

"Go ahead, Brad," responds Lopez.

"We've found the kidnapped scientists and we think we know where Brooks is hiding. He maybe in something called an incubation chamber and it should be close to your position."

"Great, can you tell us how to get there?"

"Do you see any wall monitors in your area?"

Lopez looks around then spots one of the monitors and walks over to it, "Yes I see a terminal here."

"Punch in 3389. You should be able to locate it from there."

"Got'cha, call you when we've bagged him. Out!"

Lopez and his squad are at the far edge of the forest biome near the exit. He inputs the access code and pin points the incubation chamber on the monitor.

"This is where we're headed. Alright men, we're moving up two levels. Groups of four and check your flanks," states Lopez.

Troy comes up from the rear and joins Lopez, "What's up?"

"Brad thinks he knows where Brooks is. Some area called the incubation chamber. Its two levels up from here. We're gonna make a run for it."

"Well you can count me in," he says as he switches off the safety on his rifle and pulls back the bolt to chamber a round.

Lopez looks at him and sees the eager determination in Troy's eyes, "Hey slow down, buddy. We'll get him. But just take it easy."

"Not this time Miguel. I want that bastard. You hear me? I want Brooks! And nothing is going to stop me!" He walks off toward the exit with his weapon braced against his shoulder in ready position.

Lopez shakes his head then gives the order to ascend the next two levels.

The squad moves up the stairwell in groups of four. Lopez and Troy are in the second group to move up the stairs. They slowly and cautiously move up the stairs until they reach a white door marked with a sign.

Lopez stands in front of the door and addresses his men, "This is it gentlemen. Check your weapons and stay sharp we may have company on the other side," he then turns to Troy, "Make sure you have those grenades of yours ready."

"Got'cha," responds Troy.

Lopez gives a signal to one of his men who then proceeds to place C-4 explosive charges around the door.

The soldiers cock their weapons and spread out away from the blast area.

"Stay behind me. You understand?" Lopez says to Troy who responds with a nod.

On Lopez's signal the door is blown inward. Four soldiers, two on each side of the door rush in with their weapons raised.

Rat! Tat! Tat! Tat! Tat!

Bam! Bam! Bam!

Rat! Tat! Tat! Tat! Tat!   Rat! Tat! Tat! Tat! Tat!

Bam! Bam!

Bam!

The room erupts in a blaze of gunfire. Two of the four soldiers fall the minute they enter the room. Lopez grabs a fragmentation grenade from his vest and pulls the pin. With his back against the wall he blindly throws the grenade into the room.

Boom!

Another soldier on the other side of the door throws a flash bang stun grenade into the room.

Poof!

A bright light flashes from inside the room.

Lopez, Troy and the rest of the squad sit quietly with their weapons raised on both sides of the door. They wait listening for any signs of movement from within the room. After a minute or so they hear nothing. Lopez signals his men and they all pour into the room with weapons blazing. When they stop they realize that they have hit nothing.

They're in a large semi-circular room filled with all sorts of monitoring equipment. There is a hallway to the left, one to the right and a third straight up ahead. Along the outside of the room are a series of six ten-foot windows that look out in a much larger room on the other side in which this room is suspended above.

The soldiers begin to slowly fan out in the room peering cautiously behind each piece of equipment.

One of the soldiers turns to Lopez, "Lieutenant, there's nobody here!"

Just as he makes the statement a large hand grabs him from behind and another hand grabs him by the jaw and twists his head around sharply, snapping his neck. His body falls to the floor like a ragdoll. Standing over the body is a hulking seven-foot-tall super soldier. The squad members aim their weapons and prepare to open fire when five more super soldiers appear from all sides of the room at once. One leaps twenty feet through the air onto the back of one of the Special Forces soldiers, driving an eight-inch blade into his neck. All mayhem breaks loose as Special Forces fight in close quarters with the Super Soldiers. Lopez and Troy duck behind a desk as Lopez opens fire on the attacking horde. Troy sits with his back to the desk, his hands trembling uncontrollably. He sits there listening to the squad's men dying around him. He reaches deep down inside his gut for the courage to face this unstoppable threat. For an instant his mind goes blank. He can hear nothing. Everything seems to be happening in slow motion. In the distance he hears his grandfather's voice.

"It's up to you now, my son. They're counting on you. You have the strength. You have the knowledge. Use it, use it, use it!"

The voice drifts off into the distance, and then disappears; suddenly Troy is snapped back into the reality of the fire fight.

Lopez is standing over him firing bursts of five to six shots before ducking back down behind the desk. All around them is the sound of gunfire and the screams of the wounded. The sounds of ricocheting bullets, shattering glass and breaking objects resound throughout the room. Troy sits there on the floor with his back to the desk gripping his rifle tightly. To his left he sees another soldier behind another desk across the room. The man reaches into his vest and pulls out a fragmentation grenade. He pulls the pin, stands up and cocks his arm back to throw when first one then two and then a third bullet rip through his body causing him to fall back and drop the grenade behind him. Lopez notices what has happened along with Troy and reacts instinctively. He pulls Troy to the ground and throws his body on top of him.

KaBooom!

Red hot pieces of shrapnel jet out in all directions along with chunks of burning flesh, bone and clothing. Lopez again stands up using the desk as protection and fires at the aggressors.

Bam! Bam! Bam! Bam!

But this time he's not quick enough to evade the return fire.

A bullet tears through his right shoulder with such force that Troy could hear the bones in his shoulder break. Lopez falls to the ground in pain next to Troy holding his wound as blood sprays from between his fingers.

"Run Troy. Run," says Lopez in a low shaky voice, "get out of here."

Troy fingers the trigger on his rifle, he takes a deep breath and jumps up from behind the desk, takes aim and squeezes.

Bam! Bam! Bam! Bam!   Bam! Bam!
Bam! Bam! Bam! Bam!

He hits an advancing Super Soldier in the leg and arm. It stuns the man for a short time but he soon regains his footing and returns fire.

Rat! Tat! Tat! Tat! Tat!   Rat! Tat! Tat! Tat! Tat!

Troy ducks back down and covers Lopez with his body as bullets whiz over his head, some of the rounds hit the desk sending splinters flying through the air.

Lopez looks up at Troy, "We're getting our asses kicked! You have to pull back."

"I'm not leaving without Brooks. He's here, I know he's here!" Troy reaches down into his backpack and pulls out one of the infrasonic grenades.

"You can't use that! My men are in here. We're too close. You saw what happened the last time and they don't have any ear plugs."

"If we don't what other plan do you have? They'll be on us in a minute."

Lopez thinks for a moment then turns to see another of his men fall dead, "Alright, alright do it!"

He covers his ears as Troy turns the switch and tosses the grenade behind him over the top of the desk. He hears the cylinder hit the floor and counts.

"Three, Two, One"

BOOOOOOM! Craaaaash!

Instantly after the sonic blast the large windows around the room shatter then the room instantly falls silent. Troy and Lopez stand up slowly and look over the damage. No one else has survived. They are the only ones left. Troy walks through the room toward the windows. All around him are the bodies of the Super Soldiers along with the remains of the valiant men of the United States Special Forces. All around the room are body parts, entrails, blood and shattered equipment. Troy walks up to the broken windows and looks out. Below him he sees a huge room filled with rows of six-foot glass cylinders; each one has dozens of tubes and wires running out of top and into some sort of monitoring device. Inside of each cylinder is a chimpanzee. The animals seem to be sedated and their arms and legs are shackled to the inside of the tube. All of the apes also appear to be pregnant. There are EKG probes attached to all of the animal's heads and chests. Troy looks down in amazement; there are hundreds of these cylinders throughout the entire room.

Lopez, holding his wounded shoulder, hobbles next to Troy. He looks down into the room full of cylinders and says, "What the Hell is this?"

"This area's called the incubation chamber so these must be vessels," responds Troy.

"Vessels? For what?"

"I don't know. Clones maybe."

Suddenly a voice from behind them startles them both.

"Provectus Homo Eximius Sapiens--the next step in human evolution!"

Both men spin around to see standing at the entrance to the hallway at the back of the room, a tall pale-skinned man with long straight white hair tied in a pony tail that reaches his waist. He has a long narrow face with a pointy chin and deep set dark piercing eyes accented with high arched eyebrows, giving him a sinister appearance. He's dressed in a black turtle neck sweater with black pants and boots.

"Troy. Phillip. It's a pleasure to finally meet you in person. I've been a fan of yours for a very long time."

He steps forward and looks around the room, "I see that you are indeed the genius I thought you to be. How may I ask did you defeat my creations?"

"Fuck you, Brooks!" shouts Troy as he raises his weapon and takes aim, "I should kill you where you stand!"

"Then why don't you?" says Brooks as he opens his arms and walks slowly towards the two men.

"I need to know how to counter act SF-20, you fucking bastard!"

Brooks still approaching says, "You can't. It has already mutated over a dozen times. Reshaping the world as it changes."

"What about the inoculations you were giving your workers?"

"Simply protection against mutation."

"There must be some way to stop this. Damn it, millions of people are dying!"

"Billions, my boy, billions," says Brooks as he stops and slowly raises his arms, "And from the ashes new life will grow anew."

Troy grits his teeth and points his rifle at Brooks' head, "The whole world is destroyed because of you!"

"I didn't destroy the world Troy, and you know it! The world's been dying for years and not by my hand."

"You're the one that created SF-20!"

"I thought of all people you would understand my actions."

"How's that?"

Lopez turns to Troy, "Fuck this shit, Troy. Shoot this motherfucker!"

Troy waves off Lopez, "Wait a minute, Miguel," he continues to address Brooks, "What do you mean I should understand?"

"Come on, Troy look around you. Man has made this planet his personal toilet for generations. The other species never had a chance. Look at whaling, over fishing and deforestation, the overuse of fossil fuels, the dumping of toxin waste into our lakes and streams. Man is not the only inhabitant on this planet you know!"

Troy slowly lowers his weapon as Brooks paces back and forth and he continues his speech.

"It's because of man that the Mountain Gorilla is almost extinct. It's because of man more than half of the rainforests around the world are gone, eliminating an untold number of species. It's man that has caused the polar caps to melt, it's man that has scarred the land while looking for precious metals, and has recklessly depleted the ozone layer."

He stops in front of Troy and looks him straight in the eyes, "You're a scientist. How many types of marine animals and birds were killed in '89 when the Exxon Valdez dumped over 32 million gallons of oil off the coast of Alaska? Huh? What about in 2010 when the Deepwater Horizon oil rig leaked over 100 million gallons into the Gulf of Mexico? How many helpless creatures died then? In '86 the Chernobyl Nuclear Power plant in the Ukraine leaked radiation into the Earth's atmosphere. Tell me Troy, how many lives were affected by that? How many innocent people were killed or suffered from radiation poisoning or cancer because of MAN? And you accuse me of being a murderer. Who's really the murderer here?" he snarls.

Both Troy and Lopez glance at each other.

Brooks continues, "All I did was give nature a fighting chance. I gave them the ability to fight back, after centuries of abuse at the hands of humankind," he raises his hands high into the air and says, "Blessed are the meek for they shall inherit the earth," he looks back at Troy and says, "Matthew 5:5," with a smirk.

"You're crazy," says Lopez, "You're fucking crazy!"

"Am I? Everything that I've told you is true," Brooks says to Lopez. Then he turns back to Troy and says," Isn't it, Troy?"

"Yeah it's true but there are other solutions that don't include creating killer mutants," Troy then walks over to the edge of one of the broken windows and looks down, "And what about this? How does manipulating DNA and creating hybrid humans help to heal the world?"

Brooks walks over to the edge of one of the other windows and looks down at the cylinders, "This is my gift to a new earth, a stronger, faster, smarter human, one that will live with nature not against it. A new race of human beings created in my image."

Troy looks at him, "In your image?"

"Why not? I've cleansed the world of the virus known as Homo Sapiens. Why shouldn't I be the one to reshape it as I see fit?"

"What the fuck?" says Lopez, "Now he thinks he's God!"

"Now I know what's really wrong with you, you have NPD," says Troy.

"NPD?" asks Brooks.

"Yeah, narcissistic personality disorder," says Troy sarcastically.

Lopez gives a little chuckle but it hurts him to laugh.

Brooks glances at him with a look of loathing.

Troy continues, "And that's not all, your experiment down there," Troy points down to the cylinders, "it's flawed. You're using apes to incubate your embryos. Using animal surrogates for human fetuses has never been successful. The placental tissue of the mother and the fetus won't match, causing massive rejection. None of these chimps will ever give birth."

"You underestimate me, Troy. I've long since solved that problem. These children WILL be born and will do MY bidding. I offer you a final chance to join me here in this New Garden of Eden to start the world over."

"What? You must be out of your damn mind. I'm bringing you in to stand trial for what you've done."

"Ha Ha. Stand trial where? There's no one left. You know you're only chance for survival is here with me. This is your last chance. You're either with me or you die."

Troy and Lopez give each other a puzzled look. Troy raises his rifle and points it at Brooks, "Are you forgetting who's holding the gun?"

Brooks raises his hands slowly, "No, not at all," he says as he nods his head slowly. Troy feels the hair on the back of his neck raise as if something were behind him. He spins around just as a Super Soldier lunges for him. He falls back while squeezing the trigger and empting the clip into its chest. The wounded Super Soldier still manages to grab Troy by the throat and begins choking the life out of him. The grip this creature has is like a vice and Troy can do nothing to pry its hand from around his neck. He begins to black out when all of a sudden the Super Soldier releases his grip. Troy falls to the floor and fights to catch his breath. When his eyes begin to clear he sees Lopez standing behind the monster pulling his bayonet out of the back of its neck. The beast falls to the floor with a heavy thump. That's when Troy realizes that Brooks is gone.

"Look, he's down there!" shouts Lopez, pointing down into the room filled with the incubation cylinders. Brooks is running towards an exit at the far end of the room. Troy turns and looks at Lopez's injured shoulder.

Lopez says to Troy, "Don't worry about me! Get 'em!"

Troy without hesitation jumps down into the room and runs after Brooks.

"Brad! Brad! Come in, this is Miguel," Lopez screams into his com link.

"Go ahead, Miguel," responds Brad.

"All of our men are dead but we've found Brooks. Troy is in pursuit. He's going to need some help. He's on level two heading out the back of the incubation chamber. "

"We're on our way. Are you okay?"

"I'm still in the incubation chamber. Caught a bullet, but I'll live. Don't worry just help Troy!"

"We're on it! Sending the medic to you're location. Out!"

Meanwhile, on the lower level Troy races after Brooks through the maze of halls that interconnect the various parts of New Eden. Brooks has about a fifty yard lead on him and Troy at age twenty-five thinks to himself how amazing it is that this man in his late fifties can move so fast. He's having a hard time keeping up with him. When Brooks crashes through another exit and descends to the ground level, Troy rips off his backpack and vest and discards them. He looks over the railing of the stairwell and sees Brooks scampering down the stairs. Troy takes aim and fires.

Bam! Bam! Bam!

He misses and Brooks enters the next level. Troy races down the stairs to follow. When he exits the stairwell he finds himself in a large equipment room full of snow gear and equipment. There's an exit door across the room that leads outside. It's marked in big red letters, 'Caution – Extreme Cold - Wear proper clothing before opening door.'

In the room near the exit door is a row of parkas hanging on a wall rack. Troy notices that there is one missing from the middle. He walks cautiously through the dimly lit room and passes a row of storage lockers. Suddenly one of the locker doors swings open. Brooks jumps out and hits Troy in the back with a three foot long ice axe. The pick end of the axe embeds itself into Troy's upper back just below the right shoulder causing Troy to fall to the ground and drop his rifle. Brooks pulls the axe out and prepares to strike again. Troy reaches for his weapon and holds it up to block the blow. Brooks comes down hard and makes contact with the rifle and breaks it in two. He raises the axe up over his head again. Troy holds his hands up in a defensive manner, preparing himself to be struck by the axe again.

Bam! Bam!

The sounds of gunshots ring out from behind Brooks. Troy turns to see Brad, with his gun raised, coming through the door with Hill. Brooks is only grazed by a bullet. He glances angrily back at his assailants. Brooks then turns back to Troy and raises the axe high up over his head.

Bam! Bam! Bam! Bam! Bam! Bam! Bam! Bam!

This time both Brad and Hill open fire hitting Brooks several times. He stumbles back towards the outer door. Remarkably he still manages to throw the axe at his attackers. Brad dives out of the way but Hill isn't as quick and the axe embeds itself in her left thigh. She drops her gun and falls hard to the ground, grimacing in pain as Brad turns and runs to her side.

In the confusion Brooks opens the outer door and runs out into the storm.

Hill on her back and holding her impaled leg looks up at Brad, "Don't worry about me! I'm okay! Check Troy!"

As the howling winds rush into the room through the opened door Brad runs over and helps Troy to his feet, "You alright?" he asks after seeing blood on Troy's back.

"I'm okay but Brooks is getting away!"

Hill, holding her leg with a scowl on her face from the pain says from the floor, "It's over Troy. He can't survive outside for long. Not in this weather. Come on let's get out of here."

"She's right, Troy," adds Brad as he attempts to help Troy along.

Troy pushes him away, "You don't understand. He's genetically enhanced himself. That's why he's so fast and so strong. Look at how many times you hit him and he's still going," Troy grabs a parka and a safety belt off the rack near the outer door and quickly puts them on, "I'm going after him. I'm putting an end to this now!" Without another word he rushes out into the storm.

"Troy, wait!" yells Hill but it's too late he disappears into the blinding snow.

"Brad he went out there without gloves or face protection," screams Hill.

"I know, I know but first we need to get you some help."

Hill pulls back her sleeve and shows him her com link, "I'll be alright. Just get him Brad! Get Troy!"

Brad nods then grabs some gear from the room. Before he leaves he stops at the door and looks back at Hill, "You better stay right here and call for backup."

"I promise just bring Troy back alive."

Brad salutes then dashes off into the blizzard.

As Troy runs through the near blinding storm he hits a metal safety line and uses the hook on his safety belt to latch onto the cable. Troy squints trying to find Brooks through thick swirling snow but suddenly feels the line vibrate from up ahead. *"It's Brooks,"* he thinks to himself and quickens his pace. The temperature has dropped dangerously low and the steel cable that makes up the safety line begins sticking to his bare hands, ripping the skin from his palms. But he doesn't feel a thing because his hands have become numb and his mind is focused on one thing,

Brooks. He's only minutes away from frost bite but his adrenaline keeps him moving forward.

As he runs a sudden gush of wind knocks him off balance. Troy slips and is carried into the air a short distance. The safety line pulls taunt and jerks him back to the ground. He falls onto the hard frozen ice and snow knocking the wind from his lungs and cracking a rib. Intense pain surges through his body. He struggles to pull himself back up. He grabs the safety line but the extreme cold and the wound in his back are making it difficult to maintain a grip. Strips of skin begin to peel away from his bare hands and stick to the frozen metal safety cable as he makes his way hand over hand down the line. He finally makes it back on his feet and continues his chase. After several minutes he reaches the end of the cable. There's nothing there but a metal pole in the ground. No Brooks, Nothing. Troy frantically searches through the swirling snow for his adversary.

Then as if moved by the will of his mind the storm slowly begins to clear. Visibility gradually increases and he can make out a faint figure in the distance.

"*Brooks!*" he says to himself. He unlatches himself from the safety line and takes off in pursuit. He's running on pure will power now. His cracked ribs are making it hard for him to breath and the gash in his back is sending a burning sensation throughout his entire body. But none of the pain he feels can stop him from going after Brooks.

The figure up ahead, climbs up a small hill and Troy follows. When he reaches the top he finds Brooks standing there at the edge of a cliff looking down. Troy pulls his 9mm handgun from his holster and aims it at Brooks with shaking hands.

"I got you. You son of a bitch," he snarls.

Brooks slowly turns around to face Troy. Without saying a word he lunges at the young man like a crazed animal. Troy falls back off balance and fires his gun but the bullet just misses its mark. Brooks slams Troy to the ground, causing him to drop to his weapon. His already injured body is now screaming out in searing pain. He's dazed and finds it hard to focus. Brooks grabs him by the collar of his parka and punches him hard in the face blooding his lip. He strikes him again this time breaking his nose. Blood gushes down his throat causing him to choke. Again and again Brooks pounds him in the face. Troy's not sure how much more he can take. When Brooks raises his hand one more time to strike Troy grabs his bayonet from his belt and quickly drives it up under Brooks' rib cage. Brooks freezes in place, his hand still raised. Blood begins to trickle down from his mouth. His eyes roll back in his head. He slowly stands up and grabs the knife sticking out of his side in a vain attempt to pull it out. He pulls and pulls and finally removes the knife from his body. Blood sprays out of the wound as Brooks looks down at Troy and gives him a smile as blood continues to pour out of his mouth.

"You see you can't kill me. I'm the superior race," he mumbles as he stands there holding the knife.

"The only thing you are is *DEAD!*" exclaims Troy as he rolls over in the snow and quickly picks up his gun. Troy aims and squeezes the trigger over and over.

Bang! Bang! Bang! Bang! Bang!

The bullets find their mark dead center of Brooks' chest. Troy continues as he empties the clip.

Bang! Bang! Bang! Bang! Bang!

With each shot Brooks' body shakes and he stumbles back towards the edge of the cliff.

Bang! Bang! Bang!

Bang!

The last shot finally sends Brooks over the edge and into a deep dark abyss.

Troy struggles to his feet just as he hears a voice call out his name.

"Troy! Troy!"

It's Brad; he appears at the top of hill and runs to Troy's side, "Jesus, Troy are you all right?"

Troy, out of breath and holding the pistol at his side, nods that he is okay.

"Brooks, where's Brooks?"

Troy leads Brad over to the edge of the cliff and points down into the chasm.

"Looks like the storm's clearing. Let me get you back. It's over, Troy. It's finally all over."

Troy looks up to Brad and stares him straight into his eyes and says, "No, it's not over. This is only the beginning."

The difference between animals and humans is that animals change themselves for the environment, but humans change the environment for themselves.
~ Ayn Rand

The earth we abuse and the living things we kill will, in the end, take their revenge; for in exploiting their presence we are diminishing our future.
~Marya Mannes, 1958

Epilogue

It's twelve o'clock in the afternoon and a group of young children are playing stick ball in a lightly wooded area. There's a little boy of Asian descent, about ten years old, holding a rubber ball and imitating the moves of a professional baseball pitcher. Directly across from him, standing in front of a large tree is a 9-year-old boy holding a wooden stick over shoulder like a baseball bat. Determined brown eyes framed by thick, dark lashes in a coffee-brown face, he is in batter's stance and completely focused. Behind the pitcher are two young girls, an 8-year-old black girl with thick pigtails and an auburn-haired 9-year-old with fair skin and large, piercing hazel eyes. The two girls flank the young pitcher on either side and playfully glance at one another between mock tobacco chewing and other "professional" behavior. They are all wearing multi-colored clothing that upon close inspection is skillfully wrought patchwork of myriad pieces of fabric.

"Come on, strike him out Chang!" yells the girl with the hazel eyes.

"Not this time," replies the batter, swinging the stick back and forth. "Go ahead, let it rip Chang--I'm ready!"

"Alright, Cliff you asked for it," says Chang.

Chang reaches back and throws the ball with all his might at the big tree. Cliff swings the stick.

Whiff!

The blue ball flies past his stick and bounces off the tree.

"*Ssstrike* one," yells the little black girl, complete with the authentic umpire's stance and gestures. She looks over at the redheaded child, mock-chewing tobacco with the lazy jaw action of a sleepy cow.

The two girls start to giggle, much to the irritation of Chang and Cliff, who are trying to have a serious game.

"Oh shut up, Nevaeh," shouts Cliff. He picks up the ball and throws it back to Chang.

Chang winds up again and lets the ball fly.

Whiff!

Cliff misses again.

"*Sssstrike* two," yells the little white girl, hunkering down into an umpire's stance. Her pigtailed friend does the same. Now there are two umpires, one on either side of the pitcher. They start trying to communicate with one another in umpire language, signaling at one another with their fingers.

The two girls again begin to giggle annoyingly.

"That's alright, Zion. I was just getting warmed up," says Cliff to the little girl with long auburn braids. Zion just giggles before stretching her face into the sober face of an officious umpire.

Feeling embarrassed now, Cliff grips the stick extra-tight after he throws the ball back to Chang.

Again Chang goes through the motions. He winds up and throws a hard fast ball. Cliff holds the stick as far back as he can then swings fast and hard.

SMACK!

The ball flies high over the heads of the two open-mouthed girls and into the woods behind them. They race into the bush to find it.

After a while the girls have still not returned with the ball.

"Come on, hurry up and get the ball. We have to go eat lunch soon," yells Chang.

"Okaaaay," Zion yells back.

"What's the matter, can't find it? I told you I'd hit a big one," yells Cliff as the two boys share a laugh together by the large tree, "If you want I can loan you my Grandmother's glasses, ha ha ha ha."

The two boys continue to laugh heartily, Chang bending over double and Cliff tearing up with mirth. When he had caught his breath, Chang straightens, shaking his head and muttering "Girls!" Cliff shakes his head in agreement. "Yeah," he says disgustedly, "Girls!"

"We can hear you," Nevaeh cries.

The two boys grin, and Cliff continues to swing his wooden stick, re-enacting how he connected with the ball.

In the meantime, the girls are walking through the woods, bending over and pushing apart bushes and shrubs as they diligently look for the ball. While looking behind a small evergreen bush Nevaeh says to Zion, "That Cliff can really get on my nerves."

"Both of them are pains. Boys!" responds Zion.

Nevaeh, smiles and repeats, "Boys!"

The two girls giggle as they walk through the woods. Soon they come to a small clearing in the forest. There's a six foot long mound of earth in the center of the clearing, marked with a small sign at one end of the mound. The two girls look at each other then approach the mound slowly.

"What's this?" asks Zion.

"I don't know. I've never come this far before," answers Nevaeh.

A voice from behind them startles the two girls, causing them to jump.

"It's your great-grandfather's grave, my dear."

They turn to see Jaclyn Taylor standing behind them.

"Granny!" Shouts the two girls as they run over to hug the woman.

"We were looking for our ball," Zion explains, tugging on one red pigtail.

"You mean this one," says Jaclyn as she holds out a small blue rubber ball.

"Hey, how did you find it?" asks Nevaeh.

"Oh when I was your age finding lost balls in the woods was my specialty," she smiles.

She hands the ball to Zion just as the two boys run up to join them. Nevaeh looks up at Jaclyn and asks, "Granny?"

"Yes, dear?"

"What was my great-grandfather like?"

Jaclyn smiles as she looks down into the young girl's eyes.

"Come, come all of you and sit down here."

The children and Jaclyn all sit on the ground in a small circle, the children looking up at her with dutiful attentiveness, eyes round and expectant.

"Now listen carefully. This is the grave of a great man. His name was Professor Richard Hamilton. He was Nevaeh's father's grandfather and it's because of him that we all came to live here in New Eden. He helped save us from the world outside."

Chang raises his hand.

"Yes, dear?" says Jaclyn.

"What's it like outside? We've only seen it in books and on video." Chang says in an innocent voice.

"Yeah, and when can we go out there?" asks Cliff.

"Oh my, so many questions. I'll tell you what, let's go have some lunch and while we eat I'll tell you a story about how and why we came to New Eden. It's a story of love, of adventure and courage. Would you like to hear it?"

The children all scream together, "Yes, Granny, Yes!"

"Okay. Let's go get that lunch and I'll tell you all about it."

When they get up to leave another woman appears from behind a bush; it's Debra Hill.

Zion runs over to her, "Mommy, Mommy! Granny's going to tell us a story about how we got here."

Hill looks at Jaclyn, "You think they're ready for that?"

"Well they found Hamilton's grave and started asking a lot of questions, so I figured this is as good a time as any. We were just going in to have some lunch want to join us? After all you're one of the stars of the story."

"Sure, why not."

"You're in the story, Mommy?" asks Zion.

"Yes sweetie. And so are Chang's parents and Nevaeh's mom and dad and even Cliff's parent's are in it."

"Wow!" exclaims Zion.

"My mom and dad are in the story too. Wow, I want to hear this!" shouts Cliff, balancing and hopping on one leg with sheer glee.

Hill looks down at the young boy, "That's right, Cliff they are. And so is your daddy's best friend. And I bet you can't guess what his name was?" Cliff shrugs his shoulders and Hill smiles, "It was Cliff...just like yours."

A big smile stretches across Cliff's face, "Wow, did you hear that! Come on let's eat. I want to hear more!"

"Last one to the cafeteria's a rotten egg!" says Chang as he rushes through the woods. The other children run off after him.

Jaclyn turns to Hill and says, "You know the children wanted to know when they could visit the outside world."

"I know, they're getting curious. But what can we do? We don't know what's happened out there."

"It's been ten years. Who knows how things have changed. It could be for the better or for the worst. All I know is that right now this has truly become a Garden of Eden for them and for us. But they're still curious." She turns to Hill with a knowing glance. "And one day they will want to satisfy that curiosity."

"I know Jackie. I know. I believe that someday we all will have to leave here and return. And God only knows what will be waiting for us when we do."

Just then Zion rushes back through the bushes and startles the two women.

"Oh dear, what is it sweetie?" asks Jaclyn.

"I forgot to ask you, what are we having for lunch?"

"Uh, today we're having tuna salad."

"Great, that's my favorite!" Zion shouts as she scampers off into the woods.

Hill smiles even as her eyes begin to tear up, "Just like her father. God how I miss that man."

"I know you do dear. I know you do," says Jaclyn as she puts her arm around Hill, "Someday all of this will make sense," she remarks as the two women walk slowly through the artificial forest towards the exit.

About the Author

As a cum laude graduate from Mercy College with a Bachelor's degree in Computer Information Systems and a Master's degree in Special Education, this grandson of the famed Bedford Stuyvesant community leader Herbert Von King, brings with him over 20 years of experience in the fields of technology and education covering a wide range of disciplines including but not limited to, science, biology, early childhood development, sociology, psychology, computer graphics and systems integration.

H.V. Lyons grew up in Queens, New York. Growing up he was heavily influenced by the works of Edgar Allan Poe, H. G. Wells, Jules Verne, Octavia E. Butler, Michael Crichton, Steven King, Arthur C. Clarke and Isaac Asimov.

He also heavily involved in politics and community involvement. He was the recipient of the 1997 Manhattan Borough President's Volunteerism Award and in 2004 ran for the New York State Assembly Office of District leader for Crown Heights, Brooklyn.

He presently is CEO/founder of Lyons & Grant Multimedia LLC and also works as a New York City Special Education and Science Teacher.

Other books available from
Lyons & Grant Multimedia LLC

Supernature by H.V.Lyons
Science Fiction
$14.95
978-0-9837172-0-1

Casualty of Silence by Ernestine Moore
Autobiography
$12.95
978-0-9837172-7-0

There's no vacation from desire by Bruce Jarish
Drama
$12.95
978-0-9837172-5-6

Chained Gun Vol.1 by Donny Frank Morris
Graphic Novel
$12.95
978-0-9837172-1-8

Chained Gun Vol.2 by Donny Frank Morris
Graphic Novel
$12.95
978-0-9837172-8-7

Visit our website at www.lgmmedia.net
All major credit cards accepted